Siberia

Alaska

CANADA

The Bering Sea

USA

MEXICO

The California Gray Whale

Migration Route

The Gray Whale
Nursery Lagoons

To learn more, visit Zonk at Zonktheturtle.com

Zonk and the Gray Whales' Birthday Party

by David Hoobler

This is a story about Zonk, an adventurous little Sonoran desert tortoise who wanted
to be a sea turtle. Zonk dreams of swimming in the ocean with the fishes and whales.
One day he is washed into a river and out to sea in a flash flood. His dream came true.
This is the third book in Zonk's adventure.

Zonk and the Gray Whales' Birthday Party

by David Hoobler

A special thanks to my friend, Jerrilyn Ruest, for all her help and support.

Thank you to these contributors, whose generosity made the publishing of this book possible:

Art Lover and Zonk Collector Level

Oliver Edmunds   Nam Anh and Ross Margo   Jerrilyn Ruest   Ron Zamir

Benefactor Level

The Burkes   Jerry and Roberta Hoobler   Jim and Rennie Kirby   Mary Kay Wright

Donor Level

GiGi Anber   Sonya Hoobler   Adrian Moore   Ava Stone
Cheryl Azoff   Stephen Hoobler   Alexander Moore   Kathy Tennant
Joany Callahan, for Maggie William Gerald Hoobler   Nancy Purkey   Aidan Warner
Carolyn Daniels   Zoey Florene Hoobler   Alexander Smith   Nadia Warner
Brooke Dawson and Mark   Sophie Lindner   Alyssa Smith   Paula Weightman
Jordyn Goldsmith   Jillian Luton

And thank you to Nancy Baer for her much needed assistance.

Zonk and the Gray Whales' Birthday Party by David Hoobler
Copyright 2013 by David Hoobler
All rights reserved including rights of reproduction,
in whole or in part, in any form or media.
First edition, first printing 2013
Summary: Zonk searches for a way back home and attends the gray whales' birthday party.
ISBN 978-0-9706537-3-4

Other books by David Hoobler:
Zonk, the Dreaming Tortoise   ISBN 0970653700
Zonk and the Secret Lagoon   ISBN 0970653719

Zonk books and art may be purchased at **www.zonktheturtle.com**

The Gulf of California and Sonoran Desert

The Sonoran Desert and the Gulf of
California are very special places,
full of wonderful creatures.
This is where Zonk's adventure take place.

To Georgia,
+ Soren,

A whale tale,
with a whale
tail!

"How will I ever get back home
to the desert?" Zonk asked himself.

Zonk and his new friends, Manta,
Fish, and Emily were on a great adventure.
With the ancient Elephant Cactus watching and
guiding them, they were exploring the Gulf of California.

Washed out to sea in a flash flood, Zonk had become a
"sea tortoise", his dream had come true. But he missed his
family and old friends, Bunny, Snake and Coyote, back
home in the desert. It was winter. If Zonk were home, he
would be nestled in a nice, warm burrow, out of the cold.

Zonk and his friends were trying to find the river
that had washed him out to sea. If he could find the
river, maybe he could follow it back home.

Suddenly Emily became very excited and shouted,
"Look, look!" She had spied another sea turtle.
It was an enormous leatherback sea turtle!

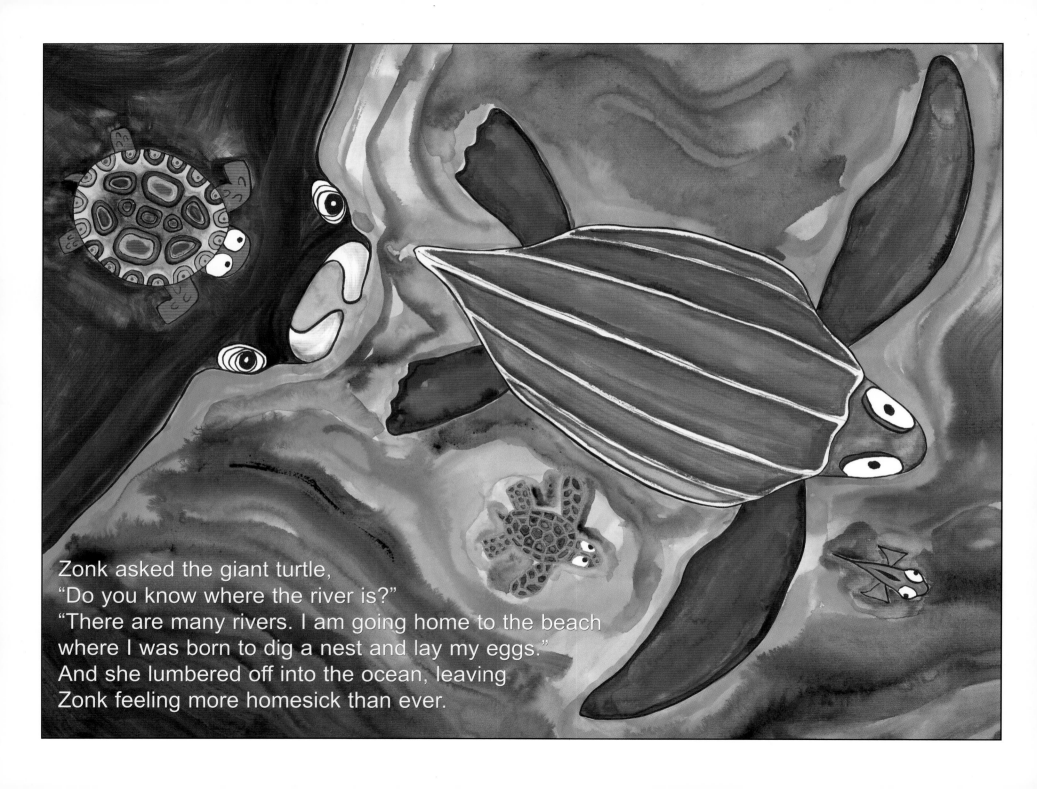

Zonk asked the giant turtle,
"Do you know where the river is?"
"There are many rivers. I am going home to the beach
where I was born to dig a nest and lay my eggs."
And she lumbered off into the ocean, leaving
Zonk feeling more homesick than ever.

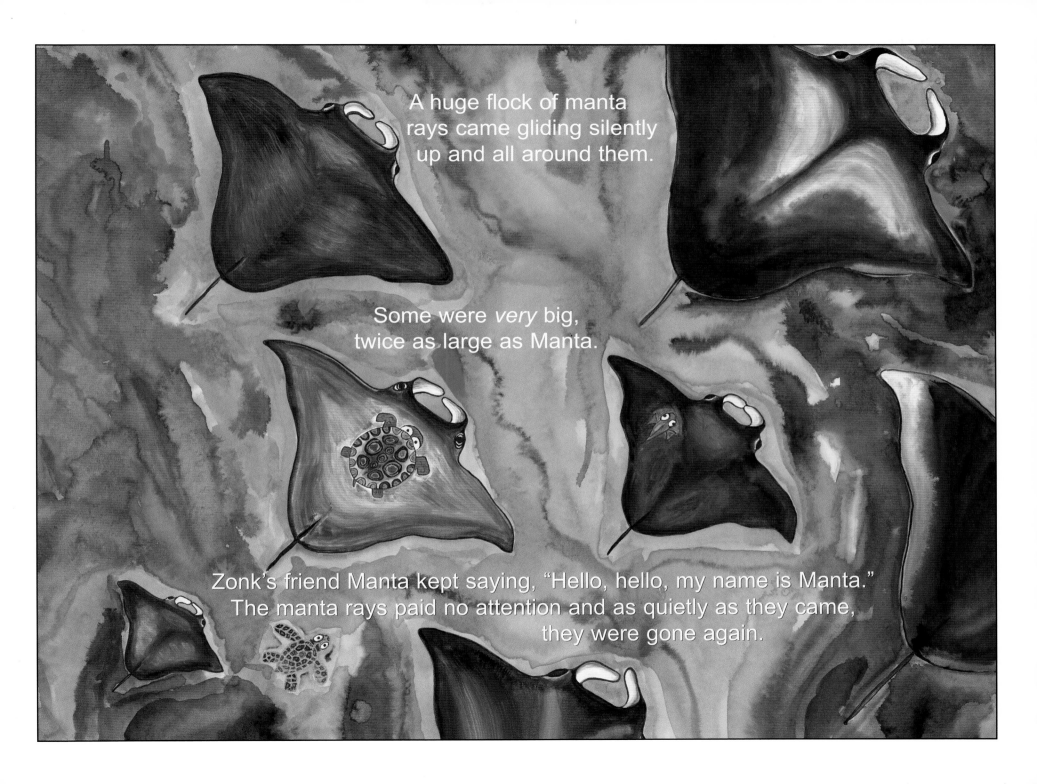

A huge flock of manta
rays came gliding silently
up and all around them.

Some were *very* big,
twice as large as Manta.

Zonk's friend Manta kept saying, "Hello, hello, my name is Manta."
The manta rays paid no attention and as quietly as they came,
they were gone again.

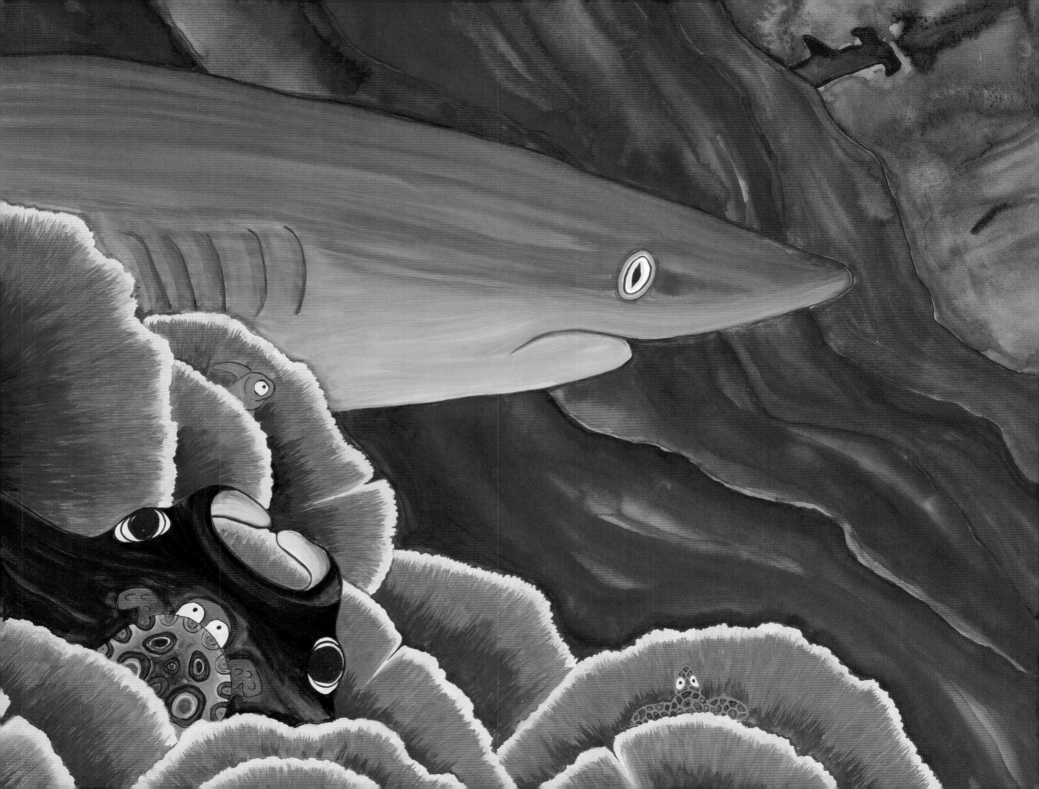

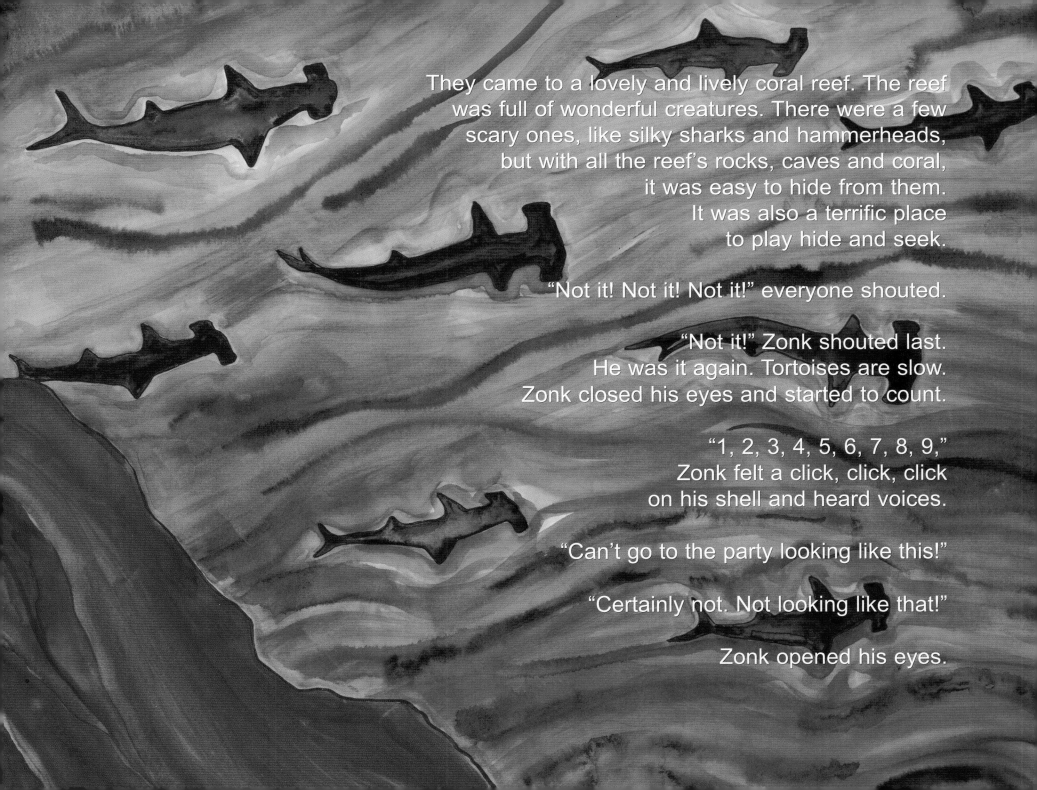

They came to a lovely and lively coral reef. The reef
was full of wonderful creatures. There were a few
scary ones, like silky sharks and hammerheads,
but with all the reef's rocks, caves and coral,
it was easy to hide from them.
It was also a terrific place
to play hide and seek.

"Not it! Not it! Not it!" everyone shouted.

"Not it!" Zonk shouted last.
He was it again. Tortoises are slow.
Zonk closed his eyes and started to count.

"1, 2, 3, 4, 5, 6, 7, 8, 9,"
Zonk felt a click, click, click
on his shell and heard voices.

"Can't go to the party looking like this!"

"Certainly not. Not looking like that!"

Zonk opened his eyes.

"What are you doing?" Zonk asked, a little startled. Two skunk shrimp and two rainbow wrasses, reef cleaner fishes, were polishing Zonk's shell.

"Cleaning you up for the party, of course."

"What party?" Zonk just loved a good party.

"The birthday party, silly!" But then, a sudden movement on the reef scared the shrimps and wrasses away.

"A birthday party. I wonder whose birthday it is." And Zonk went to find his hiding friends.

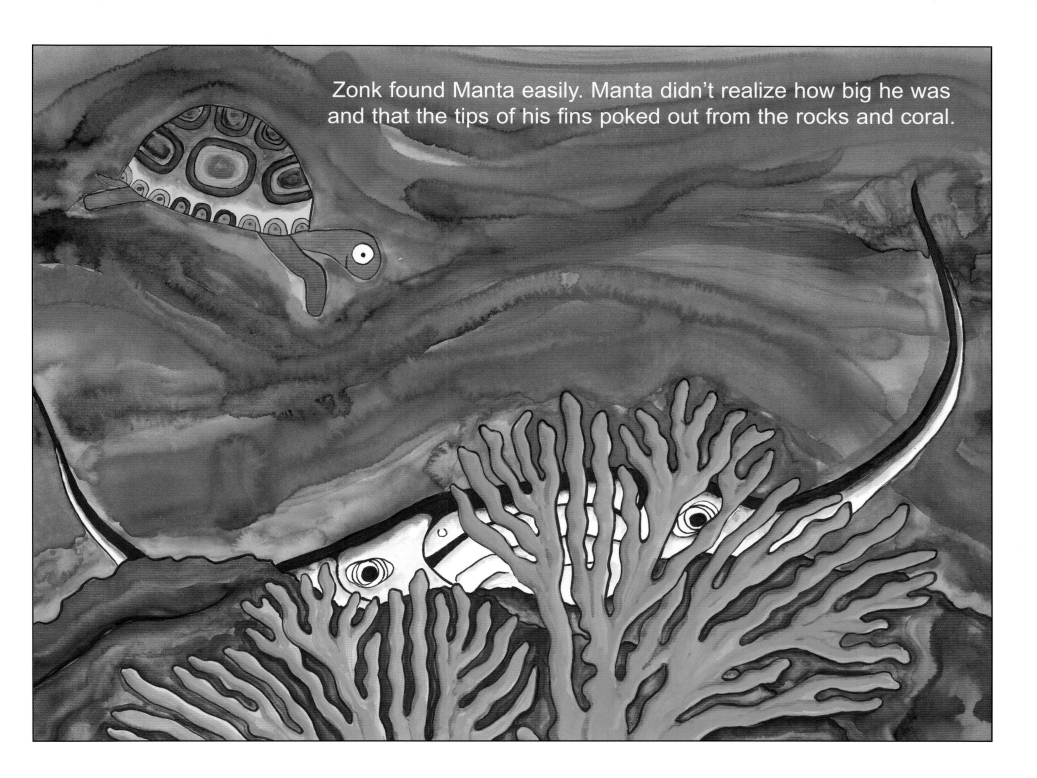

Zonk found Manta easily. Manta didn't realize how big he was and that the tips of his fins poked out from the rocks and coral.

Fish was so silly; he thought he could blend into any ol' passing school of fish.

Zonk found his friends floating on the waves. He decided he would start across the desert for home. Zonk began to say goodbye to his friends when a shadow raced across the water, and with a loud "Thump!" a large albatross landed on Zonk's shell.

"Hi, going to the party?" asked the huge bird.

"Hey!" Zonk shouted in surprise. The bird had scared him. "Do you go around dropping in on just anyone, anytime you like? Whose party?"

"It's the Gray Whales' Birthday Party. The gray whales come all the way from arctic oceans to have their babies. It's the biggest party in the world! Everyone is invited!"

"I can't go, I am trying to get home. We have been looking for the river that brought me here," Zonk replied.

"Maybe the river that empties into the whale lagoon will take you home."

"There's a river? Where?" asked Zonk.

"Come to the party, I'll tell you about it," answered the albatross. "But first you need to get your party hats. They are handing them out down on the reef. Let's go!" And using Zonk's head for a launching pad, the bird ran across the water, furiously flapping his wings until he awkwardly lifted into the air.

Zonk's friends looked at Zonk to see what he wanted to do.

"Maybe I can find my way back home," said Zonk. "Let's get some hats and go to the party."

Zonk and his friends went down to the reef. Everyone had heard about the party and was tearing about getting ready. Some were getting a final polish from the cleaner fish. Others were lined up for hats at a rocky outcropping.

A large grouper was selecting slimy, but very pretty nudibranchs in brilliant plumage as hats for each of the partygoers.

They were very strange hats indeed. Zonk got the Clown Nudibranch; Emily, the Mexican Dancer; Fish, the Sea Lemon Nudibranch; and for Manta, a flock of Red-tipped Sea Goddesses.

Off they went, with Zonk leading the way. They knew they were close when they heard the whales singing.

As they entered the lagoon, Zonk asked, "What is that smell? Phew!"

"Whale breath, you get used to it." Albatross had come down to the waves. "After the party, follow the lagoon and you will find the river. Oh, and watch out for happy whales."

"What does that mean, 'watch out for happy whales'?" asked Zonk. But the albatross was already gone.

Then they saw the whales. There were big whales and baby whales.
Boy whales, girl whales, spouting whales, breaching whales…whales, whales, whales!

Everywhere they looked, there were California Gray Whales.

Just then, a thunderous wave pitched Zonk up into the air as the joyful whales breached. The splashing knocked off everyone's nudibranch hats. Nobody seemed to mind.
Ah ha! 'Happy whales'.

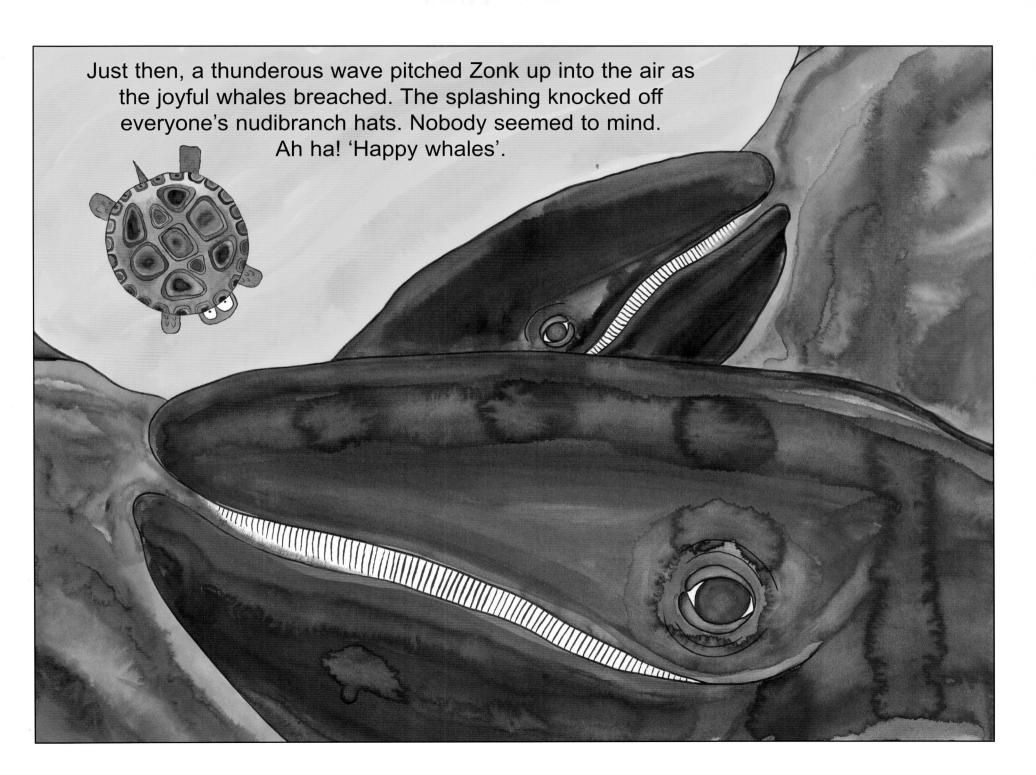

At the party they played whale games, like spyhopping. The whales poked up their heads and looked around. Zonk and his friends did too, but it seemed like a silly game.

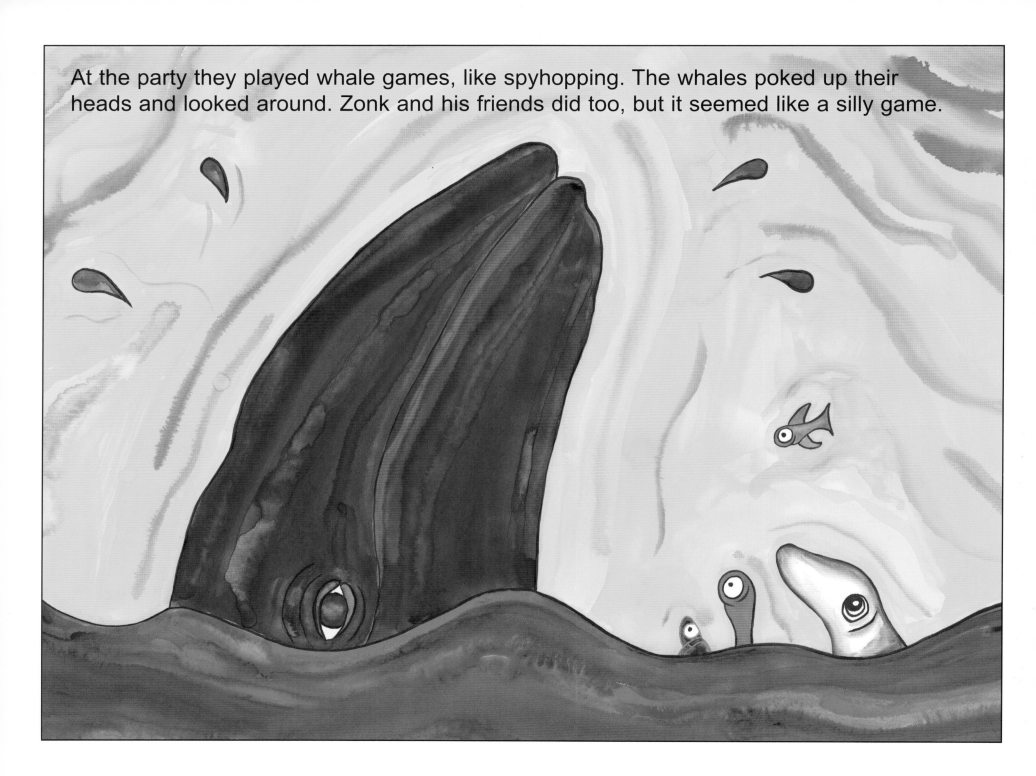

Another game was fluking, with the whales waving their giant flukes in the air. So Zonk and his friends joined in, waving *their* flukes in the air.

They played and sang on and on until the sun began to set. Even though Zonk was having a good time, seeing the whales with their families and old friends made Zonk realize how much he missed *his* family and old friends.

Zonk climbed a dune on the beach and began to say goodbye. Everyone was sad now that Zonk was really going to leave. Emily cried, "I'm going to miss you, Zonk."

"I am going to miss you too Emily, I'm going to miss all of you," said Zonk.

Zonk thanked his friends for all of their help. Manta, Fish and Emily turned and sadly headed back to the reef. Zonk went to make his bed on the beach. He would find the river in the morning.

Zonk awoke to pelicans swooping low over the waves and the sun burning through the morning fog. The air was wet, and Zonk felt lonely all by himself.

Zonk trudged along the shore of the lagoon, searching for the river. The wind whistling through the cactus seemed to say, "Zonk." It got louder "Zonk!" and louder, "ZONK!" Zonk looked up. There on a ridge were his old friends, Bunny, Snake and Coyote!

Everyone was overjoyed! Zonk, Bunny, Snake, and Coyote all danced with glee.

"How did you get here?" Zonk asked.

"It has been a very long walk. We're a little lost," said Coyote.

"I made it to the ocean. I went to a whale party. I made new friends - manta rays, fishes, sea turtles. I..."

"Let's go home," said Bunny. "You can tell us all about it on the way."

With the sun warming his shell and his old friends around him, Zonk felt like he was already home. Zonk looked back one more time and thought about his adventure.

Zonk didn't find the river, but he found something even better; old friends to share his journey back home.

For parents and teachers to discuss with your children.

Cabo Pulmo Reef

The reef in the story was inspired by the reef at Cabo Pulmo National Preserve at the southern end of the Gulf of California. Today Cabo Pulmo is one of the most successful marine preserves in the world, though it was nearly destroyed by over-fishing. The Preserve was established through the efforts of the villagers of Cabo Pulmo who came together to save their reef. This story demonstrates what people working to save their planet can accomplish.

Glossary

Breaching: Refers to a whale leaping out of the water.

Fluking: Not a scientific term, a whale lifting its tail/fluke up into the air.

Nudibranch (nu-de-brank): A group of soft-bodied colorful sea mollusks.

Reef cleaner fishes: Reef inhabitants that remove various parasites from other passing fish.

Spyhopping: When a whale pokes its head up out of the water to "look around."

CLINICALLY RELEVANT
ELECTROCARDIOGRAPHY

PQRST and U

CLINICALLY RELEVANT
ELECTROCARDIOGRAPHY

PQRST and U

WILLIAM A. SCHIAVONE, DO, FACC
Director, Non-Invasive Cardiology
Geisinger Health System
Danville, Pennsylvania

2006
BC Decker Inc
Hamilton

BC Decker Inc
P.O. Box 620, L.C.D. 1
Hamilton, Ontario L8N 3K7
Tel: 905-522-7017; 800-568-7281
Fax: 905-522-7839; 888-311-4987
E-mail: info@bcdecker.com
www.bcdecker.com

05 06 07/WPC/9 8 7 6 5 4 3 2 1

ISBN 1-55009-342-8
Printed in the United States

Sales and Distribution

United States
BC Decker Inc
P.O. Box 785
Lewiston, NY 14092-0785
Tel: 905-522-7017; 800-568-7281
Fax: 905-522-7839; 888-311-4987
E-mail: info@bcdecker.com
www.bcdecker.com

Canada
BC Decker Inc
5 King Street East
P.O. Box 620, LCD 1
Hamilton, Ontario L8N 3K7
Tel: 905-522-7017; 800-568-7281
Fax: 905-522-7839; 888-311-4987
E-mail: info@bcdecker.com
www.bcdecker.com

Foreign Rights
John Scott & Company
International Publishers' Agency
P.O. Box 878
Kimberton, PA 19442
Tel: 610-827-1640
Fax: 610-827-1671
E-mail: jsco@voicenet.com

Japan
Igaku-Shoin Ltd.
Foreign Publications Department
3-24-17 Hongo
Bunkyo-ku, Tokyo, Japan 113-8719
Tel: 3 3817 5680
Fax: 3 3815 6776
E-mail: fd@igaku-shoin.co.jp

UK, Europe, Scandinavia, Middle East
Elsevier Science
Customer Service Department
Foots Cray High Street
Sidcup, Kent
DA14 5HP, UK
Tel: 44 (0) 208 308 5760
Fax: 44 (0) 181 308 5702
E-mail: cservice@harcourt.com

Singapore, Malaysia, Thailand, Philippines, Indonesia, Vietnam, Pacific Rim, Korea
Elsevier Science Asia
583 Orchard Road
#09/01, Forum
Singapore 238884
Tel: 65-737-3593
Fax: 65-753-2145

Australia, New Zealand
Elsevier Science Australia
Customer Service Department
STM Division
Locked Bag 16
St. Peters, New South Wales, 2044
Australia
Tel: 61 02 9517-8999
Fax: 61 02 9517-2249
E-mail: stmp@harcourt.com.au
www.harcourt.com.au

Mexico and Central America
ETM SA de CV
Calle de Tula 59
Colonia Condesa
06140 Mexico DF, Mexico
Tel: 52-5-5553-6657
Fax: 52-5-5211-8468
E-mail: editoresdetextosmex@prodigy.net.mx

Brazil
Tecmedd Importadora E Distribuidora De Livros Ltda.
Avenida Maurílio Biagi, 2850
City Ribeirão, Ribeirão Preto – SP – Brasil
CEP: 14021-000
Tel: 0800 992236
Fax: (16) 3993-9000
E-mail: tecmedd@tecmedd.com.br

India, Bangladesh, Pakistan, Sri Lanka
Elsevier Health Sciences Division
Customer Service Department
17A/1, Main Ring Road
Lajpat Nagar IV
New Delhi – 110024, India
Tel: 91 11 2644 7160-64
Fax: 91 11 2644 7156
E-mail: esindia@vsnl.net

Contents

List of Abbreviations

AJR	accelerated junctional rhythm		HR	heart rate
AMI	acute myocardial infarction		HTN	hypertension
ASMI	anteroseptal myocardial infarction		ICD	implantable cardioverter-defibrillator
AV	atrioventricular		ICU	intensive care unit
AVNRT	atrioventricular nodal reciprocating or reentrant tachycardia		IMR	immediate mechanical reperfusion
AVRT	atrioventricular reentrant or reciprocating tachycardia		INR	international normalized ratio
BBB	bundle branch block		IRBBB	incomplete right bundle branch block
CABG	coronary artery bypass graft		IV	intravenous
CAD	coronary artery disease		IVCD	intraventricular conduction delay
CCU	coronary care unit		JVP	jugular venous pulse or jugular venous pressure
CHB	complete heart block		LA	left atrium
CHD	coronary heart disease		LAD	left anterior descending
CHF	congestive heart failure		LAE	left atrial enlargement
CMR	cardiac magnetic resonance		LAFB	left anterior fascicular block
COPD	chronic obstructive pulmonary disease		LAH	left anterior hemiblock
CVD	cardiovascular disease		LBBB	left bundle branch block
DCC	direct current cardioversion		LCA	left coronary artery
DCM	dilated cardiomyopathy		LCx	left circumflex coronary artery
DDD	(a pacemaker code)		LPH	left posterior hemiblock
DDDR	(a pacemaker code)		LV	left ventricle *or* left ventricular
DOO	(a pacemaker code)		LVA	left ventricular aneurysm
ECG	electrocardiogram		LVEDP	left ventricular end-diastolic pressure
ED	emergency department		LVEF	left ventricular ejection fraction
EPS	electrophysiologic studies		LVH	left ventricular hypertrophy
GNT	giant negative T wave		MAT	multifocal atrial tachycardia
HCM	hypertrophic cardiomyopathy		MCL1	modified central lead 1
HCM	hypertrophic cardiomyopathy		MI	myocardial infarction
HOCM	hypertrophic obstructive cardiomyopathy		MRI	magnetic resonance imaging

NBG	NASPE/BPEG generic code for pacemaker	RV	right ventricle *or* right ventricular
	NASPE - North American Society of Pacing and Electrophysiology	RVH	right ventricular hypertrophy
	BPEG - British Pacing and Electrophysiology Group	RVOT	right ventricular outflow tract
NQMI	non-Q-wave myocardial infarction	SA	sinoatrial
NSIVB	nonspecific intraventricular block	SSS	sick sinus syndrome
NSR	normal sinus rhythm	STEMI	ST elevation myocardial infarction
PAC	premature atrial contraction	SVT	supraventricular tachycardia
PCI	percutaneous coronary intervention	UAP	unstable angina pectoris
PJRT	permanent junctional reciprocating tachycardia	VA	ventricular aneurysm or ventriculo-atrial
PMHR	predicted maximal heart rate	VCD	ventricular conduction defect
PVC	premature ventricular contraction	VDD	(a pacemaker code)
RA	right atrium	VPB	ventricular premature beat
RAE	right atrial enlargement	VPR	ventricular-paced rhythm
RAO	right anterior oblique	VT	ventricular tachycardia
RBBB	right bundle branch block	VVI	(a pacemaker code)
RCA	right coronary artery	VVIR	(a pacemaker code)
rSR	a different appearance of the QRS complex in RBBB	WP	Wenckebach period
RSR'	a different appearance of the QRS complex in RBBB	WPW	Wolff-Parkinson-White
rSR	an appearance of the QRS complex in RBBB		

Foreword

I was honored when Dr. Schiavone asked me to write this foreword, especially so since we are not personally acquainted and even more so because his book is an excellent and quite original accomplishment. This is also a particularly timely book, which Dr. Schiavone has precisely named "Clinically Relevant Electrocardiography" since it presents a wide range of choice and informative tracings at a time when learning (and teaching!) electrocardiography has fallen to a very low level. (The Board of Cardiovascular Disease, having understood this, has for some time insisted that candidates for certification must pass a separate examination on electrocardiography as well as the Board examination proper.)

One fault of contemporary medical writing is prolixity, which Dr. Schiavone avoids by concentrating a consistently high volume of fact and analysis within a readable economy of words. The ECGs are full-sized tracings, with their analyses on facing pages in a concise format that stimulates and teaches the reader: Clinical Presentation; Description of Electrocardiogram (12-lead and rhythm strips); Interpretation; Learning Points: Suggested Readings. Each encapsulated case history is followed by its electrocardiogram and, in many, follow-up tracings where these are relevant. "Suggested Readings" presents carefully chosen references from books and articles, which Dr. Schiavone fully annotates so that readers will know what to expect in each.

I must confess that, despite having published at least 200 articles and book chapters on various aspects of electrocardiography and having taught it to everyone from medical students to nurses to faculty and practitioners, I learned from Dr. Schiavone's efforts. This book is a triumph of teaching, which will be useful at all levels of knowledge and sophistication and would make a dandy gift for a favored friend or colleague.

David H. Spodick MD, DSc
August 2005
Worcester, MA

Preface

The ability to read an electrocardiogram is essential for good patient care. This skill is applied at every turn in the daily management of illness. In the evaluation of chest pain in the emergency room, where time is of the essence, no tool gives more objective information in so short a time than the electrocardiogram.. In the office, the family practitioner, nurse practitioner, physician assistant, internist, and cardiologist use electrocardiography to assess all matters of the heart, so to speak, from palpitations to angina pectoris to the effectiveness of a therapeutic trial. The anesthesiologist and nurse anesthetist with good electrocardiogram-reading ability can better screen the preoperative patient and better manage that patient intraoperatively. The nurse, intern, or resident who knows electrocardiography will feel less daunted when called to see the patient who has chest pain or an arrhythmia. The patient will also rest easier in clinically competent hands.

Learning electrocardiography takes time, diligence, and hard work. The best teacher is experience. The next best teacher is a researched sample case. The use of example electrocardiograms categorized by their teaching points, with clinical vignettes and often with serial follow-up tracings, makes for good teaching that is clinically relevant. The addition of annotated references offers a historical perspective, detail, and insight for the student in search of more depth of understanding.

It is the purpose of this book to offer readers of various educational levels and clinical foci the opportunity to learn electrocardiography, beginning with basic recognition and familiarity with tracings and terminology and progressing to a more detailed understanding of some finer detail.

In this text, a case number refers to a particular patient. When the same patient has more than one 12 lead ECG or 3 lead rhythm strip, the second or third tracing for the patient is given the number of the case (patient) plus a letter, in alphabetical sequence (ie 50, 50a, 50b). Thus there are 74 patients and 99 tracings presented, interpreted, highlighted with learning points, discussed, and referenced (with annotation). The ECG is presented on the right hand page and the description is on the facing left hand page. For readers who wish to view an ECG as an unknown, it is best to cover the left hand page until the interpretation, discussion and references are desired. Abbreviations are used extensively throughout the text. A list of these abbreviations and their meanings are provided in the beginning of the book.

Finally, this book is dedicated to all students of electrocardiography but especially to the cardiology fellows at Geisinger Medical Center. Their enthusiasm for learning, their insight, and their industry are an inspiration. Working with them has been a personal renaissance.

William A. Schiavone, DO

1

Normal Electrocardiogram

Case 1

Clinical Presentation

The patient is a 50-year-old female planning an elective lipoma removal.

Description of Electrocardiogram (12 Leads)

This is a normal ECG. It is important to look at the standardization to see if it is full standard, half standard, or double standard. In full standard, 10 mm = 1 mV. The standard paper speed is 25 mm per second. The paper size is 8.5 × 11 inches; with a small margin on either side of the tracing, there is room for 10 seconds of recording. The HR can be estimated by counting the number of boxes between R waves when the rhythm is regular. When the R–R interval is 1 large box, the HR is 300/min; when 2 boxes, 150/min; when 3 boxes, 100/min; when 4 boxes, 75/min, and so on. The number of large boxes is divided into 300 to find the HR. There are five small boxes per large box. The number of small boxes is divided into 1,500 to more accurately find the HR. When the rhythm is irregular, count the number of QRS complexes across the 10-second strip and multiply by 6 to find the HR. In this case, the HR is 62/min. The rhythm is sinus because the P waves are upright in leads 1, 2, and V_6. Normal sinus rhythm falls between HRs of 60/min to 100/min; < 60/min is bradycardia, and > 100/min is tachycardia. The P–R interval is normally between 120 and 200 msec. If it is < 120 msec, consider preexcitation; if > 200 msec, one must deal with AV block. In this case, the P–R interval is 176 msec.

The QRS duration is 84 msec, falling normally < 120 msec. When the QRS interval is > 110 msec but < 120 msec, the term "incomplete bundle branch block" (BBB) or "borderline intraventricular conduction delay (IVCD) is used. If the QRS duration is too short or too long, be sure to check the paper speed.

The QRS axis is 31° (positive is assumed if no sign precedes the value). The normal QRS axis lies between −30° and 90° in the adult. (Calculating the axis will be dealt with later in this book.) The T waves are concordant with the major QRS deflection. The T waves are usually inverted in leads aVR and V_1. In this case, the T wave is upright in V_1, and this may be seen in normal tracings. The ST segment is normal, concave, and on the same baseline as the T–P and P–R segments. The Q–T interval is 408 msec and corrects to 414 msec, considering that the HR is > 60/min. (Calculation of the correction of the Q–T interval will follow a later tracing.)

Interpretation

NSR (rate, 62/min); normal ECG

Learning Points

ECG voltage standardization

ECG paper speed

Methods of HR determination

Diagnostic criteria for NSR, sinus bradycardia, and sinus tachycardia

Measurement of P–R interval

Measurement of QRS duration

Definition of normal QRS axis

Determination of ST segment baseline in relationship to T–P and
 P–R segments

Suggested Reading

Meek S, Morris F. ABC of clinical electrocardiography. introduction. I. Leads, rate, rhythm and cardiac axis. BMJ 2002;324:415–8. A concise pictorial review.

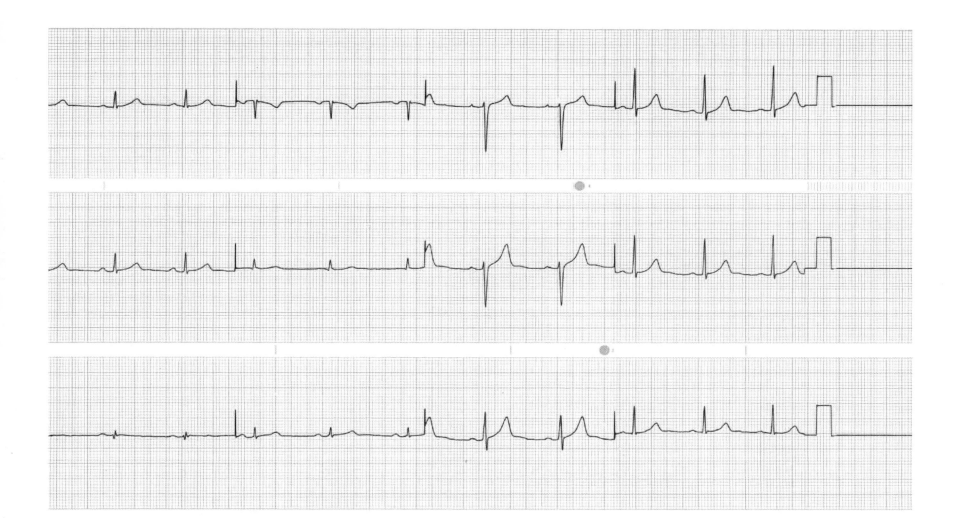

2

Atrial Abnormalities and Atrial Arrhythmias

Case 2

Clinical Presentation

The patient is a 60-year-old male with mitral valve prolapse and mitral regurgitation treated with a β-blocker to control symptoms of chest pain and palpitations.

Description of Electrocardiogram (12 Leads)

The rhythm is sinus because the P waves are upright in leads 1, 2, and V_6. The rate is 59/min, so this is sinus bradycardia. The P waves are more than three little boxes wide and are notched in lead 2, biphasic in lead V_1, and broad and notched in V_5. These findings fulfill the criteria for LAE. This pattern is also called P mitrale because it reflects mitral valve disease. The P waves are "M"-shaped. Because the sinus node is in the high RA, the first half of this P wave reflects the depolarization of the RA and the second half reflects depolarization of the LA. The P–R interval is 240 msec, so this is first-degree AV block. The remainder of the ECG is normal. Note that the T wave in V_1 is equivocal or inverted; this is normal.

Interpretation

Sinus bradycardia with LAE and first-degree AV block; abnormal ECG

Learning Points

Determination of sinus rhythm

Diagnostic criteria for LAE (P mitrale)

Separation of the RA and LA components of the P wave in LAE

Determination of first-degree AV block (> 200 msec from the start of the P wave to the Q wave)

Normal patterns for the T wave in V_1

Suggested Readings

Jose VJ, Krishnaswami S, Prasad NK, et al. Electrocardiographic left atrial enlargement—correlation with echo. J Assoc Physicians India 1989;37(8):497–9. Among 600 patients studied, LAE as reflected by P terminal force in V_1 had a sensitivity of 79%, a specificity of 91%, a predictive value of 85%, and an accuracy of 86%.

Josephson ME, Kastor JA, Morganroth J. Electrocardiographic left atrial enlargement. Electrophysiologic, echocardiographic and hemodynamic correlates. Am J Cardiol 1977;39(7):967–71. Among 21 patients studied, the prolongation of interatrial conduction time was consistently related to the electrocardiographic pattern of LAE.

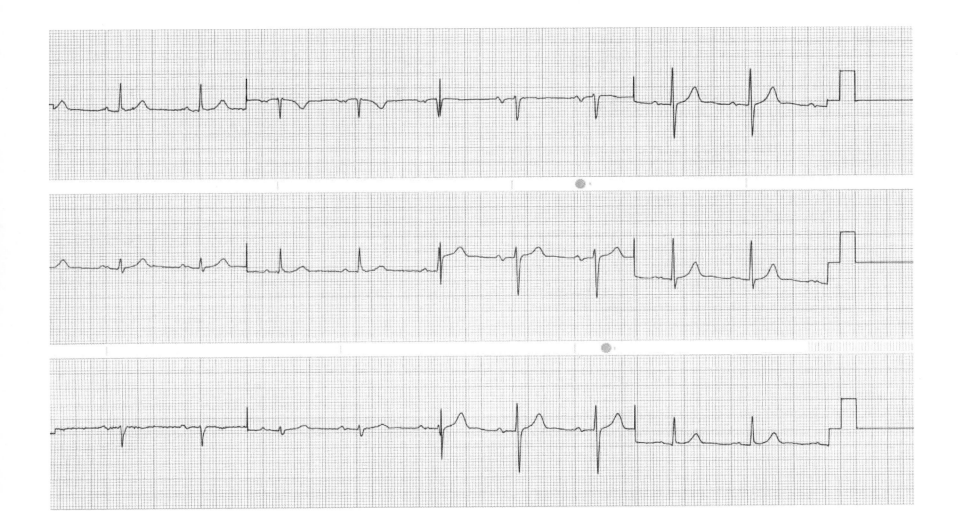

Case 3

Clinical Presentation

The patient is a 69-year-old female with episodes of spontaneous dizziness.

Description of Electrocardiogram (12 Leads)

The HR is 82/min. The P waves are inverted in leads 2 and leads V_5 and V_6. The P–R interval is 95 msec. The lower limit of normal for the P–R interval is 120 msec. Therefore, this is junctional rhythm—accelerated junctional rhythm, because the standard junctional escape rate is 40/min to 60/min and junctional tachycardia exceeds 100/min. The QRS axis is −20°, which is normal. There are no delta waves (slurred upstrokes to the initial QRS complexes), which should be sought when there is a short P–R interval. Delta waves signify preexcitation, which must be recognized before choosing a pharmacologic therapy for an arrhythmia. There are no other abnormalities on this tracing.

Interpretation

AJR; abnormal ECG

In a young person, this rhythm may be transient and may be seen when there is no cardiac abnormality; at this patient's age, it usually suggests that a pathologic process is afoot. In this case, this was a manifestation of SSS, with the AJR picking up for resting sinus bradycardia. Another cause can be toxicities from drugs such as digitalis or cocaine. In other cases SSS can be seen following coronary heart surgery, or following radiofrequency ablation of the AV node. In this case, the episodic dizziness was found (during a Holter monitor recording) to be due to sinus arrest with slow junctional escape. It responded to a DDD pacemaker insertion.

Learning Points

Junctional escape rhythm
AJR
Junctional tachycardia
Delta waves

Suggested Readings

Kerr CR, Mason MA. Incidence and clinical significance of accelerated junctional rhythm following open-heart surgery. Am Heart J 1985;110(5):966–9. Ten of 30 valvular heart surgery patients and 4 of 30 coronary heart surgery patients exhibited AJR, and 9 of the14 AJR patients required inotropic or pacemaker support.

Thibault B, deBakker JM, Hocini M, et al. Origin of heat-induced accelerated junctional rhythm. J Cardiovasc Electrophysiol 1998;9(6):631–41. AJR observed during heat and radiofrequency ablation in the AV nodal area results from the effect of heat on AV nodal cells with underlying pacemaker activity.

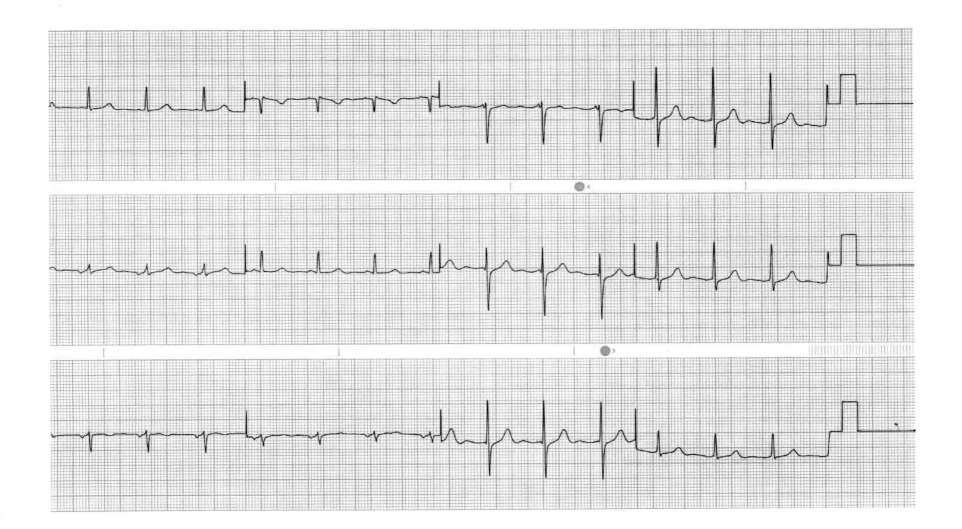

Case 4

Clinical Presentation

The patient is a 69-year-old female with tachycardia, anorexia, and nausea.

Description of Electrocardiogram (12 Leads)

In this tracing, there is tachycardia at 120/min. P waves are difficult to discern in lead 2, but in lead V_1, a P wave precedes each QRS complex. But why is the HR so fast? The PMHR for someone this age is 220 minus 69, or 151/min. When we look at lead V_6, the P waves are inverted; therefore, the rhythm is not sinus. The patient is just lying in the bed; there is no fever or pain or fear driving this HR. It must be an atrial arrhythmia. When looking closely at lead V_1 with calipers in hand, one notices a positive deflection in the T wave that might just be another P wave. The distance between the P wave that just precedes the QRS and the one that deforms the next T wave is equal to the distance between this T-deforming P wave and the P wave that just precedes the following QRS. This is a regular atrial tachycardia at 240/min. Because there are two atrial waves for each QRS complex, this should be called atrial tachycardia with 2:1 conduction. This arrhythmia can be seen in digitalis toxicity. Notice the slurred concave ST segments in leads 2, 3, aVF, and leads V_5 and V_6. This is called the digitalis effect and further supports the diagnosis of digitalis toxicity. That the patient has anorexia and nausea also points toward digitalis toxicity.

Interpretation

Atrial tachycardia with 2:1 conduction, digitalis effect; abnormal ECG. Consider digitalis toxicity

Remember that sinus rhythm will not normally exceed the PMHR and that atrial flutter has a rate of 250 to 350/min. Atrial tachycardia falls between sinus tachycardia and atrial flutter (in this case, atrial rates between 151/min and 250/min). As there was no hemodynamic compromise, no demonstrated malignant arrhythmia, and no angina pectoris from the tachycardia, the patient was not treated with digitalis antibodies. Simple withdrawal of the digoxin and hydration resulted in the resumption of sinus rhythm and the resolution of appetite and gastrointestinal upset in 24 hours.

Learning Points

Atrial tachycardia with 2:1 conduction
Digitalis toxicity
Digitalis effect
Digitalis antibodies

Suggested Readings

Antman EM, Wenger TL, Butler VP Jr, et al. Treatment of 150 cases of life-threatening digitalis intoxication with digoxin specific Fab antibody fragments. Final report of a multicenter study. Circulation 1990;81(6):1744–52. Hallmark article on the clinical indications and uses of digitalis antibodies.

Goodacre S, Irons R. ABC of clinical electrocardiography—atrial arrhythmias. BMJ 2002;324:594–7. A comparative description of atrial arrhythmias, with a list of clinical causes of atrial tachycardia.

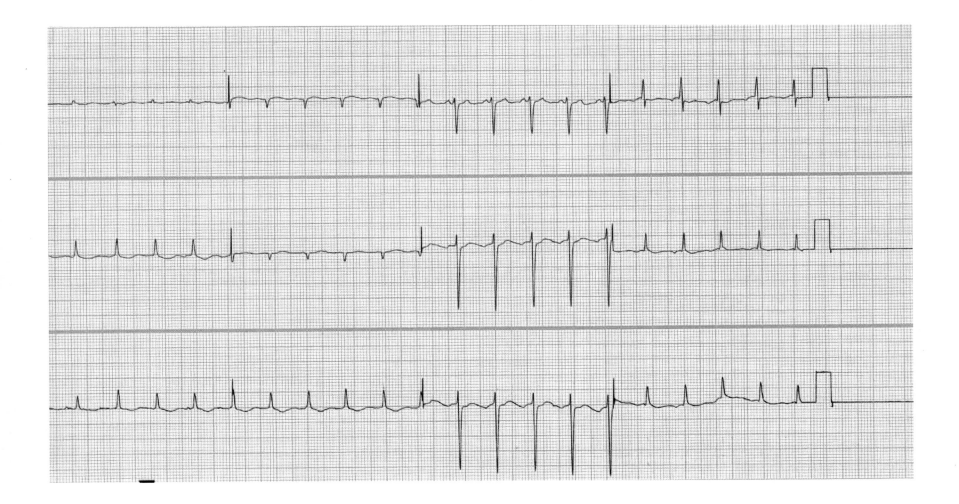

Case 5

Clinical Presentation

The patient is a sedentary 68-year-old male with waxing and waning bradycardia.

Description of Electrocardiogram (12 Leads)

This ECG shows LBBB. (This conduction abnormality will be discussed in depth later.) The HR is slow and occasionally irregular. The P waves are upright in leads 1, 2, and V_6; therefore, this is sinus rhythm. One would consider calling this sinus bradycardia with PACs, but the P waves of the premature beats are the same as those that would not be considered premature. A PAC must be premature and have a different P-wave morphology from that of the sinus P waves. Close scrutiny of the cadence of these P waves will show that the premature beats occur at twice the rate of the others. What is at work here is sinoatrial exit block. The sinus node is firing at about 95 beats/min, but only 1of 2 of these sinus firings exits the sinus node to depolarize the atrium, whereupon a P wave is inscribed. Every P wave is conducted across the AV node. The QRS axis is abnormal at −53°.

Interpretation

Sinus rhythm at 95/min with intermittent 2:1 Mobitz type II sinoatrial block, abnormal left axis, LBBB; abnormal ECG. (A three-lead rhythm strip follows.)

This patient was asymptomatic. However, with this sinus node dysfunction and LBBB in the absence of a medication known to cause sinus node dysfunction (adenosine, digitalis, β-blocker, nondihydropyridine calcium blocker, sotalol, amiodarone, etc), there was a manifestation of SSS. Upon his first dizzy spell, the patient underwent electrophysiologic studies that showed prolonged sinus node recovery time, and a DDD pacemaker was implanted. In addition to being caused by medications and SSS, sinoatrial block can be found in normal young subjects, (especially) during sleep, and as a result of sleep apnea.

Learning Points

P-wave morphology

PACs

Mobitz type II sinoatrial block

SSS

Suggested Readings

Becker H, Brandenburg U, Peter JH, Von Wichert P. Reversal of sinus arrest and atrioventricular conduction block in patients with sleep apnea during nasal continuous positive airway pressure. Am J Respir Crit Care Med 1995;15(1):215–8. A subject of importance in this era of obesity and inpatient units with electrocardiographic monitoring.

Bjornstad H, Storstein L, Meen HD, Hals O. Ambulatory electrocardiographic findings in top athletes, athletic students and control subjects. Cardiology. 1994;84(1):42–50. The sinus node slows and can demonstrate exit block in normal subjects, especially in sleep.

Snedden JF, Camm AJ. Sinus node disease. Current concepts in diagnosis and therapy. Drugs. 1992;44(5):728–37. An authoritative overview of diagnosis and therapy.

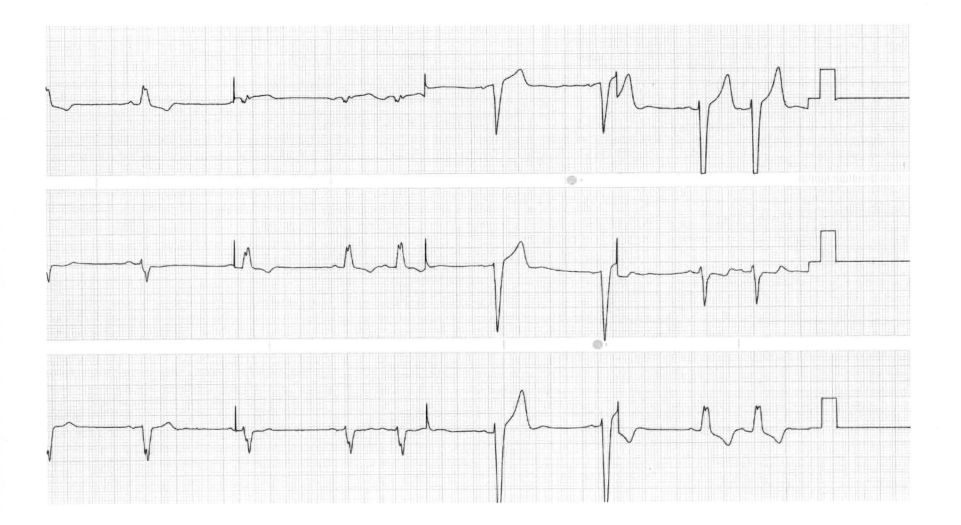

Case 5a

Rhythm Strip Interpretation

This three-lead rhythm strip will convince you that the P waves are indeed the same and that these are not PACs. Notice that the P–R interval of the P waves that are conducted in close succession is longer than it is when there is a long R–R interval. This reflects the delayed conduction rate of the AV node when the HR is increased, which is especially well demonstrated in patients who are old or who have conduction disease demonstrated elsewhere on the ECG, in this case, the LBBB. The best leads to use for rhythm strips are those used here, namely, V_1, 2, and V_5. These leads let the interpreter determine if there is sinus rhythm and if there is an RBBB or an LBBB. When the HR is slow, rhythm strips are necessary to see multiple beats in the same lead.

Learning points

Physiology of AV nodal conduction

Ideal leads for rhythm strips: V_1, 2, and V_5

Suggested Reading

Rashidi A, Khodarahmi I. Nonlinear modeling of the atrioventricular node physiology in atrial fibrillation. J Theor Biol 2005;232(4):545–9. There is an increase in the refractory period of the AV node because of rapid bombardment from the atria. The entry speed of atrial impulses into the AV node in atrial fibrillation is inversely proportional to the ventricular rate.

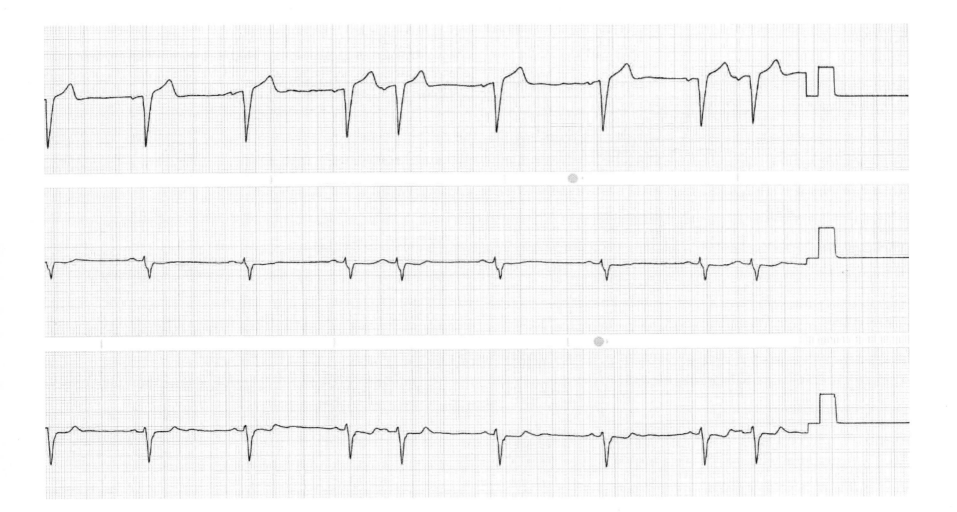

Case 6

Clinical Presentation

The patient is a 68-year-old male with an irregular rhythm.

Description of Electrocardiogram (12 leads)

There are groups of sinus beats that seem to accelerate, and then there is a pause. The P waves all have the same morphology, and the P–R intervals are constant at 178 msec. As in the last tracings, the P-wave morphology does not change despite variation of the P-wave rate. In this case, the long P–P intervals are not multiples of the P–P cycles of the basic rhythm. This is Wenckebach (Mobitz type I) SA block. The P–P intervals preceding the longer pause become progressively shorter until a dropped beat occurs. As with AV nodal Wenckebach block, there are groups of beats that accelerate to a pause. In addition, there are Q waves in leads 2, 3, and aVF, tall R waves in V_1 and V_2, and upright T waves in V_1 and V_2, meeting the criteria for an inferoposterior MI of indeterminate age. There are lateral ST segment T-wave changes, and the Q–T interval is prolonged at 480 msec (not needing correction because the mean HR is 60/min).

Interpretation

Sinus rhythm with SA Wenckebach block (mean rate, 60/min) with an inferoposterior infarction of indeterminate age, and with lateral ST segment T-wave changes and Q–T prolongation; abnormal ECG

Learning points

Wenckebach (Mobitz type I) SA block
Inferoposterior MI, age indeterminate
Q–T prolongation

Suggested Readings

Le Heuzey JY, Caron J, Guize L, et al. Wenckebach periods in sinoatrial block: experimental and clinical evidence. Pacing Clin Electrophysiol 1991;14(6):1032–9. The theory of SA Wenckebach block, tested in an animal model and demonstrated in one patient.

Oreto G. Recognition of first-degree sinoatrial block in the standard electrocardiogram. G Ital Cardiol 1982;12(10):762–6. An in-depth and clear description of the criteria for SA block originally described by Shamroth.

Yeh SJ, Lin FC, Wu D. Complete sinoatrial block in two patients with bradycardia-tachycardia syndrome. J Am Coll Cardiol 1987;9(5):1184–8. Careful studies of sinus node electrograms in patients with tachycardia-bradycardia syndrome (SSS).

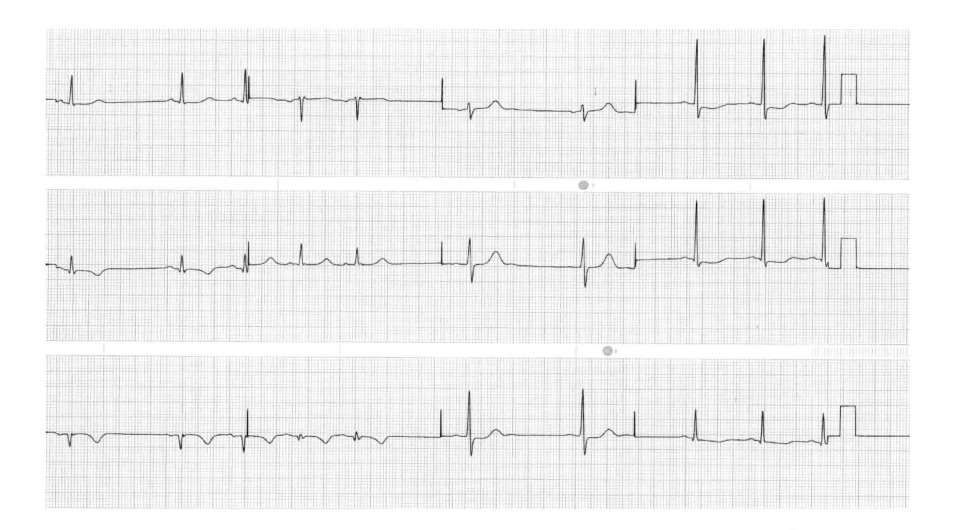

Case 6a

Rhythm Strip Interpretation

This is a three-lead standard rhythm strip of the preceding 12-lead ECG. The grouped beating of the Wenckebach SA block is apparent, and the uniformity of the P-wave morphology is clear. This is different from sinus arrhythmia because in SA Wenckebach block, the change in rate is abrupt and usually occurs in elderly patients or in patients receiving antiarrhythmic medicines. Sinus arrhythmia is usually seen in young patients and is phasic with respiration.

Learning Points

Grouped beating
Sinus arrhythmia

SA Wenckebach block often occurs transiently and is commonly seen in inferior-wall MI, in acute myocarditis, in digitalis or quinidine toxicity, as the effects of other antiarrhythmic drugs such as amiodarone, and in hyperkalemia. When it is due to increased vagal tone, it may respond to atropine. As in other forms of SSS, if it is persistent and symptomatic, it may require a pacemaker. This pertained to this patient when his telemetric monitoring showed an 8-second sinus pause with no escape rhythm coincident with the time he had syncope while lying in bed.

Suggested Reading

Morady F. An electrocardiogram that demonstrates grouped beating: what is the rhythm? J Cardiovasc Electrophysiol 1996;7(6):581–2. A case presentation with discussion to further prompt recognition.

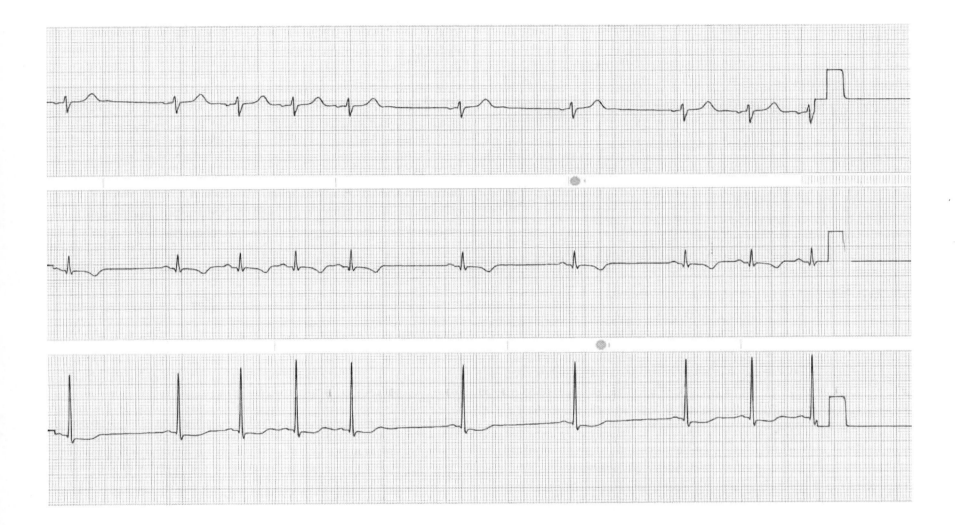

Case 7

Clinical Presentation

The patient is a 65-year-old female with tachycardia having a mean rate of 132/min.

Description of Electrocardiogram (12 Leads)

Whereas this might be sinus tachycardia, it is not possible to see P waves except in lead V_1; there, the P waves are discrete, uniform, and equidistant from each other by seven small boxes. The atrial rate is 214/min; this is clearly beyond the rate for sinus tachycardia for a patient of this age and slower than the rate for atrial flutter. There is a flat baseline between atrial waves. This is atrial tachycardia. The P–R interval is not constant; in fact, it increases up to the point of a nonconducted P wave and then repeats itself. This is atrial tachycardia with Wenckebach AV conduction. The QRS voltage when summing the R and S waves in leads 1, 2, and 3 is 13 mm. A sum of < 15 mm is called low QRS voltage, as long as normal standardization is used. Other criteria for low QRS voltage are R + S < 5 mm in all limb leads and < 10 mm in all precordial leads. I favor the former limb-lead-only criterion. The QRS axis is −19°, leftward but not abnormal. There are Q waves in leads 1, aVL, and V_1 to V_3, diagnostic of an anterolateral MI. The ST segments are largely at baseline; therefore, this is not an acute MI. The QRS duration is normal at 80 msec, but the Q–T interval is 320 msec. The corrected Q–T (Q–Tc) interval of 477 msec is prolonged. Calculating the Q–Tc interval indexes the Q–T interval to an HR of 60/min. To calculate the Q–Tc interval, one must measure the absolute Q–T interval and divide it by the square root of the R–R interval (in seconds) that precedes the Q–T interval in question. When the rhythm is irregular, one must determine the Q–Tc interval for at least three representative R–R intervals and average them. The normal Q–Tc interval is ≤ 440 msec. When measuring the Q–Tc interval in a wide QRS complex (LBBB, RBBB, pacemaker rhythm), the Q–Tc interval may be normal up to 500 msec.

Interpretation

Atrial tachycardia with Wenckebach AV block at a mean ventricular rate of 132/min, with a leftward axis and low QRS voltage and an old anterolateral MI; prolonged Q–T interval; abnormal ECG

Learning Points

Atrial tachycardia with Wenckebach AV conduction
Low-voltage QRS
Anterolateral MI, old
Calculation of Q–Tc interval

Suggested Readings

Al-Khatib SM, Allen-LaPointe NM, Kramer JM, Califf RM. What clinicians should know about the QT interval. JAMA 2003;289:2120–7. A summary of clinical data on the Q–T interval and torsades de pointes, and recommendations for the use of medications that prolong the Q–T interval.

Spodick DH. Low voltage with pericardial effusion; complexity of mechanisms. Chest 2003;124:2044–5. An analysis of associations between size of effusion, P–R segment depression, and QRS voltage in 121 patients with pericardial disease.

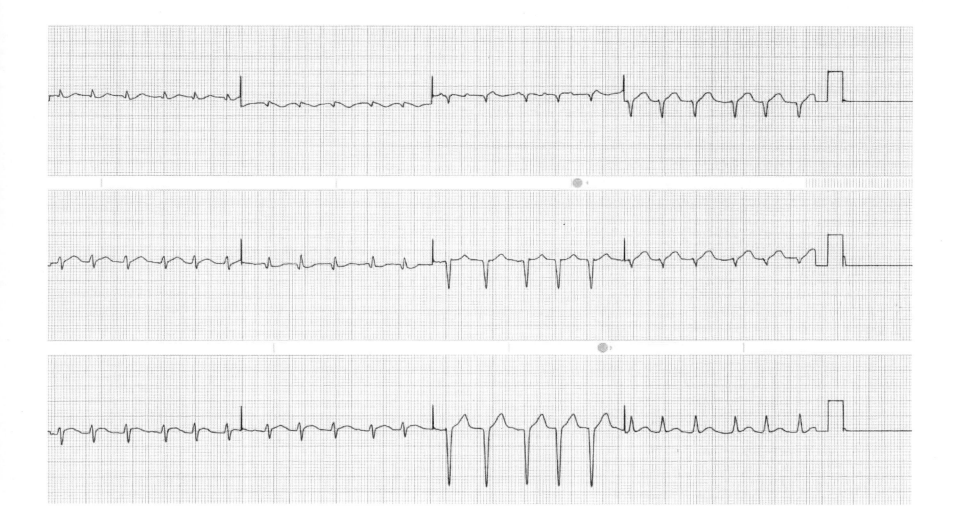

Case 7a

Rhythm Strip Interpretation

In this three-lead rhythm strip of the last tracing, the P waves of atrial tachycardia are easily seen in lead V_1. (Starting at the extreme left side of the recording, the first two P waves are conducted, but the P–R interval prolongs. The third P wave directly follows the QRS complex and is blocked. This is 3:2 Wenckebach AV conduction. In the rest of the strip, there are also examples of 4:3 AV block). As in SA Wenckebach, the tip-off to the diagnosis of AV Wenckebach periodicity is grouped beating.

Learning Point for Cases 7 and 7a

In addition to pericardial disease, causes of low QRS voltage include obesity, COPD, cardiomyopathy, amyloidosis, sarcoidosis, hypothyroidism, and anasarca. This patient had a cardiomyopathy (ischemic cardiomyopathy).

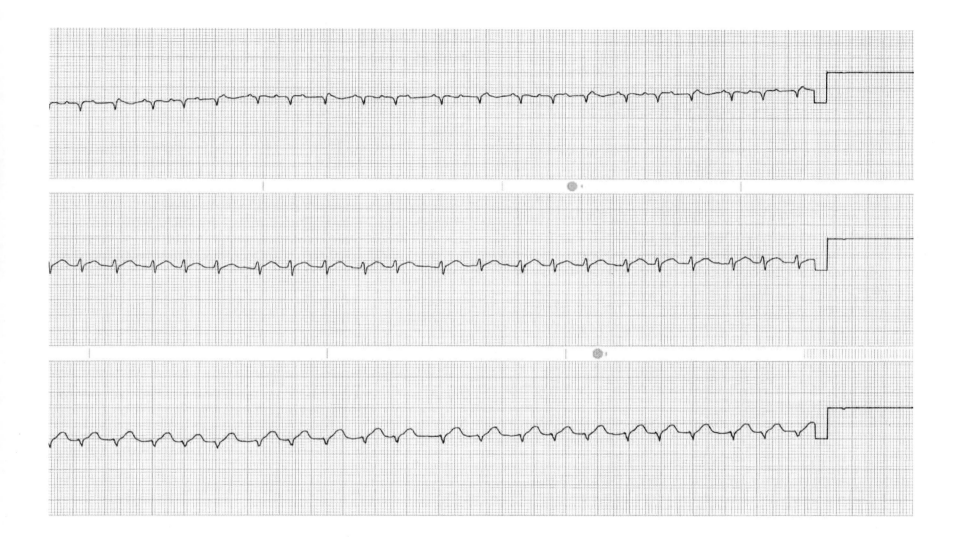

Case 8

Clinical Presentation

The patient is an 88-year-old male retired coal miner with dyspnea and tachycardia.

Description of Electrocardiogram (12 Leads)

The HR is fast and averages 186/min. It is too fast for the PMHR for this man; it must be an arrhythmia. As it is irregularly irregular (unlike Wenckebach periodicity, which is regularly irregular), one must consider atrial fibrillation with rapid ventricular response. What is different from atrial fibrillation is that there are identifiable P waves. They occur rapidly as in atrial tachycardia but are not uniform in morphology. At least four different morphologies of P waves are demonstrated (the sinus P wave and at least three other P wave morphologies). This best fits the description of MAT. Every P wave is conducted across the AV node (quite a feat in an elderly man). The QRS axis is −55°, there are no Q waves in the limb leads, and the QRS duration is normal. This is LAH. Surprisingly, for the HR and this patient's age, there are no ST segment shifts to suggest ischemia or injury.

Interpretation

MAT with a conduction rate of 186/min, with LAH; abnormal ECG

Learning Points

MAT

LAH

Patients with MAT most often have COPD, sometimes in conjunction with infection or cardiac decompensation. It is often seen in association with hypoxemia and respiratory acidosis. The use of bronchodilators may contribute to the development of MAT. This patient was treated cautiously with intravenous metoprolol and intravenous diltiazem, and he experienced prompt control of HR and relief of dyspnea.

Suggested Readings

Adcock JT, Heiselman DE, Hulisz DT. Continuous infusion diltiazem hydrochloride for treatment of multifocal atrial tachycardia [abstract]. Clin Res 1994;42:430A. An effective treatment for rate control without the risk of inducing bronchospasm.

Ansura EL, Solar M, Lefkin AS, et al. Metoprolol in the treatment of multifocal atrial tachycardia. Crit Care Med 1987;15(6):591–4. Metoprolol is effective in the acute and chronic treatment of MAT.

Shine KI, Kastor JA, Yurchak PM. Multifocal atrial tachycardia. Clinical and electrocardiographic features in 32 patients. N Engl J Med 1968;279(7):344–9. The initial description of this entity.

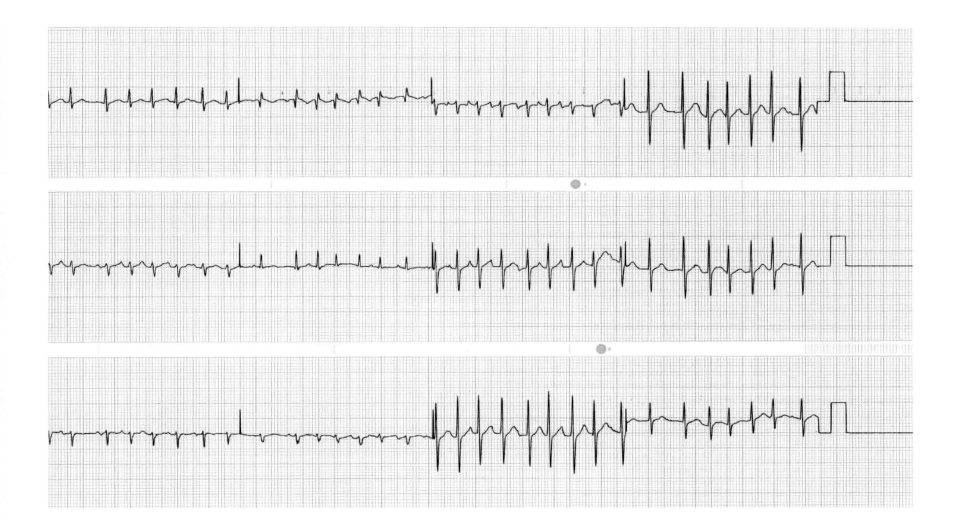

Case 9

Clinical Presentation

The patient is a 66-year-old male with a regular tachycardia and angina pectoris.

Description of Electrocardiogram (12 Leads)

The HR is 109/min and regular. The P waves are seen best in lead 2 but not in V_1. The P waves in leads 2, 3, and aVF come to a point downward, like saw teeth. These waves are inverted in V_6. This is not sinus rhythm. There are three of these saw teeth per QRS complex. The interval between each saw tooth is less than five little boxes. Their rate calculates to 327/min, in the upper rate range for atrial flutter (250–350/min). The 3:1 conduction is unusual for a patient who is not medicated with an AV nodal blocking drug. In this case, however, the rate of the flutter waves is such that in order to conduct them in a 2:1 fashion across the AV node, the HR would need to be 163/min, which would be faster than the patient's PMHR. Perhaps that is why the flutter-to-R wave interval appears to vary in this case. There are S waves in leads 1 and V_6 and an rSR in lead V_1, with a QRS duration of 112 msec, consistent with IRBBB. There are Q waves in leads V_1 and V_2, due to an anteroseptal-wall MI of indeterminate age. The ST segments in V_1 through V_4 are depressed more than one would expect for the usual IRBBB repolarization. This represents ischemia.

Interpretation

Atrial flutter with 3:1 conduction, rate 109/min with IRBBB, an anteroseptal MI of indeterminate age, and peri-infarction ischemia; abnormal ECG

Learning Points

Atrial flutter

Anteroseptal MI

IRBBB

This patient needed relief of his angina pectoris, and the most effective method was to convert the rhythm to sinus rhythm. As the duration of the atrial flutter was uncertain, he was anticoagulated with intravenous heparin, underwent transesophageal echocardiography to be certain that there was no thrombus in the left atrial appendage, and was electrically cardioverted with 100 Joules to sinus rhythm at a rate of 65/min. His angina was relieved, and the ST segment depression in V_1 to V_4 diminished. He was treated with warfarin and kept on heparin until the PT/INR (international normalized ratio) was > 2.0. There are also pharmacologic and radiofrequency ablative methods for converting atrial flutter to sinus rhythm.

Suggested Readings

Pinski SL, Sgarbassa EB, Ching E, Trohman RG. A comparison of 50-J versus 100-J shocks for direct-current cardioversion of atrial flutter. Am Heart J 1999;137(3):439–42. In 330 consecutive patients with atrial flutter divided to receive an initial shock of 50 J or 100 J, those who received an initial shock of 100 J had more effective restoration of sinus rhythm and the need for fewer shocks.

Slama R, Leclercq JF, Coumel P, Bouvrain Y. [2 or 3 level blocks in the Tawara node during atrial tachycardia.] Arch Mal Coeur Vaiss 1978;71(12):1322–40. A complex explanation of the three levels of AV nodal block that account for the various atrioventricular conduction ratios.

Waldo AL. Pathogenesis of atrial flutter. J Cardiovasc Electrophysiol 1998;8 Suppl:S18–25. An explanation of the reentrant circuit of atrial flutter.

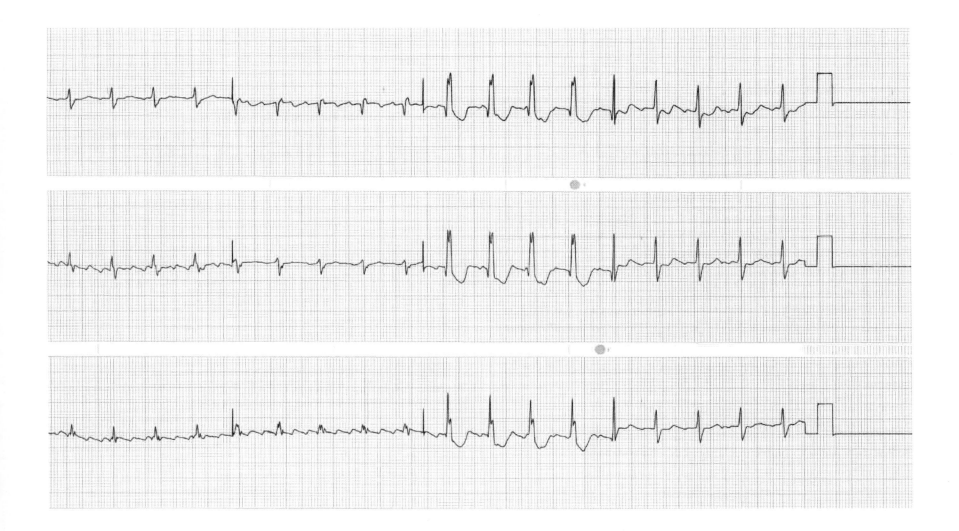

Case 10

Clinical Presentation

The patient is a 60-year-old male with an intermittent irregular rhythm.

Description of Electrocardiogram (12 Leads)

The rhythm is regular at a rate of 100/min. It is NSR at the upper rate limit of normal for sinus rhythm. The first P wave shows RAE because with full standardization of 10 mm = 1 mV, this P wave is > 3 mm high and is peaked like a tepee in leads 2 and 3 (and also in aVF in other beats). This is also called P pulmonale because it is seen in patients with pulmonary disease. The next P wave shows LAE or P mitrale (3 mm wide in leads 2 and 3 and notched like an "m"). As there is no change in the rhythm despite the change in the morphology of the P waves, this is not a PAC but rather a change in the interatrial conduction. It is likely that both atria are enlarged. The QRS voltage is at the lower limit of normal. That low voltage is seen in pulmonary disease and that most of the P waves recorded are tall and peaked speak for the presence of pulmonary disease. There are no other abnormalities on this ECG.

Interpretation

NSR at 100/min with biatrial enlargement; abnormal ECG

Learning Points

P pulmonale (RAE)
P mitrale (LAE)

This patient indeed had biatrial enlargement due to floppy mitral and tricuspid valves with chronic mitral and tricuspid regurgitation. He had a barrel chest with an increased anteroposterior diameter that accounts for the relatively low voltage. The intermittent irregular rhythm was atrial fibrillation. Some authors refer to these atrial electrographic patterns as right atrial abnormality and left atrial abnormality because the true cause of the electrocardiographic findings may be abnormalities of size, thickness, or electrical conduction. In this case, there is echocardiographic demonstration of biatrial enlargement. When dealing with RAE, the magnitude of peaking of the P waves in lead 3 can vary from the presentation after effective treatment of the acute pulmonary illness. Peaking of P waves can transiently be seen during stress electrocardiography in patients with right heart strain.

Suggested Reading

Yue P, Atwood JE, Froelicher V. Watch the P wave: it can change! Chest 2003;124(2):424–6. An editorial that reviews the several factors that influence the dynamic morphology of the P wave.

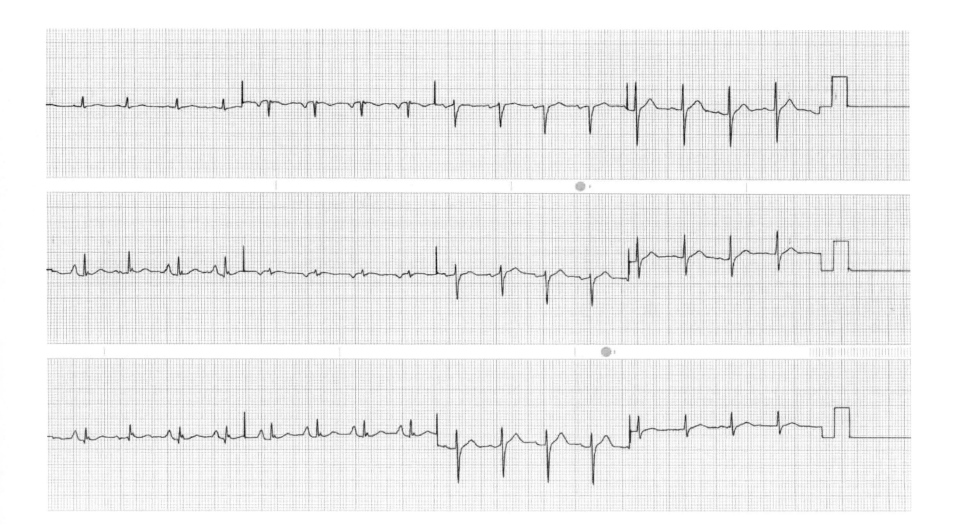

Case 11

Clinical Presentation

The patient is a 63-year-old male complaining of sudden onset of tachycardia.

Description of Electrocardiogram (12 Leads)

The HR is 227/min and regular. The T waves are deformed by retrograde P waves that are inverted in leads 2, 3, and aVF and that are upright in lead aVR and precede the QRS complex. There is a long R–P interval and a short P–R interval. The QRS complexes are uniform and narrow. In narrow-QRS tachycardias that are regular and have a visible P wave (with one P wave for each QRS) and an R–P interval longer than the P–R interval, the differential diagnosis is atrial tachycardia, PJRT, or atypical AVNRT. That the QRS complexes are narrow favors SVT. If the QRS complex were wide, it would be difficult to differentiate SVT with BBB aberrancy from ventricular tachycardia.

Interpretation

Long R–P SVT (rate, 227/min), atypical AVNRT; abnormal ECG

Learning Points

SVT

Long R–P interval

AVNRT may be induced by nicotine, alcohol, stimulants, exercise, or surges in vagal tone. It is sudden in onset and termination. Symptoms such as dyspnea and/or chest pain are related to HR and the presence or absence of underlying heart disease. Occasionally, there is associated polyuria due to high RA pressure from the arrhythmia that releases atrial natriuretic peptide. The typical AVNRT has slow anterograde (long P–R) and fast retrograde (short R–P) conduction. In this case of atypical AVNRT, there is fast anterograde (short P–R) and slow retrograde (long R–P) conduction. Treatment with electrical cardioversion or adenosine (intravenous bolus) is often successful in acute termination. Chronic treatment includes flecainide or amiodarone, but the most effective treatment is radiofrequency ablation.

Suggested Readings

Blomstrom-Lundqvist C, Scheinman MM, Aliot EM, et al. Management of patients with supraventricular arrhythmias. J Am Coll Cardiol 2003;42:1493–531. American College of Cardiology/American Heart Association/European Society of Cardiology guidelines, with good tables and algorithms.

Karas BJ, Grubb BP. Reentrant tachycardias—a look at where treatment stands today. Postgrad Med 1998;103(1):84–6, 93–6, 98. A review of the diagnosis and pharmacologic and radiofrequency ablative treatment of reentrant SVT.

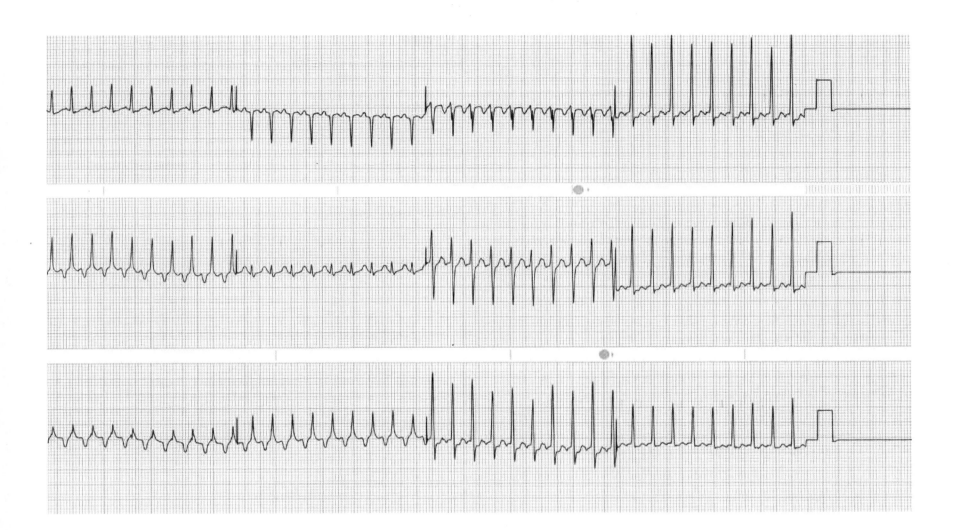

Case 11a

Clinical Presentation

The patient is a 63-year-old male complaining of sudden onset of tachycardia, after conversion to sinus rhythm.

Description of Electrocardiogram (12 Leads)

This is the ECG of the same 63-year-old male of Case 11, after conversion of SVT to sinus rhythm through administration of 6 mg of intravenous adenosine. The HR is 131/min. The P waves and the P–R interval are normal. The QRS axis is similar to that of this patient in SVT, with a rate of 227/min.

Determining the QRS axis is an important skill to master. It is a vectorial calculation to find the direction of the electrical current of the heart. The normal range is between $-30°$ and $90°$. More negative than $-30°$ is an abnormal left axis, and more positive than $90°$ is an abnormal right axis. The direction of lead 1 is $0°$, that of lead 2 is $60°$, lead 3 is $120°$, aVR is $-150°$, aVL is $-30°$, and aVF is $90°$. The easiest approach is to look for the lead with the largest upright deflection, one where the axis is almost in the same direction as the lead. Alternately, one can look for the most negative deflection, where the axis is almost opposite in direction to the lead. Additionally, one can look for the most isoelectric lead, in which case the axis is perpendicular to the lead. In this case, the tallest lead is lead 2 ($60°$), and this is perpendicular to isoelectric lead aVL ($-30 + 90 = 60$ also). The axis is $60°$.

Interpretation

Sinus tachycardia; normal ECG

Learning Points

Determination of QRS axis
Classical frontal-lead display
Orderly frontal lead display

Suggested Readings

Pahlm US, O'Brein JE, Pettersson J, et al. Comparison of teaching the basic electrocardiographic concept of frontal plane axis using the classical versus the orderly electrocardiogram limb lead displays. Am Heart J 1997;134(6):1014–8. Students using the orderly frontal lead display to determine frontal-plane QRS axis had greater accuracy, in less time, than when they used the classical frontal lead display.

Sgarbossa EB, Barold SS, Pinski SL, et al. Twelve-lead electrocardiogram: the advantages of an orderly frontal lead display including lead –aVR. J Electrocardiol 2004;37(3):141–7. If aVR is $-150°$ and –aVR is $30°$, then –aVR fits in between lead 1 ($0°$) and lead 2 ($60°$). Using the panorama from aVL ($-30°$) to lead 1 ($0°$) to –aVR ($30°$) to lead 2 ($60°$) to aVF ($90°$), the frontal plane of the 12-lead ECG is more easily understood. This is called the orderly frontal lead display, as opposed to the classical frontal lead display that uses aVR ($-150°$). The use of the orderly frontal lead display can enhance QRS axis determination. It is used in Sweden but rarely in the United States.

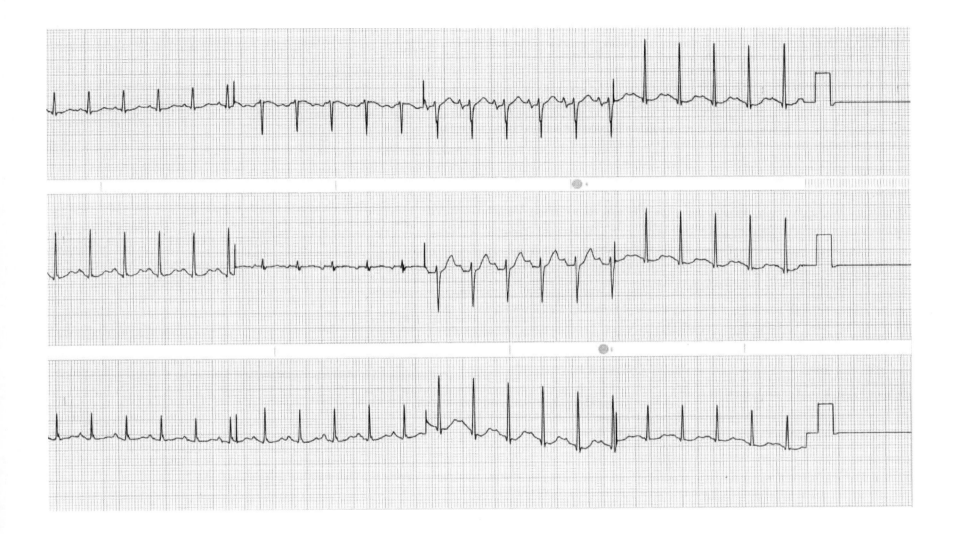

Case 12

Clinical Presentation

The patient is a 51-year-old male who passed out at home, woke up on the floor, and was taken to the hospital by the emergency medical service. He had no history of heart disease.

Description of Electrocardiogram (12 Leads)

There is a wide-complex tachycardia with an HR of 221/min. No P waves are visible, but there are small deflections in the S waves in nearly all of the limb leads. There is one deflection for each QRS complex. The QRS duration is 180 msec. With S waves in leads 1 and V_6 and an rsR' in V_1, this is an RBBB pattern. This can be SVT with RBBB or VT. An old ECG from this patient recorded when he was not in a tachycardic rhythm would be helpful. That there is no history of previous MI or structural heart disease speaks against VT.

Interpretation

SVT with RBBB, or VT; abnormal ECG

Learning Points

RBBB
Wide-complex tachycardia
SVT
VT
AVRT
Antidromic AVRT

Wide-complex tachycardias of unknown origin should be treated cautiously. If an old ECG recorded when the patient was in sinus rhythm is not available, one must consider (1) anterograde conduction down an accessory bypass tract that circumvents the AV node (antidromic AVRT) or (2) VT. The use of adenosine in these cases is unsafe. The favored pharmacologic treatments include procainamide, sotalol, and amiodarone. DCC is also safe and effective.

Suggested Reading

Blomstrom-Lundqvist C, Scheinman MM, Aliot EM, et al. Management of patients with supraventricular arrhythmias. J Am Coll Cardiol 2003;42:1493–531. American College of Cardiology/American Heart Association/European Society of Cardiology guidelines, with good tables and algorithms.

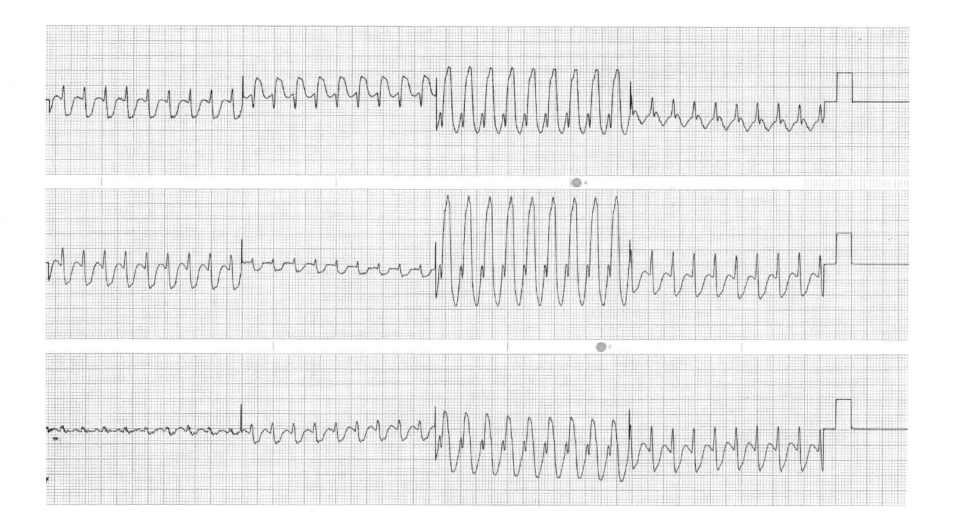

Case 12a

Clinical Presentation

The patient is the same patient as in Case 12, after conversion to sinus rhythm by DCC because of hemodynamic instability.

Description of Electrocardiogram (12 Leads)

Here the rhythm is sinus, at 88/min. The QRS axis is less rightward, but clearly there is also RBBB when in NSR. Therefore, the diagnosis for the wide-complex tachycardia was SVT. If the QRS conduction were normal when in NSR, one could consider that the tachycardia provoked aberrant conduction (SVT with aberrancy) or that the tachycardia was VT. Having access to an old ECG would have been very helpful!

Interpretation

NSR with RBBB; abnormal ECG

Learning Points

RBBB is due to the electrical block of the specialized myocardial conduction tissue that is called the right bundle. It activates the right ventricle; thus, during RBBB, the right ventricle contracts after the left ventricle. The S waves in leads 1 and V_6 and the P' in the right precordial leads (V_1–V_4) represent the late electrical depolarization of the right side of the heart, not through the specialized conduction tissue called the right bundle but through the nonspecialized myocardial tissue that conducts more slowly.

RBBB may be associated with congenital heart disease, cardiomyopathy, valvular heart disease, and coronary heart disease. In acute MI, patients with RBBB have a higher incidence of heart failure, AV block, and early and late mortality than do those without RBBB.

Suggested Reading

Melgarejo-Moreno A, Galcera-Tomas J, Garcia-Alberola A, et al. Incidence, clinical characteristics, and prognostic significance of right bundle branch block in acute myocardial infarction. A study in the thrombolytic era. Circulation 1997;96:1137–44. A study of 1,238 consecutive patients with acute MI found that the prognosis of those with RBBB is worse than those without RBBB and that the overall meaning of RBBB in acute MI has not changed in the thrombolytic era.

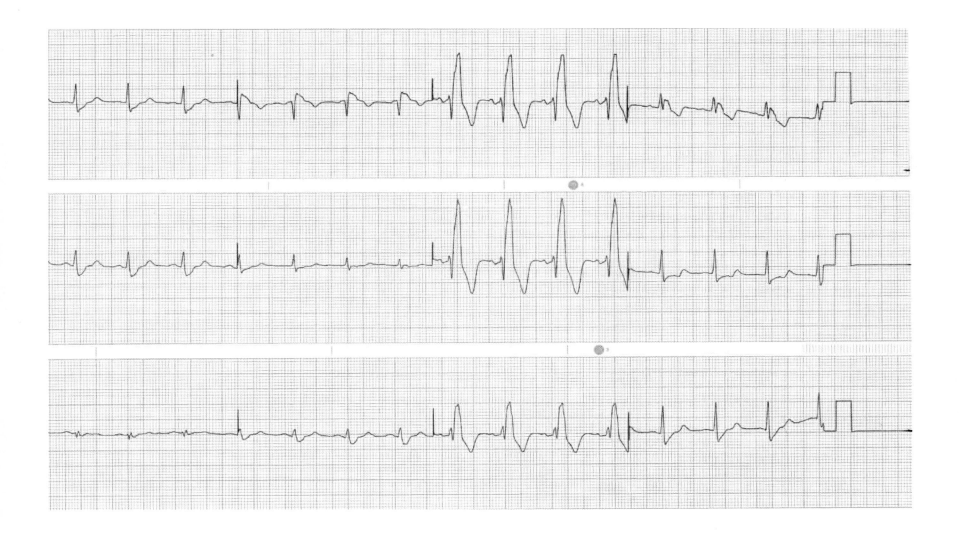

37

Case 13

Clinical Presentation

The patient is a 72-year-old male with an irregular rhythm.

Description of Electrocardiogram (Three-Lead Rhythm Strip)

The rhythm is sinus with PACs. The mean rate is 120/min. There is LAE. The PACs are followed by no change in QRS morphology except for the eighth beat on the strip. This one is conducted with RBBB aberrancy, the more common form of aberrant conduction (85% of the time). The right bundle branch is more refractory to premature conduction than the left bundle branch. Because these aberrantly conducted PACs are wider than the usual conduction, they can be misconstrued as PVCs if the preceding P wave is missed.

Interpretation of Rhythm Strip

Sinus tachycardia with LAE and PACs (one with RBBB aberrancy)

Learning Points

LAE
RBBB aberrancy
MCL1

It is important to distinguish the PAC with aberrancy from a PVC. When there are single wide-complex beats with easily identified PACs that precede the wide-complex beat and when the morphology is RBBB, it is easy. When the wide-complex beats come in groups, it can be difficult to differentiate SVT from VT. It is important to look in multiple leads for AV dissociation, the morphology of the QRS and QRS axis. Since most aberrancy has a RBBB pattern, V_1 (not MCL1) is the favored lead. Thus, if the rhythm is repetitive, there is time to record a rhythm strip of leads V_1, 2, and V_5 to ensure accuracy in rhythm diagnosis.

Suggested Reading

Drew BJ, Scheinman MM. ECG criteria to distinguish between aberrantly conducted supraventricular tachycardia and ventricular tachycardia: practical aspects for the immediate care setting. Pacing Clin Electrophysiol 1995;18(12 Pt 1):2194–208. One hundred thirty-three patients with wide-complex tachycardias were studied by surface electrocardiography leads and electrophysiologic studies. Although 10% could not be diagnosed by surface electrocardiography using established criteria, using 12 leads (and particularly lead V_1) was most valuable and was superior to using MCL1.

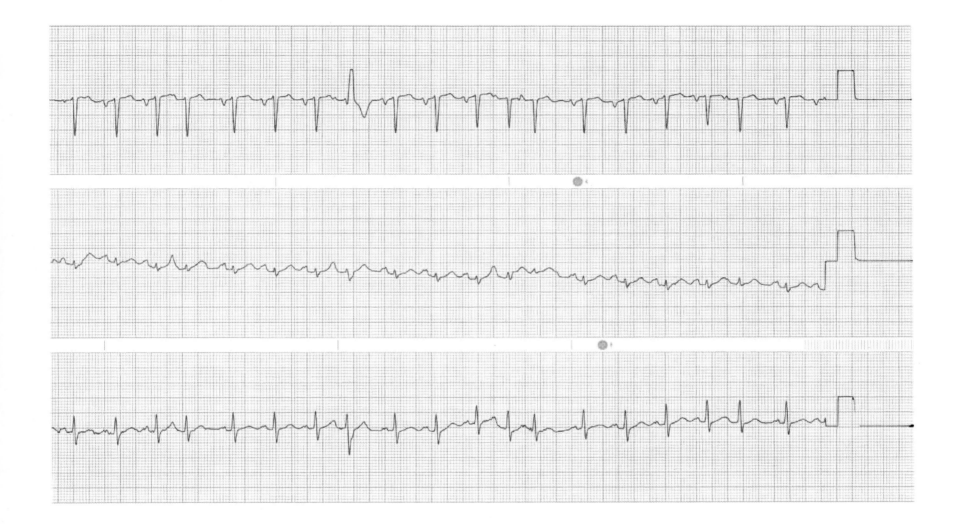

3

Ventricular Arrhythmias

Case 14

Clinical Presentation

The patient is a 23-year-old male with a dilated cardiomyopathy who suddenly felt ill and was taken to the hospital.

Description of Electrocardiogram (12 Leads)

This is a wide-complex tachycardia with an HR of 156/min. There is an extreme right axis of 264°, and there is an RBBB pattern with a QRS duration of 160 msec. VT was suspected with the patient's DCM, but a stepwise approach to making this diagnosis is warranted.

VT is diagnosed when the ventricles beat rapidly (unrelated to the atrial mechanism) and the QRS complex exceeds 120 msec and is bizarre. The onset is usually abrupt, as can be its termination. How well it is tolerated depends on its rate, its duration, and the status of ventricular function. The rate is usually between 180/min and 250/min but may be < 160/min. There usually is AV dissociation, with the atrial rate being slower than the ventricular rate. When the atrial rhythm is sinus, these sinus impulses are occasionally conducted to the ventricles and are called capture beats. No capture beats are displayed in this case. A rhythm strip follows.

Interpretation

Ventricular tachycardia (rate, 156/min) with AV dissociation; abnormal ECG

Learning Points

VT
AV dissociation
Capture beats

The Wellens criteria are based on QRS morphology and can be 80 to 90% accurate in the diagnosis of wide-complex tachycardia. Adding the presence or absence of concordance (all of the QRS complexes in the precordial leads are predominantly positive or predominantly negative) increases the accuracy to 95%. Concordance suggests VT. If the ventricular rate is faster than the atrial rate, the diagnosis of VT is clear, but if there is a 1:1 AV relationship, the diagnosis is not clear.

Suggested Readings

Brugada P, Brugada J, Mont L, et al. A new approach to the differential diagnosis of a regular tachycardia with a wide QRS complex. Circulation 1991;83(5):1649–59. Another authoritative work.

Edhouse J, Morris F. ABC of clinical electrocardiography; broad complex tachycardia—Part I. BMJ 2002;324:719–22. A simple summary with descriptive examples of VT.

Wellens HJ, Bar FW, Lie KI. The value of the electrocardiogram in the differential diagnosis of a tachycardia with a widened QRS complex. Am J Med 1978;64:27–33. A classic paper for the diagnosis of VT.

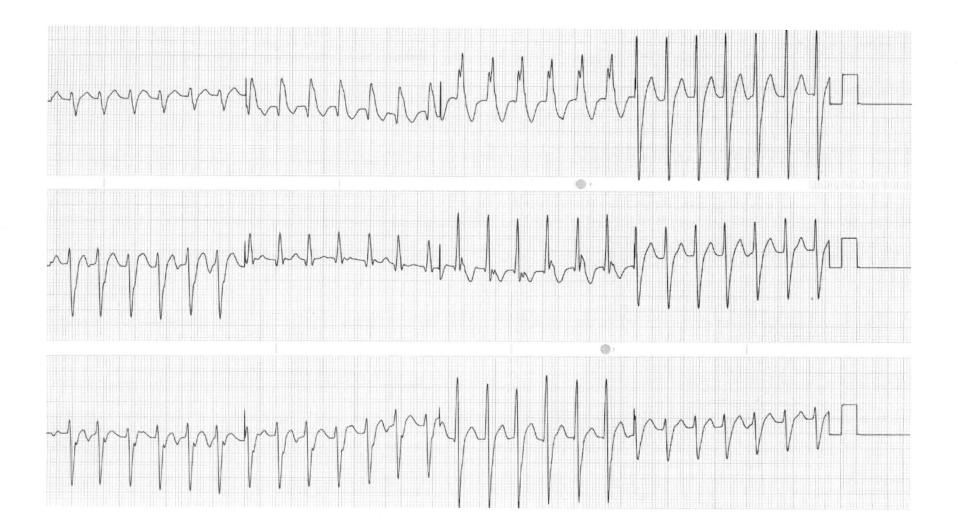

Case 14a

Description of Rhythm Strip

This three-lead rhythm strip was recorded at the same time as the 12-lead ECG of this 23-year-old male with a DCM. When counting from the right in lead 2, there are small negative deflections that occur regularly between beats 3 and 4, 7 and 8, and 11 and 12. Their rate is much slower than that of the QRS complexes and most likely represents independent atrial activity; this can be the AV dissociation that so commonly accompanies VT. The origin of the VT can often be determined from the QRS configuration. In this case, upright in V_1 and negative (downward) in V_5 suggests that the impulse originates from the LV. EPS can further localize the origin of the VT within the LV. The 12-lead ECG recorded after termination of the tachycardia can solidify the diagnosis.

Interpretation of Rhythm Strip

Left ventricular VT at 156/min, with AV dissociation

Learning Point

Left ventricular VT

Suggested Reading

Patel VV, Rho RW, Gerstenfeld EP, et al. Right bundle-branch block ventricular tachycardias: septal versus lateral ventricular origin based on activation time to the right ventricular apex. Circulation 2004;110(17):2582–7. Among 58 patients with RBBB-type VT (13 of whom did not have coronary heart disease), investigators using EPS were able to localize the origin of VT as being in the LV, where surface ECG distinctions are less identifiable.

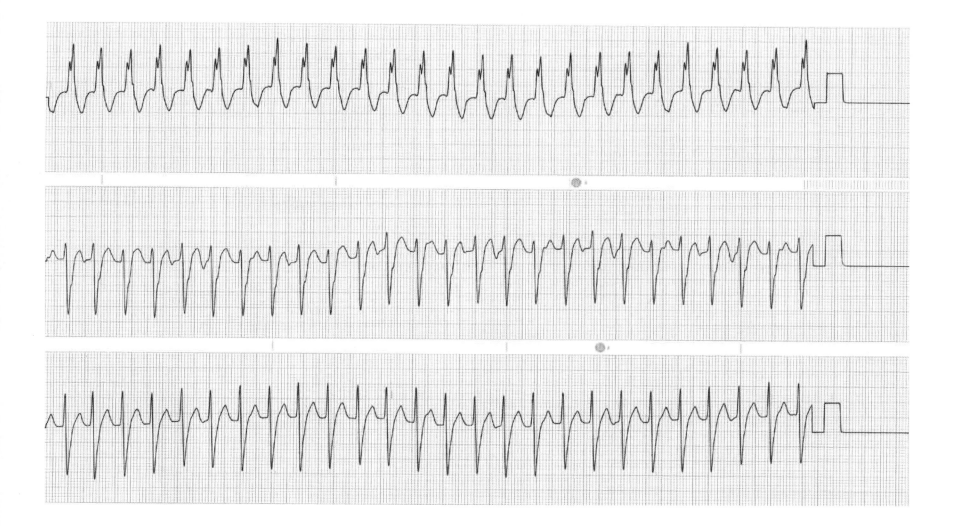

Case 14b

Clinical Presentation

The patient is a 23-year-old male who has undergone DCC.

Description of Electrocardiogram (12 Leads)

After cardioversion, the ECG shows NSR at 88/min. There are diffuse ST and T-wave changes, and there is a delayed intrinsicoid deflection characteristic of LVH. (Diagnosis of LVH will be discussed later). What is apparent is the termination of the wide bizarre QRS complexes and the resumption of AV association. The QRS axis is now normal when in NSR. Using the 12-lead ECG, the three-lead rhythm strip, and this postcardioversion ECG, one can confidently make the diagnosis.

Interpretation

Left ventricular VT (rate, 156/min) with AV dissociation now converted to NSR with LVH and nonspecific ST segment T-wave changes; abnormal ECG

Learning Points

Intrinsicoid deflection
LVH

The intrinsicoid deflection is measured in leads V_5 and V_6 as the time from the onset of the Q wave to the peak of the R wave. When it measures > 0.05 seconds, it is a minor criterion used in the diagnosis of LVH. This patient with a DCM had a laterally displaced cardiac apex on palpation, a ventricular gallop (S3) on auscultation, cardiomegaly as shown on a chest radiograph, and LVH as shown on the ECG. Treatment included angiotensin-converting enzyme inhibition, beta-blockade, and an ICD.

Suggested Reading

Josephson ME. Electrophysiology of ventricular tachycardia. Pacing Clin Electrophysiol 2003;26:2052–67. A cogent review of 30 years of interrogation of VT mechanisms with EPS, leading to lifesaving diagnoses and therapies.

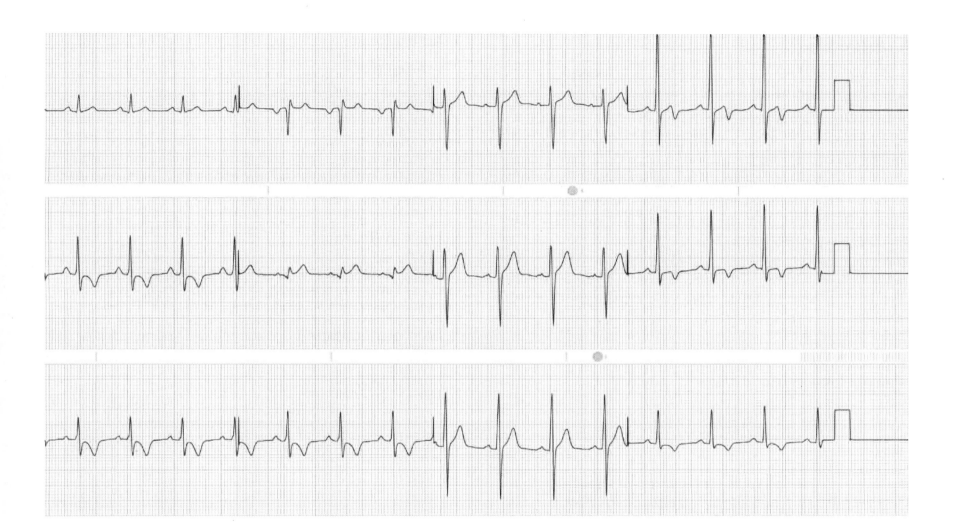

Case 15

Clinical Presentation

The patient is a 70-year-old male who stepped off the treadmill during a stress test when he felt strange. He had a remote history of MI and had just started to experience dyspnea on exertion.

Description of Electrocardiogram (12 Leads)

There is a wide-complex tachycardia; HR is 167/min. No P waves can be identified. There is an abnormal left axis. As the QRS complexes are wide, bizarre, and negative in the right precordial leads (V_1 and V_2) and upright in the left precordial leads (V_5 and V_6), this is VT originating from the RV. It resembles LBBB. Low blood pressure made it necessary to electrically cardiovert this patient to the ECG that follows.

Interpretation

Right ventricular VT (rate, 167/min)

Learning Point

Right ventricular VT

Ventricular tachycardia with an LBBB pattern can be due to an RV scar or can originate from the RVOT or another cardiac site. It is important to identify the cause of the VT if possible; treatment today includes surgical resection of an arrhythmogenic aneurysm, radiofrequency ablation of the site of origin of the VT, antiarrhythmic drugs, and (for the patient with occasional breakthrough VT) implantation of an ICD. In some cases, multiple therapeutic approaches are used.

Suggested Reading

Timmermans C, Rodriguez LM, Crijns HJ, et al. Idiopathic left bundle-branch block-shaped ventricular tachycardia may originate above the pulmonary valve. Circulation 2003;108(16):1960–7. Idiopathic LBBB-like VT is believed to originate from the RVOT or from the aortic root. These authors describe six patients with this same type of VT originating from the pulmonary trunk. Since these three regions originate from the embryonic outflow tract, a finding of pulmonary-trunk VT suggests a common embryologic etiology. If no good criteria for ablation in the RVOT are found, detailed mapping of the pulmonary artery should be performed.

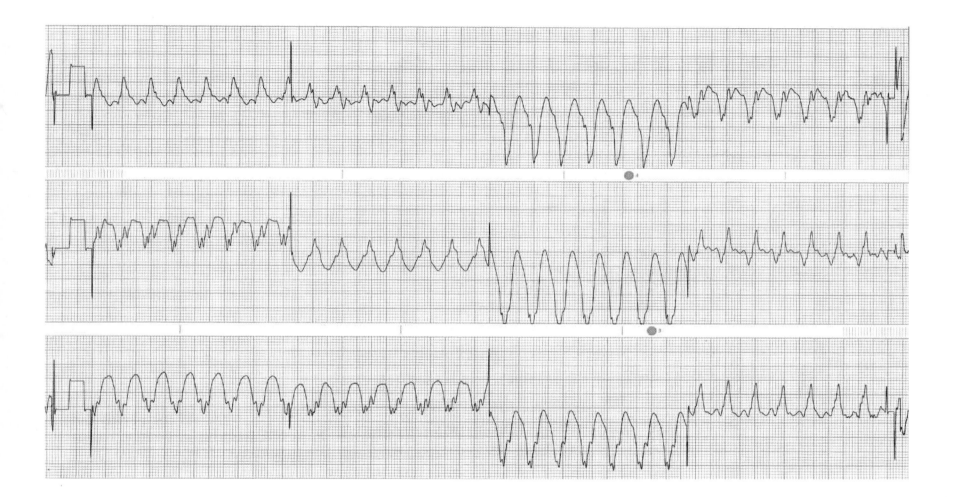

Case 15a

Clinical Presentation

This is the patient in Case 15, after electrical cardioversion.

Description of Electrocardiogram (12 Leads)

The rhythm is NSR at 77/min with a totally different QRS axis (now 20°). There is a QRS duration of 164 msec, and there are S waves in leads 1 and V_6 and an rsR' in V_1, which are the criteria for RBBB. There are Q waves in V_2 to V_6 owing to an old anterior MI. The initial R wave of the RBBB is replaced by the Q wave of this anterior MI. The persistent convex ST elevations in leads V_3 and V_4, years remote from the MI, are diagnostic for a ventricular aneurysm. There are also inferior Q waves owing to an old inferior MI. It is common for a patient with an old MI with aneurysm to have sustained VT.

Interpretation

NSR at 77/min, RBBB, old inferior MI, old anterior MI with aneurysm; abnormal ECG

Learning Points

RBBB
Ventricular aneurysm

Pathologically, a ventricular aneurysm is a wide-mouthed, scarred, and thinned myocardial segment that contains all three layers of heart muscle: endocardium, myocardium, and visceral pericardium. It must be differentiated from a ventricular pseudoaneurysm, which has a narrow mouth and represents a free-wall ventricular myocardial perforation whose wall is composed of parietal pericardium and thrombus. Electrocardiographically, a ventricular aneurysm is heralded by a wide Q wave and persistent convex-upward ST segment elevation of at least 1 mm, remote from the acute MI.

In Case 15, further studies were conducted because the VT was reproducible, the dyspnea was caused by recurrent pulmonary edema, and both were refractory to pharmacologic therapy. A cardiac magnetic resonance image showed a large and discrete anteroapical LV aneurysm with an LV ejection fraction of 0.20 and an apical thrombus. Left- and right-sided cardiac catheterization showed an LV end-diastolic pressure of 34 mm Hg, no mitral regurgitation, and no coronary stenoses in areas distant from the aneurysm. The patient underwent surgical LV thrombectomy and aneurysmectomy with cryoablation and experienced effective relief of heart failure and VT.

Suggested Readings

Demaria RG, Mukaddirov M, Rouviere P, et al. Long-term outcomes after cryoablation for ventricular tachycardia during surgical treatment of anterior ventricular aneurysms. Pacing Clin Electrophysiol 2005:28 Suppl 1:S168–71. Among 52 patients on whom this procedure was performed from 1985 to 2003, hospital mortality was 1.9%, and at 14 years, 86% of patients were free from VT or sudden death. An ICD was needed in 5 patients (9.6%), and 2 patients (3.8%) needed cardiac transplantation. The 14-year survival rate was 51.4%. The most common cause of death was CHF.

Madias JE, Ashtiani R, Agarwal H, et al. Diagnosis of ventricular aneurysm and other severe segmental left ventricular dysfunction consequent to a myocardial infarction in the presence of right bundle branch block: ECG correlates of a positive diagnosis made via electrocardiography and/or contrast ventriculography. Ann Noninvasive Electrocardiol 2005;10(1):53–9. Among 175 patients with RBBB, 28 had an old MI and ventricular aneurysm as shown by electrocardiography and one or more additional cardiac tests. Electrocardiographic criteria for ventricular aneurysm with RBBB and septal or anterior MI included ≥ 1 mm of ST elevation in V_1 to V_3 that overcomes the usual ST depression in these leads with RBBB. This was precisely the presentation of Case 15/15a.

Wellens F, Geelen P, Demirsoy E, et al. Surgical treatment of tachyarrhythmia due to postinfarction left ventricular aneurysm with endoaneurysmorrhaphy and cryoablation. Eur J Cardiothorac Surg 2002;22(5):771–6. Among 31 patients thus treated for ventricular arrhythmias and CHF, there was (just as in Case 15/15a) excellent arrhythmia control and good clinical and hemodynamic outcomes.

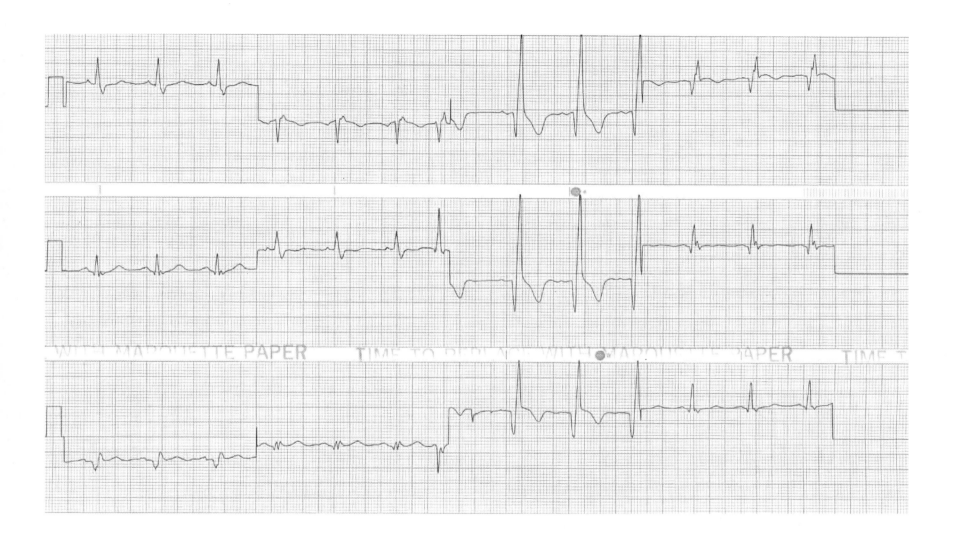

4

Hemiblocks and Bundle Branch Blocks

Case 16

Clinical Presentation

The patient is a 76-year-old male with HOCM.

Description of Electrocardiogram (12 Leads)

The rhythm is sinus, and the rate is 53/min owing to beta-blockade used to control the HR and left ventricular outflow tract obstruction. As is common in patients with HOCM, this patient has LBBB. The P–R interval is 160 msec, and the QRS duration is 136 msec. The QRS axis is −16°. There is no Q in leads 1, aVL, or V_4 to V_6. The R-wave progression is poor (or frankly a Q wave) in leads V_1 and V_2, and there are T inversions in leads 1, aVL, V_5, and V_6. These are the criteria for LBBB.

The most important electrocardiographic finding in LBBB is a reversal of the initial vector during ventricular septal activation. The initial septal activation begins from right to left instead of the normal direction of left to right. This is responsible for the absence of the physiologic (septal) Q waves in leads V_4 to V_6. In LBBB, the QRS axis can be normal but more often has an abnormal left axis. When a right-axis deviation is present, coexisting RVH should be suspected.

Interpretation

Sinus bradycardia at 53/min, LBBB; abnormal ECG

Learning Points

LBBB
HOCM
Direction of septal activation

While the QS pattern is usually seen with a septal infarction, it can occur with anatomic changes (such as the vertical axis of hyperinflation lung disease), LVH, intraventricular conduction defects (such as left anterior fascicular block, LBBB, and Wolff-Parkinson-White syndrome), or hypertrophic cardiomyopathy.
In HOCM, HR control is necessary for reduction of outflow tract gradient and symptoms of dyspnea, angina, and syncope. β-Blockers are first-line therapy.

Suggested Reading

Maron BJ. Hypertrophic cardiomyopathy: a systematic review. JAMA 2002;287:1308–20. A thorough review by one who has dedicated his career to this disease.

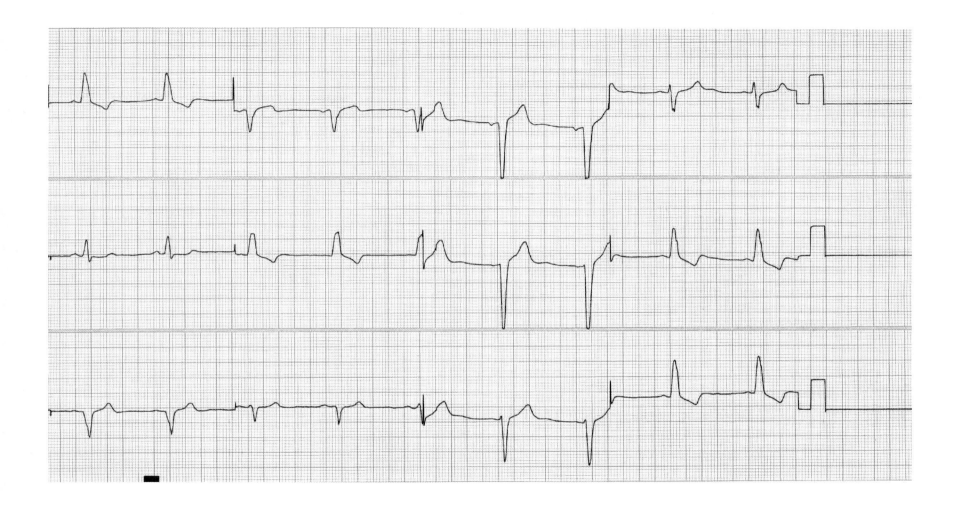

Case 17

Clinical Presentation

The patient is an 82-year-old female with acute chest pain.

Description of Electrocardiogram (12 Leads)

The rhythm is sinus, and the HR is 86/min. The P–R interval is 180 msec, and the P-wave morphology is normal. The QRS duration of 136 msec; the QRS axis of $-18°$; the absent Q waves in leads 1, aVL, V_5, and V_6; the poor R-wave progression; and the T inversion in leads 1, aVL, V_5, and V_6 meet the criteria for LBBB. What is additionally abnormal in this case is the dramatic ST elevation in leads V_2 to V_4. This, coupled with the patient's acute chest pain symptoms, makes the diagnosis one of acute anterior MI. The diagnosis of MI is often difficult or even impossible in the presence of LBBB because the characteristic abnormal Q waves may not appear on the ECG. The alterations in ST segments and T waves, not Q waves, are most important for the diagnosis of acute MI in the presence of LBBB.

Interpretation

NSR (rate, 86/min) with LBBB and acute anterior MI; abnormal ECG

Learning Point

Acute MI in LBBB

It is difficult to diagnose any MI in the presence of LBBB. In the Global Utilization of Streptokinase and Tissue Plasminogen Activator for Occluded Coronary Arteries (GUSTO-1) trial, 131 (0.5%) of 26,003 patients with acute MI also had LBBB. The analysis of these 131 ECGs and control LBBB ECGs allowed the following three electrocardiographic criteria to be formulated for making highly specific diagnoses of acute MI in patients with LBBB and acute chest pain:

1. ST elevation ≥ 1 mm concordant (in same direction) with QRS complex
2. ST depression ≥ 1 mm in V_1, V_2, or V_3
3. ST elevation ≥ 5 mm discordant (in opposite direction) with QRS complex

With > 5 mm discordant ST elevation in V_3, Case 17 demonstrates criterion 3.

Suggested Reading

Sgarbossa EB, Pinski SL, Barbagelata A, et al. Electrocardiographic diagnosis of evolving acute myocardial infarction in the presence of left bundle-branch block. N Engl J Med 1996;334:481–7. The landmark paper on the subject (abstracted above) from the Cleveland Clinic electrocardiography laboratory headed by Don Underwood, a master electrocardiographer.

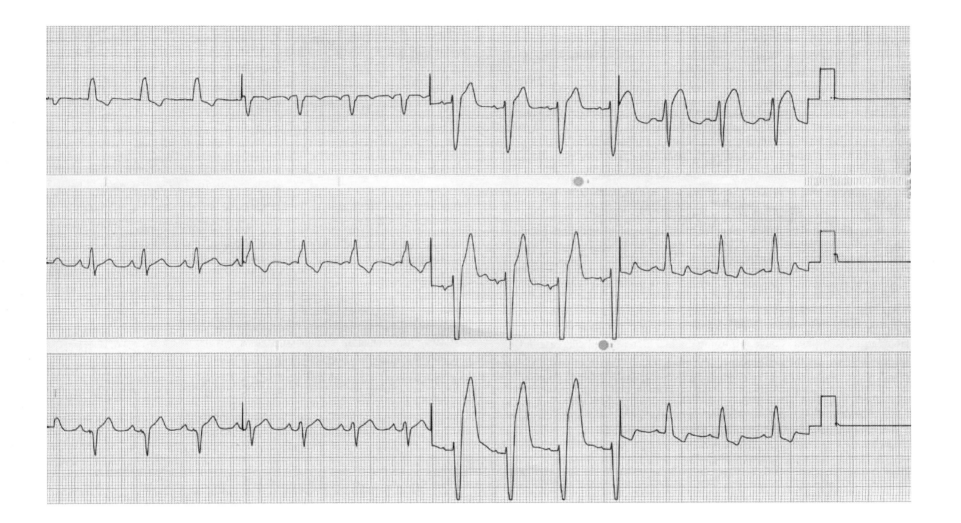

Case 18

Clinical Presentation

The patient is a 68-year-old female with a fever and obvious discomfort.

Description of Electrocardiogram (12 Leads)

The rhythm is sinus, and the rate is 133/min. The P–R interval is 144 msec, and the QRS duration is 104 msec. The Q–T interval is normal. The QRS axis is markedly rightward, 154°. This ECG fits the diagnostic criteria for LPH, which are as follows: marked right-axis deviation (105°–180°), which should not be measured with large Q waves; small R in lead 1 and small Q in lead 3; QRS duration < 110 msec; and the absence of other factors responsible for right-axis deviation (such as RVH or acute pulmonary embolism). In this case, the tachycardia makes one suspect acute pulmonary embolism, but it was not present. The fever and discomfort were caused by an intra-abdominal abscess. In addition to the tachycardia, tachypnea is indicated by the gradual increase and decrease in QRS voltage, best seen in the right precordial leads V_1 to V_3.

Interpretation

Sinus tachycardia (rate, 133/min), LPH; abnormal ECG

Learning Points

LPH

QRS electrical alternans (not demonstrated in this case)

Electrical alterans is defined as alternating higher and lower voltage in an every-other-beat fashion. Electrical alternans of the QRS may be due to pericardial effusion, SVT or VT, hypertension, rheumatic or coronary heart disease, or heart failure. The gradual change in QRS voltage demonstrated in this case is due to deep respirations at about 24 per minute.

The "father" of hemiblocks is Mauricio Rosenbaum, of Argentina. In 1970, he published "The Hemiblocks," which shed light on a widespread and previously misunderstood aspect of the cardiac conduction system. His other notable work was on the cardiomyopathy of Chagas' disease in 1964 (a turning point in his country's campaign to control the disease), the introduction of amiodarone in 1970 for the treatment of cardiac arrhythmias, and the concept of T-wave and cardiac memory in 1982. When he died in 2003, the world lost a giant in electrocardiography.

Suggested Readings

Elizari MV. In memoriam: Mauricio B. Rosenbaum, MD: a revolutionary electrocardiologist from the southern hemisphere, 1921-2003. Circulation 2003;108:780. Elizari's tribute to the great electrocardiographer with whom he worked for 30 years.

Rosenbaum MB. The hemiblocks: diagnostic criteria and clinical significance. Mod Concepts Cardiovasc Dis 1970;39(12):141–6. The seminal work that includes discussion of LPH and LAH.

Rosenbaum MB, Blanco HH, Elizari MV, et al. Electrotonic modulation of the T wave and cardiac memory. Am J Cardiol 1982;50(2):213–22. A description of the T-wave changes that may persist for days or weeks after a provoking stimulus such as temporary pacing or transient LBBB when the QRS narrows and the T waves invert in the anterior precordial leads.

Spodick DH. Electric alteration of the heart: its relation to the kinetics and physiology of the heart during cardiac tamponade. Am J Cardiol 1962;10:155–65. The pre-echocardiography explanation for electrical alterans provides great insight.

Usher BW, Popp RL. Electrical alterans: mechanism in pericardial effusion. Am Heart J 1972;83:459–63. Building upon Dr. Spodick's work, the mechanism of electrical alterans became more clear with the advent of echocardiography.

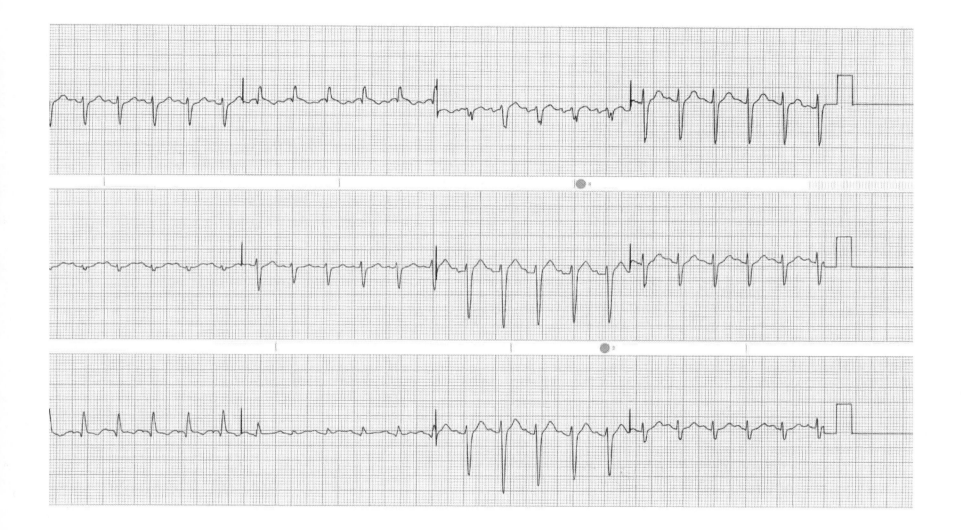

Case 19

Clinical Presentation

The patient is a 74-year-old male with known CAD who presents without chest pain for a scheduled office visit.

Description of Electrocardiogram (12 Leads)

The rhythm is sinus and averages 72/min. The P waves are normal, and the P–R interval measures 168 msec. The QRS duration is 144 msec, and the S waves in leads 1 and V_6 and the rsR' in V_1 and V_2 indicate the diagnosis of RBBB. Counting from the left, beats 1, 4, 5, and 12 are different from the others; they show Q waves diagnostic of an inferior MI of indeterminate age. The other beats are preceded by a small R wave in lead 3 and a marked left axis of –60°, with normal ST segments and T waves. These are the diagnostic criteria for left anterior hemiblock (LAH). The QRS duration exceeds 110 msec owing to RBBB. This is a form of bifascicular block. The instructive point for this case is the total obscuring of the inferior MI by the LAH. The fact that it can alternate from beat to beat in the same patient truly drives home this point: be wary of a patient with suspected CAD who presents with an ECG with LAH; there might be an inferior MI lurking!

Interpretation

NSR (rate, 72/min) with intermittent LAH masking an inferior MI of indeterminate age, RBBB, bifascicular block, lateral T-wave abnormality; abnormal ECG

Learning Points

LAH
RBBB
Inferior MI masked by LAH
Bifascicular block

"Bifascicular block" is a term used when two fascicles are blocked simultaneously, most commonly (as in this case) LAH and RBBB, but it also may be seen as LPH and RBBB. Since the left posterior fascicle is larger and has a dual blood supply, LPH is much less common than LAH.

Suggested Readings

Archbold RA, Sayer JW, Ray S, et al. Frequency and prognostic implications of conduction defects in acute myocardial infarction since the introduction of thrombolytic therapy. Eur Heart J 1998;19(6):893–8. Bifascicular block represented 2.9% of 1,225 patients with acute MI treated in a London hospital from 1988 through 1994. This represents a small decline in the incidence of severe conduction defects when compared to previous studies, possibly reflecting beneficial effects of thrombolytic therapy on infarct size. Conduction defects complicating acute MIs had a graded impact on short- and long-term prognoses (advanced bundle branch involvement fared worst).

Cristal N, Ho Winston Gueron M. Left anterior hemiblock masking inferior myocardial infarction. Br Heart J 1975;37(5):543–7. This case emphasizes the need for careful evaluation of patients with chest pain and LAH.

Khair GZ, Tristani FE, Brooks HL. Recognition of myocardial infarction complicated by left anterior hemiblock: a diagnostic dilemma. J Electrocardiol 1980;13(1):93–8. A more complicated case with an acute anterior MI and an old inferior MI that develops LAH that masks the evidence of the old and the acute MIs.

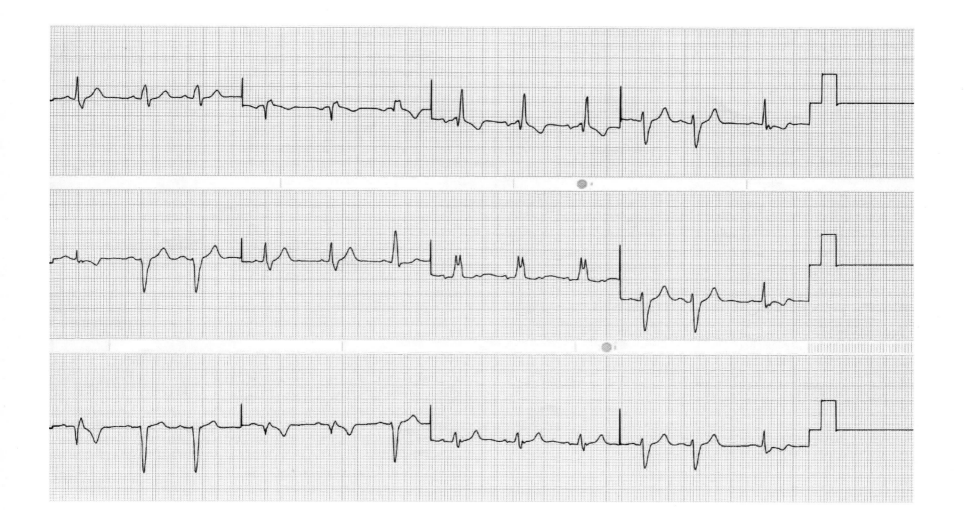

Case 20

Clinical Presentation

The patient is a 57-year-old male with acute gastrointestinal hemorrhage.

Description of Electrocardiogram (12 Leads)

The rhythm is sinus at 119/min. It is regular, and each beat is conducted across the AV node in 148 msec. The predominant QRS duration is 132 msec with a QRS axis of 0°. This meets all the criteria for LBBB, but there are three beats that are conducted with a narrow QRS complex. These three beats have an abnormal left axis and a QRS duration of 88 msec and might represent LAH. The last narrow-complex beat in the left precordial leads (V_4–V_6) shows the poor R-wave progression that is probably the expression of an old anterior MI. That the LAH and anterior MI are demonstrated in one beat and masked by LBBB in the next beat on the same ECG makes the point that an old MI cannot be diagnosed in the presence of LBBB. Under the circumstances of anemia and fright, this patient had tachycardia but fortunately no angina. It could be that a slower HR would be conducted with a narrow QRS complex and that the LAH and anterior MI would not be obscured. No old ECGs were available.

Interpretation

Sinus tachycardia (rate, 119/min) with LBBB that masks LAH and an old anterior MI; abnormal ECG

Learning Points

LAH
LBBB
LBBB masking LAH and old anterior MI

Suggested Readings

Candell-Riera J, Oller-Martinez G, Pereztol-Valdes O, et al. Usefulness of myocardial perfusion SPECT in patients with left bundle branch block and previous myocardial infarction. Heart 2003;89(9):1039–42. Stress-rest single-photon emission computed tomography (SPECT) was conducted in 72 patients with permanent LBBB and previous MI. The results were compared to those of coronary arteriography. The positive predictive values were high in all coronary distributions, as follows: circumflex (96%), left anterior descending (LAD) (93%), and right coronary artery (RCA) (89%). This is a good test when an old MI is suspected in a patient with LBBB.

Kindwall KE, Brown JP, Josephson ME. Predictive accuracy of criteria for chronic myocardial infarction in pacing-induced left bundle branch block. Am J Cardiol 1986;57(15):1255–60. An elegant study of RV pacing induction of LBBB in 47 patients with known MI and 28 patients without MI failed to discern a reliable indicator in the pattern of LBBB that would differentiate those with LBBB with an old MI from those with LBBB without an old MI. This further supports how effectively LBBB can mask an old MI. The ECG in Case 20 looks as if an RV pacemaker was turned on and off three times in the same tracing.

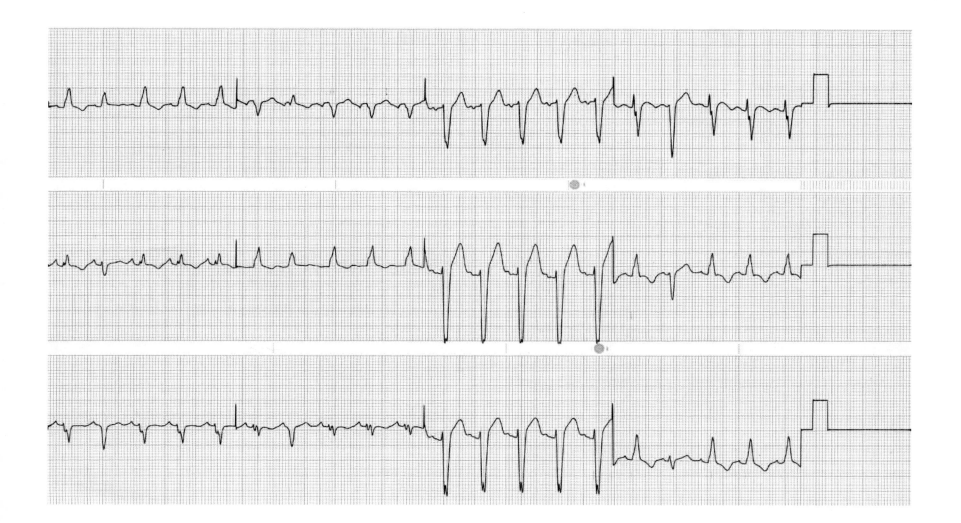

Case 21

Clinical Presentation

The patient is a 53-year-old male in the CCU who is experiencing chest pain and an elevation of cardiac enzymes.

Description of Electrocardiogram (12 Leads)

The rhythm is sinus at 84/min, and the P–R interval measures 160 msec. The predominant QRS duration is 75 msec. In the inferior leads (2, 3, and aVF), the T waves are inverted, suggesting ischemia (especially in a CCU patient). This must always stimulate the reader to glance at the T waves in leads V_1 and V_2 to see if there is posterior involvement. The T wave in V_1 can be upright and be normal, but the R wave progression is a bit early, or taller, than usual. The first two beats in the right precordial leads (V_1–V_3) are conducted with a QRS duration of 119 msec and an RSR' pattern of incomplete RBBB. The T waves are usually inverted in leads V_1–V_3 with RBBB. In these two beats, the T waves are upright in leads V_2 and V_3. These are primary T-wave abnormalities for an RBBB and indicate the diagnosis of an inferoposterior MI. Here, the IRBBB helps uncover the MI.

Interpretation

NSR (rate, 84/min) with an inferoposterior MI of indeterminate age, with intermittent IRBBB; abnormal ECG

Learning Points

IRBBB

Inferoposterior MI

IRBBB has all of the features of RBBB except that it has a QRS duration of < 120 msec. IRBBB with primary T-wave changes helps uncover a posterior MI. The T waves are usually inverted in leads V_1 to V_3 and V_4 with RBBB and IRBBB. These are T-wave changes that are secondary to the QRS alteration. They are also seen with LVH, RVH, LBBB, WPW syndrome, and PVCs. A primary T-wave change is present when the T wave abnormality occurs independently of the depolarization process (independently of the QRS change).

An inferoposterior MI has changes in both the inferior and posterior distributions, expressed as Q-wave and ST elevation and T-wave inversion inferiorly (2, 3, aVF) and as tall R-wave and ST depression and upright T waves posteriorly (V_1, V_2). Both myocardial distributions are often supplied by the same coronary artery.

Suggested Reading

Madias JE, Bravidis D, Attari M. Posterior myocardial infarction and complete right bundle-branch block. Chest 2002;122:1860–4. Just as in Case 21, the two patients described had posterior MI and developed RBBB. Their ECGs showed primary T waves upright in the right precordial leads owing to the repolarization consequences of the posterior MI, thus aiding rather than obscuring the diagnosis of acute posterior MI.

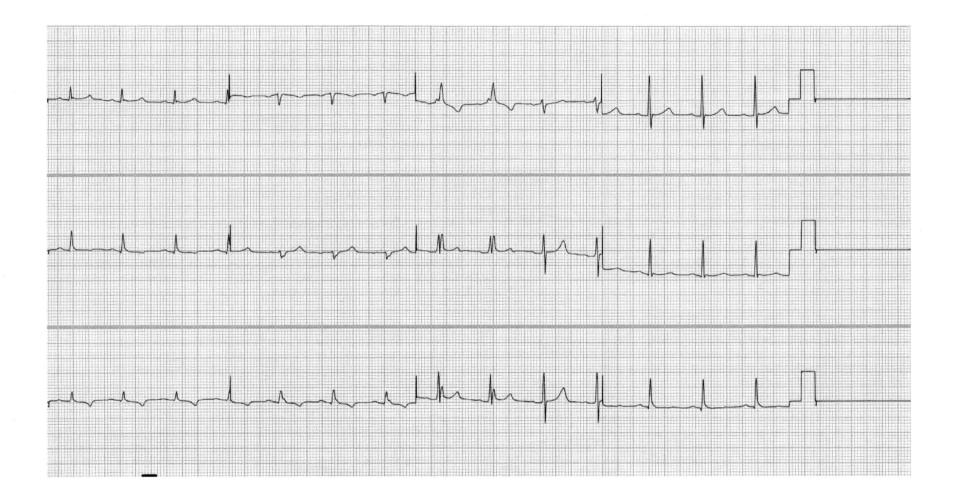

Case 22

Clinical Presentation

The patient is a 51-year-old male with long-standing hypertension.

Description of Electrocardiogram (12 Leads)

The rhythm is sinus (rate, 83/min). There is LAE and first-degree AV block with a P–R interval of 210 msec. The QRS axis is leftward but normal at −15°. The QRS duration is 136 msec. At first look, this appears to be LBBB, but there is a Q in leads 1 and aVL. This suggests normal (left-to-right) septal depolarization and rules out LBBB. An MI cannot be localized with certainty. Therefore, this is an NSIVB.

Interpretation

NSR (rate, 83/min), left atrial enlargement, first-degree AV block, NSIVB; abnormal ECG

Learning Points

First-degree AV block
LAE
NSIVB

NSIVB and IVCD are diagnosed when the criteria for RBBB or LBBB are not met but the QRS duration is prolonged. In Case 22, the presence of the Q waves in 1 and aVL do not meet the septal depolarization criterion for LBBB although there are the poor R-wave progression and T-wave inversion in V_6. Because what is indicated is not just typical LVH with strain pattern with QRS widening, it is not called LVH with IVCD. It looks like an LBBB, but it is not and is thus considered to be NSIVB. NSIVB can be seen after MI or as a result of class I antiarrhythmic drugs, LVH, and hyperkalemia. (Class IA drugs include quinidine, diisopyramide, and procainamide; class IB drugs include lidocaine, tocainide, and mexiletine; and class IC drugs include flecainide, encainide, and propafenone.)

After years of uncontrolled hypertension, the patient of Case 22 had developed a dilated cardiomyopathy and heart failure in addition to his ECG findings. He was not prescribed a class I antiarrhythmic drug at the time this ECG was made.

Suggested Readings

Peichl P, Kautzner J, Cihak R, Bytesnik J. The spectrum of inter- and intraventricular conduction abnormalities in patients eligible for cardiac resynchronization therapy. Pacing Clin Electrophysiol 2004;27(8):1105–12. A timely review of the association of bundle branch blocks and IVCD and NSIVB with the timing of regional intraventricular electrical conduction in patients with dilated cardiomyopathy in the presence or absence of coronary artery disease in an effort to predict efficacy of biventricular pacing.

Willems JL, Robles de Medina EO, Bernard R, et al. Criteria for intraventricular conduction disturbances and pre-excitation. World Health Organization/International Society and Federation for Cardiology Task Force Ad Hoc. J Am Coll Cardiol 1985;5(6):1261–75. Standardized criteria for the diagnosis of intraventricular conduction disturbances.

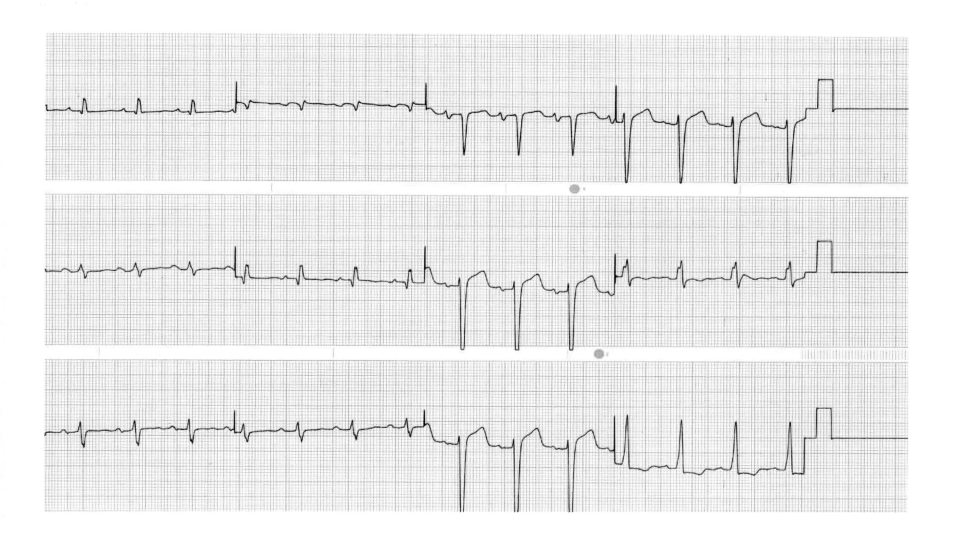

Case 23

Clinical Presentation

The patient is a 54-year-old male patient in the CCU who is experiencing chest pain and has elevated cardiac enzymes.

Description of Electrocardiogram (12 Leads)

The rhythm is sinus, and the HR is 54/min. The P–R interval is 212 msec, and the QRS duration is 160 msec. The QRS voltage in leads 1, 2, and 3 adds up to 12 mm, diagnostic of low QRS voltage at this full standardization. The Q–T interval corrects to 477 msec, which would be prolonged were it not for the widened QRS. Here, with the QRS duration of 160 msec, the corrected Q–T (Q–Tc) interval is < 500 msec and is normal. The QRS configuration is that of LBBB, but the ST segment and T wave changes in leads V_1 to V_4 are not usually found in LBBB. These are primary ST segment and T wave changes, caused in this case by ischemia.

Interpretation

Sinus bradycardia at 54/min with first-degree AV block, low QRS voltage, LBBB, and primary anterior ST-segment and T-wave changes suggesting ischemia or infarction; abnormal ECG

Learning Points

First-degree AV block
LBBB
Primary ST segment and T-wave changes
Q–Tc interval

Suggested Reading

Hands ME, Cook EF, Stone PH, et al. Electrocardiographic diagnosis of myocardial infarction in the presence of complete left bundle branch block. Am Heart J 1988;116(1 Pt 1):23–31. Among 985 patients presenting within 18 hours of the onset of ischemic chest pain, 35 had complete LBBB. These eminent authors include primary ST-segment and T wave changes in two or more adjacent leads among the diagnostic criteria for MI in the presence of LBBB. While suggestive of ischemia, such changes do not fulfill the later criteria for MI in the presence of LBBB as set forth by Sgarbossa and colleagues in 1996 from the larger GUSTO-1 trial data.

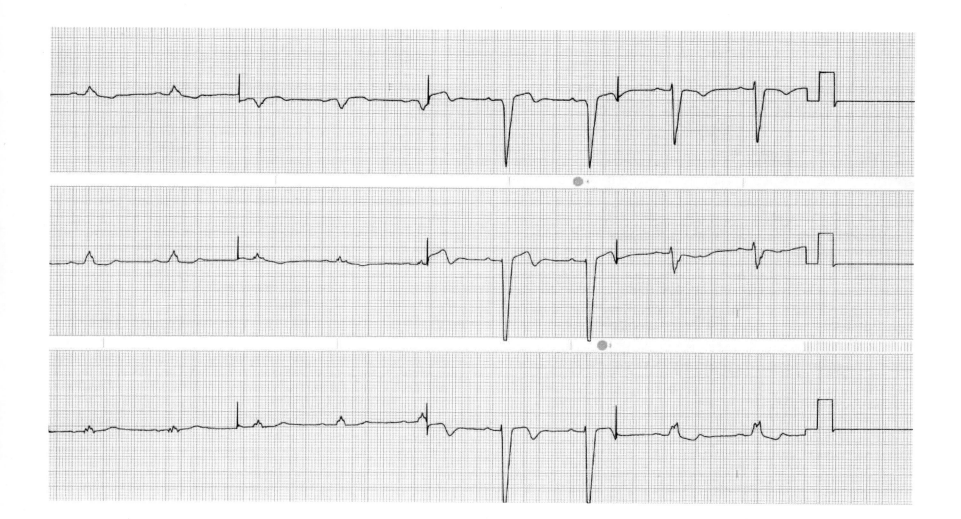

Case 24

Clinical Presentation

The patient is a 69-year-old male with the murmur of aortic stenosis.

Description of Electrocardiogram (12 Leads)

The rhythm is sinus, and the rate is 74/min. The P–R interval is normal at 136 msec, and the QRS duration is toward the upper limits of normal, at 96 msec. The QRS axis is −45°, just leftward enough to call LAH. There are small Q waves in leads V_1 to V_3, which suggests an anteroseptal MI; in the presence of LAH, however, small Q waves occasionally appear in leads V_1 and V_2 because of reflection of the initial negative forces on these leads, for the same reason that there are small Q waves in leads 1 and aVL. If the electrodes for V_1 and V_2 are placed one interspace lower, these small Q waves disappear in uncomplicated LAH. The S-wave voltage (12 mm) in lead 3, plus the R plus S (18 mm) in V_3 equaling 30 mm (Gertsch and colleagues' criteria) and the intrinsicoid deflection (50 msec) in lead V_5 suggest LVH, as do the T inversions in leads V_5 and V_6. The Q–T interval is normal.

Interpretation

NSR (rate, 74/min), LAH, LVH; abnormal ECG

Learning Points

Small anterior Q waves can be seen in uncomplicated LAH
Other mimics of CAD
LVH diagnosis in the presence of LAH
Incidence of LAH in patients with aortic stenosis

Suggested Readings

Gertsch M, Theler A, Foglia E. Electrocardiographic detection of left ventricular hypertrophy in the presence of left anterior fascicular block. Am J Cardiol 1988;61(13):1098–101. By the use of voltage criteria of S3 + (R + S) maximal precordial ≥ 30 mm to diagnose LVH (and proven by echocardiography), it was found that specificity was 87%, sensitivity was 96%, positive predictive value was 89% and negative predictive value was 95% in a sample of 50 patients with LAH but without MI and without RBBB. With the use of other electrocardiographic criteria for LVH, the presence of LAH limits a reliable diagnosis. These criteria diagnose LVH here in Case 24.

Kalusche D, Betz P, Roskamm H. [Disorders of intraventricular conduction in patients with calcified aortic valve diseases: pre- and postoperative incidence and effect on prognosis following aortic valve replacement.] Z Kardiol 1986;75(3):147–50. The authors of this article (in German) studied 210 patients who underwent aortic valve replacement between 1978 and 1983. Preoperatively, LAH was the only intraventricular conduction disorder in 9.6% of patients, more common than LBBB (1.9%), RBBB (1%), and LAH plus RBBB (1.0%). Indeed, LAH is commonly seen in patients with aortic stenosis, such as the patient in Case 24.

Levine HJ. Mimics of coronary heart disease. Postgrad Med 1978;64(1):58–62, 65–67. This famous name in cardiology enumerated disorders that mimic chronic coronary artery disease. In addition to the LAH and LVH that are seen in Case 24, disorders that demonstrate Q waves include Wolff-Parkinson-White syndrome and asymmetric septal hypertrophy.

Shettigar UR, Pannuri A, Barbier GH, Appunn DO. Significance of anterior Q waves in left anterior fascicular block—a clinical and noninvasive assessment. Clin Cardiol 2002;25(1):19–22. The study's hypothesis was that anterior Q waves in the presence of LAFB (LAH) may not be indicative of MI. From 1990 to 1997, 236 male patients in a Veterans Administration medical center who had LAH were studied. Of these 236 patients with LAH, 61 (26%) had Q waves in the V leads, but benign Q waves were seen in just 5.3% of patients. The authors concluded that patients with LAH in the absence of MI may have Q waves in the V leads that are approximately 0.02 sec in duration and restricted to one or two leads (benign Q waves). They suggested that this anomaly may represent a variation of conduction in the initial 0.02 sec QRS vector because of LAH.

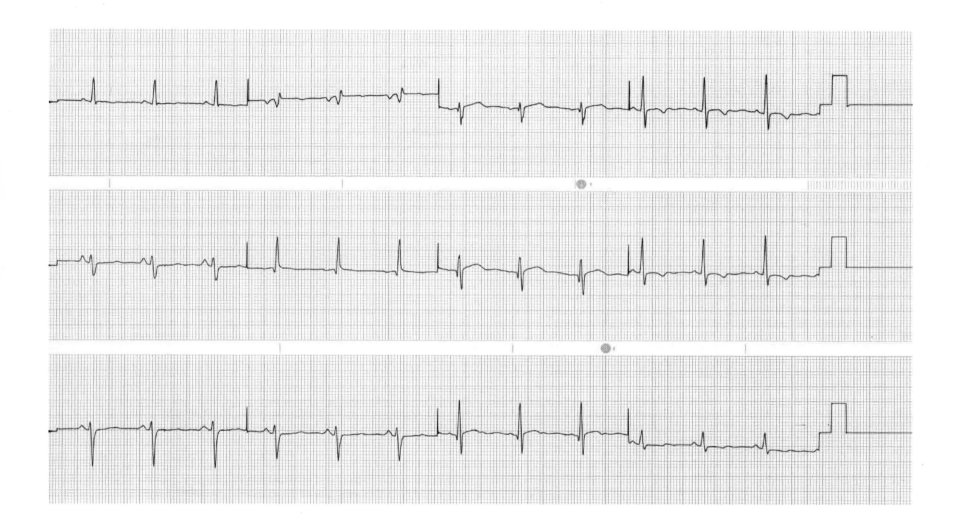

5

ST- and T-Wave Changes

Case 25

Clinical Presentation

This 58-year-old male with long-standing hypertension who is in the CCU with chest pain has a sudden increase in heart rate. Although he is nauseated, he is not on digitalis.

Description of Electrocardiogram (12 Leads)

The heart rate is 91/min and regular. The P waves are inverted in leads 2, 3, aVF, and V_6. The rhythm thus is not sinus but can be junctional or low atrial because the direction of atrial depolarization is toward the right shoulder (opposite the direction of lead 2 and toward the sinus node rather than away from it). Junctional rhythm can have three patterns for the P wave, depending on whether (1) current arrives in the atrium before it arrives in the ventricle (inverted P preceding the QRS), (2) current arrives in the ventricle before it arrives in the atrium (inverted P following the QRS), or (3) current arrives simultaneously in the atrium and ventricle (P wave is buried in the QRS and is not visible). With junctional rhythm, when the P wave precedes the QRS, the P–R interval must be ≤ 120 msec. If it is > 120 msec, it is a low atrial rhythm. Here the P–R interval is 118 msec and fits with junctional rhythm (AJR, as the rate is > 60/min and < 100/min). The Q waves in leads 3 and aVF with ST elevation and T inversion and the elevated troponin in this setting of chest pain indicate the diagnosis of an acute inferior MI. This is the likely cause of this AJR. The sinoatrial node usually gets its blood supply from the right coronary artery. When its blood supply is lost, the sinoatrial node will malfunction; if sinus bradycardia or sinus arrest ensues, AJR can result. Digitalis intoxication is another cause of AJR, but does not pertain to this case. There are ST and T-wave changes, voltage criteria, and delayed intrinsicoid deflection criteria for LVH (the Romhilt-Estes criteria). The ST and T-wave changes of LVH seen in the left precordial leads (V_5 and V_6) are often called the "strain pattern." It is associated with reciprocal ST elevation in the right precordial leads (V_1 and V_2).

Interpretation

AJR (rate, 91/min), acute inferior MI, LVH with strain; abnormal ECG

Learning Points

AJR
Inferior MI
LVH: methods of diagnosis

Suggested Readings

Casale PN, Devereux RB, Alonso DR, et al. Improved sex-specific criteria of left ventricular hypertrophy for clinical and computer interpretation of electrocardiograms: validation with autopsy findings. Circulation 1987;75(3):565–72. The Cornell voltage criteria (RaVL + SV3 exceeds 28 mm in men and exceeds 20 mm in women) improve the sensitivity of electrocardiography for LVH. Paul Casale is a fine interventional cardiologist.

Edhouse J, Thakur RK, Khalil JM. ABC of clinical electrocardiography—conditions affecting the left side of the heart. BMJ 2002;324:1264–7. A concise review of the criteria for LVH.

Okin PM, Devereux RB, Nieminen MS, et al. Electrocardiographic strain pattern and prediction of cardiovascular morbidity and mortality in hypertensive patients. Hypertension 2004;44:48–54. The finding of LVH with strain in patients with hypertension was a significant predictor of cardiovascular death, fatal and nonfatal MI, and fatal and nonfatal stroke.

Romhilt DW, Estes EH Jr. A point-score system for the ECG diagnosis of left ventricular hypertrophy. Am Heart J 1968;75(6):752–8. Still a valuable tool that integrates QRS voltage, strain pattern, LAE, left-axis deviation, QRS duration > 0.09 sec, and intrinsicoid deflection in V_5 or V_6 > 0.05 sec. The point system emphasizes voltage, strain pattern, LAE, and left axis. It worked for diagnosing LVH in Case 25.

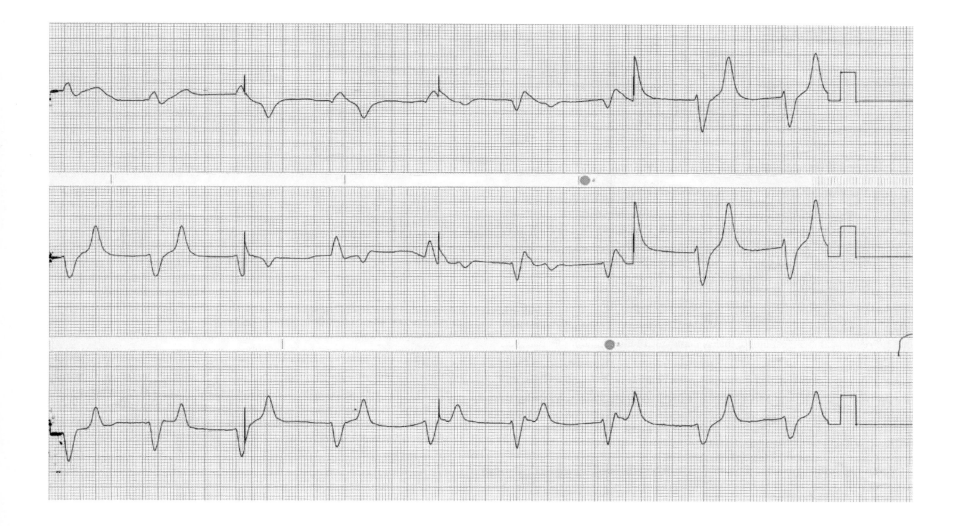

Case 27

Clinical Presentation

The patient is a 59-year-old thin male with chest pain that becomes worse with inspiration and when lying supine.

Description of Electrocardiogram (12 Leads)

The rhythm is sinus (rate, 76/min). The P waves are normal, and the P–R interval is 136 msec. The QRS duration is 96 msec, and the QRS axis is 32°. Both are normal. The QRS voltage is high but is normal for a thin male. The Q–T interval is normal. The ST segments are elevated in all leads but are depressed in leads aVR and V_1. This is acute pericarditis. It is sometimes accompanied by P–R segment depression; that is absent here. The ST elevation of acute pericarditis is always coupled with an upright T wave, unlike the T inversion that accompanies the ST elevation of acute MI. The ST elevation of acute pericarditis is diffuse and has no reciprocal changes, unlike that of acute MI. In the evolution of acute pericarditis, the ST segments return to baseline, then the T inverts and does so in the same diffuse manner. This phase of pericarditis is difficult to diagnose without the preceding ECG because it looks like so many nonspecific T wave-change ECGs.

Interpretation

NSR (rate, 76/min), acute pericarditis; abnormal ECG

Learning Points

Acute pericarditis versus acute MI

Acute pericarditis versus early repolarization

ST segment elevation in conditions other than acute MI

P–R segment depression in acute pericarditis

Suggested Readings

Beljepally R, Spodick DH. PR-segment deviation as the initial electrocardiographic response in acute pericarditis. Am J Cardiol 1998;81(12):1505–6. It was observed that P–R segment deviations precede the classic ST segment shifts in acute pericarditis. This finding was attributed to the superficial myocarditis, which accounts for the electrocardiographic changes, first encompassing the thin atrium. Dr. Spodick has focused on the pericardium for most of his academic career.

Spodick DH. Differential characteristics of the electrocardiogram in early repolarization and acute pericarditis. N Engl J Med 1976;295(10):523–6. Among 96 patients evenly divided between the two diagnoses, all 48 patients with acute pericarditis had limb lead ST segment deviations whereas only 27 of 48 patients with early repolarization demonstrated this pattern. ST segment depression in V_1 was more common in pericarditis. The combination of ST deviations and P–R segment deviations in both limb and precordial leads and ST depression in V_1 favors acute pericarditis.

Wang K, Asinger RW, Marriott HJL. ST-segment elevation in conditions other than acute myocardial infarction. N Engl J Med 2003;349(22):2128–35. In this era of rapid presentation of patients with chest pain and ST segment elevation, one must carefully assess the clinical presentation of the patient to be sure that pericarditis, myocarditis, pulmonary embolism, hyperkalemia, recent transthoracic cardioversion, Prinzmetal's angina, and normal ST segment elevation variants are considered and rejected before settling on a diagnosis of acute MI and administering thrombolytic therapy.

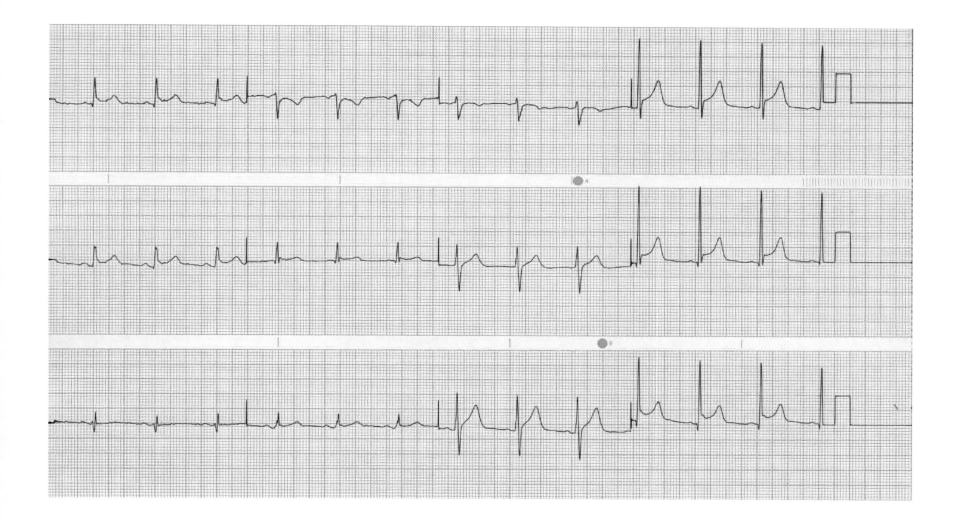

Case 28

Clinical Presentation

The patient is a 61-year-old female with muscle weakness after 3 days of diarrhea.

Description of Electrocardiogram (12 Leads)

The rhythm is sinus (rate, 56/min). The P–R interval, QRS duration, and QRS axis are all normal. Especially in leads V_2 and V_3, there are ST segment and T-wave changes. In leads 2, V_5, and V_6, prominent U waves are visible. The T waves fuse into the U waves. The Q–T interval is prolonged. These are the findings of hypokalemia. (potassium measured 3.0 mEq/L in this case). The cause of the diarrhea was viral gastroenteritis. The muscle weakness responded to intravenous fluids and potassium replacement.

This is an opportunity to learn more about Q–T intervals and how to calculate the corrected Q–T (Q–Tc) interval. The normal Q–T interval is < 440 msec when corrected for a HR of 60/min (Q–Tc). It is measured from the onset of the Q wave at baseline to the point where the terminal portion of the T wave crosses the baseline. In lead V_4, using the first beat, the absolute Q–T interval is 620 msec. To correct it to a HR of 60/min or an R–R interval of 1 second, one must divide 620 msec by the square root of the R–R interval (1.030 s), which here equals 1.015. The quotient of 620 msec divided by 1.015 is 611 msec. The Q–Tc is less than the measured Q–T when the HR is < 60/min, and the Q–Tc is greater than the measured Q–T when the HR is > 60/min. It is important to recognize Q–T prolongation because whether due to electrolyte abnormalities, drug effects, or a congenital abnormality, it can be the harbinger of malignant ventricular arrhythmias.

Interpretation

Sinus bradycardia, long Q–T with T–U fusion due to hypokalemia; abnormal ECG

Learning Points

Hypokalemia
U waves
Q–T prolongation
Q–Tc calculation (also see Case 7)

Suggested Readings

Bromstrom-Lundqvist C, Caidahl K, Olsson SB, Rudin A. Electrocardiographic findings and frequency of arrhythmias in Bartter's syndrome. Br Heart J 1989;61(3):274–9. Bartter syndrome is a disorder associated with chronic potassium deficiency. The authors studied 20 patients with this disorder by electrocardiography and 24-hour ECGs. Whereas the ST segment and T-wave changes and the U waves and Q–T prolongation associated with hypokalemia were seen, these patients had only slight electrocardiographic changes when compared with those changes seen in other patients with the same degree of hypokalemia. On the basis of the 24-hour ECG recordings, these Bartter syndrome patients also were found to have fewer arrhythmias than would be expected. The authors postulated an adaptation of the myocardium to hypokalemia.

Helfant RH. Hypokalemia and arrhythmias. Am J Med 1986;80(4A):13–22. The focus of this article is hypokalemia, its electrophysiologic properties, and clinical arrhythmias. Hypokalemia increases the resting membrane potential and increases both the duration of the action potential and the duration of the refractory period. The combination fosters reentrant arrhythmias. Hypokalemia also increases the threshold potential as well as automaticity, thus favoring automatic arrhythmias. Correcting the potassium level in patients who demonstrate these arrhythmias causes the arrhythmias to disappear. When potassium-wasting diuretics are used in clinical practice, there are obvious clinical implications.

Reinig MG, Harizi R, Spodick DH. Electrocardiographic T- and U-wave discordance. Ann Noninvasive Electrocardiol 2005;10(1):41–6. Of 18,750 ECGs reviewed, 143 were found to have prominent U waves; these 143 patients and their ECGs were studied. The authors propose the analysis of U waves in respect to their accompanying T waves. In such analysis, patterns of discordance between the polarity of T waves and U waves can suggest the clinical etiology of the U waves (ie, LVH vs CAD).

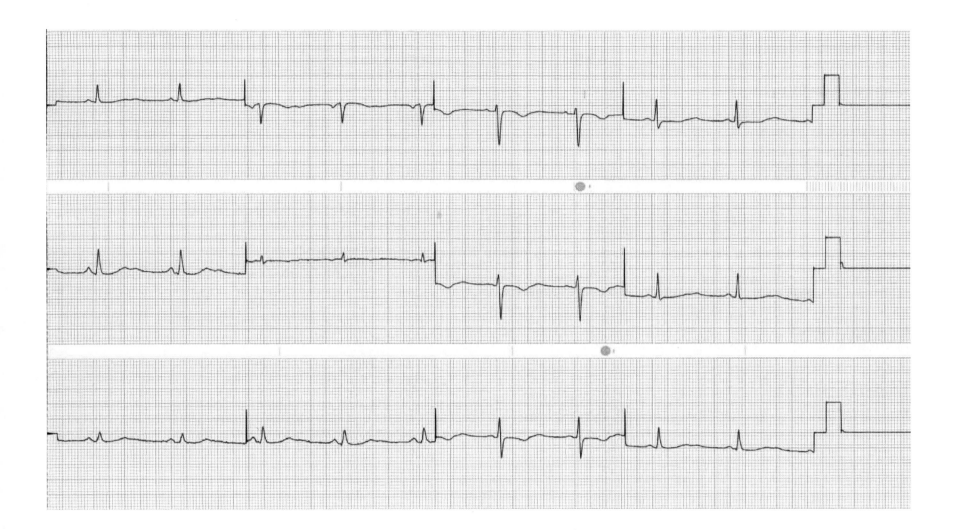

Case 29

Clinical Presentation

The patient is a 26-year-old female, pregnant and near term with her first child. She has never before undergone electrocardiographic examination.

Description of Electrocardiogram (12 Leads)

The rhythm is sinus; HR, 87/min. The P waves and the P–R interval are normal. The QRS complexes are normal in duration and axis. The T waves are inverted in lead V_2 and flat in lead V_3. The T inversion is neither symmetrical nor deep. There is no abnormality with the heart. It may be that the heart is displaced upward by the diaphragm (in this case, by pregnancy). Because this T-wave pattern is seen in ECGs made in adolescence and childhood, it is called the juvenile T-wave pattern and is normal. As regards the Q–Tc interval, the measured Q–T is 400 msec, the R–R interval is 0.670 sec, the square root of 0.670 is 0.818, and 400 msec divided by 0.818 is 489 msec. The Q–Tc interval is 489 msec and prolonged.

Interpretation

NSR (rate, 87/min) with juvenile T-wave pattern, Q–T prolongation; abnormal ECG

Learning Points

Juvenile T-wave pattern
ECG in pregnancy

The ECG of a patient with a normal heart during a normal pregnancy can exhibit minor changes in the ST segments and T waves, as well as QRS axis shifts to the right or to the left, but the axis usually remains normal. Like other patients with increased abdominal distention, the third-trimester pregnant woman can have a small Q in lead 3 that can vary in size with respiration and can disappear when she changes from a supine position to a standing position.

Suggested Readings

Assali AR, Khamaysi N, Birnbaum Y. Juvenile ECG pattern in adult black Arabs. J Electrocardiol 1997;30(2):87–90. In a group of 50 "black Arabs" (negroid bedouins) nearly equally divided between the sexes, a juvenile T-wave pattern was observed in 21% of the women but in none of the men. There is a female predominance of juvenile T-wave pattern in other studies as well, and this is thought to be related to cardiac position. In Case 29, this T-wave pattern can be attributed to pregnancy, but the pattern persisted 1 month post partum. The patient was indeed tall and thin. The Q–T interval normalized post partum, but no cause for its prolongation during pregnancy was determined.

Das BB, Ray M, Mohapatra SK, Das SP. Juvenile T waves (a study of 100 normal subjects). Indian J Physiol Pharmacol 1984;28(4):291–8. This pattern of T inversion in the precordial leads was seen mostly in young patients who were tall and thin. In those subjected to exercise electrocardiography, the T-wave inversion in leads V_1 to V_3 showed slight flattening during exercise.

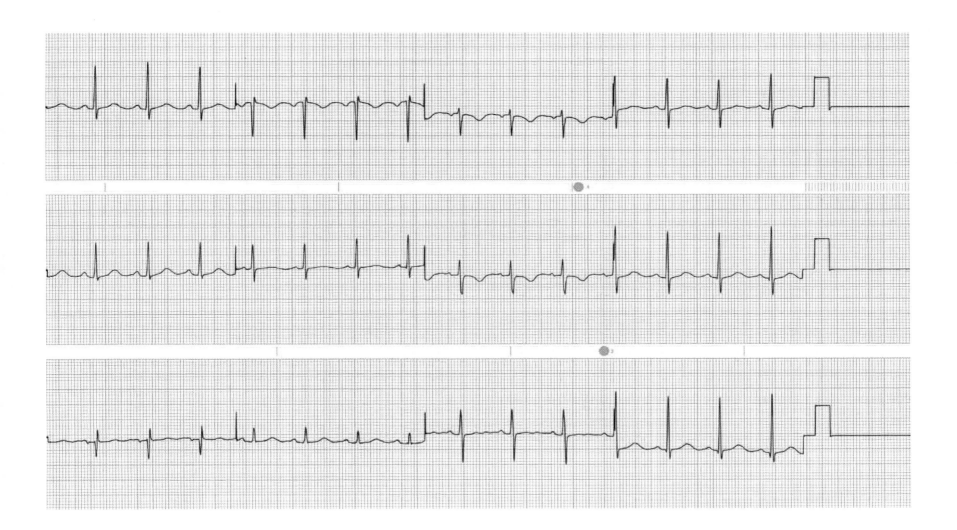

Case 30

Clinical Presentation

The patient is a 20-year-old female military applicant.

Description of Electrocardiogram (12 Leads)

The rhythm is sinus at 78/min. The P waves, P–R interval, and QRS duration and axis are normal, and the Q–T interval is normal. The T waves are flattened in leads V_2 and V_3 and although less pronounced than in Case 29, constitute a juvenile T-wave pattern. The R-wave progression from V_2 to V_3 appears to be abnormal; rather than being due to cardiac position, a conduction abnormality, or an anterior MI, here it is due to a decrease in voltage, as the V_3 electrode is placed on top of the left breast. It is not the absolute R-wave magnitude but rather the R-to-S ratio that should increase as the leads move leftward across the precordium. In this case, the R-to-S ratio increases normally despite the localized lower voltage.

Interpretation

NSR (rate, 78/min), juvenile T-wave pattern, breast-attenuation artifact; normal ECG

Learning Points

Breast-attenuation artifact
Poor R-wave progression
Juvenile T-wave pattern

This military recruit had a normal cardiac examination and underwent stress echocardiography with ECG precordial lead placement under the left breast. The V_3 R-wave voltage increased, and the R-wave progression was normal, but the juvenile T-wave pattern persisted. Echocardiographically, there was normal anterior-wall motion at rest and with exercise. Her work capacity was high, and there was no sign of ischemia shown by stress electrocardiography. She passed her physical examination and was inducted.

Suggested Readings

Colaco R, Reay P, Beckett C, et al. False positive ECG reports of anterior myocardial infarction in women. J Electrocardiol 2000;33 Suppl:239–44. Among 84 women recruited to a study in which chest electrodes were placed strictly in adherence with recommendations to use the fourth and fifth intercostal spaces as references and also to use the more widely adopted technique of placing electrodes V_3 to V_6 under the left breast, it was found that measurements recorded on the breast by electrode V_3 have a significantly smaller R-wave magnitude when compared with corresponding measurements below the breast.

Gami AS, Holly TA, Rosenthal JE. Electrocardiographic poor R-wave progression: analysis of multiple criteria reveals little usefulness. Am Heart J 2004;148(1):80–5. Excluding subjects with Q-wave anterior MI, BBB, or WPW syndrome, these authors found that poor R-wave progression criteria for diagnosing anterior MI did not improve the accuracy of diagnosis over the accuracy expected by chance.

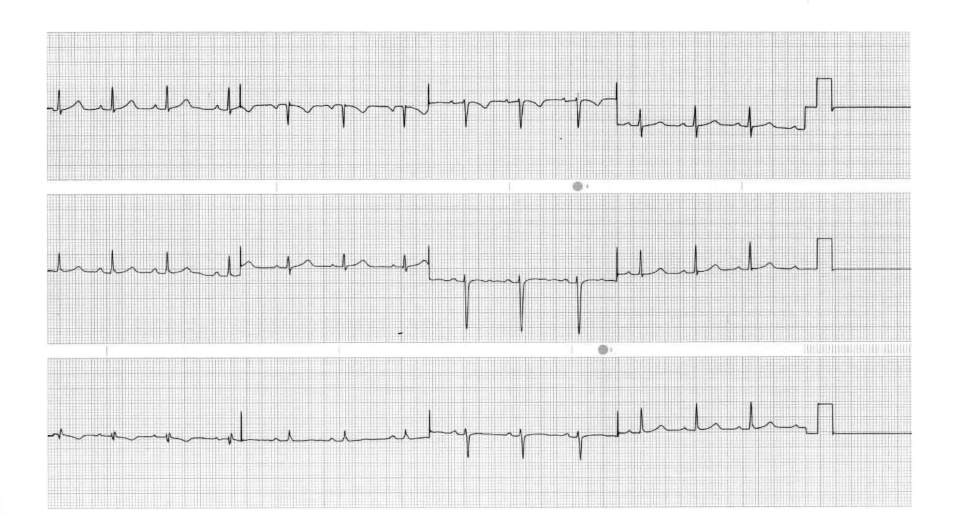

Case 31

Clinical Presentation

The patient is a 48-year-old female found to have a regularly irregular rhythm during preadmission testing for elective surgery.

Description of Electrocardiogram (12 Leads)

The rhythm is sinus with trigeminal (every third beat) unifocal (with fixed coupling and uniform morphology) PVCs with a mean HR of 78/min. With this normal standardization, the QRS voltage is at the lower limit of normal. The narrow QRS complexes are normal, but the PVCs have broad Q waves in the inferior leads. This may be a hint for occult right coronary artery disease that is expressed only by the prematurity of the ventricular depolarization. Remember that the second PVC is a chimera because it falls directly on the change-of-leads marker. The T waves are variable from beat to beat in the same lead. The T waves in the beats that follow the PVCs are inverted. This is called the postectopic T-wave change and is believed to be caused by alteration of ventricular repolarization related to the postectopic pause. It is important to recognize because it almost always indicates organic heart disease. This patient's elective surgery should be postponed until her heart is further evaluated.

Interpretation

Sinus rhythm with trigeminal PVCs (mean rate, 78/min); postectopic T-wave change and PVC morphology suggesting CAD; abnormal ECG

Learning Points

Unifocal PVCs
Fixed coupling
Change-of-leads marker
Postectopic T-wave change
PVC as a diagnostic aid

Suggested Readings

Rosen MR. The electrocardiogram 100 years later: electrical insights into molecular messages. Circulation 2002;106:2173–9. This is a valuable work that traces the history of electrocardiography with science, anecdotes, and insights. Descriptions of T-wave memory and the postectopic T-wave change (with references on the subject dating back to1944) are included.

Wang K, Hodges M. The premature ventricular complex as a diagnostic aid. Ann Intern Med 1992;117(9):766–70. This is an elegant article for the clinician. The PVC can give clues of an MI when the sinus complex fails to do so. The PVC can also have a compensatory pause that allows normal conduction of the next QRS complex in a patient with a rate-dependent LBBB. This narrow QRS may contain important diagnostic findings, such as an MI that is masked by the conduction block. In the pause that follows a PVC, one may also visualize P waves that will uncover the supraventricular mechanism that drives a tachycardia.

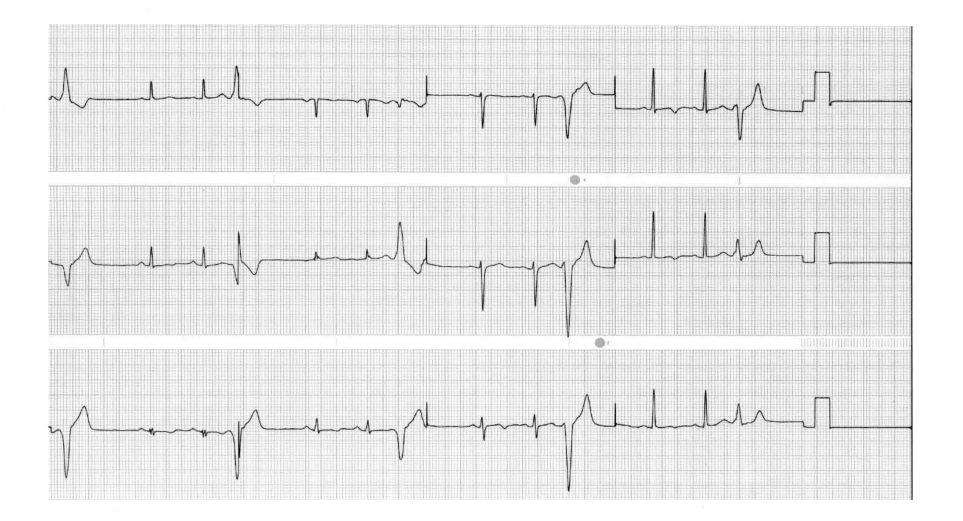

Case 31a

Description of Rhythm Strip

This is the three-lead rhythm strip of the previous ECG. The postectopic T-wave change is more apparent in a longer strip, as is the uniformity of the PVCs. It is interesting to consider how this phenomenon would be missed were the PVCs bigeminal (every other beat), as each narrow QRS complex would follow a PVC. The organic abnormality would not be missed, however, because every T wave of a sinus beat would be abnormal and would require an explanation.

Interpretation of Rhythm Strip

Sinus rhythm with trigeminal PVCs and postectopic T-wave change

Learning Point: Classification of PVCs

Ventricular ectopy can be single, paired, trebled, or in groups. It can be unifocal or multifocal. It can have fixed coupling, or variable coupling intervals can be seen. It can be followed by a compensatory pause, or it can be interpolated. It can be parasystolic (PVCs equidistant from one another without fixed coupling to normally conducted beats). It can be an escape rhythm or one that overtakes the sinus rhythm, such as accelerated ventricular rhythm or VT. It can be R-on-T–induced VT. It can be multifocal VT (torsades de pointes). It can be sustained VT or intermittent. It can be ventricular flutter or ventricular fibrillation.

Suggested Reading

Lown B, Calvert AF, Armington R, Ryan M. Monitoring for serious arrhythmias and high risk of sudden death. Circulation 1975;52(6 Suppl):III189–98. The "father of the CCU" offers his classification of VPBs in patients with CAD, based on frequency, multiformity, repetitive pattern, and degree of prematurity, as an aid to identifying patients at risk for sudden death.

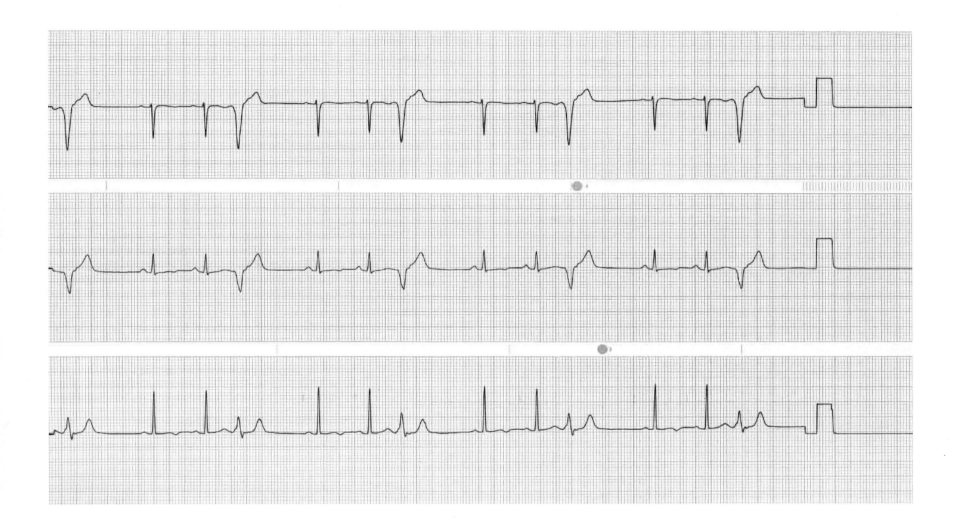

Case 32

Clinical Presentation

The patient is a 24-year-old healthy male professional football player undergoing a preemployment physical examination.

Description of Electrocardiogram (12 Leads)

The rhythm is sinus, and the rate is 52/min and regular. The P–R interval and the QRS duration are normal. The QRS axis is 83° and normal. The voltage standardization is full (10 mm = 1 mV), and the QRS voltage is high (just enough to indicate LVH by Cornell criteria [R aVL + S V_3 > 28 mm], considering that the S in V_3 is truncated), but this is commonly found in such athletes. The ST elevation in the lateral precordial leads, J-point elevation in V_4 to V_6, ST elevation in V_1 and V_2, and minimal ST elevation in the limb leads constitute a pattern called an *early repolarization pattern* and is considered to be a normal variant. Of course, it must be differentiated from acute pericarditis (see Case 27) and acute MI, but the clinical setting and repeat electrocardiography 1 hour later (or referring to an old ECG) can help in this differentiation. Accuracy in reading ECGs is important—especially when one may have to deliver bad news to a defensive lineman! This time the news is good.

Interpretation

Sinus bradycardia, early repolarization pattern; normal ECG

Learning Points

Early repolarization
Electrocardiographic patterns in trained athletes
Acute pericarditis
Cornell criteria for LVH

Suggested Reading

Pelliccia A, Maron BJ, Culasso F, et al. Clinical significance of abnormal electrocardiographic patterns in trained athletes. Circulation 2000;102:278–84. Among 1,005 trained athletes studied, 603 had a normal ECG or an ECG with minor alterations. Of the 603, 28% had an R or S measuring 23 to 28 mm, 24% had an early repolarization pattern, and 61% had sinus bradycardia (all of which were demonstrated in Case 32). The authors concluded that these patterns and most of the abnormal patterns seen in the 402 remaining athletes were indicative of physiologic cardiac remodeling.

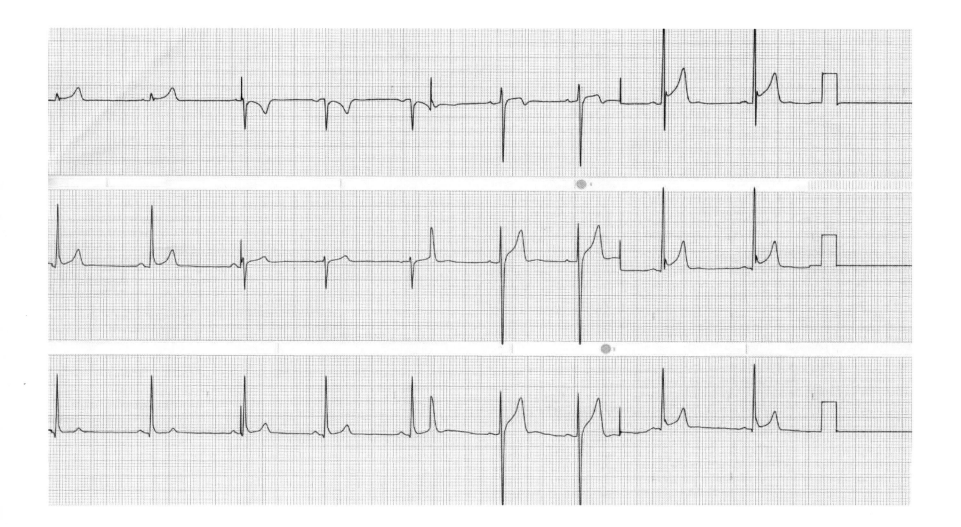

Case 33

Clinical Presentation

The patient is a 52-year-old male with chest pain at the time he had a fever from a cellulitic reaction to a diabetic foot ulcer.

Description of Electrocardiogram (12 Leads)

The HR is 118/min. The rhythm is sinus, and the P–R interval is normal. The QRS axis is $-4°$, and the QRS duration is 84 msec. The Q–Tc interval is 425 msec. All intervals are normal. The ST segments in leads 1, aVL, and V_3 to V_6 are depressed about 3 mm. This suggests subendocardial ischemia; this fits best with CAD in this setting. If sustained over time, this can lead to myocardial injury. The stimulus provoking the tachycardia must be removed. An antipyretic, oxygen, nitroglycerin, aspirin, and metoprolol were administered, affording relief of the chest pain and improvement in the ST depression on he ECG. The infection was treated, and the CAD was further investigated.

Interpretation

Sinus tachycardia (rate, 118/min), marked lateral ST depression suggesting ischemia; abnormal ECG

Learning Points

Subendocardial ischemia

Positive stress electrocardiography for ischemia

Suggested Reading

Li D, Li CY, Yong AC, Kilpatrick D. Source of electrocardiographic ST changes in subendocardial ischemia. Circ Res 1998;82:957–70. To clarify the source of electrocardiographic ST depression associated with ischemia, a sheep model in which simultaneous epicardial and endocardial ST potentials were mapped was developed. Ischemia was produced in different territories of the same animal by partially constricting in sequence the LAD coronary artery and the LCx artery. In all, 36 sheep were studied. The distributions of epicardial potentials from either ischemic source were very similar; both showed ST depression on the free wall of the left ventricle and no association between the ST depression and the ischemic region. Endocardial potentials, however, showed that ST elevation was directly associated with the region of reduced blood flow. Increasing the percentage of stenosis of a coronary artery increased epicardial ST depression at the lateral boundary and resulted in ST elevation, starting from the ischemic center as ischemia became transmural. This explains why body surface ST depression does not localize cardiac ischemia in humans. The ECG in Case 33 looks like a positive stress ECG at the peak of exercise, when the patient complains of angina pectoris. When the patient steps off the treadmill, the HR slows and the ST segments return to baseline and then develop a negative slope with inverted T waves before returning to the preexercise tracing. The duration of the ST depression is related to the severity of ischemia. If the ST depression persists without the rate's slowing to decrease myocardial oxygen demand, subendocardial injury will result. Depression of ST segments is a marker for ischemia, but it does not localize the territory of ischemia, as explained in the article by Li and colleagues, cited above.

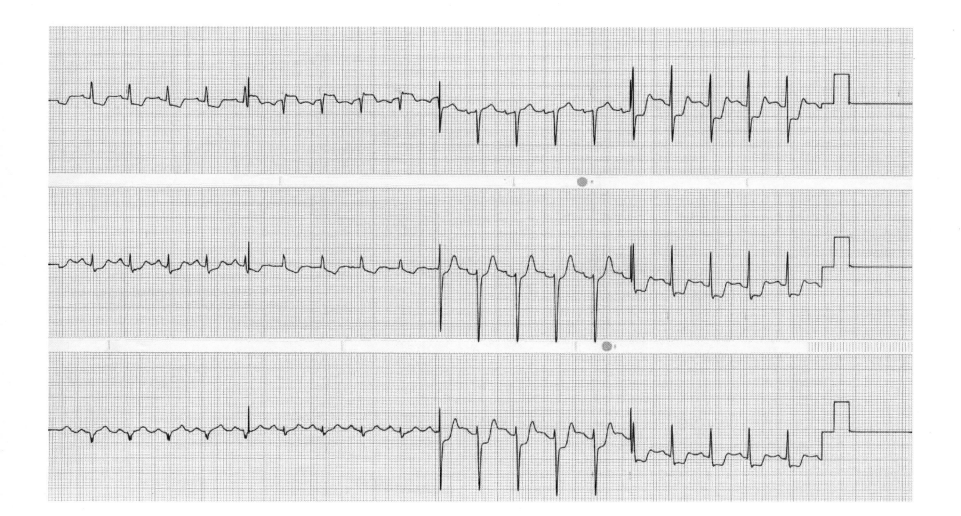

Case 34

Clinical Presentation

The patient is a 52-year-old male who is in the CCU because he had chest pain at home while reading the newspaper.

Description of Electrocardiogram (12 Leads)

The HR is 68/min, the P–R interval is 160 msec, and the QRS duration and Q–Tc interval are normal. The T waves in leads V_3 to V_5 are abnormal, biphasic or inverted, and are due to subepicardial or transmural myocardial ischemia. There is minimal ST segment elevation, but there is no loss of R wave. Coronary arteriography in this setting often shows $\geq 90\%$ stenosis in an anterior coronary artery.

Interpretation

NSR (rate, 68/min), anterior T-wave changes due to subepicardial or transmural ischemia; abnormal ECG

Learning Points

Subepicardial or transmural ischemia
Coronary arteriography

Transmural ischemia is present when ischemia extends to the subepicardial region. As explained in the above-mentioned article by Li and colleagues, as the degree of stenosis increases, the ischemia becomes transmural and ST elevation begins in the center of the ischemic zone. Unlike subendocardial ischemia that cannot be localized, subepicardial ischemia can be localized, and here the ischemic zone is in the anterior myocardium and is due to a tight stenosis in the LAD coronary artery.

Suggested Reading

Boden WE, Bough EW, Benham I, Shulman RS. Unstable angina with episodic ST segment elevation and minimal creatinine kinase release culminating in extensive, recurrent infarction. J Am Coll Cardiol 1983;2(1):11–20. In 1983, prior to percutaneous coronary intervention and intracoronary stenting, treatment options were medication, intraaortic balloon pump and coronary bypass surgery. This article portrays the frustration of the authors with limited treatment options in dealing with patients with high-grade proximal LAD coronary artery stenosis whose ECGs were like that of Case 34.

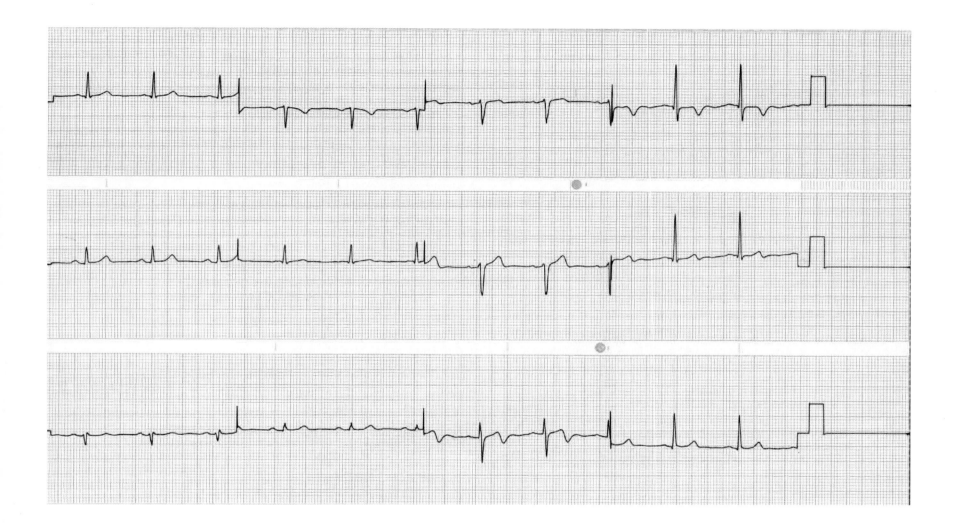

Case 35

Clinical Presentation

The patient is a 76-year-old female at a routine check-up for her cardiac arrhythmia.

Description of Electrocardiogram (12 Leads)

The rhythm is irregularly irregular, and the mean HR is 103/min. There are no discrete P waves; rather, the baseline is irregular between R waves. The R–R interval is inconsistent. This is atrial fibrillation.

The QRS duration is 92 msec, the QRS axis is 15°, and the Q–Tc interval is 379 msec. The QRS voltage is normal. The rate of atrial activity in atrial fibrillation often is 500/min, exceeding that of atrial flutter. In patients with normal AV nodal conduction, the ventricular response to this rapid atrial rate is fast and poorly tolerated. It requires a pharmacologic treatment that will slow AV conduction, thus improving ventricular filling and cardiac output, blood pressure, and the feeling of palpitations. Digitalis is such a medication. The mark it leaves on the ECG must be recognized so that it is not confused with ischemia. With therapeutic doses, the *digitalis effect* is recognized by the scooping ST segments seen here in leads 1, 2, V_5, V_6, and aVR.

Interpretation

Atrial fibrillation with rapid ventricular response (rate, 103/min), digitalis effect; abnormal ECG

Learning Points

Atrial fibrillation
Digitalis effect

Today, digitalis is nearly always prescribed as digoxin, a form of digitalis glycoside that is renally cleared. It is used to control the HR in atrial fibrillation and to provide inotropic support in patients with systolic dysfunction. It has a narrow therapeutic range and is prone to accumulation to toxic levels in elderly persons and in those who develop renal insufficiency. Certain drugs taken in conjunction with digoxin necessitate that its dosage be adjusted downward; these drugs include verapamil, amiodarone, quinidine, and diltiazem. When the level of digoxin in the blood increases into the toxic range, the patient may develop subtle adverse symptoms such as anorexia, visual changes, or abdominal pain. If the patient does not complain, these symptoms may only be sought by an astute electrocardiographer when a digitalis-intoxicated rhythm is recognized. Since excessive digitalis levels increase the automaticity of the atria, the AV junction, and the ventricles and also prolong AV nodal conduction time, these rhythms cover the spectrum from PVCs to VT, to AJR, to atrial tachycardia with 2:1 block, to first-degree AV block, to second-degree AV block, and to complete heart block. (See Case 4 for a discussion of the treatment of life-threatening digitalis toxicity.) In Case 35, there is no arrhythmia caused by digitalis, just the ST segment scooping that the esteemed cardiologist J. Willis Hurst described to me as the appearance of a round digitalis pill having been put into the ST segments. Like patients with LVH, LBBB, a permanent pacemaker, or WPW syndrome, patients whose ECGs show the digitalis effect will have abnormal ST segment depression during stress electrocardiography. This ST segment depression cannot be differentiated from that seen in cases of CAD. Such differentiation requires that an imaging modality be coupled with the stress electrocardiography.

Suggested Readings

Eagle KA, Berger PB, Calkin H, et al. ACC/AHA guideline update for perioperative cardiovascular evaluation for noncardiac surgery—executive summary. J Am Coll Cardiol 2002;39(3):542–53. For patients with important abnormalities on their resting ECGs (eg, LBBB, LVH with strain pattern, or the digitalis effect), other techniques such as exercise echocardiography or exercise myocardial perfusion imaging should be considered.

Hauptman PJ, Kelly RA. Digitalis. Circulation 1999;99(9):1265–70. A review of the history, clinical applications, pharmacology, manifestations of toxicity, and efficacy of digitalis, with a focus on the Digoxin Investigation Group data.

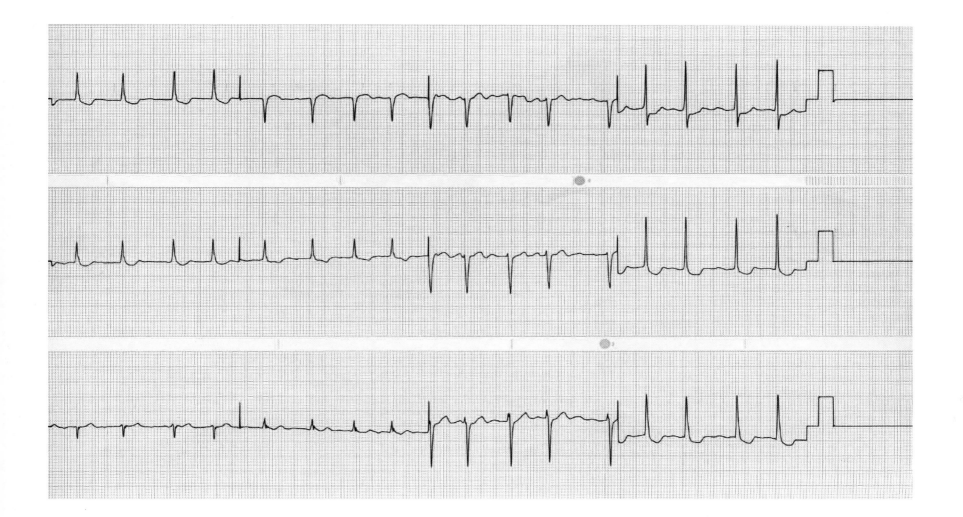

6

Atrioventricular Blocks

Case 36

Clinical Presentation

The patient is a 66-year-old female who is taking digoxin.

Description of Electrocardiogram (12 Leads)

The HR is 76/min, but the rhythm is difficult to discern. The only lead in which P waves are clearly seen is V_1. The P–R interval is 440 msec, and each P wave is followed by a QRS with an unvarying P–R interval. Measuring 440 msec from the QRS in leads V_6 and 2 gives one the impression that there are P waves, and they are upright. This is most likely sinus rhythm. There are small Q waves in the inferior leads, but as they are not 40 msec wide nor one-third the height of the coinciding R wave, the criteria for the diagnosis of an inferior MI are not met. There are T-wave inversions in leads 1, aVL, and V_3 to V_6 and ST changes that are consistent with the digitalis effect. The long P–R interval is at least in part due to digitalis as well. The QRS duration and Q–T interval are normal.

Interpretation

Sinus rhythm with long first-degree AV block, anterolateral T-wave abnormality, digitalis toxicity; abnormal ECG

Learning Points

First-degree AV block
Digitalis toxicity
Criteria for diagnosis of Q-wave MI

In the absence of other cardiac disease, the auscultatory finding of first-degree AV block is a soft first heart sound (S_1). Normally, S_1 should be louder than the second heart sound (S_2) at the lower left sternal border and sixth intercostal space in the left midclavicular line. With this long P–R interval, S_2 is louder than S_1 at the lower left sternal border, and at the left upper sternal border, S_2 is loud and S_1 is inaudible. The reason for the soft S_1 is that the onset of ventricular systole follows atrial systole by such a long time that the mitral and tricuspid valves drift closed prior to ventricular systole, and their short excursion of closure fails to generate much of a sound.

Suggested Readings

Keller KB, Lemberg L. Q and non-Q wave myocardial infarctions. Am J Crit Care 1994;3(2):158–61. Previously, the classification of MI into transmural and subendocardial types has been based on the presence or absence of abnormal Q waves. The pathologic anatomy of necrosis in MI does not necessarily correspond to these electrocardiographic criteria. Thus, it is more appropriate to describe myocardial infarcts as Q-wave or non-Q-wave infarcts. The importance of this classification is underscored by their clinical and pathologic differences and the tendency for a more serious prognosis in the case of non-Q-wave infarcts. It should be noted that in Q-wave infarcts, the volume of necrosis is usually greater than that in non-Q-wave infarcts.

Kelly RA, Smith TW. Recognition and management of digitalis toxicity. Am J Cardiol 1992;69(18):108G–19G. The symptoms of digitalis toxicity are protean. Other cardiac diseases or concomitant noncardiac diseases may share symptoms with digitalis toxicity, but when the toxic rhythm disturbances are recognized, it is easier to focus on digitalis as the cause of the symptoms. The ECG can be the key. Conventional therapy for digitalis toxicity remains the maintenance of serum potassium levels ≥ 4 mEq/L, reversal of decompensated CHF or overt myocardial ischemia, attention to serum magnesium levels and the patient's acid-base status, appropriate antiarrhythmics in the event of ventricular arrhythmias, and a temporary pacemaker for high-grade AV block. The addition of digitalis-specific antibodies provides a safety net for difficult-to-manage and life-threatening digitalis toxicity rhythms.

Mymin D, Mathewson FA, Tate RB, Manfreda J. The natural history of primary first-degree atrioventricular block. N Engl J Med 1986;315(19):1183–7. The long-term prognosis of first-degree heart block was studied in a 30-year longitudinal study that included 52 cases present on entry into the study and 124 incident cases during follow-up. The incidence steadily rose in the years over the age of 40 years. Progression to higher grades of heart block occurred in only two cases. The authors concluded that primary first-degree heart block with moderate P–R prolongation (up to 0.23 seconds) is a benign condition but that this conclusion may not apply to persons with more marked prolongation of the P–R interval, a rare condition, as seen in Case 36.

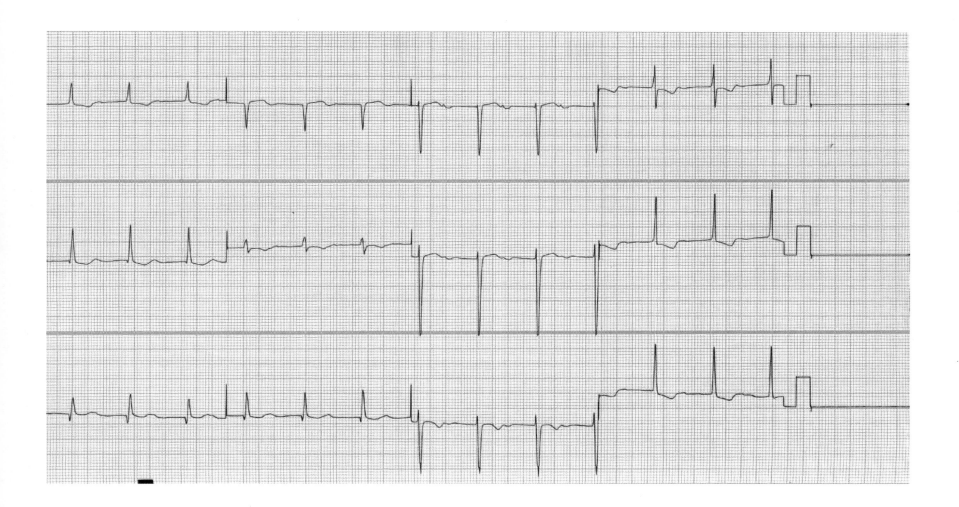

Case 36a

Description of Rhythm Strip

This is the three-lead (V_1, 2, and V_5) rhythm strip of the preceding ECG. It is clear that there is a P wave before each QRS and that the P–R interval is constant. The strip is long enough to pick up a long-cycle Wenckebach AV block, were one present. One might consider AJR, but the R–P interval would be quite long, and the P waves do not appear to be inverted in leads 2 and V_5.

Interpretation of Rhythm Strip

Sinus rhythm with long first-degree AV block

Learning Points

First-degree AV block
AJR
Long-cycle Wenckebach AV block

Suggested Readings

Silverman ME, Upshaw CB Jr. Walter Gaskell and the understanding of atrioventricular conduction and block. J Am Coll Cardiol 2002;39(10):1574–80. The subject of this article is the nineteenth-century British physiologist whose investigations became central to our understanding of cardiac physiology. His contributions include the concept of heart block and the elucidation of the sequence of cardiac contraction, rhythmicity, excitability, contractility, conductivity, and tonicity.

Strasberg B, Amat-Y-Leon F, Dhingra RC, et al. Natural history of chronic second-degree atrioventricular nodal block. Circulation 1981;63(5):1043–9. This report documents the authors' experience with documented chronic second-degree AV block (proximal to the bundle of His) in 56 patients. The ECGs of all the patients demonstrated episodes of type I second-degree block; five patients also had periods of 2:1 block. For 19 patients who had no organic disease, the mean follow-up was 1,395 days, during which one patient required a permanent pacemaker because of bradycardia with symptoms and two patients died (not suddenly). Of 37 patients with organic heart disease who were followed for a mean of 1,347 days, 10 patients were implanted with pacemakers (for CHF in 8 and for syncope in 2) and 16 patients died (3 suddenly, 7 of CHF, 2 of acute MI, and 4 of causes unrelated to cardiac disease). In summary, chronic second-degree AV nodal block has a relatively benign course in patients who do not have organic heart disease; in patients with organic heart disease, however, the prognosis is poor and is related to the severity of the underlying heart disease.

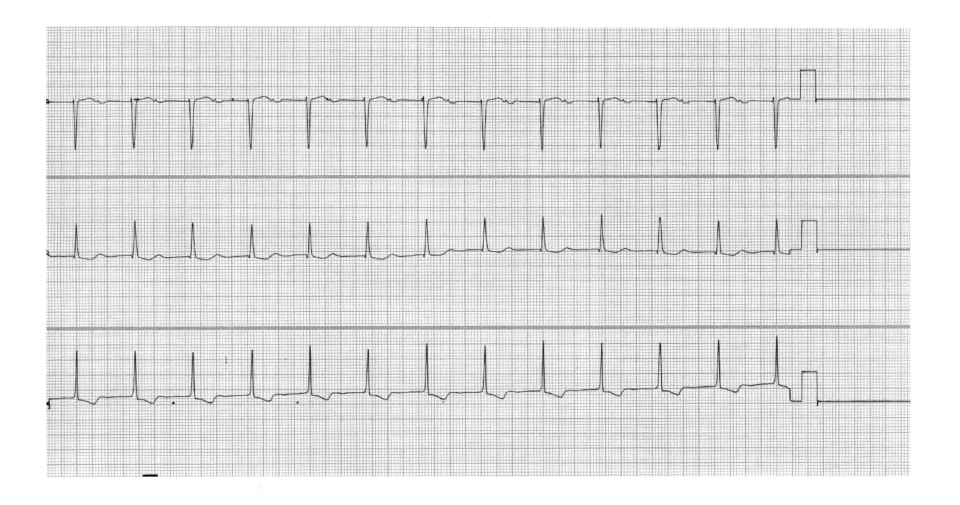

Case 37

Clinical Presentation

The patient is a 97-year-old female with syncope whose family notes that she has a slow regular pulse.

Description of Electrocardiogram (12 Leads)

There is sinus rhythm at a rate of 83/min, but there are at least two P waves for each QRS, and the P–R intervals for the P waves that precede the QRS complexes are not uniform. What is uniform is the R–R interval. The QRS complexes are not wide, nor is the axis abnormal; this fits with a slow junctional escape. The QRS voltage is low, but the corrected Q–T (Q–Tc) interval is normal.

Interpretation

Sinus rhythm (rate, 83/min), with slow junctional escape rhythm at 33/min, with CHB, low QRS voltage; abnormal ECG

Learning Points

Complete heart block
AV dissociation
Junctional escape rhythm
Third-degree AV block

This is AV dissociation but also CHB (third-degree AV block) because the sinus rate of 83/min should have been conducted 1:1, even by a patient well past 100 years of age. The term "AV dissociation without CHB" is used when the sinus or atrial rate is too fast to be conducted by the patient according to age, or when the junctional or ventricular rate is faster than the sinus or atrial rate.

In this patient, the CHB and low QRS voltage should make one consider hypothyroidism in addition to AV nodal blocking drugs (including β-blocker eyedrops), but regardless, it appears that a permanent dual-chamber pacemaker is in her future. She did not have hypothyroidism and was not using a β-blocker by any route of administration.

Suggested Readings

Harrigan RA, Perron AD, Brady WJ. Atrioventricular dissociation. Am J Emerg Med 2001;19(3):218–22. A concise description of the classifications of AV dissociation and the special form known as complete heart block.

Silverman ME, Upshaw CB, Lange HW. Woldemar Mobitz and his 1924 classification of second-degree atrioventricular block. Circulation 2004;110:1162–7. Woldemar Mobitz analyzed arrhythmias by graphing the relationship of changing atrial rates and premature beats to AV conduction. Through a mathematical approach, he was able to classify second-degree AV block into two types subsequently referred to as Mobitz type I (Wenckebach) and Mobitz type II (Hay). Type I was often due to digitalis and was reversible. There were no associated pathologic findings. Type II AV block frequently progressed to complete AV block and was associated with syncope (as seen in Case 37), seizures, death, and pathologic findings. Mark Silverman is a master teacher who values the contributions of great predecessors.

Sokoloff NM. Bradyarrhythmias: AV conduction disturbances. Geriatrics 1985;40(8):83–6. It should be noted that "high-grade" type II block is not usually the result of a transient process but rather of a chronic progressive infranodal disease. This means that it is more likely to progress to CHB and to require permanent pacing.

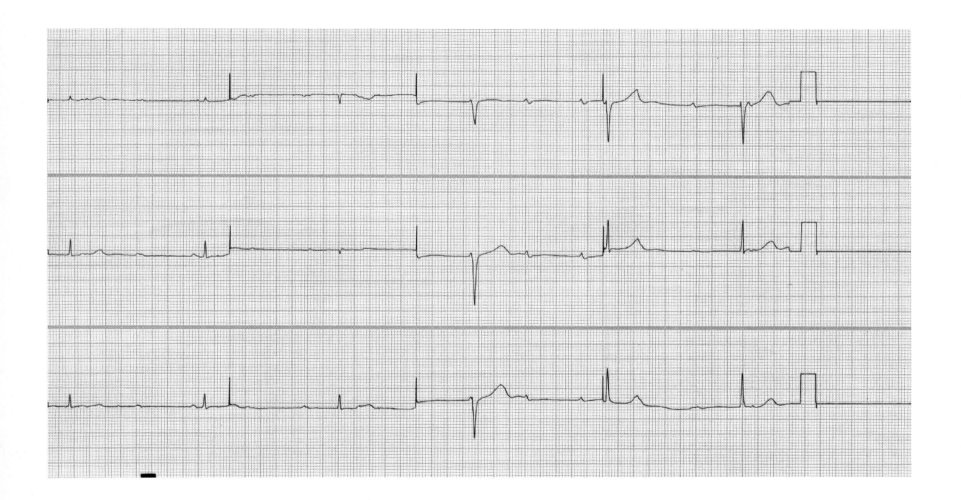

Case 38

Clinical Presentation

The patient is a 55-year-old male in the pacemaker clinic, where his pacemaker is being reprogrammed.

Description of Electrocardiogram (12 Leads)

With a ventricular rate of 30/min, the QRS complexes are wide and are preceded by a pacemaker spike. There are P waves that are upright in leads 2 and V_6, are regular, and have a rate of 93/min, but they are dissociated from the paced QRS complexes (the interval from the P wave to the pacer spike varies from beat to beat). The paced beats have no acute ST changes, nor are they excessively wide. The rate of the pacemaker was intentionally slowed to 30/min to determine whether there was any intrinsic AV conduction. If there are native QRS complexes, one can learn more about the status of the heart than could be learned from paced QRS complexes. Pacemaker rates usually cannot be programmed to < 30/min; in this case, there is no intrinsic AV conduction, and there are thus no native QRS complexes, even at this slow pacemaker rate.

Interpretation

Sinus rhythm at 93/min, with an implanted ventricular pacemaker rate of 30/min with high-grade AV block; abnormal ECG

Learning Points

Ventricular pacemaker
AV dissociation
High-grade AV block
Pacemaker reprogramming (slowing) to uncover intrinsic QRS complexes

Suggested Readings

Gregoratos G, Abrams J, Epstein AE, et al. ACC/AHA/NASPE 2002 guideline update for implantation of cardiac pacemakers and antiarrhythmia devices—summary article. J Am Coll Cardiol 2002;40(9):1703–19. The guide to implantation indications and follow-up of patients with pacemakers.

Rosenqvist M, Edhag KO. Pacemaker dependence in transient high-grade atrioventricular block. Pacing Clin Electrophysiol 1984;7(1):63–70. In a prospective study with median follow-up of 62 months, 6 of 16 patients who had been given a pacemaker for symptomatic high-grade AV block and whose conduction had been recovered later went on to have recurrent episodes of pacemaker dependence. The authors conclude that pacing introduced because of symptomatic high-grade AV block should not be discontinued even if a conducted heart rhythm has been established and maintained for long periods.

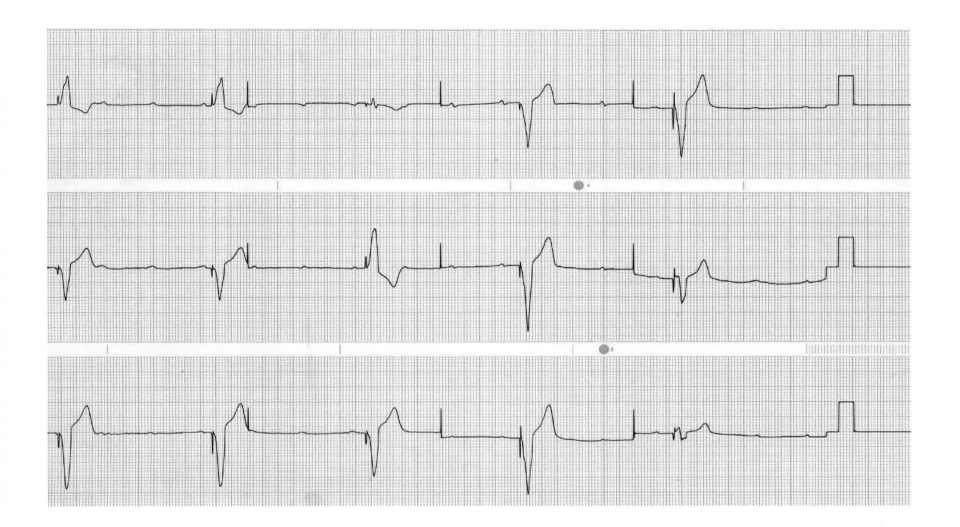

Case 38a

Description of Rhythm Strip

This is the rhythm strip for the 55-year-old patient in Case 38. It is clear that the P–P intervals are constant and that the pacemaker spikes are equidistant. The interval from the P wave to the pacemaker spike is variable; thus, they are not associated. Association between P waves and ventricular pacing spikes requires two pacemaker wires, one in the right atrium and one in the right ventricle. The pacemaker generator then serves to coordinate AV synchrony. In this case, there are three P waves that precede each pacemaker spike; that certainly represents some form of high-grade AV block, but because one is unable to see the native escape rhythm, one cannot say this indicates CHB (although it is assumed when the escape rate is < 30). When a pacemaker lead located in the right ventricle fires, the QRS complex will usually have an LBBB pattern because it first captures the right bundle and because the heart muscle in the distribution of the left bundle is depolarized without the use of this specialized conduction bundle. Accordingly, the QRS complex is wide and looks like LBBB.

Interpretation of Rhythm Strip

Sinus rhythm at 93/min with RV pacemaker at 30/min, with high-grade AV block

This is a ventricular demand inhibited (VVI) pacemaker, but because this strip does not demonstrate its ability to sense intrinsic ventricular rhythm, it can only be called a ventricular pacer.

Learning Points

RV endocardial pacing has an LBBB pattern

LV endocardial pacing is prone to cause arterial emboli

Suggested Readings

Schiavone WA, Castle LW, Salcedo E, Graor R. Amaurosis fugax in a patient with a left ventricular endocardial pacemaker. Pacing Clin Electrophysiol 1984;7(2):288–92. The causes of the electrocardiographic RBBB pattern in cardiac pacing and the usefulness of echocardiography in evaluating pacing catheters are discussed.

Yang YN, Yin WH, Young MS. Safe right bundle branch block pattern during permanent right ventricular pacing. J Electrocardiol 2003;36(1):67–71. It is known that electrocardiography after transvenous RV pacing should yield an LBBB QRS pattern. When RBBB pacing morphology appears in a patient with a permanent or temporary transvenous RV pacemaker, myocardial perforation or malposition of the pacing lead must be ruled out even though the patient may be asymptomatic. There are exceptions to this rule, however.

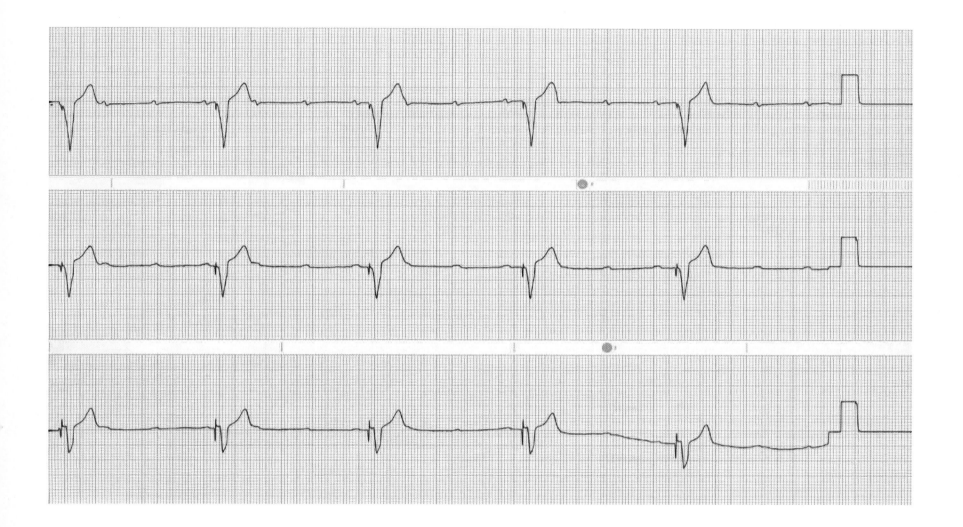

Case 39

Clinical Presentation

The patient is a 64-year-old male who has had a permanent pacemaker in place for 7 years and who likes to chop firewood. He says that he is starting to get dizzy again, as he had prior to the implantation of his pacemaker.

Description of Electrocardiogram (12 Leads)

This is an early computerized format. Three leads were recorded simultaneously, followed by a dense line 280 msec in duration, right in the center of the recording paper. During the inscription of this dense line, there was no record of intrinsic electrical activity, but the timing of events was accurate. When changing from the augmented limb leads to the three right precordial leads, a spike was inscribed and time elapsed that was not recorded. Thus, in this format, the P–P and R–R intervals can be measured only before or after the spike. From the last four P waves in leads V_3 and V_6, one can determine that there is sinus rhythm at 70/min and junctional escape at 41/min. There are LPH, RBBB, LVH, a long Q–Tc interval (530 msec), and AV dissociation.

Interpretation

Sinus rhythm at 70/min with junctional escape at 41/min, CHB; LPH, RBBB, LVH with ST segment and T-wave changes, long Q–T interval; abnormal ECG

There were no pacemaker spikes. The battery was totally depleted. Chest radiography showed a wire to be broken where it crossed under the clavicle, a common site for lead fracture. From then on, the patient had to buy firewood.

Learning Points

Pacemaker lead fracture
Pacemaker battery depletion
LVH
RBBB
LPH
CHB
AV dissociation

Suggested Readings

Antonelli D, Rosenfeld T, Freedberg NA, et al. Insulation lead fracture: is it a matter of insulation coating, venous approach or both? Pacing Clin Electrophysiol 1998;21(2):418–21. Lead insulation material and implant route have a major impact on lead reliability and durability. By studying 290 leads followed for a mean of 57 months, the authors compare the incidence of lead insulation failure resulting from both the venous approach and the type of insulation. Their conclusion was that insulation failure was more common when the subclavian venous route was chosen rather than the cephalic venous approach. In Case 39, perhaps the proximity of the subclavian vein to the clavicle and the repetitive injury caused by the clavicle-lead apposition during the chopping motion resulted in lead fracture.

Grieco JG, Scanlon PJ, Pifarre R. Pacing lead fracture after a deceleration injury. Ann Thorac Surg 1989;47(3):453–4. Unlike in Case 39, in which chronic repetitive injury was the cause of the problem, pacemaker lead fracture can occur acutely during deceleration injury to the chest.

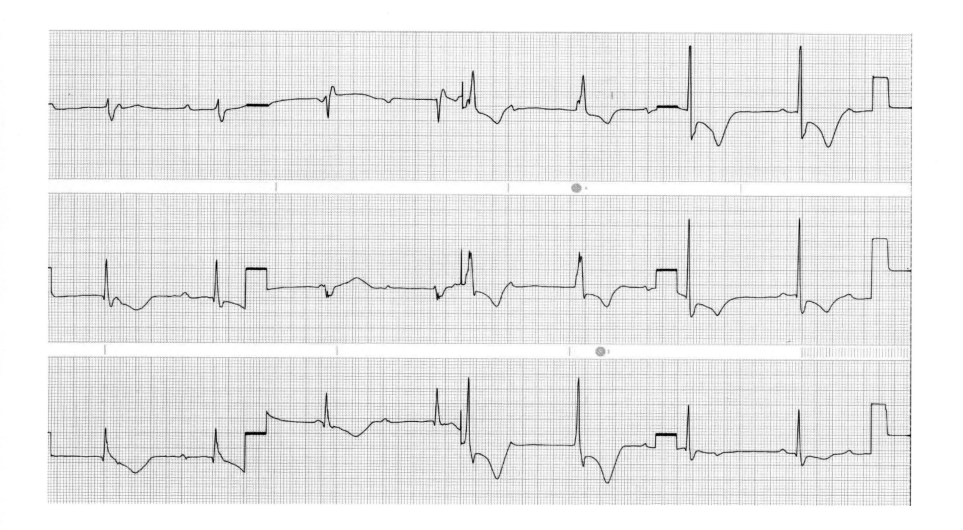

7

Pacemakers

Case 40

Clinical Presentation

The patient is a 65-year-old male with a ventricular pacemaker and weakness.

Description of Electrocardiogram (12 Leads)

The HR is about 60/min. As the QRS complexes have an LBBB pattern, the pacemaker is a RV pacemaker. Because there is no demonstration of a sensed ventricular event, one can say only that this is a ventricular pacemaker. If there were sensed intrinsic ventricular beats, one could say that this is a ventricular demand inhibited (VVI) pacemaker. The method of pacemaker nomenclature is the following: the first "V" stands for where the pacemaker paces, the second "V" indicates where it senses, and the "I" indicates the pacemaker's response to sensing. A VVI pacemaker, which is the type of pacemaker used in patients with chronic atrial fibrillation who have slowing of atrioventricular conduction, paces in the ventricle (V), senses in the ventricle (V) and inhibits (I) its pacing when it senses. There is no atrial activity just preceding the paced QRS complexes, but notice the inverted P waves best seen in leads 2 and V_1. These represent retrograde ventriculo-atrial (VA) conduction.

Interpretation

RV pacemaker (rate, 60/min) with 1:1 VA conduction; abnormal ECG

Learning Points

Pacemaker nomenclature (NBG code)

Ventriculo-atrial conduction

Suggested Readings

Bernstein AD, Camm AJ, Fletcher RD, et al. The NASPE/BPEG generic pacemaker code for antibradyarrhythmia and adaptive-rate pacing and antitachyarrhythmia devices. Pacing Clin Electrophysiol 1987;10(4 Pt 1):794–9. The North American Society of Pacing and Electrophysiology (NASPE)/British Pacing and Electrophysiology Group (BPEG) Generic Code was developed to permit extension of the generic-code concept to (1) pacemakers whose escape rate is continuously controlled by monitoring some physiologic variable rather than determined by fixed escape intervals measured from stimuli or sensed depolarizations and (2) antitachyarrhythmia devices, including cardioverters and defibrillators. The NASPE/BPEG Generic (NBG) Code incorporates an "R" in the fourth position to signify rate modulation and uses one of four letters in the fifth position to indicate the presence of antitachyarrhythmia-pacing capability or of cardioversion or defibrillation functions.

Bernstein AD, Daubert JC, Fletcher RD, et al. The revised NASPE/BPEG generic code for antibradycardia, adaptive-rate, and multisite pacing. North American Society of Pacing and Electrophysiology/British Pacing and Electrophysiology Group. Pacing Clin Electrophysiol 2002;25(2):260–4. This revised NBG Code differs from its predecessor in two respects: position 4 specifies only the presence or absence of rate modulation, and position 5 specifies only the location or absence of multisite pacing, (biatrial or biventricular pacing, with at least two stimulation sites in each case), more than one stimulation site in any single cardiac chamber, or any combination of these.

Teplitz L. Classification of cardiac pacemakers: the pacemaker code. J Cardiovasc Nurs 1991;5(3):1–8. Familiarity with the pacemaker code is essential for nurses (and other medical personnel) caring for the patient who has a permanent pacemaker.

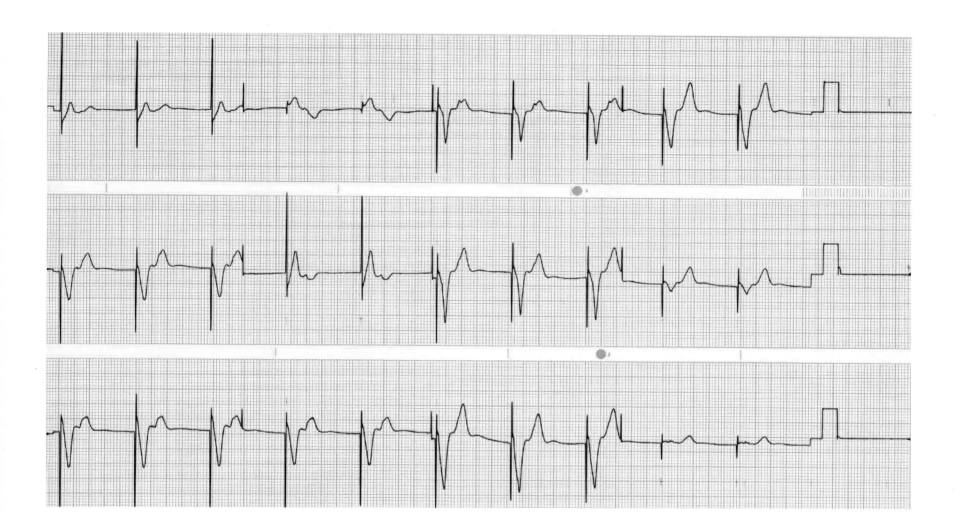

Case 40a

Description of Rhythm Strip

This is the three-lead rhythm strip for Case 40, with an RV pacemaker, rate of 60/min. The retrograde P waves are best seen in leads V_1 and 2, deforming the ST segments. That they are inverted in lead 2 suggests that they are retrograde. That there is no evidence of intrinsic sinus nodal activity makes it reasonable to expect that the electrical activity that starts in the ventricle would cross the AV node in a retrograde fashion, to electromechanically activate the atria. Since the timing of atrial contraction for each of these beats on this strip closely follows ventricular contraction, the atria will contract against closed AV valves. The force of contraction of the atria will be unable open these valves, and the blood in the atria will be propelled retrograde into the neck veins and pulmonary veins; neither of which has a valve to prevent this. Many patients will be troubled by the sensation of warmth in the neck, and some (with marginal cardiac output) will suffer with weakness owing to a further fall in cardiac output when this rhythm pertains. This is called the pacemaker syndrome, and it can be corrected by converting to a dual chamber (atrial and ventricular) pacing system.

Interpretation of Rhythm Strip

RV pacemaker (rate, 60/min), with 1:1 VA conduction, abnormal rhythm

Learning Point

Pacemaker syndrome

Suggested Readings

Ellenbogen KA, Stambler BS, Orav EJ, et al. Clinical characteristics of patients intolerant to VVIR pacing. Am J Cardiol 2000;86(1):59–63. The Pacemaker Selection in the Elderly (PASE) trial enrolled 407 patients ≥ 65 years of age in a 30-month quality-of-life trial comparing ventricular pacing with dual chamber pacing. Of the 204 patients randomized to VVIR mode, 53 patients (26%) crossed over to DDDR pacing, with significant improvement in quality of life. A decrease in systolic blood pressure during ventricular pacing, the use of β-blockers, and nonischemic cardiomyopathy correlated with a patient's intolerance of VVIR pacing.

Link MS, Hellkamp AS, Estes NA 3rd, et al. High incidence of pacemaker syndrome in patients with sinus node dysfunction treated with ventricular-based pacing in the Mode Selection Trial (MOST). J Am Coll Cardiol 2004;43(11):2072–4. Pacemaker syndrome, or intolerance to VVIR pacing, consists of cardiovascular signs and symptoms induced by VVIR pacing that include either (1) congestive signs and symptoms associated with retrograde conduction during VVIR pacing or (2) a reduction of systolic blood pressure ≥ 20 mm Hg during VVIR pacing, associated with reproducible symptoms of weakness, lightheadedness, or syncope. Pacemaker syndrome occurred early in most patients (in 13.8% at 6 months, 16.0% at 1 year, and 19.7% at 4 years). Baseline predictors of pacemaker syndrome included a lower sinus rate and a higher programmed pacemaker rate. Postimplantation predictors of pacemaker syndrome were a higher percentage of paced beats, a higher programmed low rate, and a slower underlying spontaneous sinus rate, such as was seen in Case 40. The only way to prevent pacemaker syndrome is to implant atrial-based pacemakers in all patients.

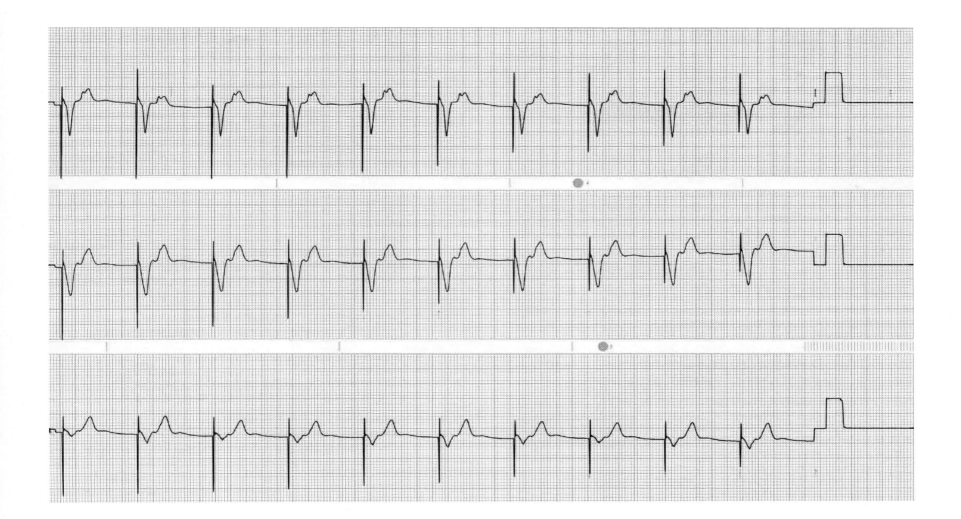

Case 41

Clinical Presentation

The patient is a 70-year-old male with largely sinus rhythm and a pacemaker.

Description of Electrocardiogram (12 Leads)

The mean HR is 84/min. The voltage standardization is normal. The P waves are broad and notched, as is seen in LAE. The change-of-leads spikes must not be confused with the pacemaker spikes. The first six P waves are followed by ventricular pacing spikes with a uniform P wave to pacer spike interval. Thus, this must be a pacemaker system with both atrial and ventricular leads. The seventh beat is a PVC that is sensed. Following the PVC, there is a pause, then an upright change of leads spike, then a P wave and an atrial spike that fires in the later half of the P wave. In this case, atrial sensing is altered following a PVC and may be normal for this pacemaker. Because this pacemaker paces in both atrium and ventricle ("D" in pacemaker code), senses in both atrium and ventricle (D), and triggers (T) in the ventricle when it senses in the atrium and inhibits (I) in the atrium and in the ventricle when the respective wire senses in its chamber, it is called a DDD pacemaker. The "D" stands for dual. In the first position the "D" means that it paces in both the atrium and in the ventricle (dual chamber pacing). In the second position the "D" means that it senses in the atrium and in the ventricle. In the third position the "D" means that it is able to respond to a sensed electrical event by either triggering pacing or inhibiting pacing (based on its programmed parameters.) If there is a fourth letter it is an R, which signifies that it is rate-responsive (it increases the pacing rate based on motion sensation or another programmable parameter that is intended to appropriately increase the rate of pacing when the demand is present and to slow the rate of pacing when the clinical demand is no longer present).

Interpretation

Sinus rhythm with PVC (mean rate, 84/min), LAE, and DDD pacemaker that fails to sense atrial activity following a sensed PVC; abnormal ECG

Learning Points

Failure to sense atrial activity
DDD pacemaker
Advantages of DDD pacing

Suggested Readings

Garson A Jr. Stepwise approach to the unknown pacemaker ECG. Am Heart J 1990;119(4):924–41. A method is presented for obtaining data about a pacemaker from a routine ECG without any prior information about the type of pacemaker or the pacemaker's parameters.

Hargreaves MR, Channon KM, Cripps TR, et al. Comparison of dual chamber and ventricular rate responsive pacing in patients over 75 with complete heart block. Br Heart J 1995;74(4):397–402. In active elderly patients with complete heart block, both DDD and VVIR pacing are associated with improved exercise performance when compared with fixed-rate VVI pacing. The convenience and reduced cost of VVIR systems, however, may be offset by a higher incidence of pacemaker syndrome. In elderly patients with complete heart block, VVIR pacing results in suboptimal symptomatic benefit and should not be used instead of DDD pacing.

Theodorakis GN, Panou F, Markianos M, et al. Left atrial function and atrial natriuretic factor/cyclic guanosine monophosphate changes in DDD and VVI pacing modes. Am J Cardiol 1997;79(3):366–70. Compared to patients with DDD pacing, patients who developed pacemaker syndrome during VVI pacing had a significant decrease in left atrial emptying fraction and a substantial increase in atrial natriuretic factor and cyclic guanosine monophosphate plasma levels. Unlike symptoms, these are objective findings of the superiority of DDD pacing.

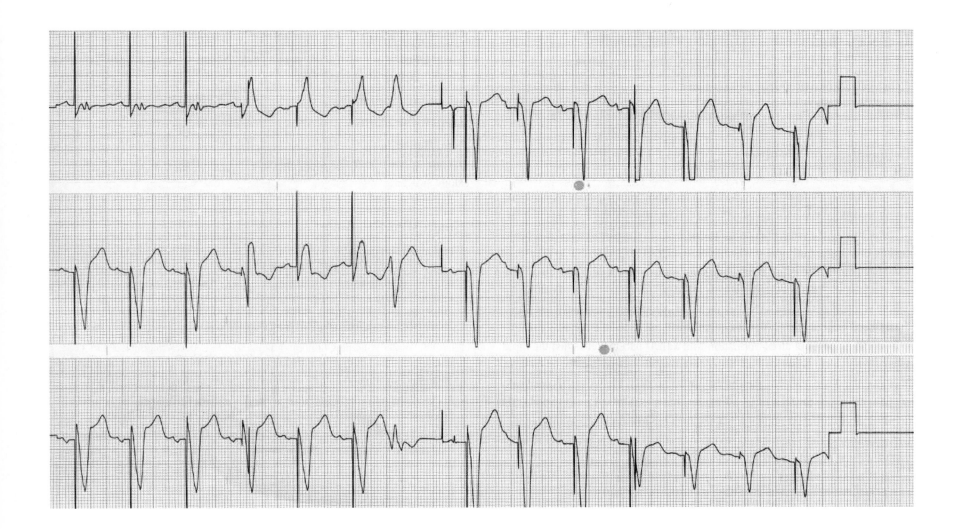

Case 42

Clinical Presentation

The patient is a 75-year-old male with a pacemaker and a new irregular rhythm.

Description of Electrocardiogram (12 Leads)

The mean HR is 84/min. There is a pacemaker, and there are change-of-leads spikes following the fourth, seventh, and tenth beats. The pacemaker spikes that trigger the QRS complexes are of different magnitudes in different leads, but this pertains even in the same lead, from beat to beat. This is due to the signal processing of a digital ECG system. The baseline is irregular and is due to coarse atrial fibrillation. The larger atrial fibrillation waves are sensed by the atrial wire and are followed by a ventricular pacing spike. When the voltage of the atrial activity is insufficient to be sensed by the atrial wire (as in the last beat on the ECG), there is atrial pacing, but of course, it will not capture if the atria are fibrillating. The danger of atrial fibrillation with a DDD pacemaker is that the rapid atrial activity might be sensed and the ventricle will be paced rapidly. In the presence of CAD, this could provoke angina (or worse, MI). Modern DDD pacemakers have the ability to sense atrial fibrillation and switch to VVI pacing mode. This is called mode-switching. One also should note the RBBB pattern to the paced QRS complexes. This might be due to intrinsic RBBB, but it is necessary to be sure that the ventricular wire is not in the left ventricle.

Interpretation

Atrial fibrillation with DDD pacer (rate, 84/min); unusual RBBB pattern for RV pacing; abnormal ECG

Learning Points

Atrial fibrillation
Varying voltage pacemaker spikes in computer-generated ECG
Mode switching

Suggested Readings

Passman RS, Weinberg KM, Freher M, et al. Accuracy of mode switch algorithms for detection of atrial tachyarrhythmias. J Cardiovasc Electrophysiol 2004;15(7):778–9. In patients with bradycardia-tachycardia syndrome and permanent pacemakers that have these mode-switching algorithms, mode-switching events are reliable surrogate markers for atrial tachyarrhythmias. Therefore, mode switching may serve as a valuable tool for clinical decisions, such as to administer antiarrhythmic drug therapy or anticoagulation.

Peters RW, Kushner M, Knapp K. Giant pacemaker spikes. An electrocardiographic artifact. Chest 1985;87(2):256–7. Because of a different type of signal processing, digital electrocardiographs show much larger spikes from pacemakers than do analog machines.

Sutton R, Stack Z, Heaven D, Ingram A. Mode switching for atrial tachyarrhythmias. Am J Cardiol 1999;83(5B):202D–10D. Mode switching was introduced in the early 1990s to prevent dual chamber pacemakers from ventricular tracking of rapid atrial rates. The authors discuss the advantages and disadvantages of the technique.

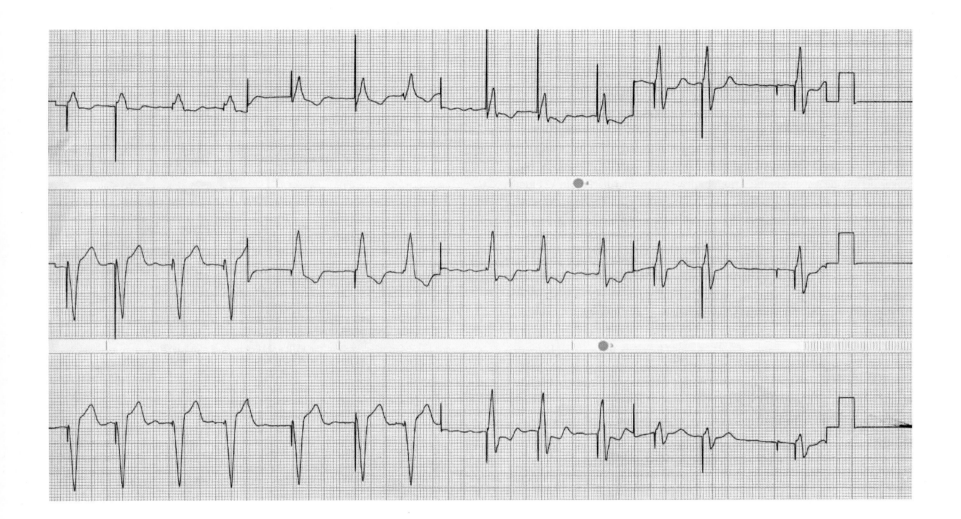

Case 42a

Description of Rhythm Strip

This is the rhythm strip for Case 42 (atrial fibrillation and a DDD pacemaker). There are no change-of-leads spikes. The varying voltage of the pacemaker spikes is more evident. When mode switching is activated on the pacemaker system, atrial fibrillation is sensed and DDD mode is converted to VVI mode, no longer permitting sensing in the atrium to drive ventricular pacing. In VVI mode, the paced beats would be at a constant programmable rate. Although the patient would still be in atrial fibrillation, the only increase in HR would be due to intrinsically-conducted beats or if there were rate responsiveness (VVIR). The importance of recognizing a pacemaker that has an RBBB pattern to paced beats is that thrombi can form on a pacemaker wire, and if the wire is in the LV, there can be systemic embolization. The pacing wire that paces the LV in a biventricular pacemaker system (used to treat certain patients who have CHF) is positioned in the coronary sinus or in a posterior or lateral cardiac vein overlying the LV. In such an LV pacing wire position, there is no problem with systemic embolization.

Interpretation of Rhythm Strip

Atrial fibrillation with DDD pacemaker (rate, 84/min), abnormal rhythm

Learning Points

Rate-responsive pacing

Biventricular pacing

Suggested Readings

Reynolds MR, Joventino LP, Josephson ME. Relationship of baseline electrocardiographic characteristics with the response to cardiac resynchronization therapy for heart failure. Pacing Clin Electrophysiol 2004;27(11):1513–8. "Cardiac resynchronization therapy" is a synonym for biventricular pacing that has inter- and intraventricular synergy as the tenets for improving cardiac output and decreasing mitral regurgitation in patients with CHF. This study analyzed preimplantation ECGs of 110 patients with ICD indications and CHF due to left ventricular systolic dysfunction. They found that electrocardiographic markers of anterior infarction and RV dilation may help identify patients who are unlikely to benefit from biventricular pacing.

Trappe HJ, Klein H, Frank G, Lichtlen PR. Rate-responsive pacing as compared to fixed-rate VVI pacing in patients after ablation of the atrioventricular conduction system. Eur Heart J 1988;9(6):642–8. In 44 patients with supraventricular arrhythmias treated with ablation of the AV conduction system and a pacemaker, half had a rate-responsive unit (VVIR) and half had a rate-programmable unit (VVI). Those with the rate-responsive units had better work capacity and less dyspnea on exertion. The VVIR units that tracked physical activity were more physiologic during stress testing.

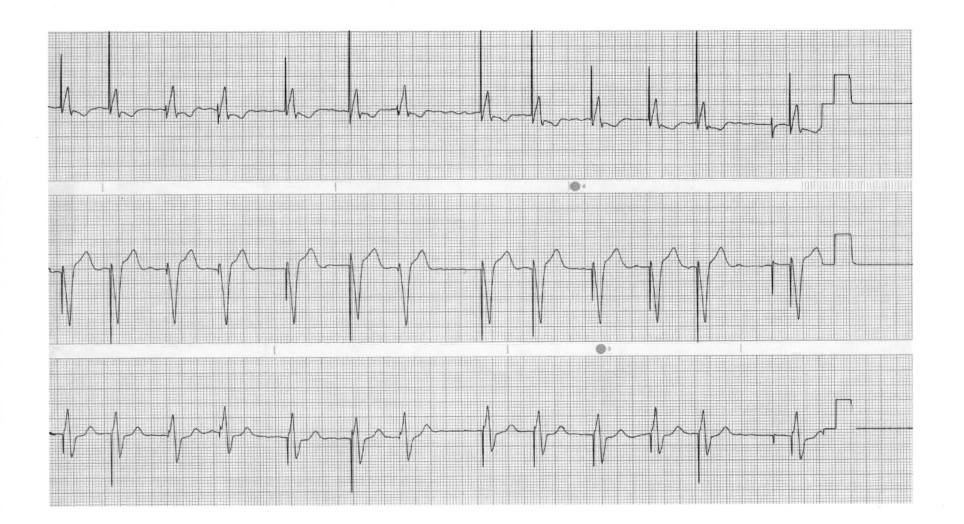

Case 43

Clinical Presentation

The patient is a 58-year-old male with a pacemaker and different widths of paced QRS complexes.

Description of Electrocardiogram (12 Leads)

The rate is 88/min. There are atrial and ventricular pacing spikes for each beat. The AV pacing delay is programmed at 160 msec. The paced QRS complexes have an LBBB pattern, which verifies RV pacing. Since every beat recorded is paced in both atrium and ventricle, this pacemaker's ability to sense is not demonstrated. It can only be called an AV sequential pacemaker or a dual chamber pacemaker. On the ECG, there are two QRS complexes—three beats before the last and one beat before the last—that are conducted with a more narrow QRS complex, even though each is still preceded by a ventricular pacer spike. This is due to the conduction of paced atrial activity across the AV node to depolarize the ventricle through the native conduction bundles and the His-Purkinje system. The pacemaker depolarizes the RV from its apex, without using the specialized electrical conduction bundles. Thus, the paced beats have a wide QRS complex. These more narrow beats that follow a ventricular pacer spike are called *pacemaker fusion beats*, the fusion of paced and intrinsic QRS conduction. The term is borrowed from the fusion of a late PVC and intrinsic QRS conduction that makes a PVC more narrow than expected.

Interpretation

AV sequential pacemaker, rate of 88/min, with occasional fusion in ventricle; abnormal ECG

Learning Point

Pacemaker fusion beats

The dual chamber pacemaker with the most programmability is the DDD pacemaker. In the absence of rate responsiveness, the rate of the pacemaker is pro-grammed for pacing in the atrium at a rate of, for example, 60/min. The patient's HR should not be less than that. If the atrial rate is sensed to exceed 60/min, the AV delay that is also programmed will pace in the ventricle after a set period of time (eg, as in this case, 160 msec). An ECG should be periodically checked to see how these programmed parameters fit with the patient's rhythm and intrinsic AV conduction. In Case 43, the two pacemaker fusion beats show that there is intrinsic AV conduction, at least in some beats, that is close to 160 msec, the programmed pacemaker AV delay. In most cases, an AV delay of closer to 200 msec is physiologic and preserves the atrial contribution to ventricular filling. Reprogramming the pacemaker AV delay to 200 msec might decrease the amount of ventricular pacing required (both fully paced and fused in the ventricle), favor native AV conduction of atrially paced complexes, improve cardiac output, and preserve pacemaker battery life. Of course, there are situations (such as DDD pacing for hypertrophic obstructive cardiomyopathy) in which a short AV delay and ventricular pacing of every beat is desirable.

If one must prove the presence of a fusion beat, it is necessary to record a His bundle electrogram, which will show the His spike that precedes the pacemaker spike and the ventricular complex that is wider than one entirely conducted through the His-Purkinje system. A complex that is fully paced in the ventricle lacks a preceding His spike.

Suggested Reading

Folino AF, Buja G, Ruzza L, Nava A. Long-term follow-up of patients with single lead VDD stimulation. Pacing Clin Electrophysiol 1994;17(11 Pt 2):1854–8. According to the pacemaker code, a VDD pacemaker only paces in the ventricle, but it senses in the atrium and in the ventricle, and it can be triggered to pace in the ventricle by a sensed atrial beat or inhibited in the ventricle by a sensed ventricular beat. A VDD pacemaker uses only a single lead that senses in the atrium and then passes through the tricuspid valve to sense and pace in the ventricle. In this study, VDD pacemakers implanted in 85 patients with second- or third-degree AV block were observed by Holter monitor every 6 months for a mean of 44 months. Among other findings that were pertinent to Case 43, persistent fusion beats were detected in 12 patients (14%). It is necessary periodically to reassess pacing characteristics and the efficacy of pacing, as well as battery life, in all patients with an implanted pacemaker. Reprogramming, when indicated, can improve cardiac function and prolong battery life.

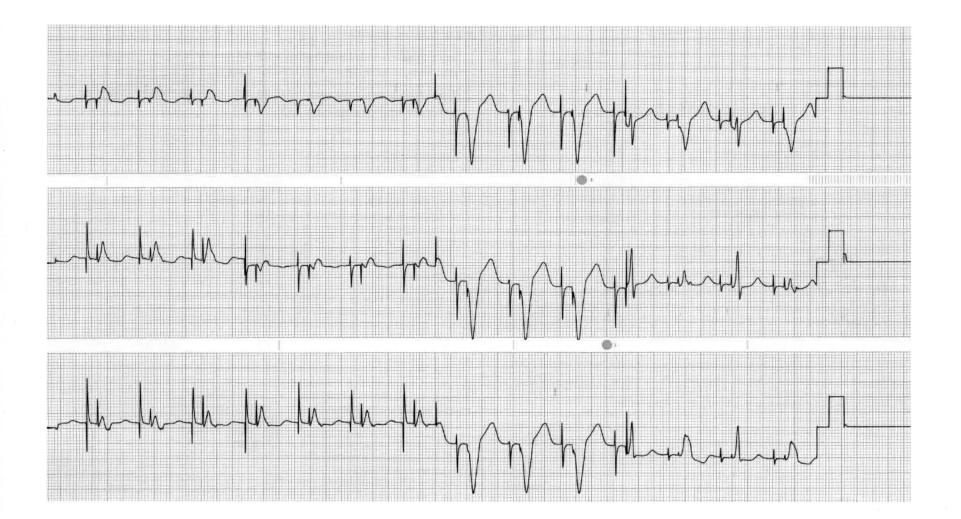

Case 44

Clinical Presentation

The patient is a 48-year-old male with a pacemaker and an irregular rhythm.

Description of Electrocardiogram (12 Leads)

There are change-of-leads spikes in the middle of the fifth QRS complex and following the eighth and twelfth QRS complexes. These confusing spikes are not encountered in the rhythm strip that follows (Case 44a, below). The mean HR is 96/min, but the pacemaker rate is 100/min at times, followed by a pause and either AV sequential pacing or *VAT pacing* (pacing in the ventricle that senses atrial activity and triggers ventricular pacing after a programmed interval measured from the sensed or paced atrial beat to ventricular pacing). This interval is known as the AV delay. The only P wave recorded is seen in the lateral precordial leads and is upright in V_6, suggesting sinus rhythm. The grouped beating is reminiscent of Wenckebach periodicity. Again, the "red flag" goes up because of the RBBB pattern to the paced ventricular beats. One must check the lateral chest radiograph to verify ventricular lead location. The T waves are a bit peaked. Hyperkalemia or ischemia/injury should be investigated.

Interpretation

Sinus rhythm with DDD pacing with intermittent pauses suggesting a Wenckebach periodicity (mean rate, 96/min); unusual RBBB pattern to paced QRS complexes; peaked T waves (consider hyperkalemia or ischemia/injury); abnormal ECG

Learning Points

VAT pacing
Upper rate behavior in dual chamber pacemakers
Wenckebach behavior in DDD pacemakers

Suggested Reading

Furman S. Dual chamber pacemakers: upper rate behavior. Pacing Clin Electrophysiol;8(2):197–214. This article is for the serious student of the subject. It discusses how a pacemaker is programmed to respond to varying atrial rates yet not pace excessively fast in the ventricle. Dr. Furman is a pacemaker pioneer.

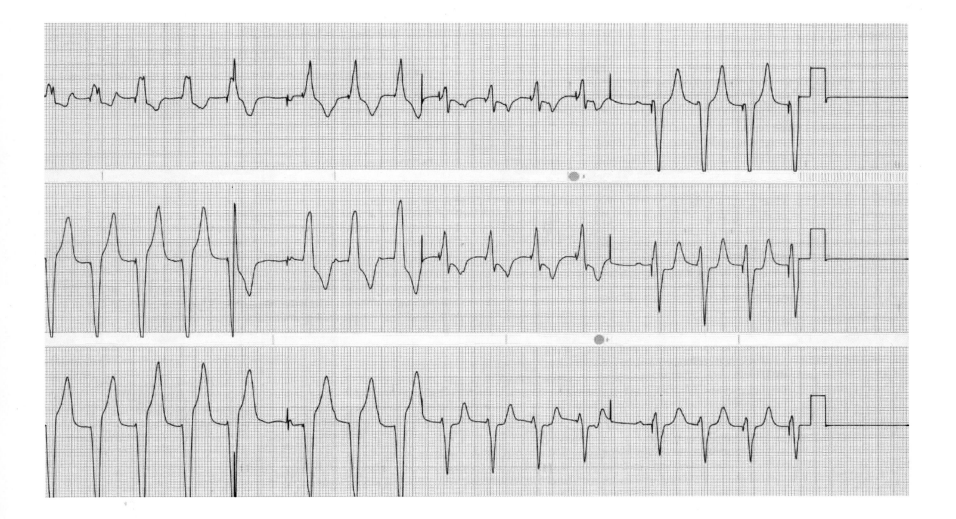

Case 44a

Description of Three-Lead Rhythm Strip

In lead V$_1$, the P waves are beautifully demonstrated. Their rate is 107/min (the P–P interval equals 14 little boxes). Starting on the sixth QRS complex, there is an atrially-paced beat with an AV delay that is slightly less than 200 msec. The AV delay of the next six beats progressively lengthens until the next P wave is not followed by a paced QRS complex. In fact, the next P wave is clearly upright in lead 2, is clearly sinus in origin (like the others), and is followed by ventricular pacing with a normal AV delay. The same pattern repeats itself. It is clear that this DDD pacemaker is programmed so that it cannot pace in a VAT (atrial tracking and ventricular pacing) fashion that will sustain an HR of 107/min. It thus is programmed to conduct this sinus tachycardia at 107/min with an 8:7 Wenckebach periodicity to effectively keep the HR at < 100/min (the upper rate limit of this pacemaker).

Interpretation of Rhythm Strip

Sinus tachycardia (107/min) with DDD pacing in VAT mode using Wenckebach-type AV conduction block to slow the ventricular pacing response to 96/min; abnormal rhythm

Learning Point

8:7 Wenckebach periodicity

Suggested Reading

Higano ST, Hayes DL. Quantitative analysis of Wenckebach behavior in DDD pacemakers. Pacing Clin Electrophysiol 1990;13(11 Pt 1):1456–65. Wenckebach-type behavior in P-synchronous pacing modes allows a gradual transition to 2:1 block. As this behavior is dependent on precise timing intervals, it can be quantitated with mathematical equations. These equations can be clinically useful. This gradual transition to 2:1 block allows sudden atrial tachyarrhythmia to have a more gentle change in HR rather than an abrupt halving of HR, which can decrease cardiac output and cause hypoperfusion symptoms.

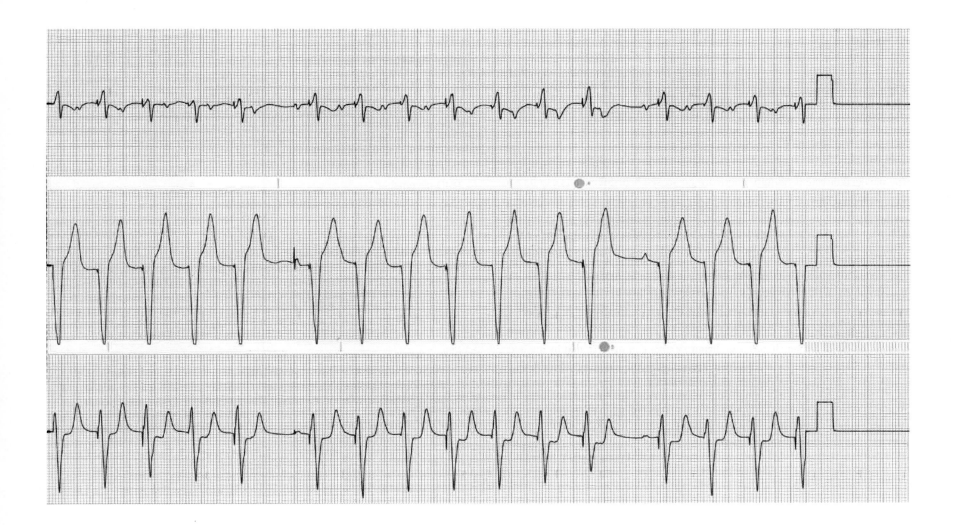

Case 45

Clinical Presentation

The patient is a 72-year-old female with a dual chamber pacemaker and backache.

Description of Electrocardiogram (12 Leads)

The pacemaker rate is 88/min. There are no sensed beats; thus, this can be a fixed-rate dual chamber pacemaker (DOO). DOO pacing is usually seen in temporary pacemakers that do not have good sensing characteristics but can also be found in permanent pacemakers when a magnet is applied over the generator and left in place. The paced QRS complexes all have the expected LBBB pattern. The one glaring abnormality is the failure to capture the ventricle in the second beat in the right precordial leads. This abnormality requires a search for lead malfunction or a change in lead impedance when a pacemaker check is performed. Battery depletion can be responsible for intermittent failure to capture. Electrolyte imbalance such as severe hypocalcemia can be heralded by the pacemaker's intermittent failure to capture. The usual prolongation of the Q–T interval has less sensitivity when the rhythm is entirely paced (up to 500 msec can be normal), but here the corrected Q–T (Q–Tc) interval is 486 msec. Hypocalcemia from acute pancreatitis was the cause of this pacemaker malfunction and was corrected in time to prevent disaster.

Interpretation

Dual chamber RV pacemaker (rate, 88/min), with intermittent failure to capture, long Q–Tc interval (consider hypocalcemia); abnormal ECG

Learning Points

Pacemaker failure to capture
Hypocalcemia
DOO pacemaker
Magnet application to a permanent pacemaker

Suggested Readings

Dohrmann ML, Goldschlager NF. Myocardial stimulation threshold in patients with cardiac pacemakers: effect of physiologic variables, pharmacologic agents, and lead electrodes. Cardiol Clin 1985;3(4):527–37. Electrolyte and metabolic abnormalities (especially hyperkalemia, alkalosis, acidosis, and hyperglycemia) increase the pacing threshold. Hypocalcemia (seen in Case 45) is a less common cause of intermittent pacemaker failure to capture in the ventricle.

Driller J, Barold SS, Parsonnet V. Normal and abnormal function of the pacemaker magnet reed switch. J Electrocardiol 1976;9(3):283–92. Application of the special test magnet over a demand pacemaker actuates a magnetic reed switch that converts the pacemaker to fixed-rate pacing (either VOO or DOO). Theoretical and practical aspects are discussed.

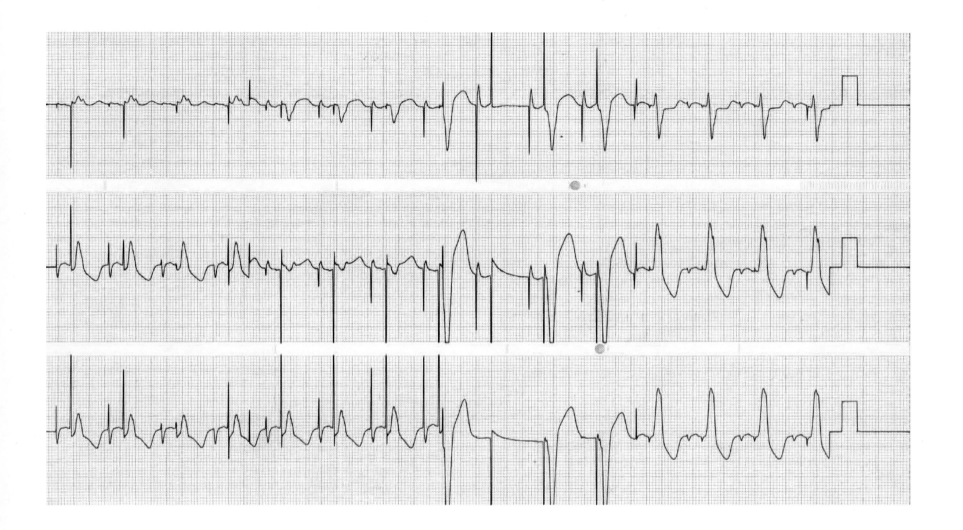

Case 46

Clinical Presentation

The patient is a 44-year-old male with chest pain in the CCU.

Description of Electrocardiogram (12 Leads)

There is no atrial activity, and there is ventricular pacing (rate, 77/min) with an LBBB pattern. There is ST elevation in leads 2, 3, and aVF, with reciprocal ST depression in leads 1 and aVL. This fits with an acute inferior MI, despite the fact that this is a ventricular-paced rhythm. As in LBBB, only an acute MI can be diagnosed with a ventricular pacemaker rhythm. Whenever one encounters an inferior MI, an RV infarction should be sought; this is demonstrated in this case by ST elevation in V_1, the lead that best reflects the RV when the standard left-sided precordial leads are used. Because the RCA occlusion in an RV infarction is most proximal in the artery and because the artery of the sinoatrial node is often a proximal branch of the RCA, it is easy to understand how this patient with an inferior/RV infarction would have sinus bradycardia or sinus arrest and need a pacemaker, because the junctional escape is not of sufficient rate.

Interpretation

RV pacemaker (rate, 77/min), with acute inferior wall and RV infarction; abnormal ECG

Learning Points

Diagnosing acute MI on a ventricular-paced ECG
RV infarction using V_1

Suggested Readings

Barold SS, Ong LS, Banner RL. Diagnosis of inferior wall myocardial infarction during right ventricular apical pacing. Chest 1976;69(2):232–5. The qR (small Q and large R) pattern in leads 2, 3, and aVF in a patient with an acute inferior-wall MI and a temporary pacemaker at the apex of the right ventricle is offered as specific for inferior-wall MI because it is never seen during uncomplicated pacing from anywhere within the RV cavity.

Barold SS, Wallace WA, Ong LS, Heinle RA. Primary ST and T wave abnormalities in the diagnosis of acute anterior myocardial infarction during permanent ventricular pacing. J Electrocardiol 1976;9(4):387–90. The authors admit that the diagnosis of MI in patients with ventricular pacemakers is often difficult. The diagnosis of acute anterior MI could be made with confidence, though, by observing the evolution of primary ST segment and T-wave abnormalities in the absence of specific QRS changes.

Chou TC, Van der Bel-kahn J, Allen J, et al. Electrocardiographic diagnosis of right ventricular infarction. Am J Med 1981;70(6):1175–80. The electrocardiographic findings in 11 cases of acute RV infarction associated with acute left ventricular inferior-wall MI are described. The diagnosis of RV infarction was proved by autopsy findings in 5 cases and supported by hemodynamic data in the other 6 cases. Transient ST segment elevation in V_1 or in other right precordial leads was present in 8 cases. Therefore, when acute inferior MI is accompanied by ST segment elevation in the right precordial leads, the coexistence of RV infarction should be suspected.

Kozlowski FH, Brady WJ, Aufderheide TP, Buckley RS. The electrocardiographic diagnosis of acute myocardial infarction in patients with ventricular paced rhythms. Acad Emerg Med 1998;5(1):52–7. The anticipated (or expected) morphology in patients with VPRs is one of QRS complex/ST segment-to-T-wave discordance. Several strategies are available to assist the physician in correctly interpreting the 12-lead ECGs of patients with permanent ventricular pacemakers. These include (1) a knowledge of the anticipated ST segment T-wave changes of VPRs and the consequent ability to recognize acute ischemic morphologies; (2) the performance of serial electrocardiography or ST segment trend monitoring, demonstrating dynamic changes encountered in acutely ischemic patients; (3) a comparison with previous ECGs; and (4) if appropriate, an analysis of the native underlying rhythm (as was done in Case 47).

Lopez-Sendon J, Coma-Canella I, Alcasena S, et al. Electrocardiographic findings in acute right ventricular infarction: sensitivity and specificity of electrocardiographic alterations in right precordial leads V4R, V3R, V1, V2, and V3. J Am Coll Cardiol 1985;6(6):1273–9. Among 43 patients with a diagnosis of acute RV MI studied with electrocardiography and by autopsy, ST segment elevation in leads V_1 to V_3 had a sensitivity of 79% for that diagnosis. The sensitivity of ST segment elevation in V_4R was 100%.

Madias JE. The nonspecificity of ST-segment elevation ≥ 5.0 mm in V1-V3 in the diagnosis of acute myocardial infarction in the presence of ventricular paced rhythm. J Electrocardiol 2004;37(2):135–9. The author points out that the criterion of ST segment elevation ≥ 5.0 mm in leads V_1 to V_3 for the diagnosis of acute MI lacks specificity because it is also encountered in patients who have pacemakers and QRS complexes with large amplitudes in these same leads but who do not have an acute MI. Remember that in 1976, Barold concentrated on the evolution of primary ST and T-wave changes in the absence of specific QRS changes. A series of ECGs is always helpful in the diagnosis of MI, but in the era of thrombolytic therapy and percutaneous catheter coronary intervention, one or two tracings are often all that time allows. Thus, the diagnosis must be made quickly by coupling the ECG(s), current and old if available, with the patient's symptoms.

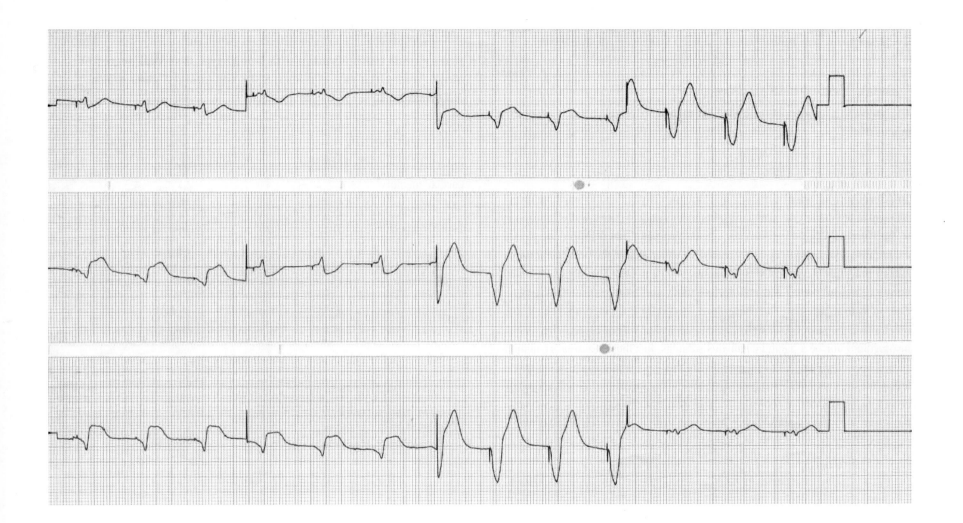

Case 47

Clinical Presentation

The patient is a 65-year-old male with a permanent pacemaker that is not programmable.

Description of Electrocardiogram (12 Leads)

To determine what was the underlying (intrinsic) rhythm and to study the morphology of the native QRS complexes, cutaneous pacing (chest-wall stimulation) was performed with a temporary pacemaker generator that delivered the electrical impulses via suction-cup leads placed on either side of the permanent pacemaker unit while the patient was positioned supine in bed. The rate of the temporary cutaneous pacing was 100/min, certainly above the permanent pacing rate, so as to suppress it. The energy level was set for the temporary pacing so that it would be sensed by the permanent pacemaker yet not capture the myocardium nor be a painful cutaneous stimulus. Just these features are demonstrated here. The change-of-leads spikes are those 9.5 mm upright spikes that follow the intrinsic QRS complexes 1, 3, and 5. The cutaneous stimuli are smaller and occur at a rate of 100/min. With the permanent pacemaker suppressed, the intrinsic rhythm is sinus rhythm at 88/min, with 2:1 AV block (Mobitz type I or, more likely, II) with RBBB and lateral T abnormality (which may be due to cardiac memory).

Interpretation

Sinus rhythm (rate, 88/min), with Mobitz type II second-degree AV block (ventricular rate, 44/min); RBBB and lateral T abnormality; abnormal ECG

Learning Points

Chest wall stimulation to inhibit a permanent pacemaker
Cardiac memory

Suggested Readings

Shvilkin A, Danilo P Jr, Wang J, et al. Evolution and resolution of long-term cardiac memory. Circulation 1998;97(18):1810–7. "Cardiac memory" refers to T-wave changes induced by ventricular pacing or arrhythmia that accumulate in magnitude and duration with repeated episodes of abnormal activation. In this dog study, the authors conclude that cardiac memory is a dynamic process for which the T vector is predicted by the paced QRS vector and that is associated with significant changes in epicardial and endocardial (but not midmyocardial) cell action potential duration, such that the transmural gradient of repolarization is altered. It is unaccompanied by evidence of altered hemodynamics or flow.

Staessen J, Ector H, De Geest H. The underlying heart rhythm in patients with an artificial cardiac pacemaker. Pacing Clin Electrophysiol 1982;5(6):801-7. Underlying heart rhythms were evaluated by electrocardiography in 142 patients with AV block and a permanent pacemaker during chest-wall stimulation, to determine if the patients were pacemaker dependent. Since the advent of rate-programmable pacemakers, this technique is seldom used today.

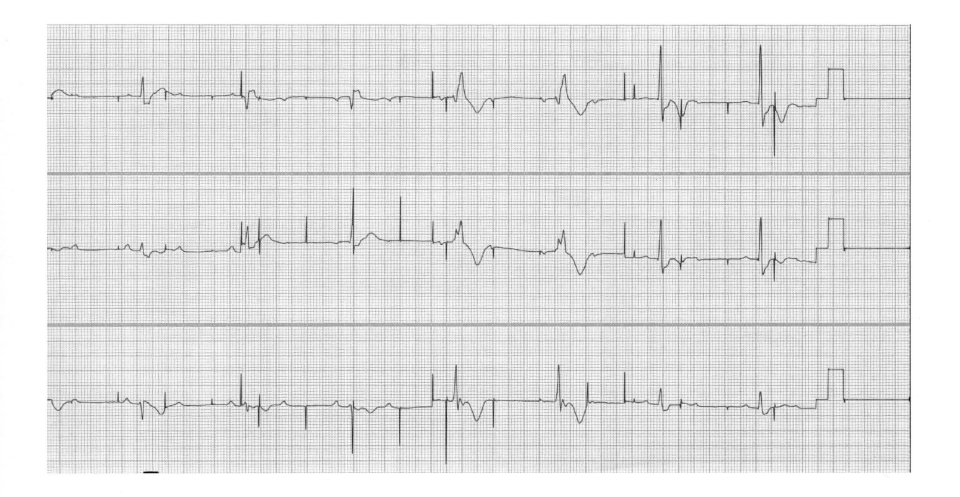

8

Acute Myocardial Infarction

Case 48

Clinical Presentation

This 56-year-old male is stoic and presents to the emergency department with stuttering chest pain. When he had waves of dizziness, he decided to seek attention.

Description of Electrocardiogram (12 Leads)

The HR is 53/min and regular. No P waves are visible, and the QRS complexes are narrow and equidistant from each other, indicating this to be junctional rhythm. That there is no sinus or other atrial rhythm and that the junctional rhythm is < 60/min indicates that this is junctional escape rhythm. There are Q waves in leads 3 and aVF, with ST elevation in leads 2, 3, and aVF. Reciprocal ST depression in leads 1 and aVL is pronounced. The QRS duration and corrected Q–T (Q–Tc) interval are normal. This is an acute inferior MI, and the next regions of myocardial injury to be ruled out are posterior and RV. An acute posterior MI has ST depression and upright T waves in leads V_1 and V_2. Over the ensuing days, the ST segments in leads V_1 and V_2 return to baseline and the R waves become taller than before the posterior MI. The T waves remain upright. By standard 12-lead electrocardiography, an acute RV MI has ST elevation in V_1 and V_2 without loss or augmentation of the R wave. Neither a posterior nor RV MI is present in this case.

Interpretation

Junctional escape rhythm (rate, 53/min); acute inferior MI, abnormal ECG

Learning points

Junctional escape rhythm
Acute inferior MI
Evolution of posterior MI
Diagnosis of acute RV MI from standard 12-lead ECG

Suggested Readings

Iseri LT, Humphrey SB, Siner EJ. Prehospital brady-asystolic cardiac arrest. Ann Intern Med;88(6):741–5. Among 13 coronary causes of death proved by autopsy, 10 (77%) were due to fresh thrombus, and 7 (54%) were due to an occluded proximal right coronary artery, suggesting a causal relationship to this type of arrest.

Randall WC, Wehrmacher WH, Jones SB. Hierarchy of supraventricular pacemakers. J Thorac Cardiovasc Surg 1981;82(5):797–800. Definitive subsidiary atrial pacemakers exist within the crista terminalis and in the atrial free wall at the junction of the inferior vena cava and the inferior right atrium. These pacemakers are capable of maintaining cardiac rhythm at a rate intermediate between that of the sinoatrial node and atrioventricular junctional pacemakers upon default of the normal sinoatrial nodal cells. Perhaps these too are injured with an inferior MI caused by a proximal RCA thrombosis.

Schuger CD, Tzivoni D, Gottlieb S, et al. Sinus node and atrioventricular nodal function in 220 patients recovering from acute myocardial infarction. Cardiology 1988;75(4):274–82. Sinus node recovery time and total recovery time were significantly longer in patients with an inferior or non-Q-wave infarct than in patients with an anterior infarct.

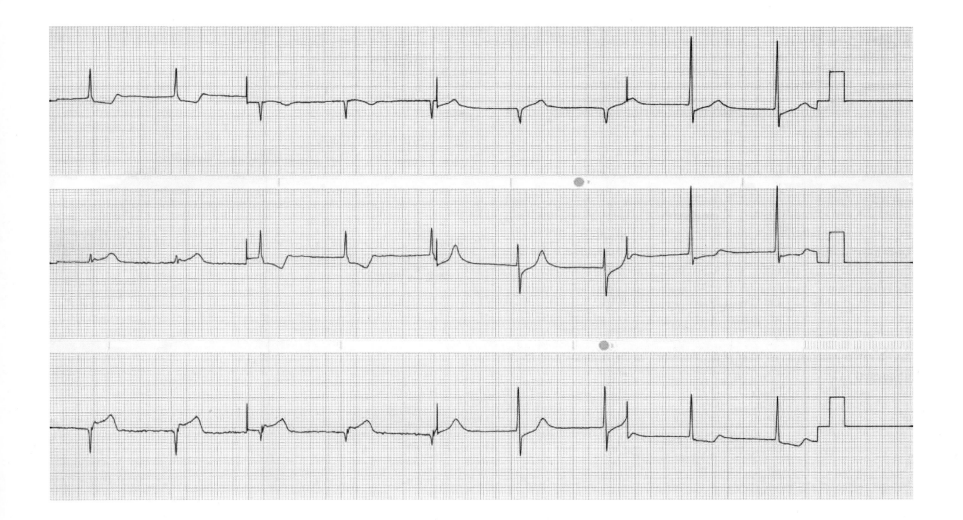

Case 49

Clinical Presentation

The patient is a 56-year-old male who developed chest pain while undergoing a right coronary angioplasty.

Description Of Electrocardiogram (12 Leads)

The rhythm is accelerated junctional at 74/min. There is ST elevation in leads 2, 3, and aVF, and in leads V_1 and V_2. There is reciprocal ST depression in leads 1, aVL, and V_6. This is the pattern of an acute inferior and RV MI. The QRS axis and Q–Tc interval are normal. After balloon dilatation of a proximal RCA lesion, a large coronary artery dissection was noted. An RV branch was lost because of the dissection. Despite stenting of the RCA, the patient sustained an MI.

Interpretation

Accelerated junctional rhythm (rate, 74/min); acute inferior and RV MI; abnormal ECG

Learning points

Accelerated junctional rhythm
Acute inferior and RV MI
Proximal RCA stenting

Suggested Readings

Ando' G, Gaspardone A, Proietti I. Acute thrombosis of the sinus node artery: arrhythmical implications. Heart 2003;89(2):E5. During RCA angioplasty with stent placement, intermittent occlusion of the sinus nodal artery led to sinus arrest and junctional escape rhythm. The authors conclude that sinus node dysfunction may be an unrecognized marker of coronary artery disease (as seen in Cases 48 and 49).

Mikdadi G, Wadgaonkar SU, Dhurandhar RW, Quintal RE. Right ventricular infarction complicating right coronary angioplasty. Catheter Cardiovasc Interv 1999;47(3):327–30. In a case very similar to Case 49, an RV infarction was demonstrated electrocardiographically.

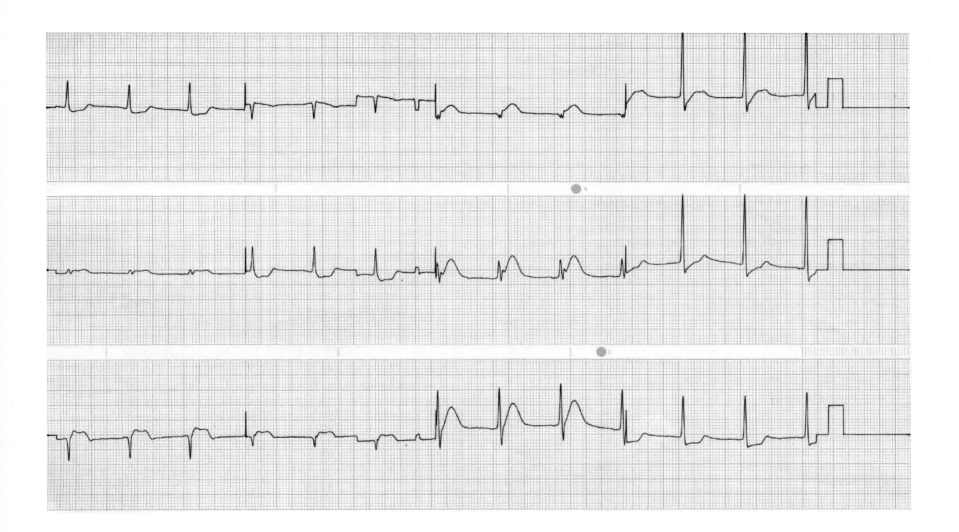

Case 49a

Clinical Presentation

The patient is the same 56-year-old male (Case 49) with the inferior and RV MI. He is still having chest pain.

Description of Electrocardiogram (12 Leads)

The right precordial leads were taken 77 minutes after the previous tracing.

The limb leads are normally placed and continue to show the signs of an acute inferior MI, but the precordial leads are right-sided, that is to say, V_1-R is where V_2-L is placed, and V_2-R is where V_1-L is placed. Leads V_3-R, V_4-R, V_5-R, and V_6-R are placed across the right side of the chest in a mirror image of the standard left-sided precordial leads that have the same number. Notice that the ST elevation in leads V_1-R and V_2-R has resolved, but in V_4-R and V_5-R, there are Q waves and ST elevation. It is ST elevation in lead V_4-R that is the most sensitive for RV infarction. Patients with an RV infarction have jugular venous distention, a palpable RV heave, and intolerance to intravenous nitroglycerin. Hypotension responds to intravenous saline infusion.

Interpretation

Right-sided precordial leads: accelerated junctional rhythm (rate, 79/min) with acute inferior and RV infarction; abnormal ECG

Learning points

RV infarction
Right-sided precordial leads
Clinical signs of RV infarction

Suggested Readings

Braat SH, Brugada P, de Zwaan C, et al. Value of electrocardiogram in diagnosing right ventricular involvement in patients with an acute inferior wall myocardial infarction. Br Heart J 1983;49(4):368–72. When electrocardiograms are recorded in patients with an acute inferior-wall infarction within 10 hours after the onset of chest pain, additional RV infarction can easily be diagnosed by recording lead V_4R. ST elevation of ≥ 1.0 mm in leads V_3R, V_4R, V_5R, and V_6R is a reliable sign of RV involvement (as it is in Case 49a).

Fijewski TR, Pollack MI, Chan TC, Brady WJ. Electrocardiographic manifestations: right ventricular infarction. J Emerg Med 2002;22(2):189-94. Diagnosis of RV infarction in the presence of acute inferior-wall MI is made by using right-sided chest leads with high sensitivities and specificities. The proper recognition of RV infarction can allow rapid implementation of treatment that often involves a temporary pacemaker, an intraaortic balloon pump, and percutaneous coronary intervention.

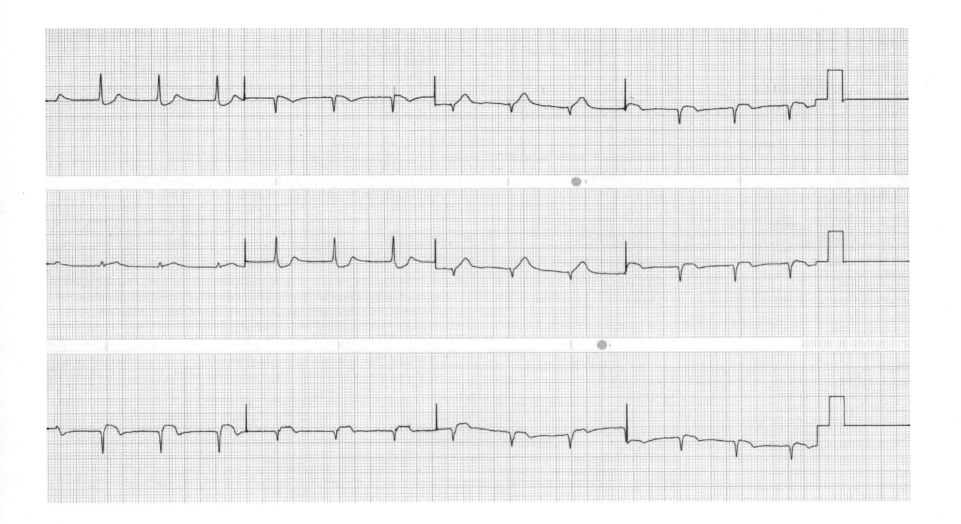

Case 50

Clinical Presentation

The patient is a 49-year-old male with an acute inferior/RV infarction. This is the first of three ECGs.

Description of Electrocardiogram (12 Leads)

Standard limb leads and right-sided chest leads were used

There is sinus rhythm (rate, 93/min). The P–R interval is normal, but there is QRS prolongation owing to RBBB. The Q–Tc is slightly prolonged at 473 msec, but this is within normal range (up to 479 msec for this RBBB). There is ST elevation in leads 2, 3, and aVF and reciprocal ST depression in leads 1 and aVL. In leads V_2R through V_6R (but especially V_4R), there is ≥ 1.0 mm ST elevation.

Interpretation

Right-sided chest leads: NSR (rate, 93/min), RBBB, acute inferior/RV infarction; abnormal ECG

Learning Points

Right-sided chest leads
RV infarction
RBBB
Q–Tc with RBBB

Suggested Readings

Das G. QT interval and repolarization time in patients with intraventricular conduction delay. J Electrocardiol 1990;23(1):49–52. In this study of 72 subjects with various types of IVCD, the Q–Tc interval was 470 ± 9.1 msec in patients with RBBB (as in Case 50) and 489 ± 6.9 msec in those with LBBB. The prolongation of the Q–Tc interval in each category of IVCD subjects was entirely secondary to a prolonged depolarization time. A control group of 33 healthy individuals with no IVCD was used for comparison.

Rautaharju PM, Zhang ZM, Prineas R, Heiss G. Assessment of prolonged QT and JT intervals in ventricular conduction defects. Am J Cardiol 2004;93(8):1017–21. The JT interval, or Bazett's Q–Tc-QRS, has been advocated for the detection of prolonged repolarization in VCDs, but it has not been validated. The authors developed formulas for males and for females in order to detect prolonged repolarizations in VCDs by using the JT interval or a bivariate model for QT with R–R and QRS intervals as covariates. They studied 11,739 adult males and females with normal ventricular conduction and 1,251 subjects with major VCDs.

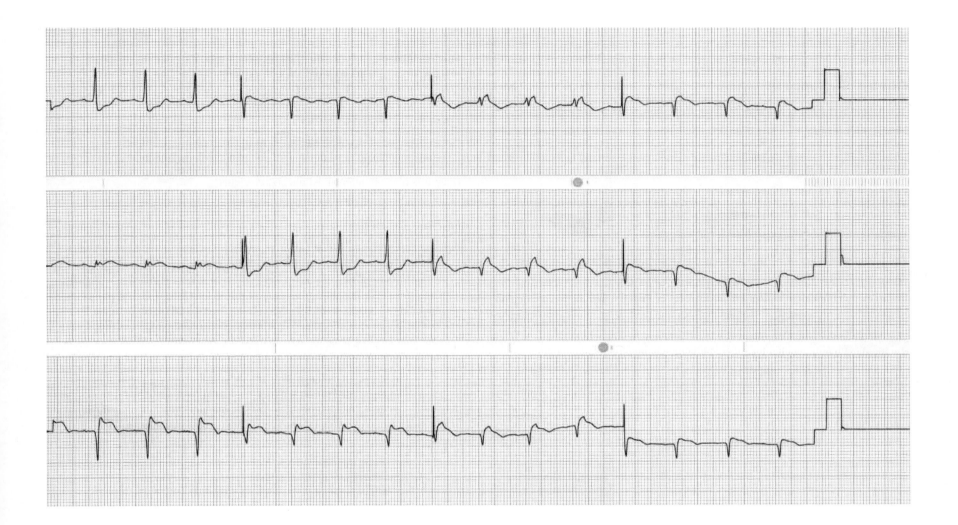

Case 50a

Clinical Presentation

The patient is a 49-year-old male with an acute inferior/RV infarction (Case 50). Shortly after his first ECG was recorded, he developed marked sinus bradycardia and hypotension that was refractory to intravenous atropine and saline. A temporary pacemaker was inserted.

Description of Electrocardiogram (12 Leads)

Standard limb leads and precordial leads were used.

The pacemaker is set at 77/min and has the LBBB pattern of an RV pacemaker. There is a P wave visible following the third paced beat. It is not conducted; thus, there is sinus node dysfunction and some form of AV node dysfunction as a result of this inferior/RV infarction. Despite the pacemaker rhythm, there is ST elevation in leads 2, 3, and aVF, with reciprocal ST depression in leads 1 and aVL. Using the standard left precordial leads, the RV infarction cannot be diagnosed although there might be mild ST elevation in V_1.

Interpretation

Marked sinus bradycardia with AV block and RV pacemaker (rate, 77/min); acute inferior MI; abnormal ECG

Learning Points

Sinus node and AV node dysfunction with inferior infarction
Postinfarction IVCD
Diagnosis of acute inferior MI during ventricular pacing

Suggested Readings

Pagnoni F, Finzi A, Valentini R, et al. Long-term prognostic significance and electrophysiological evolution of intraventricular conduction disturbances complicating acute myocardial infarction. Pacing Clin Electrophysiol 1986;9(1 Pt 1):91–100. After studying 59 patients with postinfarctional isolated IVCDs who survived the acute stage of MI for a mean of 11.4 months and comparing them to a control group of survivors of MI with normal QRS duration, the authors conclude that prolongation of H–V intervals in patients with an isolated IVCD is correlated with a worse prognosis. They conjecture that this reflects the wider anatomic damage in comparison to patients with normal H–V intervals.

Sinker D, Parameswaran R, Goldberg H. Sinus and A-V nodal dysfunction following myocardial infarction. J Electrocardiol 1975;8(3):281–3. Transient or permanent sinus bradycardia and/or AV block with syncope following MI suggest that the dysfunction may be due to ischemic damage. Symptoms disappear following the insertion of a permanent demand pacemaker.

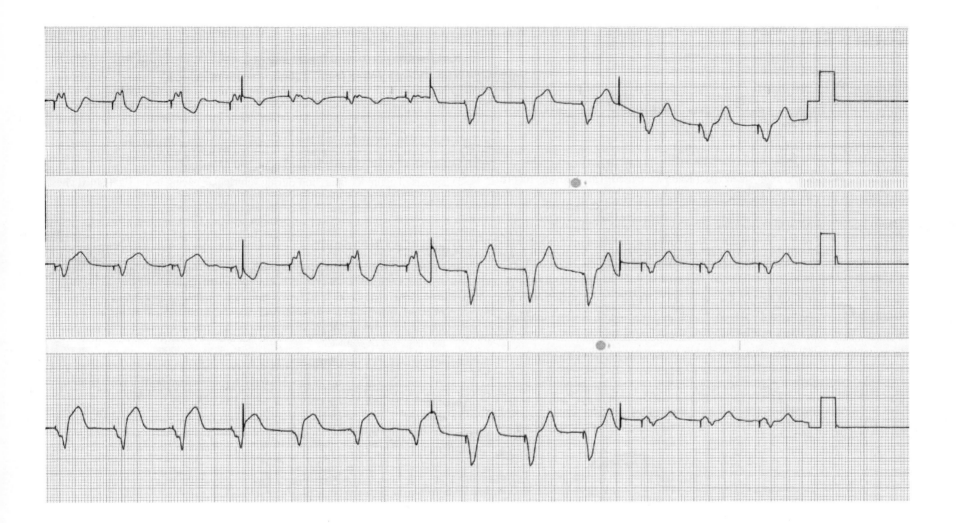

Case 50b

Clinical Presentation

The patient is a 49-year-old male with an acute inferior/RV infarction (Case 50).

Description of Electrocardiogram (12 Leads)

Standard limb leads and right-sided chest leads were used. This ECG was recorded 3 minutes after the ECG described in Case 50a.

It takes just about 3 minutes to switch the precordial leads from the left side to the right side. The only P wave again is seen following the third paced QRS complex. There are the same ST elevation and reciprocal ST changes of inferior MI seen in the previous tracing, but the ST elevation in V_3R through V_6R allows the diagnosis of RV infarction despite the paced QRS complexes. Therefore, with a ventricular pacemaker and the standard limb lead placement, one can diagnose an acute inferior MI. With special right-sided precordial lead placement, one can diagnose an acute RV infarction, even with a ventricular pacemaker rhythm.

Interpretation

Right-sided precordial leads: marked sinus bradycardia with AV block with RV pacemaker (rate, 77/min); acute inferior/RV infarction; abnormal ECG

Learning Points

Diagnosis of acute inferior MI during ventricular pacing
Diagnosis of acute RV infarction during ventricular pacing using right-sided chest leads

Suggested Readings

Kochiadakis GE, Kaleboubas MD, Igoumenidis NE, et al. Electrocardiographic diagnosis of acute myocardial infarction in the presence of ventricular paced rhythm. Pacing Clin Electrophysiol 2001;24(8 Pt 1):1289–90. ST segment deviation was recently described as the only electrocardiographic finding that was useful in the diagnosis of acute MI during RV pacing. This report shows that the same sign may also indicate the amount of myocardium in jeopardy and the coronary artery responsible.

Sgarbossa EB, Pinski SL, Gates KB, Wagner GS. Early electrocardiographic diagnosis of acute myocardial infarction in the presence of ventricular paced rhythm. GUSTO-I investigators. Am J Cardiol 1996;77(5):423–4. A substudy of a large multicenter trial.

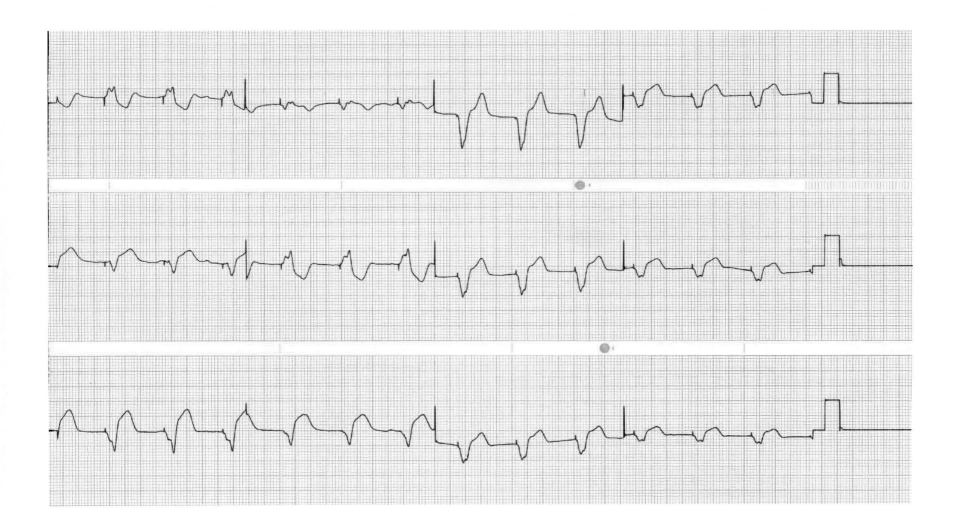

Case 51

Clinical Presentation

The patient is a 51-year-old female with acute chest pain.

Description of Electrocardiogram (12 Leads)

The rhythm is sinus, and the rate is 92/min. The P-wave morphology is normal, but the P–R interval is prolonged at 216 msec. There are Q waves and ST elevation in leads 2, 3, and aVF, with reciprocal ST depression in leads 1 and aVL. There are no signs of ST segment shifts in leads V_1 and V_2. Therefore, posterior or RV infarction do not pertain. There is T-wave flattening in leads V_5 and V_6. The QRS duration and Q–Tc are normal. Using newly developed criteria referenced below, the culprit artery (RCA vs LCx) and (if RCA is the culprit) whether it is a proximal or distal occlusion can be accurately predicted.

Interpretation

NSR (rate, 92/min) with first-degree AV block, acute inferior MI, lateral T-wave flattening; abnormal ECG

Learning Points

New criteria for predicting proximal versus distal RCA occlusion
Predicting the culprit artery for acute inferior-wall MI

Suggested Readings

Fiol M, Carrillo A, Cygankiewicz I, et al. New criteria based on ST changes in 12-lead surface ECG to detect proximal versus distal right coronary artery occlusion in case of acute inferoposterior myocardial infarction. Ann Noninvasive Electrocardiol 2004;9(4):383–8. In patients with an inferoposterior MI, the clinical outcome depends mainly on whether the occlusion of the RCA is proximal or distal. The authors used new electrocardiographic criteria—the sum of ST depression in leads 1 and aVL, and ST changes in V_1—to predict the location of RCA occlusion in 50 patients with acute inferoposterior MI. Previously established criteria use only the ST changes in lead aVL.

Isoelectric or elevated ST in V_1 allowed prediction of proximal RCA occlusion with 70% sensitivity and 87% specificity. The new criterion of the sum of ST depression in leads 1 and aVL ≥ 5.5 mm, when compared to the criterion based only on ST depression in aVL, also was more specific (91% vs 72%) for proximal RCA occlusion. (These new criteria accurately predicted that the RCA occlusion was proximal in Case 51.)

Fiol M, Cygankiewicz I, Carrillo A, et al. Value of electrocardiographic algorithm based on "ups and downs" of ST in assessment of a culprit artery in evolving inferior wall acute myocardial infarction. Am J Cardiol 2004;94(6):709–14. Acute MI of the inferoposterior wall is due to occlusion of the RCA or LCx. The outcome depends on the culprit artery and thus has clinical importance. The authors analyzed the electrocardiographic and angiographic findings of 63 consecutive patients with an acute MI with ST elevation in inferior leads (2, 3, and aVF) and with a single-vessel occlusion. The following electrocardiographic criteria were included in a three-step algorithm: (1) ST changes in lead 1, (2) the ratio of ST elevation in lead 3 to that in lead 2, and (3) the ratio of the sum of ST depression in precordial leads (V_1–V_3) to the sum of ST elevation in inferior leads (2, 3, and aVF). Application of this algorithm suggested the location of the culprit artery (RCA vs LCx) in 60 of 63 patients (> 95%) and failed only in the 3 patients with a very dominant LCx that presented with ST depression of ≥ 0.5 mm in lead 1.

In Case 51, the occlusion in the RCA was accurately predicted by this algorithm because the ST depression in lead 1 is > 0.5 mm, the ST elevation in lead 3 exceeds that in lead 2, and the sum of ST depression in leads V_1 to V_3 is less than the sum of ST elevation in leads 2, 3, and aVF. In this reference, Figure 2 on page 711 displays this algorithm.

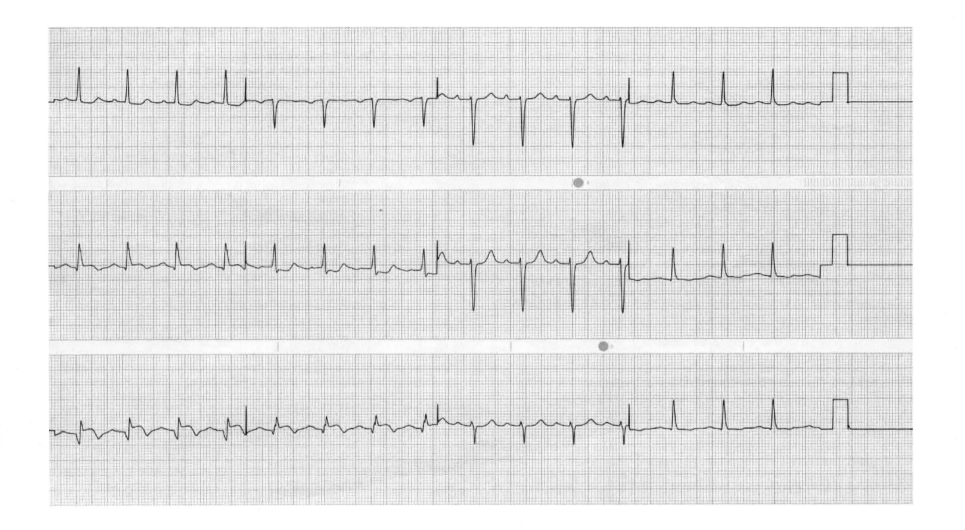

Case 52

Clinical Presentation

The patient is a 77-year-old male who is comfortable in the CCU and has minimal cardiac enzyme elevation, but 1 day earlier, he had oppressive chest discomfort that prompted his admission to the hospital.

Description of Electrocardiogram (12 Leads)

The rhythm is sinus at 56/min. The P waves are normal, and the P–R interval is normal. The QRS axis is normal at about 0°, and the QRS duration is normal. The anterolateral T waves are deeply inverted, and the Q–Tc interval is prolonged at 535 msec. There are no ST segment changes. These are the findings of severe subepicardial anterior-wall ischemia or injury. The patient was treated with aspirin and low-molecular-weight heparin, a β-blocker, and topical nitroglycerin. Plans were made for cardiac catheterization on the next day.

Interpretation

Sinus bradycardia (rate, 56/min), with deep anterolateral T-wave inversion and prolongation of the Q–T interval consistent with severe anterior-wall subepicardial ischemia or injury; abnormal ECG

Learning points

Prolongation of Q–T interval owing to ischemia
Subendocardial ischemia/injury (discussed in Cases 33 and 34)
Subepicardial or transmural ischemia

Transmural ischemia is present when ischemia extends subepicardially. The recovery of subepicardial cells is more visible than the recovery of subendocardial cells and is manifested as inversion of T waves overlying the ischemic region. This T-wave inversion is due to repolarization occurring from endocardium to epicardium during subepicardial ischemia (reversed direction of repolarization; thus, reversed direction of the T wave).

Suggested Readings

Dekker JM, Crow RS, Hannan PJ, et al. Heart rate-corrected QT interval prolongation predicts risk of coronary heart disease in black and white middle-aged men and women: the ARIC study. J Am Coll Cardiol 2004;43(4):565–71. In a study of 14,548 black and white men and women, aged 45 to 64 years, Q–Tc was measured at baseline, and the incidence of mortality from CHD and CVD was observed. Long Q–Tc is associated with increased risk of CHD and CVD mortality in black and white healthy men and women.

Hirota Y, Kita Y, Tsuji R, et al. Prominent negative T waves with QT prolongation indicate reperfusion injury and myocardial stunning. J Cardiol 1992;22(2-3):325–40. To observe the clinical course after reperfusion and recovery from myocardial stunning of the left ventricular anterior wall, the authors prospectively reviewed and analyzed cardiac enzymes, electrocardiographic changes, echocardiograms, and cineangiograms of eight patients with the acute ischemic syndrome who fulfilled the following criteria: (1) no history of previous MI, (2) repeated and/or prolonged episodes of chest pain, (3) critical stenosis of the left anterior descending artery with wall motion abnormalities, (4) successful emergency percutaneous transluminal coronary angioplasty, and (5) normal wall motion on repeat cineangiography 4 to 8 weeks later. Creatine kinase (CK), its cardiac isoenzyme (CK-MB), or both CK and CK-MB were minimally elevated in all cases. LV ejection fraction increased from 51 to 71%, and serial echocardiography showed normalization of wall motion within 4 to 28 days. T-wave inversion in the left precordial leads developed 30 minutes to 5 hours after the cessation of chest pain or successful reperfusion, and prominent negative T waves with Q–T prolongation in V_3 or V_4 reached their peak values within 1 to 5 days. Electrocardiographic abnormalities resolved after 21 to 95 days. The authors theorize that these electrocardiographic findings may indicate reperfusion injury and the presence of myocardial stunning in the anterior wall of the left ventricle.

Robbins J, Nelson JC, Rautaharju PM, Gottdiener JS. The association between the length of the QT interval and mortality in the Cardiovascular Health Study. Am J Med 2003;115(9):732–4. In a study of 5,888 community-based men and women of at least 65 years of age, a Q–Tc > 450 msec was of value in identifying all-cause and coronary heart disease mortality. A Q–Tc interval of > 450 msec should prompt clinical evaluation and possible interventions to reduce the risk of coronary events.

Rukshin V, Monakier D, Olshtain-Pops K, et al. QT interval in patients with unstable angina and non-Q wave myocardial infarction. Ann Noninvasive Electrocardiol 2002 7(4):343–8. The authors compared maximal Q–Tc interval in 52 patients hospitalized with NQMI with that in 52 patients hospitalized for UAP. Maximal Q–Tc in patients with NQMI was significantly longer than that in patients with UAP (475 vs 439 msec). Q–Tc of > 460 msec was present in 48% of patients with NQMI and in 19% of patients with UAP. Maximal Q–T prolongation was observed within 36 hours of admission, and return to normal was within 96 hours. Q–T prolongation was not associated with increased frequency of arrhythmia. The cause of Q–T prolongation in NQMI may be related to the damage to the subendocardial layer exposing the M-cell layer, which markedly prolongs action potential duration. Thus, transient Q–T prolongation is observed in about half of patients with NQMI, and this finding may help differentiate NQMI from UAP.

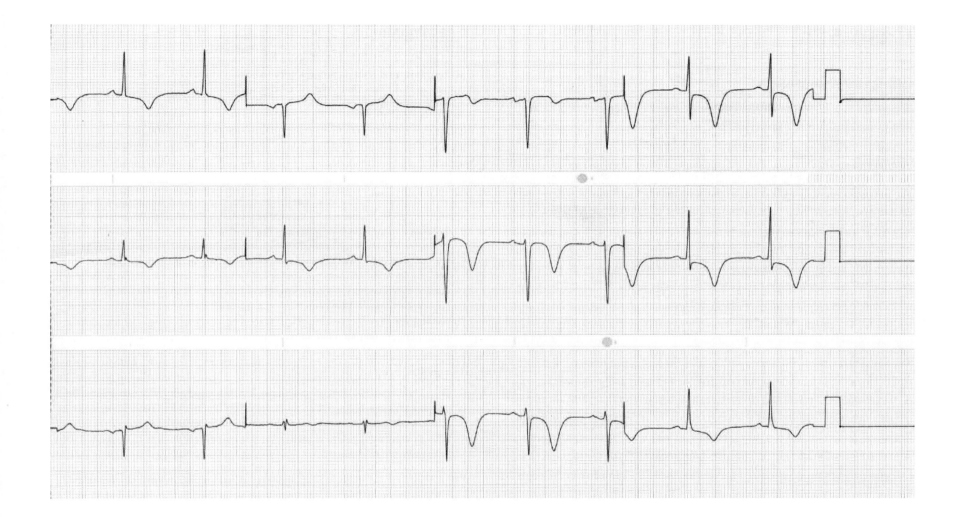

Case 52a

Clinical Presentation

The patient is a 77-year-old male with severe anterior subepicardial ischemia who is awaiting cardiac catheterization.

Description of Electrocardiogram (12 Leads)

The ECG was recorded 13 hours after the previous tracing (Case 52). Here, the rhythm is sinus at 67/min, and the P–R interval is slightly prolonged at 204 msec. Now the P wave morphology is that of LAE, most likely due to stretch of the left atrium owing to high LVEDP. The QRS duration is normal, but there is ST elevation in leads 1, aVL, and V_1 to V_6, meeting the diagnostic criteria for an acute extensive anterior MI, now a transmural MI with subepicardial injury. Because the patient was about to get onto the catheterization table when he developed the chest pain and acute ST segment elevation, this was truly acute! After the occluding thrombus was opened and circulation was reestablished, a 90% lumen-compromising lesion was found in a large LAD coronary artery after the first septal branch but before the first diagonal branch. Today, with coronary arteriography and percutaneous coronary intervention, a prediction of coronary lesion from an ECG can be verified instantly. When the occlusion is in the LAD coronary artery and is proximal to the first septal perforator, the R wave is often lost in lead V_1. Assessment of inferior ST segment depression and lateral ST elevation may shed light on the location of the LAD coronary artery occlusion and the distribution of the myocardium in jeopardy. The LAD coronary artery was dilated and stented, and the patient's ECGs slowly normalized over a few months.

Interpretation

NSR (rate, 67/min), with LAE and first-degree AV block; acute extensive anterior MI; abnormal ECG

Learning points

LAE due to acute rise in LVEDP from MI

Acute transmural subepicardial injury

Subepicardial or transmural injury is manifested by ST segment elevation.

Extensive anterior MI

LAD coronary artery occlusion proximal to first septal perforator

Evolution of anterior T-wave inversion after transmural MI

Suggested Readings

Appleton CP, Galloway JM, Gonzalez MS, et al. Estimation of left ventricular filling pressures using two-dimensional and Doppler echocardiography in adult patients with cardiac disease. Additional value of analyzing left atrial size, left atrial ejection fraction and the difference in duration of pulmonary venous and mitral flow velocity at atrial contraction. J Am Coll Cardiol 1993;22(7):1972–82. Left atrial size, left atrial ejection fraction, and the difference between mitral and pulmonary venous flow duration at atrial contraction are independent determinants of LV filling pressures in patients with coronary artery disease. What seems to be a corollary of this study is the finding (in Case 52a) of acute LAE criteria by electrocardiography in a patient with an abrupt expression of acute elevation in LVEDP owing to a large MI.

Fletcher WO, Gibbons RJ, Clements IP. The relationship of inferior ST depression, lateral ST elevation, and left precordial ST elevation to myocardium at risk in acute anterior myocardial infarction. Am Heart J 1993;126(3 Pt 1):526–35. Using technetium 99m tomographic imaging to measure the amount and location of myocardium at risk, the authors concluded that inferior ST depression in patients with transmural anterior ischemia is a reciprocal finding and does not represent inferior ischemia and that the presence of inferior ST depression or lateral ST elevation is associated with a more lateral perfusion defect.

Hamby RI, Zeldis SM, Hoffman I, Sarli P. Left atrial size and left ventricular function in coronary artery disease: an echocardiographic-angiographic correlative study. Cathet Cardiovasc Diagn 1982;8(2):173–83. Although this was not primarily an electrocardiographic study, it found a specificity of 83% for LAE in identifying an abnormal LV ejection fraction in patients with coronary artery disease (something that suddenly occurred in Case 52a).

Kosuge M, Kimura K, Ishikawa T, et al. Electrocardiographic criteria for predicting total occlusion of the proximal left anterior descending coronary artery in anterior wall acute myocardial infarction. Clin Cardiol 2001;24(1):33–8. Patients with occlusion of the LAD coronary artery proximal to both the first septal branch and the first diagonal branch may benefit most from early reperfusion therapy, owing to the extensive area at risk. The aim of this study was to examine whether 12-lead ECGs recorded in the acute phase of acute MI could identify total occlusion of the LAD coronary artery proximal to both the

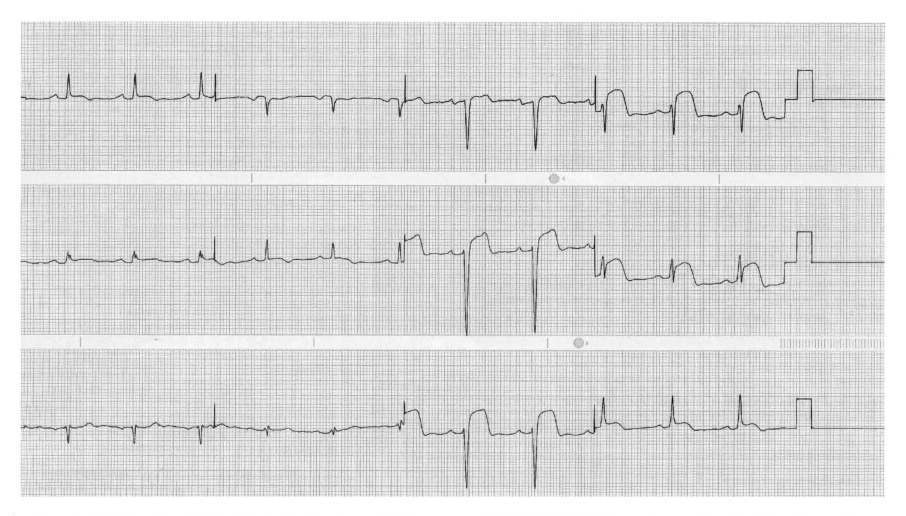

first septal and the first diagonal branch. One hundred twenty-eight patients with acute anterior MI were studied by electrocardiography and coronary arteriography within 12 hours of the onset of symptoms. The authors concluded that a greater degree of ST segment depression in lead 3 than the degree of ST segment elevation in lead aVL is a useful predictor of proximal LAD coronary artery occlusion in patients with anterior MI. Using these criteria in Case 52a (because of the lack of ST depression in lead 3), a mid-LAD coronary artery lesion was accurately predicted.

Shalev Y, Fogelman R, Oettinger M, Caspi A. Does the electrocardiographic pattern of "anteroseptal" myocardial infarction correlate with the anatomic location of myocardial injury? Am J Cardiol 1995;75(12):763–6. The current electrocardiographic definition of anteroseptal acute MI is a Q wave or QS wave of > 0.03 seconds in leads V_1 to V_3, with or without involvement of lead V_4. To verify this, the authors compared ECGs, echocardiograms, and cardiac catheterization in 80 patients with electrocardiographic findings for acute anteroseptal MI. They found that 48 of 52 patients who presented with ST elevation in V1 to V_3 had an anteroapical MI and a normal septum. In 85% of patients, the culprit narrowing was found to be in the mid- to distal LAD coronary artery. The authors concluded that the electrocardiographic pattern traditionally termed "anteroseptal MI" should be defined as extensive anterior-wall MI, associated with diffuse ST changes involving the anterior, lateral, and (occasionally) inferior leads.

Case 53

Clinical Presentation

The patient is a 57-year-old male with an irregular rhythm and a long history of coronary artery disease. He is not experiencing chest pain.

Description of Electrocardiogram (12 Leads)

The rhythm is sinus, and the P–R interval is 172 msec and constant, but the P–P interval is successively closer in a series and then is followed by a pause. After a group of beats, the pattern is repeated. This is Wenckebach sinoatrial block, and the mean HR is 90/min. There is low QRS voltage, yet an old inferior MI can be diagnosed. There is RBBB. The initial R wave of the RBBB is lost to a Q wave in leads V_1 to V_5 owing to an anteroseptal MI. Notice that the Q in leads 1 and aVL are also lost in an ASMI, as is seen in LBBB, but the QRS duration here is not wide, and it is the infarction of the proximal ventricular septum that changes the direction of septal depolarization. Temporally, this is not an acute ASMI; therefore, the ST elevation in leads V_2 to V_6 is due to an LV aneurysm.

Interpretation

Sinus rhythm with Wenckebach sinoatrial block,(mean rate, 90/min); low QRS voltage, RBBB, old inferior MI, ASMI with aneurysm; abnormal ECG

Learning points

Sinoatrial Wenckebach block

Loss of septal Q waves in ASMI

RBBB

Electrocardiographic diagnosis of LV aneurysm

Suggested Readings

Bogaty P, Boyer L, Rousseau L, Arsenault M. Is anteroseptal myocardial infarction an appropriate term? Am J Med 2002;113(1):37–41. ASMI is defined by the presence of electrocardiographic Q waves limited to precordial leads V_1 to V_2, V_3, or V_4 and (as in Case 53) lead V_5. To determine the appropriateness of the term "anteroseptal myocardial infarction," the authors sought to correlate electrocardiographic, echocardiographic, and angiographic findings in 50 consecutive patients admitted for a first acute MI with coronary arteriography during hospitalization. Their findings suggest that "anteroseptal MI" is a misnomer and that the "lead V_1 to leads V_2 to V_4," Q-wave pattern should be considered to indicate a predominantly apical and generally limited MI.

Engel J, Brady WJ, Mattu A, Perron AD. Electrocardiographic ST segment elevation: left ventricular aneurysm. Am J Emerg Med 2002;20(3):238–42. LVA is manifested electrocardiographically by varying degrees of ST segment elevation, which may be difficult to distinguish from ST segment changes caused by acute MI. In LVA, the ST segment elevation is generally associated with well-developed and completed Q waves in the anterior precordial leads, and there will not be reciprocal ST depression in the contralateral leads. This article focuses on the electrocardiographic findings of LVA and hints for distinguishing LVA from other ST segment elevation syndromes.

Madias JE, Ashtiani R, Agarwal H, et al. Diagnosis of ventricular aneurysm and other severe segmental left ventricular dysfunction consequent to a myocardial infarction in the presence of right bundle branch block: ECG correlates of a positive diagnosis made via echocardiography and/or contrast ventriculography. Ann Noninvasive Electrocardiol 2005;10(1):53–9. Generally, RBBB is associated with ST segment depression in leads V_1 to V_3. The authors hypothesized that stable ST segment elevation in leads V_1 to V_3 in patients with RBBB could be diagnostic of a VA and other severe segmental LV dysfunction. According to a sample of 4,197 files in a cardiology clinic, RBBB was detected in 175 patients. Of these, 28 patients had an old MI and had a VA diagnosed by ST segment elevation in one or more of leads V_1 to V_3. Of these 28 patients, 21 met this ST elevation criterion and 7 did not. The sensitivity for VA in this small group was 75%, and the specificity was 100%. The location of the VA was septal or anterior in those with ST elevation in V_1 to V_3. The authors concluded that a VA can be diagnosed in the presence of RBBB by the concordance of ST changes in V_1 to V_3 and that it correlates with involvement of the septal or anterior myocardial regions. They also concluded that these ST changes represent a superimposition of primary repolarization alterations of VA overcoming the secondary repolarization changes of RBBB.

Selvanayagam JB, Kardos A, Nicolson D, et al. Anteroseptal or apical myocardial infarction: a controversy addressed using delayed enhancement cardiovascular magnetic resonance imaging. J Cardiovasc Magn Reson 2004;6(3):653–61. Delayed-enhancement MRI of the heart has been shown to reliably identify areas of irreversible myocardial damage. The authors sought to determine if the term "anteroseptal MI" is appropriate by correlating electrocardiographic, angiographic, cine-MRI, and delayed-enhancement MRI findings. In all, 19 patients with their first acute anterior MI whose ECGs showed new Q waves in leads V_1 to V_4 were studied. The authors concluded that high-resolution cardiac MRI in patients with acute infarction and new Q waves in leads V_1 to V_4 demonstrates the presence of predominantly apical infarction but not isolated septal or anteroseptal infarction. Perhaps the electrical conduction abnormality of ASMI that is demonstrated by electrocardiography is not a good depiction of the true distribution of LV irreversible damage or scarring.

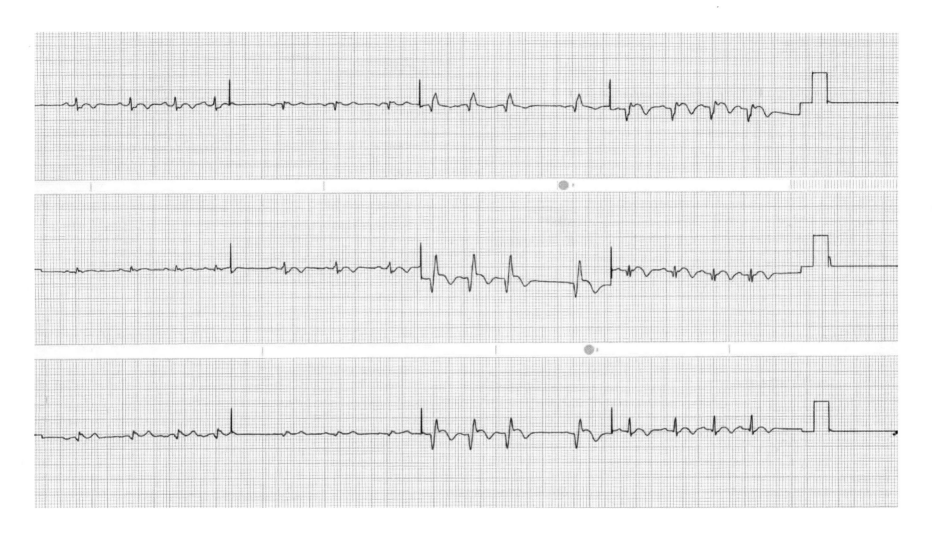

Yotsukura M, Toyofuku M, Tajino K, et al. Clinical significance of the disappearance of septal Q waves after the onset of myocardial infarction: correlation with location of responsible coronary lesions. J Electrocardiol 1999;32(1):15–20. The authors investigated the relationship between the disappearance of septal Q waves after MI and the location of the culprit lesion. In this study, 82 patients who were studied following their first ASMI had had electrocardiography performed before the MI. Septal Q waves were detectable before MI in 56 patients and disappeared after MI in 17 of those patients. The culprit lesion was located proximal to the origin of the first septal branch in 13 patients (76%). Disappearance of septal Q waves after MI predicted that the culprit lesion was proximal to the origin of the first septal branch (42% sensitivity, 84% specificity, 76% predictive value, and 61% accuracy). The authors suggest that the disappearance of septal Q waves that were detected before MI locates the LAD coronary artery lesion proximal to the origin of the first septal branch in 76% of patients and can be a clinically useful finding.

Case 53a

Description of Three-Lead Rhythm Strip

With longer strips in these three leads, the grouped pattern is more easily seen. There is a steady decrease in the P–P interval, followed by a pause that is shorter than twice the value of the preceding cycle, then a cycle longer than the one preceding the pause.

Interpretation of Rhythm Strip

Sinus rhythm with Mobitz type I, (Wenckebach) sinoatrial block; mean rate, 90/min; abnormal rhythm

Learning Point

Sinoatrial Wenckebach block

Suggested Readings

Le Heuzey JY, Caron J, Guize L, et al. Wenckebach periodicity in sinoatrial block: experimental and clinical evidence. Pacing Clin Electrophysiol 1991;14(6):1032–9. The authors observed sinoatrial WPs in a 72-year-old patient via direct recording of the sinus node electrical activity. In this patient, transient acceleration of the sinus rate seemed to be involved in the genesis of sinoatrial WP that was similar in mechanism to that of experimental sinoatrial blocks induced by superfusion of bepridil (a calcium channel blocker) in 15 preparations of isolated rabbit right atria.

Ostborn P, Wohlfart B, Ohlen G. Arrhythmia as a result of poor intercellular coupling in the sinus node: a simulation study. J Theor Biol 2001;211(3):201–17. The effects of reduced intercellular coupling in the sinus node were investigated by means of simulations. Theories of exit block are discussed in an attempt to better understand the mechanisms of rhythms seen in sick sinus syndrome.

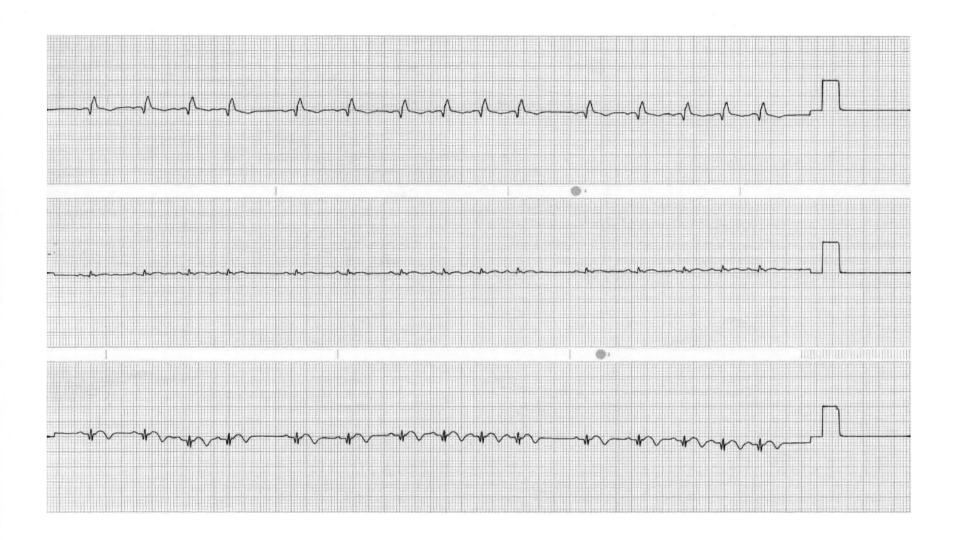

Case 54

Clinical Presentation

The patient is a 39-year-old female with acute chest pain.

Description of Electrocardiogram (12 Leads)

The rhythm is sinus, the rate is 64/min, and the P waves and P–R interval are normal. The QRS voltage and duration and the Q–T interval are normal, but there is subtle ST elevation in lead aVL and reciprocal ST depression in leads 2, 3, and aVF. This is accompanied by ST depression with upright T waves in leads V_1 to V_5. This complex of ST shifts fits with an acute posterolateral MI. The patient was taken with express to the cardiac catheterization laboratory, where an occluded posterolateral branch of the LCx was encountered and successfully stented open.

Interpretation

NSR (rate, 64/min) with an acute posterolateral MI; abnormal ECG

Learning Point

Acute posterolateral MI

Suggested Reading

Sclarovsky S, Topaz O, Rechavia E, et al. Ischemic ST segment depression in leads V2-V3 as the presenting electrocardiographic feature of posterolateral wall myocardial infarction. Am Heart J 1987;113(5):1085–90. In this study of 14 patients hospitalized with a first event of MI, maximal ST segment depression in precordial leads V_2 and V_3 was the sole electrocardiographic finding during chest pain in the first 24 hours of evolving posterolateral infarction, based on further two-dimensional echocardiographic examination and cardionuclear imaging. Delayed electrocardiographic findings compatible with posterolateral MI include the appearance of Q waves in V_5 and V_6, increased R-to-S ratio in leads V_1 and V_2, and a diminution of R-wave amplitude in leads 1, aVL, V_5, and V_6. In Case 54, these delayed findings never manifested because the MI was aborted by acute coronary intervention.

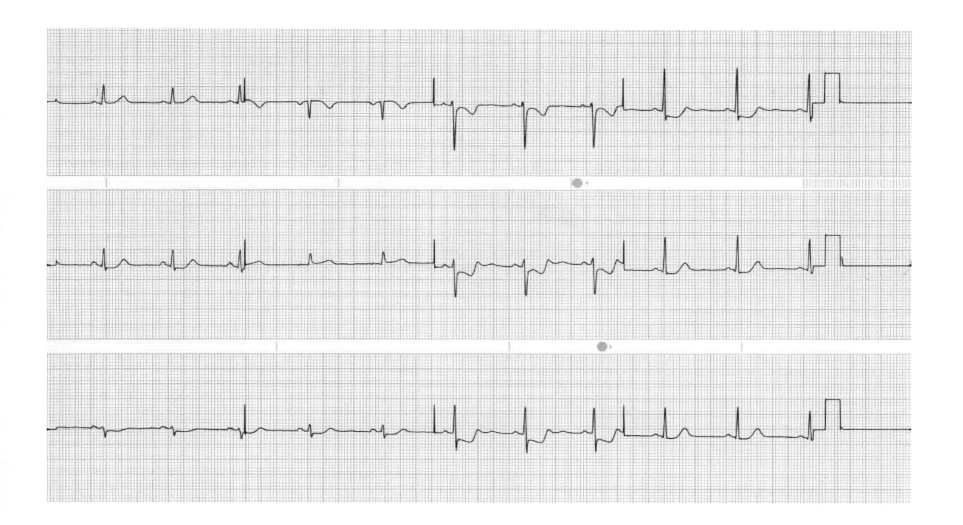

Case 54a

Clinical Presentation

The patient is a 39-year-old female with acute posterolateral MI, 3 hours after she was whisked off to the catheterization laboratory and returned pain free.

Description of Electrocardiogram (12 Leads)

The rhythm is sinus at 89/min. The P–R interval, QRS duration, and QRS axis are normal. The QRS voltage is low normal at 15 mm with full standardization. The Q–Tc is prolonged at 467 msec. The major ST segment shifts that were used to diagnose the acute MI markedly improved by the time of this tracing, such that only mild ST depression remained in leads V_2 to V_4. The late manifestations of a posterolateral MI, tall R in V_1 and V_2, and loss of R-wave amplitude in leads 1 and aVL and leads V_5 and V_6 never developed.

Interpretation

NSR (rate, 89/min) with prolongation of the Q–T interval and nonspecific posterolateral ST depression following acute coronary intervention; abnormal ECG

Learning Points

Posterior leads V_7 to V_9 (placed in the sixth left intercostal space in posterior axillary line, midscapular line, and medial to the midscapular line, respectively)

Suggested Reading

Casas RE, Marriott HJ, Glancy DL. Value of leads V7-V9 in diagnosing posterior wall acute myocardial infarction and other causes of tall R waves in V1-V2. Am J Cardiol 1997;80(4):508–9. In this study, Dr. Casas and colleagues use left posterolateral chest leads (V_7 to V_9) to help distinguish the multiple causes of tall R waves in V_1 and/or V_2, to diagnose true posterior MI when standard leads did not, and to identify the presence or absence of posterior injury in patients with inferior infarction. (Had the patient in Case 54 not been so fortunate as to have her LCx posterolateral branch promptly reperfused, these posterolateral leads might have been useful.)

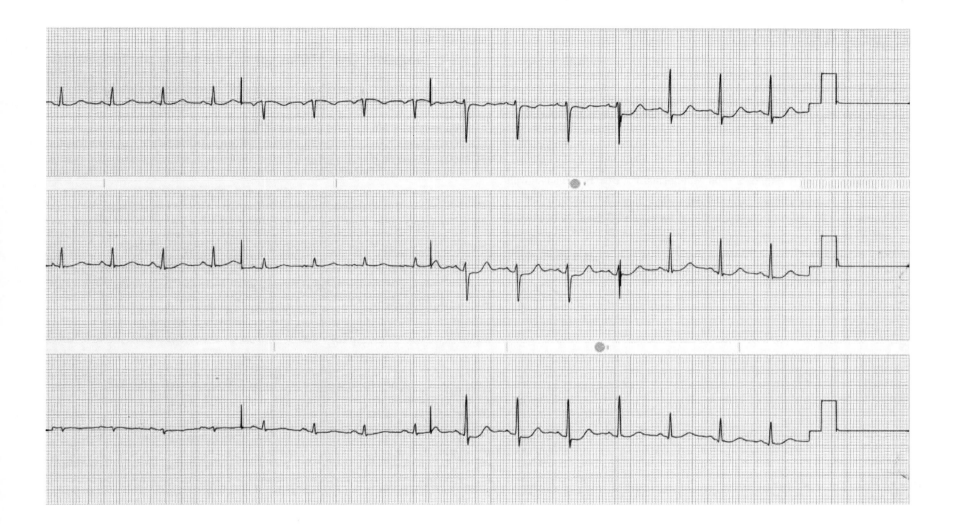

Case 55

Clinical Presentation

The patient is a 57-year-old female with acute chest pain that brought her to the ED.

Description of Electrocardiogram (12 Leads)

The ECG shows sinus rhythm at 57/min with normal P waves, P–R interval without variation, normal QRS duration and axis, and normal Q–T interval. The explanation for the patient's chest pain lies in the subtle ST elevation in leads 2, 3, and aVF and the greater reciprocal ST depression in lead aVL than in lead 1. There were no ST or T-wave changes in leads V_1 and V_2 to suggest RV or posterior involvement. She was taken to the catheterization laboratory.

Interpretation

Sinus bradycardia (rate, 57/min) with an acute inferior MI; abnormal ECG

Learning Point

Acute inferior MI

Suggested Reading

Macfarlane PW, Browne D, Devinie B, et al. Modification of ACC/ESC criteria for acute myocardial infarction. J Electrocardiol 2004;37 Suppl:98–103. The American College of Cardiology and the European Society of Cardiology recently proposed criteria for acute ST elevation MI. These criteria were based on ST elevation of > 0.1 mV in limb leads and in V_4 to V_6, or on ST elevation of > 0.2 mV in V_1 to V_3, the criteria being met in two contiguous leads. The authors added age and gender criteria that improved sensitivity and particularly specificity. (The ST elevation is subtle and barely meets the criteria for an acute ST elevation MI, but the results of RCA PCI are apparent in Case 55a.)

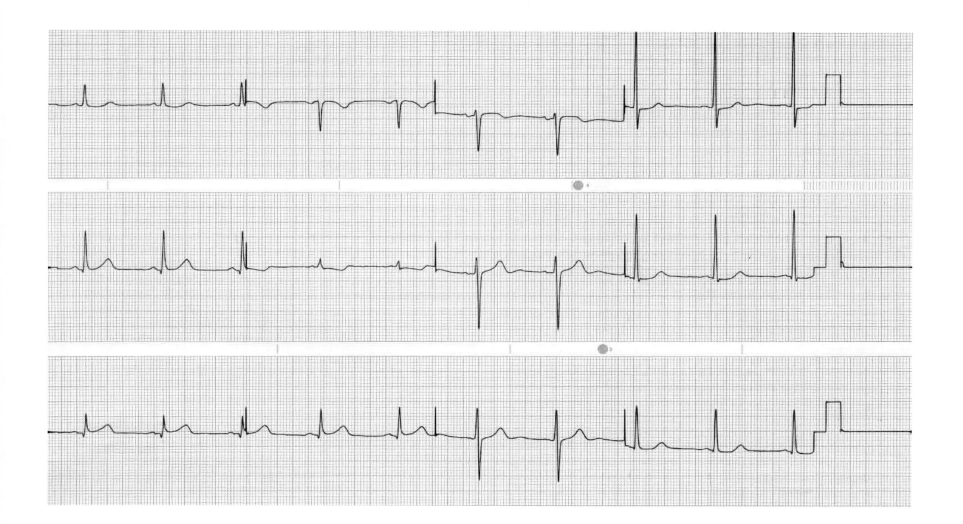

Case 55a

Clinical Presentation

The patient is a 57-year-old female who has just returned from the catheterization laboratory, where her occluded RCA was opened.

Description of Electrocardiogram (12 Leads)

The lesion was in the mid-RCA, which explains the lack of marked sinus slowing, AV block, and RV infarction that are seen with more proximal RCA lesions. The ST depression in the inferior leads (2, 3, and aVF) has largely resolved, considering the baseline drift upward to the right in these leads. In aVL, where there is no baseline drift, there is no longer any reciprocal ST depression. In the ideal world, the physician interpreting the ECG should be able to approve of its technical quality before the electrocardiographic leads are removed, to avoid having to interpret the most important aspect of this case with imperfect data. In the real world, one must be resourceful and adapt. The U waves seen here are sometimes seen in myocardial ischemia. These upright U waves are not specific. Inverted U waves are a more reliable sign of ischemia. In this case, because of the ST shifts, the U waves were not necessary for diagnosis.

Interpretation

Sinus bradycardia (rate, 53/min); reperfused acute inferior MI; normal ECG

Learning Points

Reperfused acute inferior MI
U waves
Inverted U waves of ischemia
Baseline drift

Suggested Reading

Di Diego JM, Antzelevitch C. Cellular basis for ST-segment changes observed during ischemia. J Electrocardiol 2003;36 Suppl:1–5. Transmembrane action potentials were recorded from epicardial and endocardial regions of an isolated arterially perfused canine ventricular wedge preparation. Global ischemia was induced by an abrupt interruption of coronary flow for 30 minutes. After 30 minutes of ischemia, epicardial regions repolarized after endocardial regions, causing reversal of repolarization gradients and T-wave inversion. These ischemia-induced electrophysiologic changes returned to nearly control values within 5 minutes of reperfusion (just as was seen in Case 55a).

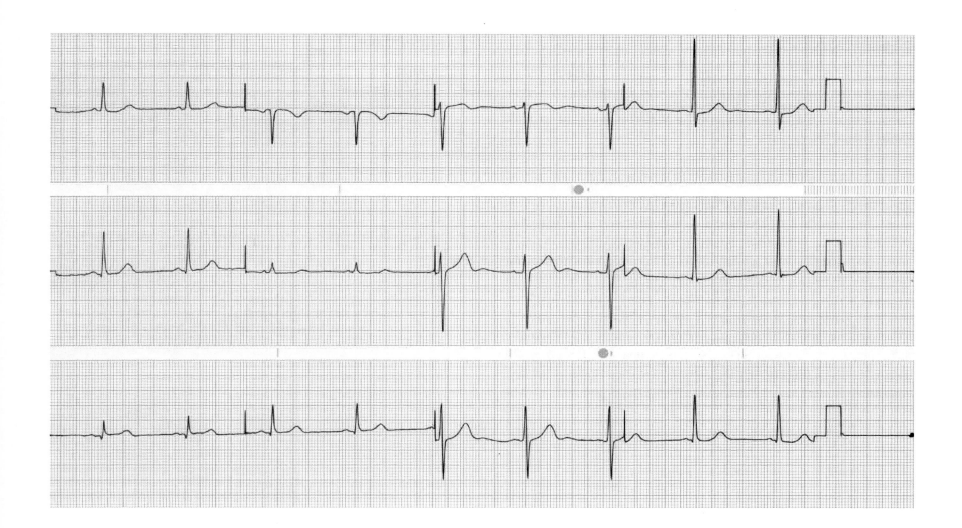

Case 56

Clinical Presentation

The patient is a 70-year-old male preparing for an elective surgery. He had an MI 5 years prior to this tracing.

Description of Electrocardiogram (12 Leads)

The rhythm is sinus with a uniform P wave and a constant P–R interval measuring 132 msec, but the P–P interval varies significantly. This is called sinus arrhythmia and can be respiratory related or nonrespiratory related. The respiratory type is related to vagal tone. The nonrespiratory type is more commonly seen in patients with increased intracranial pressure or with a previous inferior MI. It may also be seen in some patients who are being treated with morphine or digitalis. The Q waves in leads 2, 3, and aVF, the tall R waves with upright T waves in leads V_1 and V_2, and the small Q waves in V_5 and V_6, all without ST shifts, speak for an old inferoposterior MI. This location of MI accounts for the sinus arrhythmia and should warn the physicians and nurses to use morphine or digitalis with caution.

Interpretation

Sinus rhythm with sinus arrhythmia (mean rate, 66/min), old infero-posterior MI; abnormal ECG

Learning Points

Sinus arrhythmia
Old inferoposterior MI

Suggested Reading

Wolf MM, Varigos GA, Hunt D, Sloman JG. Sinus arrhythmia in acute myocardial infarction. Med J Aust 1978;2(2):52–3. Sinus arrhythmia, defined by calculation of variance of the R–R interval on admission to the hospital, was present in 73 of 176 patients with acute MI who were admitted to a coronary care unit. These patients had a lower hospital mortality. They tended to have a higher incidence of inferior infarction, a lower incidence of anterior infarction, and smaller infarcts as measured by the Norris index (a prognostic index devised in 1969 and published in *Lancet*). The main difference between patients with sinus arrhythmia and those without sinus arrhythmia was related to heart rates on admission to hospital, the patients with the former having slower heart rates at that time.

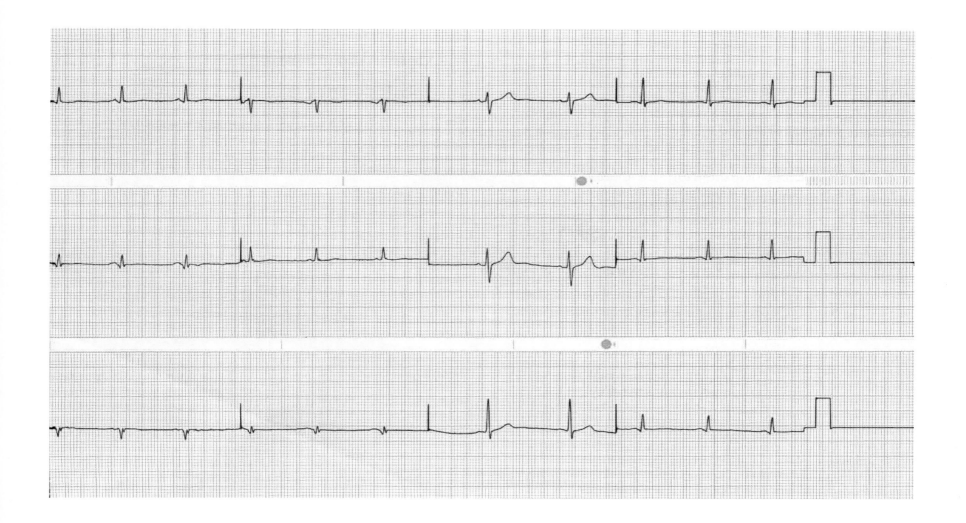

Case 57

ClinicalPresentation

The patient is a 52-year-old male who is in the catheterization laboratory after presenting to the ED with sudden onset of crushing chest pain and nausea.

Description of Electrocardiogram (12 Leads)

The rhythm is sinus, and the rate is 72/min and regular. The P waves are normal, and the P–R interval is 176 msec. The QRS axis is 74°, and the QRS duration is 88 msec; both are normal. There is ST segment elevation in leads 2, 3, and aVF, with diminutive Q waves in these same leads, no reciprocal changes, and no signs of posterior or RV involvement. The RCA was occluded in its middle third and was opened with a guidewire and stent within 2 hours of the onset of the pain at home. Because of prompt action, the patient had only a minimal cardiac enzyme rise, no complicating scar or arrhythmia, and no mitral regurgitation; this is the goal of acute coronary intervention.

Interpretation

NSR (rate, 72/min) with an acute inferior MI; abnormal ECG

Learning Points

Acute inferior MI

Acute coronary intervention

Suggested Reading

Montalescot G, Andersen HR, Antoniucci D, et al. Recommendations on percutaneous coronary intervention for the reperfusion of acute ST elevation MI. Heart 2004;90(6):e37. This paper presents the recommendations of a task force for the treatment of acute STEMI by PCI.

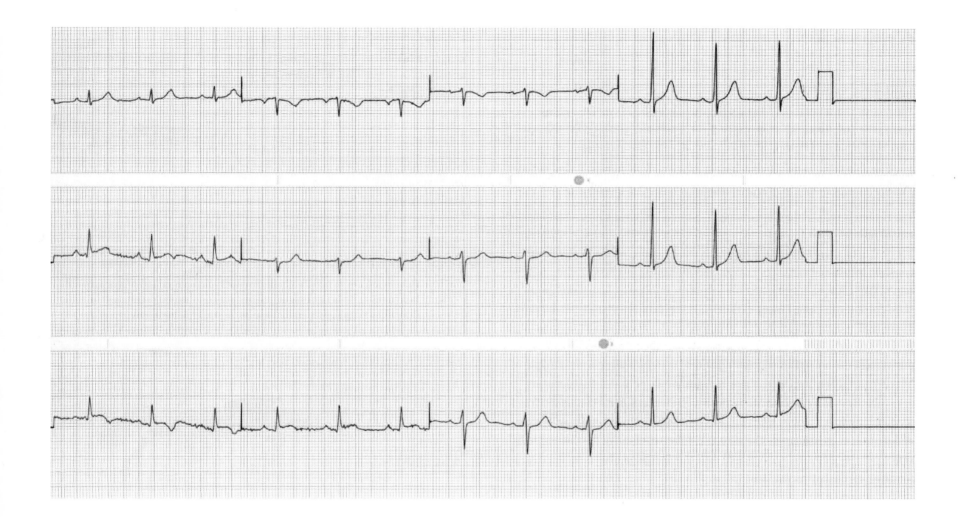

Case 58

ClinicalPresentation

The patient is a 60-year-old female who presents to the ED via Emergency Medical Services after the acute onset of chest pressure and syncope while at work. She has long-standing diabetes and is hypotensive and pale.

Description of Electrocardiogram (12 Leads)

The rhythm is rapid atrial flutter (rate, 375/min [1500/4]) with a ventricular rate of 58/min. The ratio of flutter waves to QRS complexes is not a whole number, and the flutter wave to QRS interval is not constant, yet the R–R interval is constant, suggesting that there is AV dissociation and junctional rhythm. It is the rate of the junctional rhythm and the loss of AV association that affects blood pressure and can cause syncope. The QRS complexes are 96 msec in duration. There is ST elevation in leads 2, 3, aVF, and V_6, with reciprocal ST depression in leads 1 and aVL. This is an acute inferior MI. It is the ST depression in V_1 to V_5 that is most ominous. This suggests additional anterior-wall subendocardial injury. This is often seen when there is a chronically occluded LAD coronary artery that does not cause an MI because it receives collateral circulation from the RCA. In cases like this, when the RCA is acutely occluded, multiple myocardial territories are infarcted. The altered cardiac sensation of the diabetic individual permits this to go undiagnosed until this late stage. This is an indication for acute coronary intervention.

Interpretation

Rapid atrial flutter with junctional rhythm and AV dissociation; V rate, 58/min; acute inferior MI and marked anterior subendocardial injury; abnormal ECG

Learning Points

Atrial flutter
Junctional rhythm
AV dissociation
Acute inferior MI with anterior subendocardial injury

Suggested Reading

Mirvis DM. Physiologic bases for anterior ST segment depression in patients with acute inferior wall MI. Am Heart J 1988;116(5 Pt 1):1308–22. Patients with acute inferior MI commonly have ST segment depression in the anterior precordial leads. This may reflect either reciprocal changes from the inferior ST elevation or primary ST depression from additional anterior subendocardial ischemia. As in Case 58, acute occlusion of the RCA may produce ischemia in the anterior LV wall supplied by a stenotic or previously occluded anterior descending coronary artery.

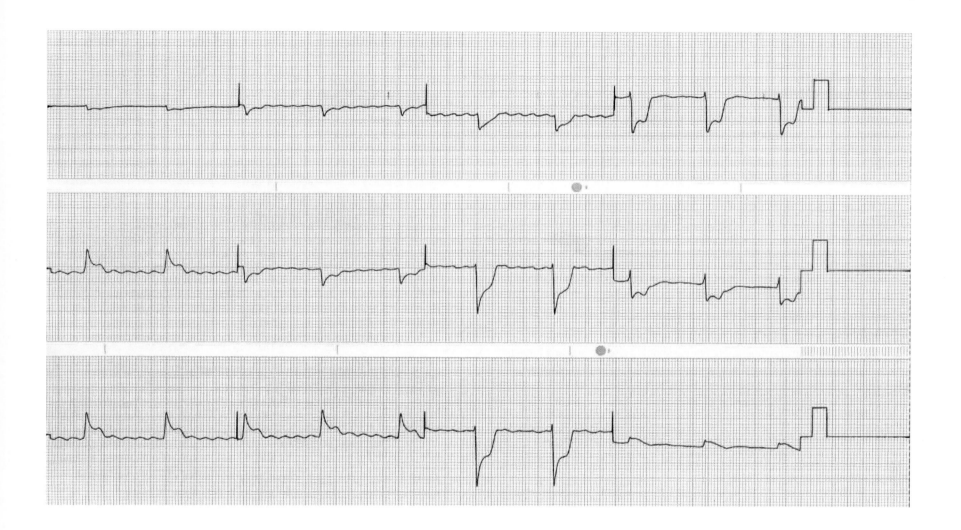

Case 59

ClinicalPresentation

The patient is a 56-year-old male who has just suffered a stroke. He had an MI years earlier and has recently been suffering from dyspnea on exertion.

Description of Electrocardiogram (12 Leads)

There is sinus rhythm at 103/min without ectopy. The P waves and P–R interval are normal. The QRS axis is −66°, and the QRS duration is 88 msec. There are Q waves in V_2 to V_6, and there is no R wave until lead V_6. The ST segments are elevated slightly in leads 1 and aVL but are more elevated in leads V_3 to V_6. The T waves in these same leads are inverted. The patient had no chest pain coincident with this tracing. Electrocardiography in this same patient 1 month after his MI did not show ST elevation. This is the electrocardiographic pattern of an LVA. An LVA is most common in the anterior wall or LV apex. Inferior wall LVAs are uncommon. This electrocardiographic finding should raise the antenna for ventricular tachycardia, left ventricle failure, and embolization of LV thrombi from the aneurysm, the latter two of which were present in this case.

Interpretation

Sinus tachycardia at 103/min with LAH and an old extensive anterior MI with aneurysm; abnormal ECG

Learning Points

LAH
Anterior MI with aneurysm
Clinical complications of LVA

Suggested Readings

Inoue T, Morooka S, Hayashi T, et al. Features of coronary artery lesions related to left ventricular aneurysm formation in anterior myocardial infarction. Angiology 1993;44(8):593–8. To determine the factors of LVA formation in acute MI, the authors studied the distribution of coronary artery lesions and the LV wall motion of 43 patients with anterior MI. Of 15 patients with aneurysm, 9 (60%) had single-vessel disease with severe stenosis of the proximal LAD coronary artery. Of 9 patients with triple-vessel disease, 8 had no aneurysm. In 23 patients with single-vessel disease, the collateral score was significantly less in patients with an aneurysm. The authors concluded that important factors for LVA formation were as follows: (1) the culprit lesion for the MI was severe, but other coronary artery lesions were mild; (2) collateral vessels were poor; and (3) the LV wall motion of the infarct area was impaired, but that of the noninfarct area was relatively good.

Levy S, Gerard R, Castellanos A Jr, et al. Pure left anterior hemiblock: hemodynamic and arteriographic aspects in patients with coronary artery disease. Eur J Cardiol 1978;8(4-5):553–63. The electrocardiographic pattern of pure LAH (without BBB) was found in ECGs of 20 of 283 (7.3%) patients who were shown to have significant CAD by coronary arteriography. Of these 20 patients, 10 had electrocardiographic features of old infarction. LAH was associated with (1) a significant lesion in the LAD coronary artery in all patients, (2) severe CAD (2.5 vessels per patient), and (3) impairment of LV contraction pattern in 14 patients, 9 of whom had a ventricular aneurysm (precisely the situation of the patient in Case 59).

Tikiz H, Atak R, Balbay Y, et al. Left ventricular aneurysm formation after anterior myocardial infarction: clinical and angiographic determinants in 809 patients. Int J Cardiol 2002;82(1):7–14. In this larger study, the conclusions that were reached were very similar to those of Inoue and colleagues; the determinants included single-vessel disease, the absence of previous angina, total occlusion of the LAD coronary artery, and (in this study) female gender.

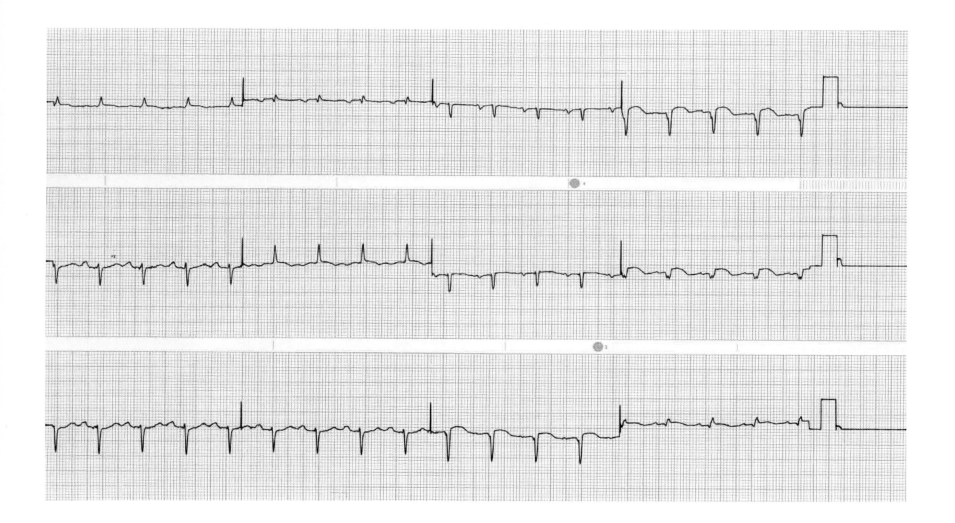

Case 60

ClinicalPresentation

The patient is a 69-year-old female with an MI of several days' duration.

Description of Electrocardiogram (12 Leads)

The rhythm is sinus at 119/min. The P waves and P–R intervals are normal. The QRS duration is 146 msec, and the QRS axis is –67°. The QRS prolongation is due to RBBB. The initial R wave in the right precordial leads is replaced by a Q wave, but the R' in these same leads and the S in lead V_6 support the presence of RBBB. This LAH and RBBB can be called a bifascicular block. This bifascicular block was not present prior to this MI. The Q waves and ST elevation in leads V_1 to V_5 and the ST elevation in leads 1 and aVL are criteria for an acute extensive anterior MI. When bifascicular block occurs as a result of an acute anterior MI, there is a high incidence of complete heart block and the need for a temporary transvenous pacemaker.

Interpretation

Sinus tachycardia (rate, 119/min) with LAH, RBBB (bifascicular block), and an acute extensive anterior MI; abnormal ECG

Learning Points

Acute MI with LAH and RBBB (bifascicular block)

Indications for prophylactic pacing in acute MI

Suggested Readings

Ryan TJ, Antman EM, Brooks NH, et al. 1999 Update: ACC/AHA Guidelines for the management of patients with acute myocardial infarction: executive summary and recommendations. Circulation 1999;100:1016–30. A class 2a indication for temporary transvenous pacing in acute MI is RBBB and left anterior or left posterior fascicular block (new or indeterminate). With the addition of first-degree AV block to this new bifascicular block in the setting of an acute MI, the indication for temporary transvenous pacing would be class 1. (In Case 60, a temporary transvenous pacemaker was inserted, but a permanent pacemaker was not needed.) The terms left anterior hemiblock and left anterior fascicular block are interchangeable, as are left posterior hemiblock and left posterior fascicular block.

Stephens MR, Fadayomi MO, Davies GJ, Muir JR. The clinical features and significance of bifascicular block complicating acute myocardial infarction. Eur J Cardiol 1975;3(4):289–96. The overall prevalence of LAH and RBBB in patients with anterior MI was 3.3%. Complete heart block was noted in 36% of these patients, and 12% of these died from this arrhythmia. These data support the guidelines of prophylactic temporary transvenous pacing for acute anterior MI complicated by new LAH and RBBB. However, it is important to note that these conduction blocks are associated with a large amount of myocardial damage, and mortality is directly related to the amount of infarcted myocardium.

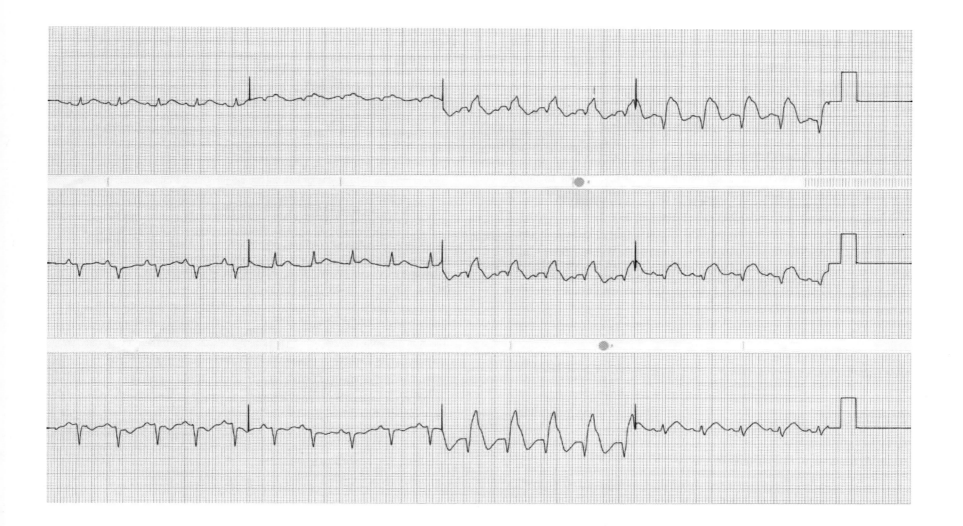

Case 61

Clinical Presentation

The patient is a 47-year-old male who had chest pain following neurosurgery.

Description of Electrocardiogram (12 Leads)

As the patient was somewhat combative, the baseline is irregular. The rhythm is sinus, and the rate is 82/min. The P waves and the P–R interval are normal. The QRS axis is 3°, and the QRS duration is 103 msec, slightly prolonged. There is ST elevation in leads 1 and aVL, with reciprocal ST depression in leads 2, 3, and aVF. There is ST depression with upright T waves in leads V_1 to V_4. This is an acute posterolateral MI. The preoperative ECG was normal. Because of the risk of intracranial bleeding, the patient had to be managed without thrombolytic therapy and without heparin. PCI was considered.

Interpretation

NSR (rate, 82/min) with an acute posterolateral MI; abnormal ECG

Learning Points

Acute posterolateral MI
Managing the acute STEMI after neurosurgery

Suggested Readings

Grzybowski M, Clements EA, Parsons L, et al. Mortality benefit of immediate revascularization of acute ST-segment elevation myocardial infarction in patients with contraindications to thrombolytic therapy: a propensity analysis. JAMA 2003;290(14):1891–8. The authors state that there are no definite recommendations for the management of AMI in patients with ST segment elevation who have contraindications to thrombolytic therapy. The goal of this paper was to determine if IMR (defined as PCI or CABG surgery) is associated with a mortality benefit in such patients. According to the National Registry of Myocardial Infarction, between June 1994 and January 2003, there were 1,799,704 patients with AMI. Of these, 19,917 patients with acute ST segment elevation were eligible for IMR but had thrombolytic contraindications. Of these 19,917 patients, 4,705 (23.6%) received IMR. The mortality rate for the IMR-treated patients was 11.1%, and that of the 15,212 non-IMR-treated patients was 30.6%. This represents a 63.7% risk reduction. Even after a further analysis using a propensity-matching score to reduce the effects of bias, the risk reduction of IMR was still 48.5%. The authors conclude that using IMR in patients with acute ST segment elevation AMI and thrombolytic contraindications should be strongly considered. (Perhaps if the patient in Case 61 had been treated with IMR, the ECG findings in the following case [Case 61a] would not have developed.)

Smith Jr SC, Dove JT, Jacobs AK, et al. ACC/AHA guidelines for percutaneous coronary intervention (revision of the 1993 PTCA guidelines)—executive summary. Circulation 2001;103:3019–41. This is an exhaustive overview of indications for PCI in acute STEMI. There are, however, no guidelines for the management of an acute MI following neurosurgery.

Clearly, exposure to any anticoagulant or antithrombotic or antiplatelet agent after neurosurgery can predispose the central nervous system to bleeding. The risks of bleeding into the brain or spinal cord and the resultant sequelae must be weighed against the risks of conservative management of the STEMI without these agents. (In Case 61, the vital signs were stable, and the chest pain could be controlled with analgesics and nitroglycerin. There were no significant arrhythmias, and there was no heart failure.)

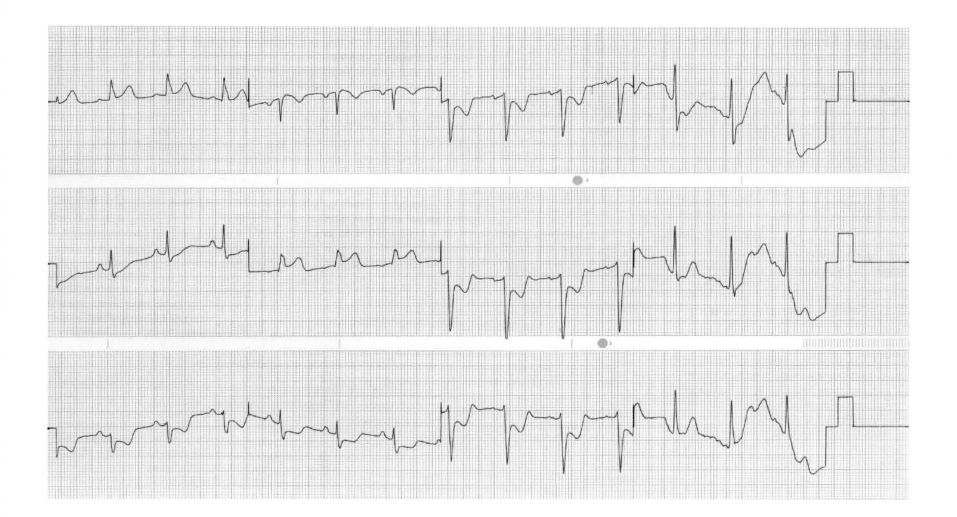

Case 61a

ClinicalPresentation

The patient is a 47-year-old male (Case 61) with acute posterolateral MI following neurosurgery, the next day.

Description of Electrocardiogram (12 Leads)

The ECG shows sinus rhythm at 101/min with a new right axis of 111° and a QRS duration of 116 msec. The P–R interval remains normal. There is a broad and deep Q wave in lead aVL, and the ST segments have returned to baseline in leads V_1 to V_4. The patient completed the posterolateral MI and developed a new right axis that fits the criteria for a left posterior fascicular block, except for the QRS duration of > 110 msec. Because the left posterior fascicle has dual circulations, the implication of this new axis and QRS widening is that of multivessel CAD.

Interpretation

Sinus tachycardia (rate, 101/min) with an abnormal right axis and QRS widening; recent posterolateral MI; abnormal ECG

Learning Points

LPH with acute lateral MI

Clinical significance of LPH in AMI

Suggested Readings

Lewin RF, Sclarovsky S, Strasberg B, et al. Right axis deviation in acute myocardial infarction. Clinical significance, hospital evolution, and long- term follow-up. Chest 1984;85(4):489–93. The incidence, in-hospital evolution, and long-term follow-up of patients who developed acute deviation of the mean (frontal) QRS axis to the right during acute MI were studied. Among 3,160 patients evaluated, 13 (0.41%) developed LPH, and 1.8% developed a lesser form of right-axis deviation. In this prethrombolytic therapy and pre-PCI era, these patients with right-axis deviation in acute MI had a 69% incidence of in-hospital CHF and an in-hospital mortality of 38.5%. In long-term follow-up, these patients had a statistically significant higher incidence of angina pectoris and CHF than a control group had.

Papa LA, Scariato A, Gottlieb R, et al. Coronary angiographic assessment of left posterior hemiblock. J Electrocardiol 1983;16(3):297–301. Among the ECGs of 1,095 patients with coronary angiographic evidence of significant CAD, 5 (0.5%) indicated LPH. Of those 5 patients, all had significant RCA disease, and all had at least 75% stenosis in one or more branches of the LCA. The authors concluded that the presence of LPH in patients with CAD is an ominous electrocardiographic finding and is associated with extensive CAD.

Wagner R, Rosenbaum MB. Transient left posterior hemiblock. Association with acute lateral myocardial infarction. Am J Cardiol 1972;29(4):558–60. An observation by those who first described the hemiblocks.

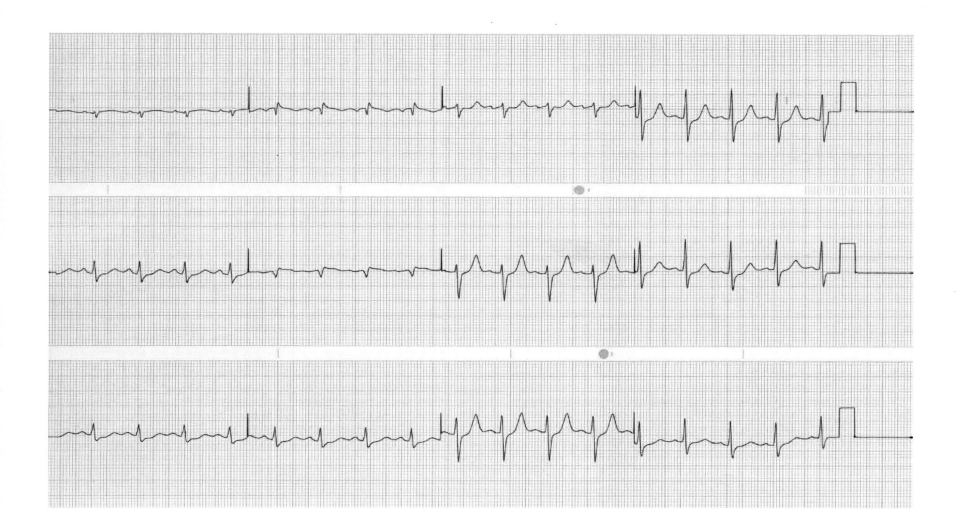

Case 62

ClinicalPresentation

The patient is a 47-year-old male (not the patient of Cases 61 and 61a) returning to his physician for an evaluation 3 months after his first MI. He is no longer able to do manual labor on the construction site, but fortunately, he can be a foreman.

Description of Electrocardiogram (12 Leads)

There is sinus rhythm at 66/min with a P–R prolongation of 240 msec. The QRS duration is 85 msec, and the QRS axis approximates 0°. There are anterior Q waves and small inferior Q waves that are seen with anteroapical infarction. The persistent ST elevation with T inversion across the precordial leads and highest in V_2 suggests an LVA. Palpation of the precordium and transthoracic echocardiography confirms this suspicion and explains his inability to continue to do vigorous physical work.

Interpretation

NSR (rate, 66/min) with first-degree AV block and an old anteroapical MI with aneurysm; abnormal ECG

Learning Points

Anteroapical MI with aneurysm
First-degree AV block

Suggested Readings

Bhatnagar SK. Observations of the relationship between left ventricular aneurysm and ST segment elevation in patients with first acute anterior Q wave myocardial infarction. Eur Heart J 1994;15(11):1500–4. In 78 consecutive survivors of a first acute anterior Q-wave MI, two-dimensional echocardiography, color Doppler echocardiography, and radionuclide angiography for the diagnosis of LV anteroapical aneurysm were performed to study the relationship of this complication to precordial ST segment elevation in these patients. The ST elevation (millimeters) in lead V_2, the maximum ST elevation in leads V_1 to V_6, and the sum of ST elevation in leads V_1 to V_6 were calculated. LVA was present in 19 patients as determined by two-dimensional echocardiography. The sum of ST elevation in V_1 to V_6 was higher in patients with an aneurysm. The mean LV ejection fraction was 23% in patients with an aneurysm as opposed to 34% in those without an aneurysm. (It is clear why the 47-year-old man in Case 62 could no longer do manual labor.)

Engel J, Brady WJ, Mattu A, Perron AD. Electrocardiographic ST elevation: left ventricular aneurysm. Am J Emerg Med 2002;20(3):238–42. LVA is manifested electrocardiographically by varying degrees of ST segment elevation, which may be difficult to distinguish from ST segment changes caused by acute MI. In LVA, the ST elevation is generally associated with well-developed completed Q waves in the anterior precordial leads, and there will not be reciprocal ST depression in the contralateral leads.

Saber W, Nishime EO, Brunken RC, et al. Does chronic ST segment elevation following Q wave myocardial infarction exclude tissue viability? Cardiology 2003;100(1):11–6. Using positron emission tomography to distinguish viable myocardium from scar, the authors studied 132 patients with chronic anteroseptal Q-wave MI; 84 of these patients had persistent ST segment elevation exceeding 1.0 mV, and the other 48 did not. No relationship was noted between chronic ST segment elevation and the presence or absence of myocardial viability. (Perhaps the patient in Case 62 may benefit from anterior-wall revascularization and regain some stamina.)

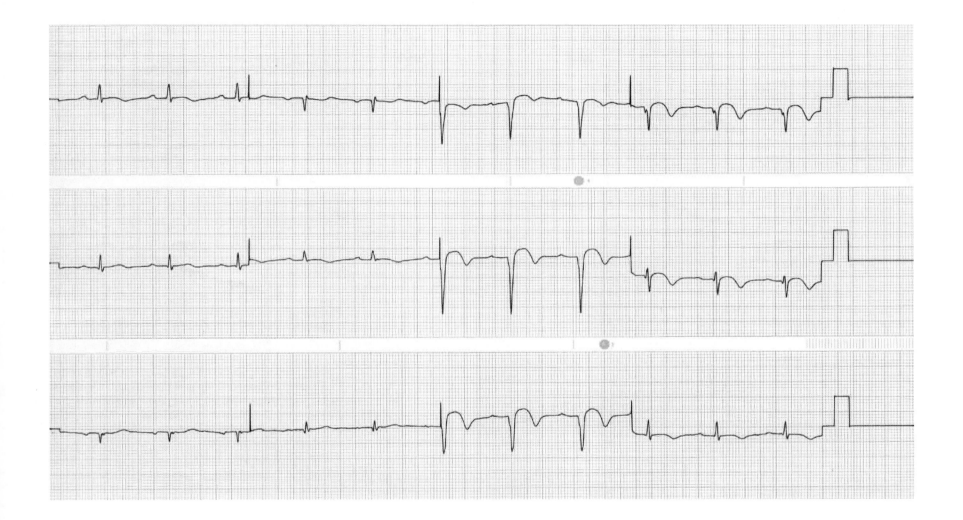

9

Ventricular Preexcitation Syndromes

Case 63

ClinicalPresentation

The patient is a 73-year-old male who presented to his physician complaining of sudden episodes of a regular tachycardia lasting 20 to 60 minutes and suddenly terminating. He has had the problem for many years, but he has started to sweat during recent episodes.

Description of Electrocardiogram (12 Leads)

The rhythm is sinus at 93/min, and the P–R interval measures 110 msec (short for this patient's age). The QRS duration is normal, and there are small inferior Q waves that do not meet the criteria for old infarction in lead aVF (one little box [40 msec] wide and at least one-third the height of the R wave). The T waves are a bit flattened in the lateral leads, but in the second beat from last, one finds a shorter P–R interval, a slurred upstroke to the R wave (delta wave), and ST–T changes distinctly different from all of the others. This one beat is *preexcited*: part of the electricity originating in the atrium bypasses the AV node and more quickly depolarizes the ventricles, and part of the electricity reaches the ventricles across the AV node. The more electricity that reaches the ventricles via the bypass tract, the larger is the delta wave and the wider is the QRS complex.

Interpretation

NSR (rate, 93/min), with a short P–R interval and one preexcited beat; abnormal ECG. (Consider WPW syndrome.)

Learning Points

Q-wave criteria for old MI
Short P–R interval
Delta wave of preexcitation
WPW syndrome

Suggested Reading

Rosner MH, Brady WJ Jr, Kefer MP, Martin ML. Electrocardiography in the patient with the Wolff–Parkinson-White syndrome: diagnostic and initial therapeutic issues. Am J Emerg Med 1999;17(7):705–14. WPW syndrome, estimated to occur in approximately 0.1 to 3.0% of the general population, is a form of ventricular preexcitation involving an accessory conduction pathway. The definition of WPW syndrome relies on the following electrocardiographic features: (1) a P–R interval of < 0.12 seconds; (2) a slurring of the initial segment of the QRS complex, known as a delta wave; (3) a QRS complex widening with a total duration > 0.12 seconds; and (4) secondary repolarization changes reflected in ST segment T-wave changes that are generally directed opposite (discordant) to the major delta wave and RS complex changes. The accessory pathway bypasses the AV node, creating a direct electrical connection between the atria and ventricles.

The majority of patients with preexcitation remain asymptomatic throughout their lives. When symptoms do occur, they are usually secondary to tachyarrhythmias, which cause disabling symptoms and, in the extreme, sudden cardiac death. The tachyarrhythmias encountered in the WPW syndrome patient include paroxysmal supraventricular tachycardia (both the narrow QRS and wide QRS complex varieties), atrial fibrillation, atrial flutter, and ventricular fibrillation. Therapy is also discussed.

All of the electrocardiographic features of WPW syndrome are shown in Case 63. Since the features are intermittent, they stand out against the normal QRS complexes in the same patient in the same 10-second period. Clinically, this patient is starting to have symptoms of diaphoresis with spells of tachycardia, perhaps because he has lost vasoconstrictive ability with age.

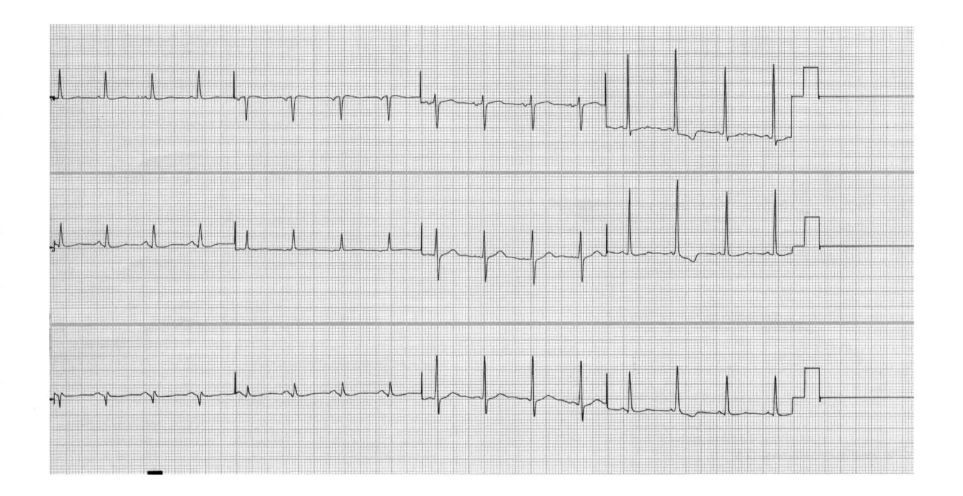

Case 64

ClinicalPresentation

The patient is an 18-year-old female in her eighth month of pregnancy who presents to the ED with tachycardia and known WPW syndrome. She has taken procainamide orally throughout her pregnancy for the control of SVT but recently discontinued it when she no longer could afford it.

Description of Electrocardiogram (12 Leads)

A six-channel electrocardiograph that allows more time for recording in each lead was used, but the second and third channels were half-standard (N/2) in order to fit on the paper. The leads are labeled. Lead V_3R is not recorded.

The rate is 188/min. No P waves are visible, the QRS complexes are 80 msec in duration, and the QRS axis is normal. There are diffuse ST segment T-wave changes. Because the QRS complexes are narrow, the bypass tract is used for retrograde conduction and the anterograde conduction is down the normal AV node His bundle route. This is called orthodromic reentrant AV tachycardia, or AVRT.

Interpretation

Reentrant (reciprocating) AV tachycardia (orthodromic); rate, 188/min; WPW syndrome; abnormal ECG

Learning Points

Orthodromic AVRT
Antidromic AVRT

But how do we know when this is or is not WPW syndrome, and what therapy to give? WPW syndrome occurs because of the presence of a rapidly conducting accessory pathway (bypass tract). In WPW syndrome, reentrant tachycardias can occur in several ways, as follows:

1. Conduction can go down the AV node and up the bypass tract (anterograde or orthodromic AVRT). Because the ventricle is depolarized through the normal conduction pathway, the QRS is narrow during SVT. Cardioversion can be accomplished with adenosine, β-blockers, calcium channel blockers, procainamide, or synchronized direct current.

2. Conduction can go down the accessory pathway and up the AV node (retrograde or antidromic AVRT). Here the ventricle is depolarized via the bypass tract, resulting in a wide QRS during SVT. In this setting, β-blockers and calcium channel blockers are contraindicated because they may increase the ventricular rate. Some authors (ie, Zehender and colleagues) consider adenosine to be a safe treatment whereas others consider it contraindicated. Procainamide or direct-current cardioversion are appropriate.

3. Atrial fibrillation and atrial flutter, although not reentrant rhythms, can occur at rates ≥ 300/min or more in patients with WPW syndrome. These rhythms tend to be wide complex since there is anterograde conduction down the bypass tract from the atrium that is fluttering or fibrillating faster than 300/min. Hypotensive or unstable patients should have direct-current cardioversion, and the more stable patient (systolic blood pressure ≥ 90 mm Hg) can be treated with IV procainamide (10 mg/kg at ≤ 50 mg/min or slower if hypotension develops). Procainamide depresses conduction across the accessory pathway (with electrophysiologic properties of ventricular myocardium), decreasing the ventricular rate response and stabilizing the hemodynamics, and may also terminate the wide-complex tachycardia.

Suggested Reading

Zehender M, Jeron A, Faber T, et al. Adenosine in treating cardiac arrhythmias. J Auton Pharmacol 1996;16(6):329–31. Adenosine is an endogenous nucleoside that causes a brief blockade of the AV nodal conduction pathway following intravenous administration. Such brief AV block can be used therapeutically for reliable termination of AVNRT and WPW syndrome reentrant tachycardia (ie, AVRT). It can also be used for unmasking atrial activity in rapid suspected SVT with a broad QRS complex or a delta wave (not present during sinus rhythm with normal AV node conduction), indicating the presence of a hidden WPW syndrome. Side effects after adenosine administration are frequent but are very transient and are rarely serious. The serious side effects, seen in 1 to 3% of cases, are status asthmaticus or ventricular fibrillation. For this reason, some other authors consider adenosine to be contraindicated with wide-complex tachycardias that are regular or irregular.

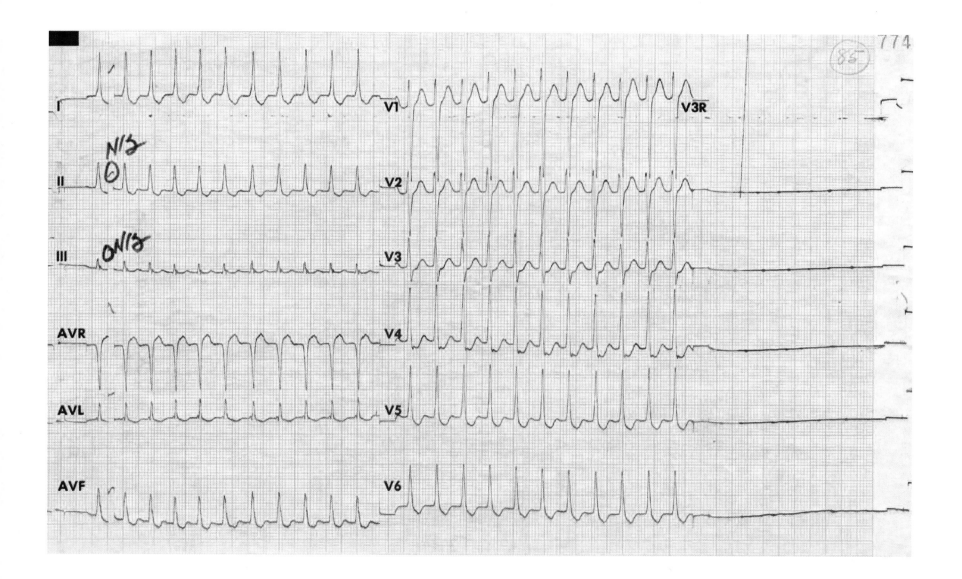

Case 64a

ClinicalPresentation

The patient is the 18-year-old pregnant woman of Case 64. Because she had been taking the oral preparation, she was given an IV infusion of 500 mg of procainamide over 1 hour (more rapid administration caused hypotension), and the rhythm converted to sinus rhythm.

Description of Electrocardiogram (12 Leads)

This is the postconversion ECG. The same six-channel recorder was used, and all leads are full standard. The rhythm is sinus at 79/min. The P waves are normal, and the P–R interval (or the P–delta-wave interval) is 100 msec. The delta waves are best seen in lead 1, but note also the inverted delta wave in aVR and the tall R wave in V_1 and V_2, also seen in preexcitation, depending on the location of the accessory pathway (bypass tract). If the patient had been unstable, the treatment would have been direct-current cardioversion. As she was stable and as the QRS in AVRT was narrow, other treatment options include vagal maneuvers, IV adenosine, IV calcium channel blockers (verapamil or diltiazem), or IV β-blockers. IV procainamide is usually reserved for wide-QRS tachycardias. For wide-QRS tachycardia with a bypass tract, avoid digitalis, calcium channel blockers, and β-blockers (and probably also adenosine).

Interpretation

NSR (rate, 79/min) with a short P–R interval and signs of preexcitation with ST segment T-wave changes; abnormal ECG

Learning Points

Treatment of SVT
Recognition of WPW syndrome

Suggested Readings

Conover MB. Diagnosis and management of arrhythmias associated with Wolff-Parkinson-White syndrome. Crit Care Nurse 1994;14(3):30–9. Because of the emergency nature of the arrhythmias associated with WPW syndrome, nurses are often called upon for diagnosis and intervention in critical care settings. This paper addresses recognition, mechanisms, and treatment.

Trohman RG. Supraventricular tachycardia: implications for the intensivist. Crit Care Med 2000;28(10 Suppl):N129–35. This article focuses on SVT patterns, mechanisms, precipitants, and treatment for the intensivist. Dr. Trohman emphasizes assessment of hemodynamics and clinical judgment in decision making for optimal patient outcomes.

Valderrama AL. Wolff-Parkinson-White syndrome: essentials for the primary care nurse practitioner. J Am Acad Nurse Pract 2004;16(9):378–83. This paper provides the nurse practitioner with a basic understanding of the pathophysiology, clinical characteristics, diagnostic methods, and management of WPW syndrome. Although many patients remain asymptomatic throughout their lives, approximately half of the patients with WPW syndrome experience symptoms secondary to tachyarrhythmias. Symptoms include palpitations, dizziness, syncope, and dyspnea. Diagnosis is usually made by electrocardiographic findings, but further testing may be required to confirm the diagnosis. In these symptomatic patients, specialist referral is warranted.

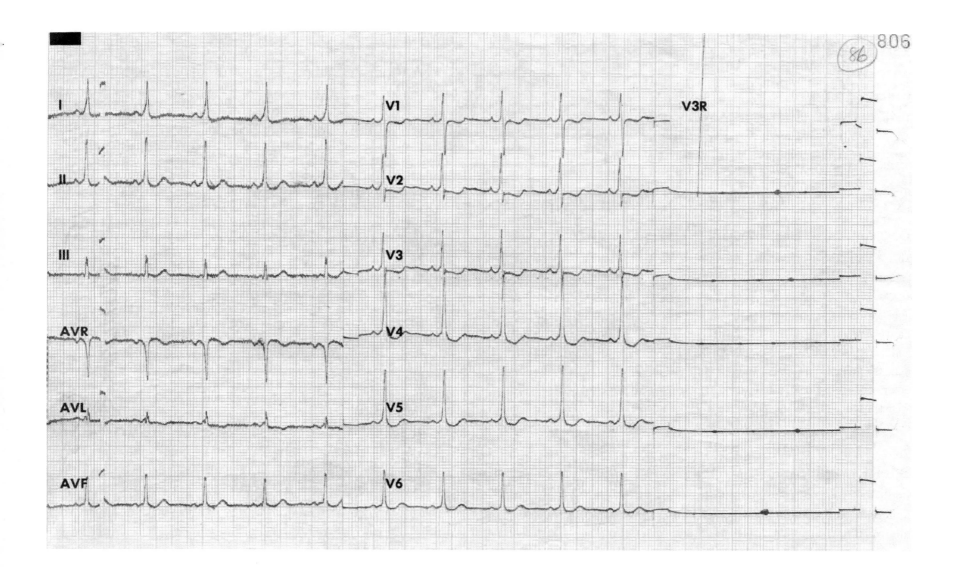

Case 65

ClinicalPresentation

The patient is a 15-year-old female with episodes of sustained tachycardia who was brought to the ED, but an ECG demonstrating the tachycardia could never be obtained prior to spontaneous conversion. Several Holter monitor recordings also failed to demonstrate the tachycardia. She is therefore brought to the electrophysiology laboratory.

Description of Electrocardiogram (12 Leads)

This ECG was recorded during rapid atrial pacing by the use of a transvenous pacing electrode positioned in the high right atrium. The pacing rate is 260/min (cycle length, 230 msec). The pacemaker spikes are best seen in leads 2, 3, and aVF. The interval from spike to delta wave is only 70 msec. The delta waves are most visible in leads 2, 3, and aVF and in leads V_4 and V_5. The QRS axis is 109°, and there is a tall R in V_1. Using the formula 220-the patient's age in years to estimate the predicted maximum HR, it is clear that this 15-year-old patient could never conduct this rapid atrial pacing 1:1 across the AV node without Wenckebach AV block. She clearly has a bypass tract. The substrate for her episodes of tachycardia was found.

Interpretation

Rapid atrial pacing at 260/min, with a short pacer spike to R interval and delta waves and an abnormal right axis owing to preexcitation; abnormal ECG

Learning Points

Electrophysiology of WPW syndrome

Predicting atrial fibrillation in WPW syndrome

Suggested Readings

Harton JM, Prystowsky EN. Electrophysiology: the Wolff-Parkinson-White syndrome. Curr Opin Cardiol 1991;6(1):40–8. Though tachyarrhythmias occur commonly in patients with WPW syndrome, many patients remain asymptomatic. Studies suggest that routine electrophysiologic testing in these individuals is of limited value. Electrophysiologic testing remains very helpful in the symptomatic patient for predicting arrhythmia recurrence and for determining accessory pathway location and function. Given the frequency of antiarrhythmic therapy for WPW syndrome, there is increasing interest in the use of radiofrequency catheter ablation of accessory pathways.

Sakabe K, Fukuda N, Nada T, et al. Atrial electrophysiologic abnormalities in patients with Wolff-Parkinson-White syndrome but without paroxysmal atrial fibrillation. Clin Cardiol 2004;27(7):396–400. In this paper, an electrophysiologic study was performed in 28 patients with WPW syndrome, 23 patients with AVNRT, and 25 patients with other arrhythmias, all of whom had no history of atrial fibrillation. The authors concluded that atrial electrophysiologic abnormalities, especially atrial conduction delays, are more prominent in patients with WPW syndrome, even if they had no previous history of paroxysmal atrial fibrillation. These abnormalities may play a role in determining the vulnerability to atrial fibrillation. Atrial fibrillation can be a lethal arrhythmia in a patient with WPW syndrome who has rapid conduction to the ventricle via the accessory pathway.

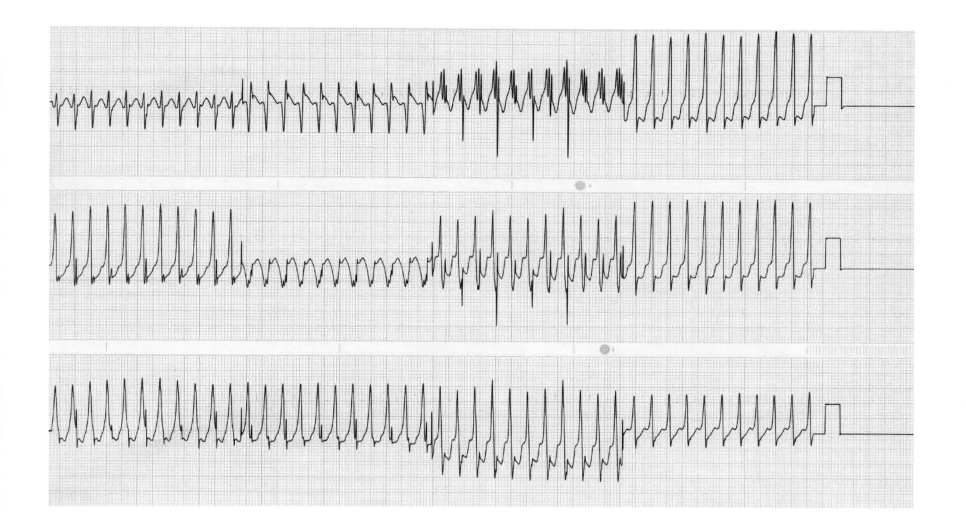

Case 66

ClinicalPresentation

The patient is a 34-year-old male with frequent symptomatic tachycardia who is undergoing mapping of his accessory pathway in the electrophysiology laboratory.

Description of Electrocardiogram (12 Leads)

There is rapid atrial pacing at a cycle length of 360 msec (HR, 167/min). In lead V_4, the interval from pacer spike to delta wave is 160 msec (not short), but the rightward axis, the QRS prolongation (including the delta wave), and the tall R in V_1 demonstrate preexcitation with a bypass tract located in the left posterolateral AV groove. Like the 15-year-old patient in Case 65 who was also proven to have a bypass tract to explain her accessory pathway substrate for episodic sustained tachycardia, this patient underwent radiofrequency ablation of the bypass tract, curing the tachycardia without the need for scores of years of pharmacologic treatments.

Interpretation

Atrial pacing at 167/min, with a rightward axis and tall R wave in V_1 and delta waves of preexcitation; abnormal ECG

Learning Points

Mapping the location of the accessory pathway
Prophylactic catheter ablation of asymptomatic patients with WPW syndrome

Suggested Readings

Chiang CE, Chen SA, Teo WS, et al. An accurate stepwise electrocardiographic algorithm for localization of accessory pathways in patients with Wolff-Parkinson-White syndrome from comprehensive analysis of delta waves and R/S ratio during sinus rhythm. Am J Cardiol 1995;76(1):40–6. The prediction of accessory pathway location prior to radiofrequency ablation has become increasingly important for patients with WPW syndrome. This study analyzes the ECGs of 369 patients with a single anterograde conducting accessory pathway who underwent successful radiofrequency ablation.

Pappone C, Santinelli V, Manguso F, et al. A randomized study of prophylactic catheter ablation in asymptomatic patients with the Wolff-Parkinson-White syndrome. N Engl J Med 2003;349(19):1803–11. Young age and inducibility of AVRT or atrial fibrillation during invasive electrophysiologic testing identify asymptomatic patients with a WPW syndrome pattern on their ECGs as being at high risk for arrhythmic events. The authors tested the hypothesis that prophylactic catheter ablation of accessory pathways would provide meaningful and durable benefits for such patients, as compared with no treatment. From 1997 to 2002, among 224 eligible asymptomatic patients with WPW syndrome, those who were at high risk for arrhythmias were randomly assigned to radiofrequency ablation of accessory pathways (37 patients) or no treatment (35 patients). Two patients in the ablation group (5%) and 21 patients in the control group (60%) had arrhythmic events. The authors concluded that prophylactic accessory pathway ablation markedly reduces the frequency of arrhythmic events in asymptomatic patients with WPW syndrome who are at high risk for such events. Perhaps the benefit of ablating the accessory pathway in the patient in Case 66 can be extended to those asymptomatic patients with WPW syndrome who are at high risk for AVRT and atrial fibrillation.

Steurer G, Frey B, Gursoy S, et al. Cardiac depolarization and repolarization in Wolff-Parkinson-White syndrome. Am Heart J 1994;128(5):908–11. Delta-wave and QRS complex polarities have been extensively studied in preexcitation syndromes. However, only limited data exist in regard to ventricular depolarization and repolarization in the setting of maximal preexcitation in relation to the site of insertion of the accessory pathway. The authors analyzed the polarity of the QRS complex and T wave on the frontal plane on the conventional 12-lead ECGs of 118 patients with maximal preexcitation during fast atrial pacing. As in Case 66, the 32 patients with a left lateral accessory pathway showed a right axis of the QRS complex with a left axis of the T wave.

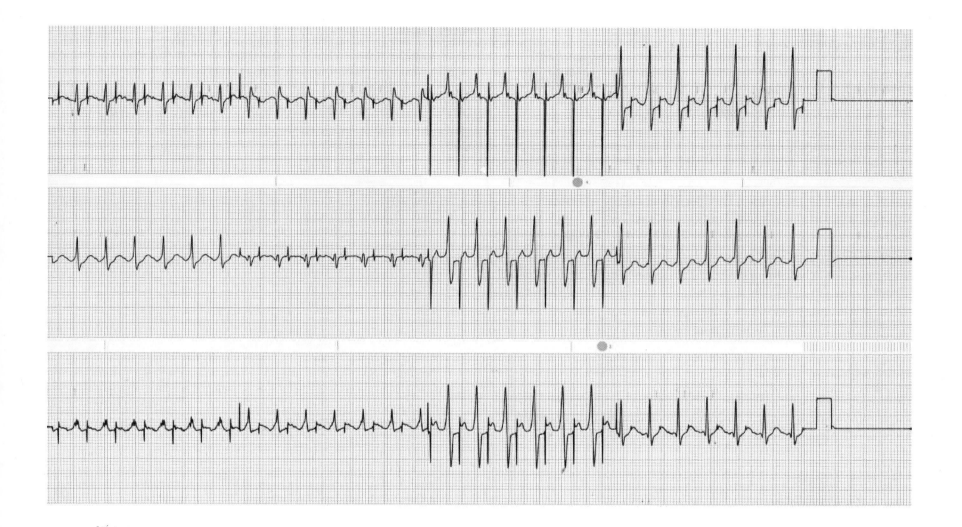

Case 67

Clinical Presentation

The patient is a 39-year-old male with acute chest pain.

Description of Electrocardiogram (12 Leads)

The rhythm is sinus at 100/min, and the P–R interval is 115 msec in the leads with evident delta waves, such as lead 1. The delta waves are inverted in leads 3 and aVF, suggesting an old inferior infarction, but there is no such history. There is ST segment elevation in leads 1, 2, 3, and aVF and in leads V_1 to V_6. The source of the patient's chest pain was correctly assumed to be an acute anterior MI. He was taken emergently for coronary arteriography, which demonstrated normal right and circumflex coronary arteries and an occluded LAD coronary artery. It was successfully balloon-dilated and stented, affording relief of the patient's pain and resolution of the anterior ST elevation. The delta waves persisted.

Interpretation

Sinus tachycardia (rate, 100/min), with a short P–R interval and delta waves of ventricular preexcitation; pseudoinferior MI pattern, acute anterior MI; abnormal ECG

Learning Points

Pseudo-MI in WPW syndrome

Acute MI in WPW syndrome

The literature contains many references describing pseudo-MI in patients with WPW syndrome. References describing cases such as Case 67 are rare. Confusion results from bypass tract–associated segmental wall-motion abnormalities demonstrated echocardiographically. When the ECG is difficult to interpret, waiting for a second set of cardiac enzymes can be an eternity when faced with a patient with chest pain; such cases are most often managed by definitive coronary arteriography and percutaneous coronary intervention when required. There are no series or review articles on the subject. With the advent of radiofrequency ablation of accessory pathways, there have been a number of case reports of postprocedural MI from which electrocardiographic changes attributable to MI can be studied.

Suggested Readings

Chatelain P, Zimmermann M, Weber R, et al. Acute coronary occlusion secondary to radiofrequency catheter ablation of a left lateral accessory pathway. Eur Heart J 1995;16(6):859–61. This report documents a case of asymptomatic acute coronary occlusion secondary to radiofrequency catheter ablation of a left lateral accessory pathway. Owing to post-procedural ST modifications of the surface ECG, coronary angiography was performed, disclosing total occlusion of the first marginal branch of the left circumflex coronary artery. Acute MI was confirmed by moderate cardiac enzyme release, an abnormal myocardial perfusion scan, and mild lateral hypokinesia found by echocardiography.

Guler N, Eryonucu B, Bilge M, et al. Wolff-Parkinson-White syndrome mimicking acute anterior myocardial infarction in a young male patient—a case report. Angiology 2001;52(4):293–5. A young male with WPW syndrome whose electrocardiographic pattern was suggestive of acute anterior MI is described. The patient had been successfully resuscitated from ventricular fibrillation and admitted to the CCU. His ECG showed ST elevation in leads V_1 to V_6. Unlike as in Case 67, the condition here was erroneously interpreted as an acute anterior MI. An MI was excluded by biochemical tests, echocardiography, and coronary angiography. On the fourth day after the patient's admission, the ST segments returned to baseline, and short P–R and delta waves were observed on the electrocardiogram, findings not present on acute presentation. Electrophysiologic study confirmed WPW syndrome with two accessory pathways. One must have a high index of suspicion when dealing with a young patient with acute ST elevation and known WPW syndrome.

Herman RL, Zoltick JM. Infarction in Wolff-Parkinson-White syndrome. Evolution of Q-wave-T-wave vector concordance. Arch Intern Med 1986;146(5):1013. WPW syndrome often mimics MI. Q wave–T wave discordance (upright T waves in the inferior leads with inferior Q waves) is normally found in WPW syndrome as a result of secondary repolarization changes. The authors evaluated Q wave–T wave concordance as a result of an inferoposterior infarction and documented it with electrocardiographic, enzymatic and catheterization data.

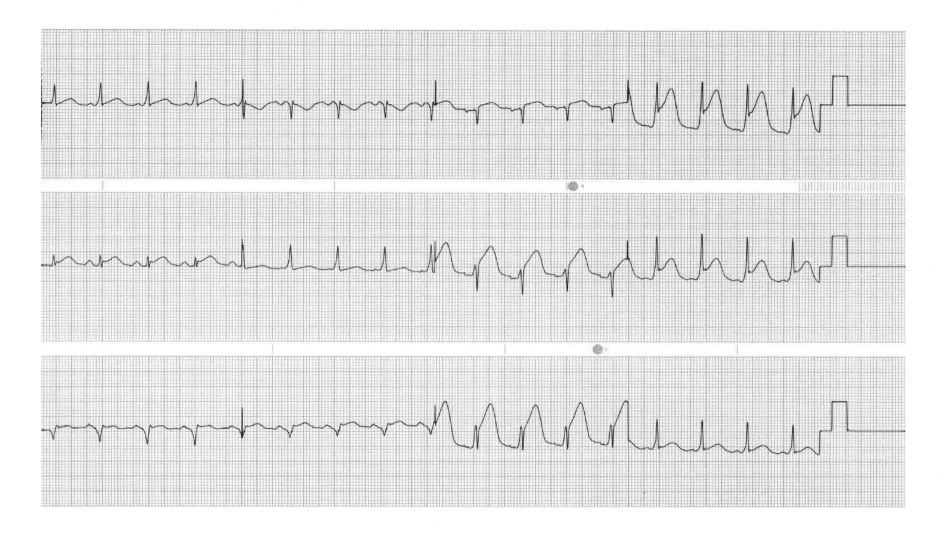

Zarebinski M, Krupienicz A, Marciniak W, Ostrowski M. Coexistence of WPW syndrome, coronary disease and segmental disorders of myocardial contraction. Diagnostic difficulties. Description of a case. Kardiol Pol 1993;38(3):217–9. A 61-year-old patient with WPW syndrome was admitted to the CCU with chest pain. The ECG continued to show a right-sided bypass tract with no evolution of MI. The cardiac enzymes remained normal. The echocardiogram, however, showed akinesis of the posterior wall and hypokinesis of the lateral wall (just as had been described in this patient 5 years previously). The first portion of the ventricles to contract was the base of the right ventricle. This case emphasizes the need for multiple diagnostic modalities when MI is considered in the presence of WPW syndrome. Cases like this do not lend themselves well to thrombolytic therapy.

10

General Interest

Case 68

Clinical Presentation

The patient is a 69-year-old female who is anticipating elective surgery and who has no cardiac history and no symptoms attributable to cardiac disease.

Description of Electrocardiogram (12 Leads)

The rhythm is sinus (rate, 55/min), with a P–R interval of 148 msec, a QRS axis of 10°, and a QRS duration of 80 msec. The Q–Tc interval measures 383 msec. The ST segments and T waves are normal. The only question is the R-wave progression across the precordium, especially from lead V_3 to lead V_4. The voltage in V_3 is barely 3 mm, and that is due to the V_3 electrode placement over a large left breast. The breast tissue increases the distance of that lead from the heart and lowers the voltage. This finding is common in leads V_3 and V_4 in women. What makes this normal is that the R-to-S ratio in each lead, from lead V_1 to V_2 to V_3 to V_4, continues to increase despite the fact that the absolute voltage may decrease from one lead to the next.

Interpretation

Sinus bradycardia (rate, 55/min), with breast attenuation artifact in V_3 and V_4; normal ECG

Learning Point

Breast attenuation is a common electrocardiographic finding and warrants repetition (see Case 30 and its references).

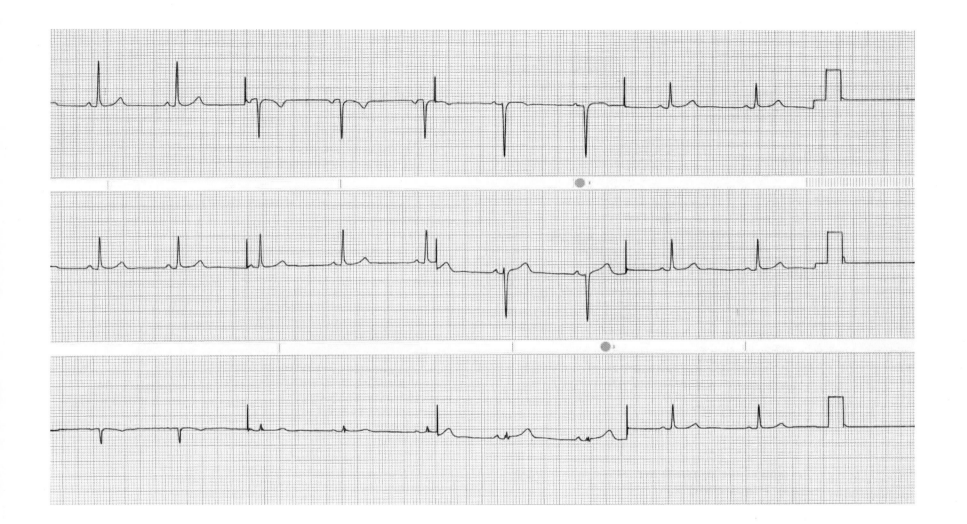

Case 69

ClinicalPresentation

The patient is a 52-year-old obese female who is being evaluated for elective bilateral knee surgery.

Description of Electrocardiogram (12 Leads)

The rhythm is sinus, and the rate is 83/min. The P waves, P–R interval, QRS axis, and QRS duration are all normal. There are diffuse T-wave changes that are not specific for any particular diagnosis. The QRS voltage appears to be low. It is necessary to note the standardization; here, it is full standard (10 mm = 1 mV). The sum of the QRS complexes (all positive and negative deflections) in leads 1, 2, and 3 is just 8 mm. When this sum is < 15 mm, the term "low voltage" is used. Notice also how the voltage decreases from lead V_2 to the subsequent left precordial leads as the electrodes are positioned over the left breast. Other more strict criteria for low voltage require the amplitude of the entire QRS complex (adding R and S) to be < 5 mm in all limb leads and < 10 mm in all precordial leads. Causes of low voltage include obesity, emphysema, pericardial or pleural effusion, hypothyroidism, marked CHF, and AMI.

Interpretation

Normal sinus rhythm (NSR) (rate, 83), with low QRS voltage and nonspecific T-wave changes; abnormal ECG

Learning Points

Low-voltage QRS definitions
Breast attenuation

This patient underwent echocardiography and was found to have a pericardial effusion without cardiac tamponade, due to hypothyroidism. Her orthopedic surgery was postponed, and the hypothyroidism was treated. At subsequent evaluation, the pericardial effusion resolved, and the electrocardiographic QRS voltage increased.

Suggested Readings

Alpert MA, Terry BE, Cohen MV, et al. The electrocardiogram in morbid obesity. Am J Cardiol 2000;85(7):908–10, A10. Electrocardiographic variables that occurred with significantly higher frequency in morbidly obese patients than in lean controls were low QRS voltage and leftward shift of the P, QRS, and T axes; there were also multiple electrocardiographic criteria for left ventricular hypertrophy and left atrial enlargement.

Casale PN, Devereux RB, Kligfield P, et al. Pericardial effusion: relation of clinical, echocardiographic and electrocardiographic findings. J Electrocardiol 1984;17(2):115–21. To evaluate the effects of pericardial effusion on the ECG, the authors compared clinical, echocardiographic, and electrocardiographic findings in 459 patients. Standard electrocardiographic criteria for low voltage (leads 1, 2, and 3 each < 5 mm or leads V_1–V_6 each < 10 mm) were extremely insensitive for detection of pericardial effusion (12%) although highly specific (94%).

Coffland FI. Thyroid-induced cardiac disorders. Crit Care Nurse 1993;13(3):25–30. Signs and symptoms of thyroid disease are varied and often vague. Patients in the ICU may have cardiac disorders that are directly related to altered levels of thyroid hormone rather than inherent cardiac disease. Cardiac manifestations of thyroid disease result from a decrease or increase in circulating hormone and are usually reversible with treatment. Accurate ongoing assessment, especially after treatment has begun, is important to help guide safe and effective therapy. Patient education is another priority of nursing care and can be a major factor in helping the patient to achieve and maintain a euthyroid state.

Lee KO, Choo MH. Low voltage electrocardiogram with tachycardia in hypothyroidism—a warning sign of cardiac tamponade. Ann Acad Med Singapore 1993;22(6):945–7. Cardiac tamponade is a rare complication of pericardial effusion associated with hypothyroidism. In myxedematous patients with pericardial effusion, the occurrence of paradoxical tachycardia may be a clue that cardiac tamponade is impending or has occurred. Of the patients presented, the authors note that the typical patient with hypothyroidism and a pericardial effusion will have low voltage and a slow or normal heart rate. It is the elevated pressure in the pericardial space that limits cardiac filling, decreasing stroke volume and dropping cardiac output, which then can only be augmented by an increase in heart rate. The drive to maintain cardiac output with an increase in heart rate in cardiac tamponade overcomes the lack of chronotropic support of hypothyroidism. In Case 69, the heart rate was 83/min, not tachycardic; nevertheless, it was faster than one would expect in a patient with hypothyroidism. Because cardiac tamponade has a spectrum of severity, even a heart rate of 83/min in a patient with hypothyroidism should raise suspicions of pericardial effusion.

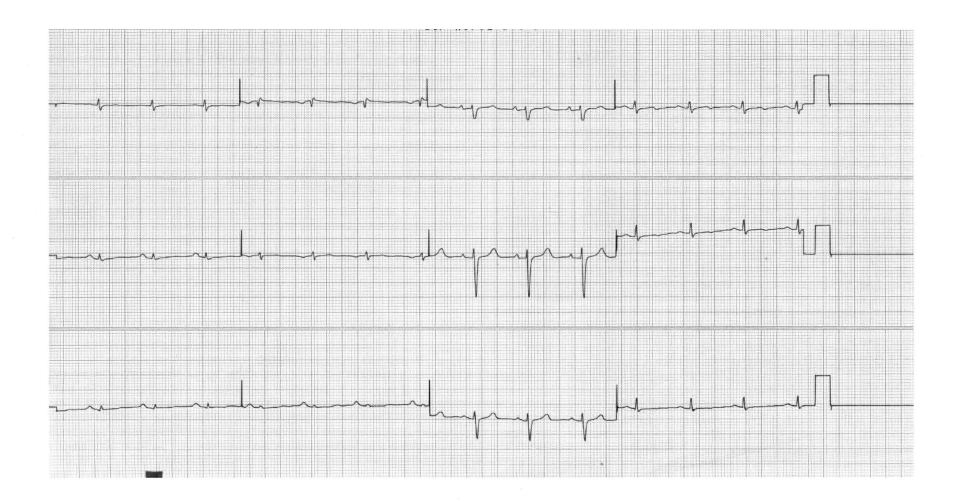

Case 70

ClinicalPresentation

The patient is a 23-year-old male who is a participant in a study of a new antihistamine medication. He has seasonal rhinitis but is otherwise healthy.

Description of Electrocardiogram (12 Leads)

The rhythm is sinus at 81/min, and the P waves, P–R interval, and QRS axis are normal. The QRS duration is at the upper limit of normal (108 msec). The Q–Tc interval is 432 msec and normal. The R-wave progression from V_1 to V_3 is abnormal, but there are no Q waves to suggest MI, and even if there were a structure separating these electrodes from the heart to decrease the voltage, the R-to-S ratio would not decrease from V_1 to V_3 like this. This really only fits with transposition of leads V_1 and V_3; just attaching one cable to the wrong electrode ensures that another cable will be mismatched. Switching leads V_1 and V_3 in one's mind will normalize the R-wave progression. This is a common technical error that must be recognized promptly.

Interpretation

NSR (rate, 81/min); probable transposition of leads V_1 and V_3; otherwise a normal ECG

Learning Point

Transposition of leads V_1 and V_3 (a technical error)

Suggested Reading

Peberdy MA, Ornato JP. Recognition of electrocardiographic lead misplacements. Am J Emerg Med 1993;11(4):403–5. Improper placement of the recording electrodes on the skin can generate misleading patterns on the ECG. Switching the arm leads will alter the P-wave axis and "create" a high lateral MI. Exchanging the leg leads will also alter the P wave axis and "create" an inferior MI. Reversing the right arm and right leg leads creates a unique pattern of diffuse low voltage in the limb leads. As is demonstrated in Case 70, precordial lead switches are common and can be recognized by the abnormal R-wave progression that is created.

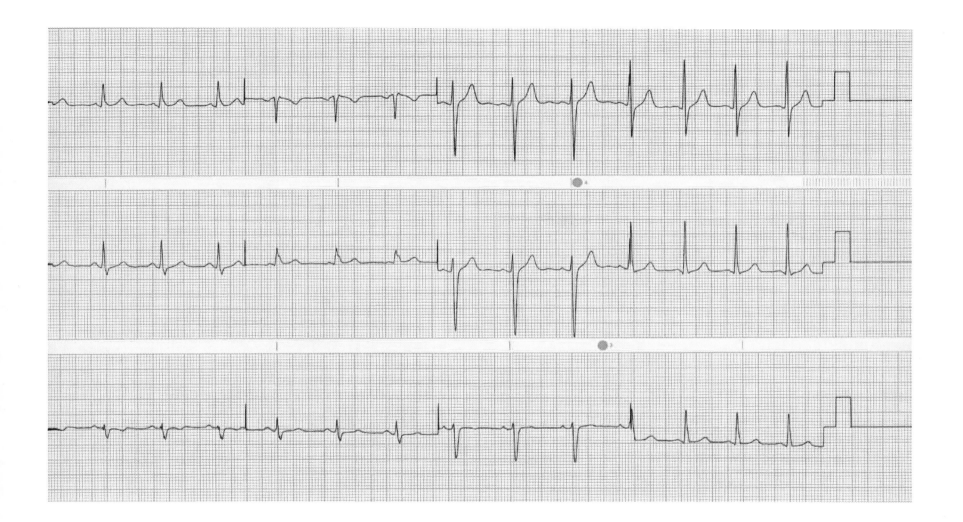

Case 71

ClinicalPresentation

The patient is a 76-year-old male who presented to his physician with nausea and anorexia he had been experiencing for a few days. He has a history of atrial flutter that was converted to sinus rhythm with digitalis.

Description of Electrocardiogram (12 Leads)

The HR is 56/min and regular. In a search for P waves, lead 2 has sharp rhythmic deflections at 240/min that are also seen in leads 1, aVR, and aVF but less so in aVL and not at all well seen in the precordial leads. Is this slow atrial flutter? In leads 3, aVL, and V_1 to V_3, there are P waves with a P–R interval of 220 msec. The QRS axis is −60°, and the QRS duration is 136 msec. The Q–T interval is prolonged, and there are ST segment T-wave changes that are seen in the digitalis effect. Turning to the bedside and observing the patient's parkinsonian tremor (in the arms) was helpful.

Interpretation

Sinus bradycardia (rate, 56/min) with first-degree AV block, abnormal left axis, and nonspecific intraventricular block; long Q–T interval; digitalis effect and somatic tremor; abnormal ECG

Learning Points

ECG tremor artifact

Digitalis effect

This is not LAH. Although the QRS axis is leftward (more negative than −45°) and not due to inferior Q waves, the QRS duration is > 110 msec.

One need not have a classic digitalis-intoxicated rhythm, such as atrial tachycardia with 2:1 AV block, or even an elevated serum digoxin level (although it was elevated in this case) to have the nausea and anorexia that are attributed to clinical digitalis toxicity. Withdrawal of the digoxin resulted in resolution of the nausea and anorexia, shortening of the P–R interval, and (unfortunately) later resumption of atrial fibrillation. Another drug had to be chosen to treat the atrial fibrillation because atrial fibrillation in this patient always resulted in heart failure.

Suggested Reading

Finsterer J, Stollberger C, Gatterer E. Oral anticoagulation for ECG tremor artefact simulating atrial fibrillation. Acta Cardiol 2003;58(5):425–9. This is a case report of the electrocardiographic misdiagnosis of sinus rhythm with an overlying somatic tremor as atrial fibrillation. Because of additional risk factors for stroke and embolism, a warfarin-type anticoagulant was prescribed. The diagnosis was changed to paroxysmal atrial fibrillation when subsequent ECGs showed sinus rhythm. The diagnosis was further questioned, and the anticoagulant was stopped when the diagnosis of Parkinson's disease was made; effective treatment alleviated the tremor, and the tremor artifact was no longer visible on the ECG. Although this is the first case report of its kind, similar cases are encountered annually in consultative cardiology practices.

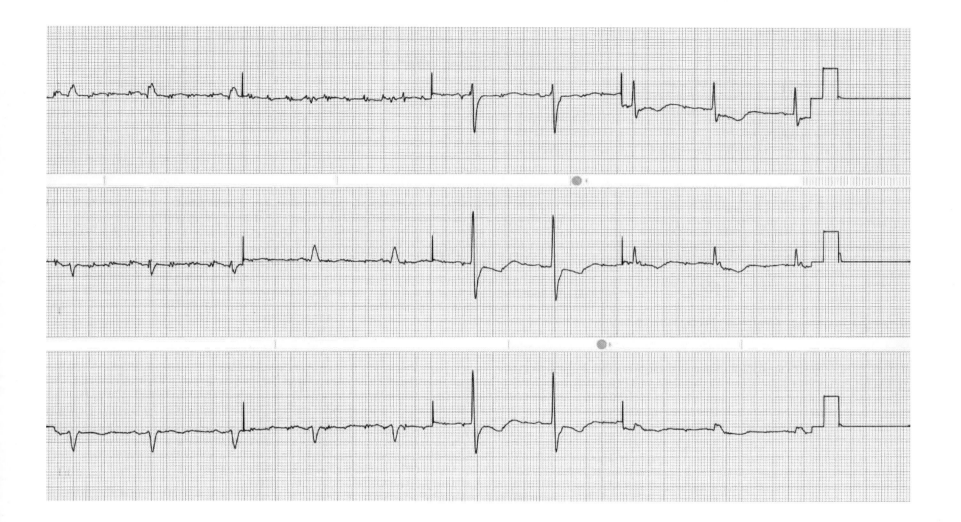

Case 71a

Description of Three-Lead Rhythm Strip

Lead V_1 clearly shows sinus rhythm with first-degree AV block, and lead 2 shows the somatic tremor that obscures the P waves. With these longer strips simultaneously recorded in leads 2 and V_1, the P waves can be separated from the somatic tremor deflections in lead 2. Although one is tempted by the history to call this atrial flutter, there is not yet a rhythm problem in this patient. He did have an elevated digoxin level, and his nausea and anorexia, ST segment T-wave changes, and P–R interval improved with hydration and with the withdrawal of the digitalis. Continued administration of digitalis would surely result in further AV block and/or tachyarrhythmias due to increased automaticity of the atria, junction, or ventricles.

Interpretation of Rhythm Strip

Sinus bradycardia (rate, 56/min) with first-degree AV block; somatic tremor mimicking atrial flutter; abnormal rhythm (due to first-degree AV block).

Learning Point

Differentiation of atrial flutter from atrial fibrillation

Suggested Reading

Knight BP, Michaud GF, Strickberger SA, Morady F. Electrocardiographic differentiation of atrial flutter from atrial fibrillation by physicians. J Electrocardiol 1999;32(4):315–9. The purpose of this study was to determine the ability of physicians to differentiate atrial flutter from atrial fibrillation on a surface ECG. A questionnaire containing three 12-lead ECGs was mailed to 689 physicians and contained multiple-choice questions asking whether the rhythm on each ECG indicated atrial flutter or atrial fibrillation. ECG 1 showed atrial fibrillation with prominent atrial activity (> 0.2 mV = > 2 mm) in lead V_1; ECG 2 displayed atrial fibrillation with prominent atrial activity (> 2 mm) in leads 3 and V_1; and ECG 3 displayed atrial flutter. The authors found that atrial fibrillation is frequently misdiagnosed as atrial flutter, and they concluded that the misdiagnosis of atrial fibrillation occurs more often when atrial activity is prominent in more than one lead on an ECG.

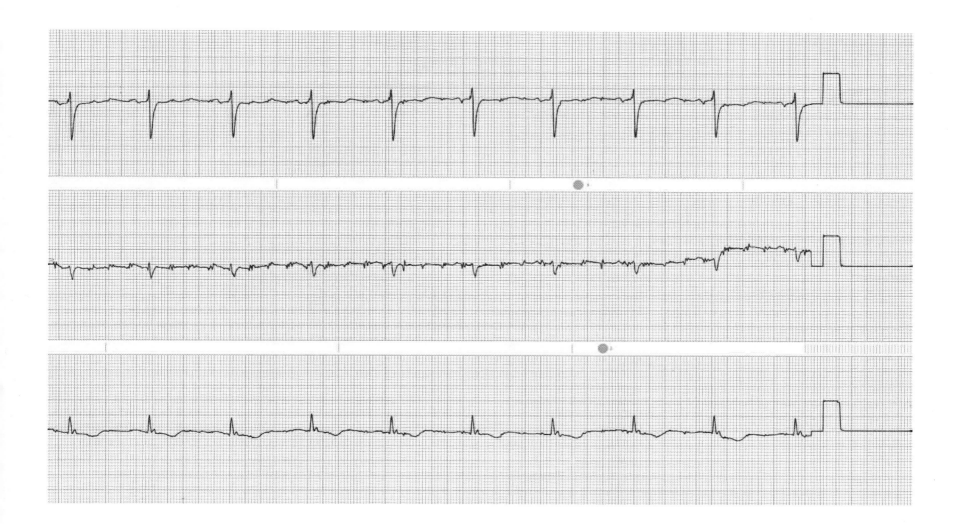

Case 72

ClinicalPresentation

The patient is a 51-year-old man in the CCU after a prolonged episode of chest pain at home. At admission to the unit, he was nauseated and was vomiting and could not take his oral medications.

Description of Electrocardiogram (12 Leads)

As in Case 71, it is difficult to discern P waves in any of the limb leads where there are perfectly rhythmic deflections at 325/min. In all of the precordial leads, the P waves are easily identified; their rate is 80/min, and the P–R interval is 160 msec. The QRS axis and duration are normal. The T waves in V_1 and V_2 are unusually upright, and those in V_5 and V_6 are abnormally inverted. These T-wave changes, along with the chest pain and cardiac enzyme elevation, suggest an MI in the circumflex territory (posterolaterally).

Interpretation

NSR (rate, 80/min) with posterolateral T-wave abnormalities suggestive of ischemia or injury; somatic tremor; abnormal ECG

Learning Points

Assessing T-wave changes through superimposed tremor artifact

Consequences of misdiagnosis of atrial fibrillation

Suggested Reading

Bogun F, Anh D, Kalahasty G, et al. Misdiagnosis of atrial fibrillation and its clinical consequences. Am J Med 2004;117(9):636–42. Computer algorithms are often used for interpreting cardiac rhythm and are subsequently corrected by an over-reading physician. The purpose of this study was to assess the incidence and clinical consequences of misdiagnosis of atrial fibrillation based on a 12-lead ECG. The authors retrieved 2,298 ECGs with the computerized interpretation of atrial fibrillation from 1,085 patients. The ECGs were reanalyzed to determine the accuracy of the interpretation. The medical records of patients for whom the interpretation was incorrect were reviewed to assess the clinical consequences resulting from misdiagnosis.

The authors found that 442 ECGs from 382 of the 1,085 patients had been incorrectly interpreted as atrial fibrillation by the computer algorithm. In the case of 92 patients (24%), the physician ordering the electrocardiogram had failed to correct the inaccurate interpretation, resulting in a change in management and in the initiation of inappropriate treatment, including antiarrhythmic medications and anticoagulation for 39 patients (10%) and unnecessary additional diagnostic testing for 90 patients (24%). A final diagnosis of paroxysmal atrial fibrillation, based on the initial incorrect interpretation of the ECGs, was generated for 43 patients (11%).

The authors concluded that incorrect computerized interpretation of atrial fibrillation, combined with the failure of the ordering physician to correct the erroneous interpretation, can result in the initiation of unnecessary and potentially harmful medical treatment as well as inappropriate use of medical resources. Further, the authors state that greater efforts should be directed toward educating physicians about the electrocardiographic appearance of atrial dysrhythmias and in the recognition of confounding artifacts (such as are seen in Cases 71 and 72).

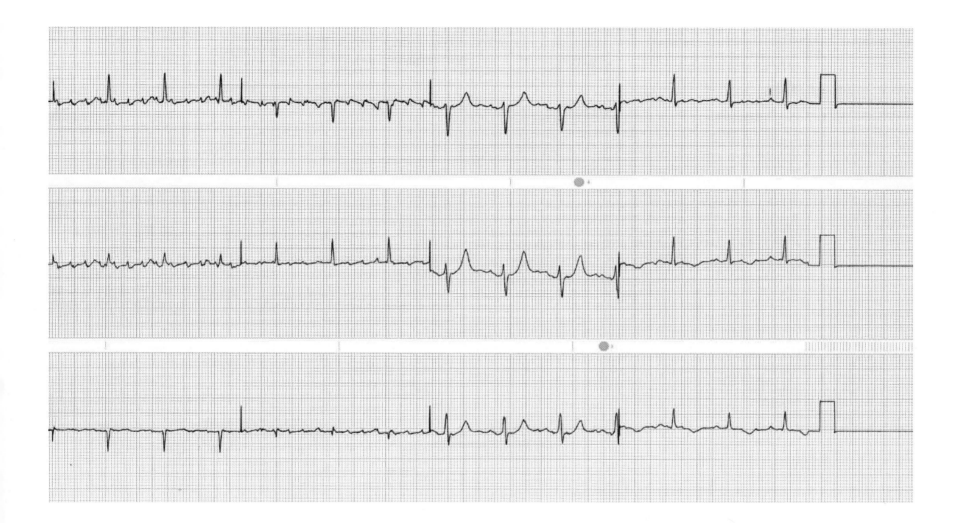

Case 72a

Description of Three-Lead Rhythm Strip

The P waves are best seen in lead V$_1$; with these as a guide, the same P waves can be seen to rise above the somatic tremor. This patient had paralysis agitans (Parkinson's disease). His inability to take his oral carbidopa/levodopa uncovered his somatic tremor. Trying to read the patient's ECG without observing his masked face and new tremor made it easy to consider new-onset atrial flutter. The tremor deflections are sometimes in synchrony with the QRS complexes, making the case all the more difficult. In addition to observing the tremor, one can note the absence of flutter waves in the JVP and the presence of an auscultated atrial gallop when the rhythm is sinus.

Interpretation of Rhythm Strip

NSR (rate, 80/min) with a somatic tremor; normal rhythm

Learning Point

If the electrocardiographic rhythm is too difficult to interpret, examine the patient.

Suggested Reading

Longhini C, Musacci GF, Portaluppi F. Polycardiographic study of atrial flutter. Acta Cardiol 1976;31(3):209–19. The modifications that atrial flutter demonstrates on phonocardiography, apexcardiography, carotid pulse tracing, jugular venous pulse tracing, and indirect (esophageal) left atrial pulse tracing were studied. During atrial flutter, there is notable variation in the intensity of the first and the second heart sounds. All mechanographic tracings correspond to the F waves on the ECG. It is clear that careful auscultation of heart sounds and careful inspection of the jugular venous pulse can help the examiner determine that (as in Case 72a) the regular baseline alteration is due to a tremor artifact and not to atrial flutter.

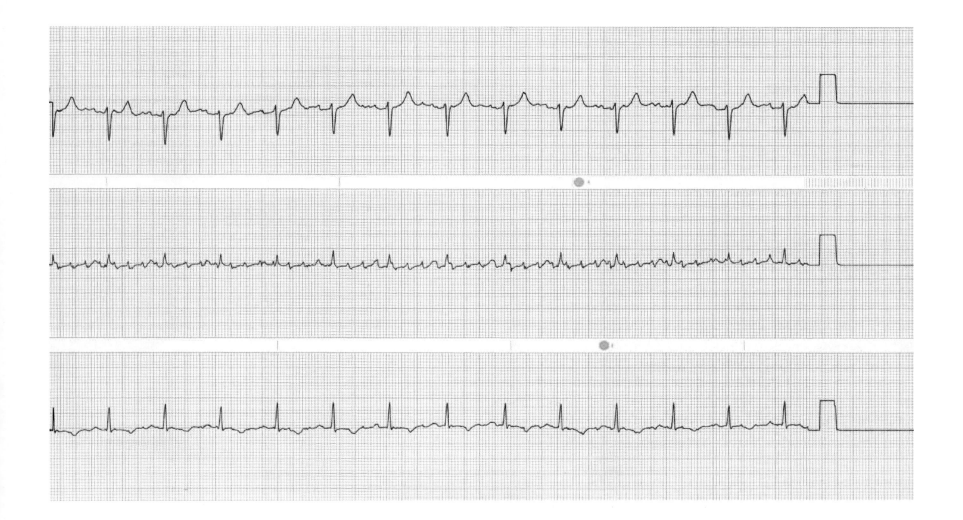

Case 73

ClinicalPresentation

The patient is a 37-year-old male who presents to the ED with chest pressure. He describes it as exertional and associated with dyspnea; it is relieved with rest. He has never before undergone electrocardiographic examination.

Description of Electrocardiogram (12 Leads)

The rhythm is sinus at 57/min. The P waves are normal, and the P–R interval is 132 msec. The QRS axis is 43°, and the QRS duration is 104 msec. The most striking abnormality is the deeply inverted T waves anterolaterally. In association are large QRS voltage (S in V_2 + R in V_5 = > 50 mm) and delayed intrinsicoid deflection (> 0.045 s) in leads V_5 and V_6, electrocardiographic findings that reliably indicate LVH with the systolic overload pattern (see Case 25 and the Romhilt-Estes criteria for LVH). Blood pressure was normal, and there was no history of HTN. There was no murmur of aortic stenosis and no murmur with the strain phase of the Valsalva maneuver. What remained to be ruled out was CAD and HCM of the apical type (Yamaguchi's disease). Echocardiography showed apical HCM, and because radionuclide stress testing has a high rate of false positives for CAD in HCM, cardiac catheterization was done. The findings, including normal coronary arteries, elevated LVEDP, and spade-shaped RAO left ventriculography also indicated apical HCM.

Interpretation

Sinus bradycardia (rate, 57/min) with LVH with strain pattern plus anterior T inversion (consider apical HCM versus ischemia); abnormal ECG

Learning Points

Diagnosing LVH

Yamaguchi's disease, apical hypertrophic cardiomyopathy

Suggested Readings

Sakamoto T. Apical hypertrophic cardiomyopathy (apical hypertrophy): an overview. J Cardiol 2001;37 Suppl 1:161–78. Clinical and laboratory data on apical hypertrophy were reviewed, based on experience with more than 200 consecutive patients, of whom 126 were followed up by the author for more than 1 year (1 to 29 years). Emphasis was placed on various aspects of electrocardiography, including the natural course and the "wax and wane" phenomenon of GNTs. The use of CMR imaging was also stressed. Apical HCM was mainly discovered by annual health checks including electrocardiography and is characterized by GNTs (−1.0 to −4.2 mV) in the left precordial leads (V_4 or V_5) in middle-aged men. (In Case 73, the T waves in V_4 measure −1.5 mV.)

Transition from normal T wave to negative T wave requires several years and usually remains unchanged thereafter. On rare occasions, this change can be rather abrupt. GNTs may also disappear slowly and progressively in patients in whom an apical aneurysm has developed. The diagnosis may be made with echocardiography, left ventriculography, or ultrafast computed tomography, but this diagnosis was most accurately made with CMR imaging, by which identification of the diversity of hypertrophy was achieved because multiple short-axis views were accurately obtained in addition to the exact long-axis view. Hypertrophy was not simple and was quite complex in both morphology and grade. Gene abnormality may be present in cases of apical hypertrophy. In Japan, the prognosis of apical hypertrophy has been benign; heart failure due to atrial fibrillation and left ventricular aneurysm due to the destruction of hypertrophied muscle are thought to have prognostic importance, but these events were rare in this series.

Sayin T, Kocum T, Kervancioglu C. Apical hypertrophic cardiomyopathy mimics acute coronary syndrome. Int J Cardiol 2001;80(1):77–9. The authors present the case of a patient who was initially thought to have an acute coronary syndrome but who was later diagnosed as having apical HCM. Unless specifically sought echocardiographically, the condition can be missed and can be diagnosed only by left ventriculography done in the RAO projection and showing the spade shape. The absence of CAD sufficient to account for the electrocardiographic abnormalities is often the impetus to look further to make the diagnosis. Clearly, apical HCM is not found in Japanese patients exclusively, and CAD can coincide in a patient with apical HCM.

Yamaguchi H, Ishimura T, Nishiyama S, et al. Hypertrophic nonobstructive cardiomyopathy with giant negative T waves (apical hypertrophy): ventriculographic and echocardiographic features in 30 patients. Am J Cardiol 1979;44(3):401–12. This is the initial report of this congenital cardiac disease that bears the name of its first author. The condition is recognized by its electrocardiographic characteristics.

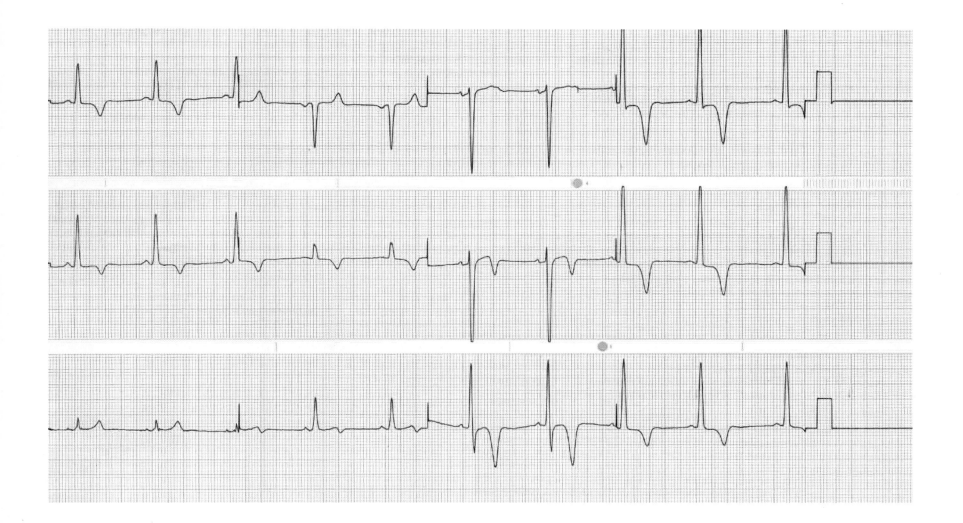

Case 74

ClinicalPresentation

The patient is a 69-year-old female with dextrocardia with situs inversus (mirror-image dextrocardia with total transposition of the abdominal viscera) and no complaints. She is undergoing a routine physical examination.

Description of Electrocardiogram (12 Leads)

Limb lead placement and left precordial lead placement were correct.

Especially with an older patient without an accessible history of dextrocardia, the first thing to check when such a rightward axis is presented is that the arm leads are not reversed. If the arm leads are correct, negative polarity of the P wave in lead 1 suggests that the atrial electrical activation is abnormal (from left to right). The QRS axis in this ECG is also markedly to the right (192°). This is further supported by the progressive loss of R-wave voltage across the precordial leads from V_1 to V_6. If one were to reverse the limb leads and position the precordial leads on the right side of the chest, this patient would have normal P-wave and QRS axes and a normal precordial R-wave progression; the ECG would look normal.

Interpretation (Standard Limb and Left Precordial Lead Positions)

NSR (rate, 67/min); dextrocardia; abnormal ECG

Learning Points

Reading the ECG of a dextrocardia patient

Tall R wave in V_1: electrocardiographic differential diagnosis

Remember that there can be dextrocardia with situs solitus (other organs in normal position), in which case the P-wave axis is normal with normal limb lead placement.

Suggested Reading

Mattu A, Brady WJ, Perron AD, Robinson DA. Prominent R wave in lead V1: electrocardiographic differential diagnosis. Am J Emerg Med 2001;19(6):504–13. A tall R wave in V_1, defined as an R-to-S ratio ≥ 1, is a common occurrence in patients in the ED. This electrocardiographic finding exists as a normal variant in only 1% of patients. Physicians should therefore be familiar with the differential diagnosis for this QRS configuration. The electrocardiographic entities that can present with this finding include RBBB, left ventricular ectopy, right ventricular hypertrophy, acute right ventricular dilation (acute right heart strain), type-A WPW syndrome, posterior MI, HCM, progressive muscular dystrophy, dextrocardia, misplaced precordial leads, and a normal variant. It is always best to corroborate the electrocardiographic diagnosis with the history and physical examination and with available laboratory tests that may have already been done or that need to be done.

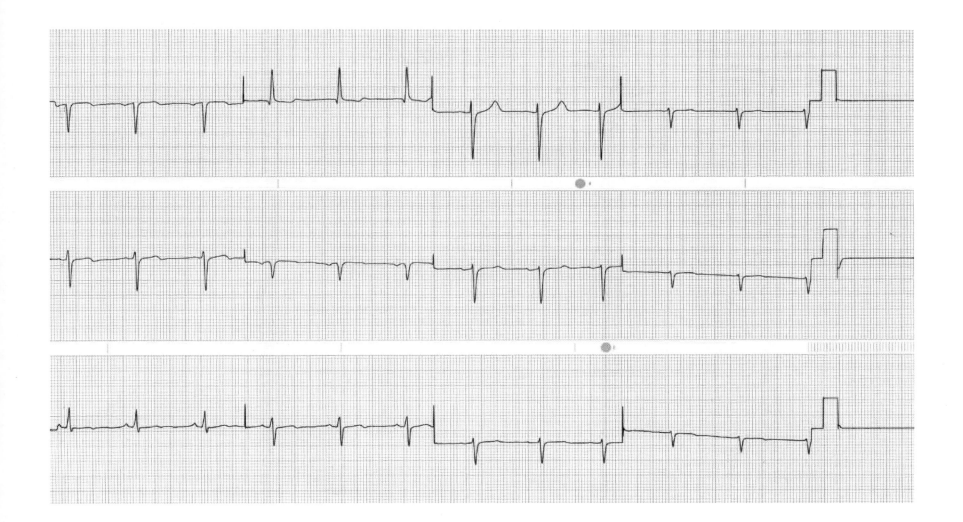

Index